Amy-Alex Campbell
THE LOWEST
REALM

AAC Publishing Australia

Maps by Amy-Alex Campbell
Cover and title page by Warren Design
Artwork by reendhanasukma

Printed in Australia
Feb 19, 2023

SECOND EDITION

ISBN 978-0-6486992-6-2

AAC Publishing Australia
Sydney, Australia

Amy-Alex.Campbell@outlook.com
www.amyalexcampbell.com

A copy of this title is available in the National Archives of Australia
Written on Dharug land
232406

Since publishing the very first version of this story, I have grown as both a person and an author. It was only fitting that I rework this story and bring it up to where it should be.

And so this second edition is dedicated to you,
my beloved readers,
who have stuck by me since that very first day.

I hope this version brings you more joy and excitement and less cringing.

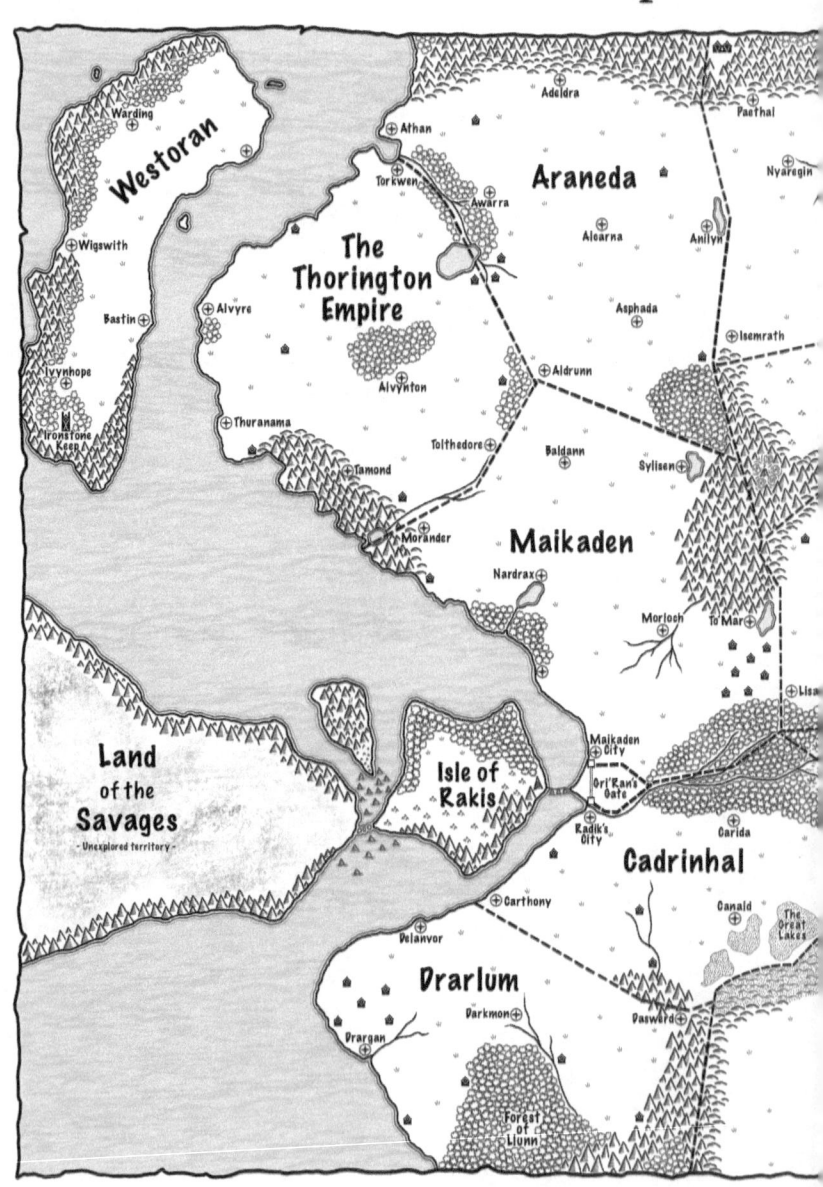

Warding

Westoran

Wigswith

Bastin

Ivynhope

Ironstone Keep

Athan

Torkwen

Awarra

The Thorington Empire

Alvyre

Alvynton

Thuranama

Tamond

Morander

Nardrax

Adeldra

Paethal

Araneda

Nyaregin

Alcarna

Anilyn

Asphada

Isemrath

Aldrunn

Tolthedore

Baldann

Sylisen

Maikaden

Morloch

To Mar

Lisa

Land of the Savages
- Unexplored territory -

Isle of Rakis

Maikaden City

Orl'Ran's Gate

Radik's City

Garida

Cadrinhal

Carthony

Ganald

The Great Lakes

Delanvor

Drarlum

Prargan

Darkmon

Daeword

Forest of Llunn

Lands of Ayrillis

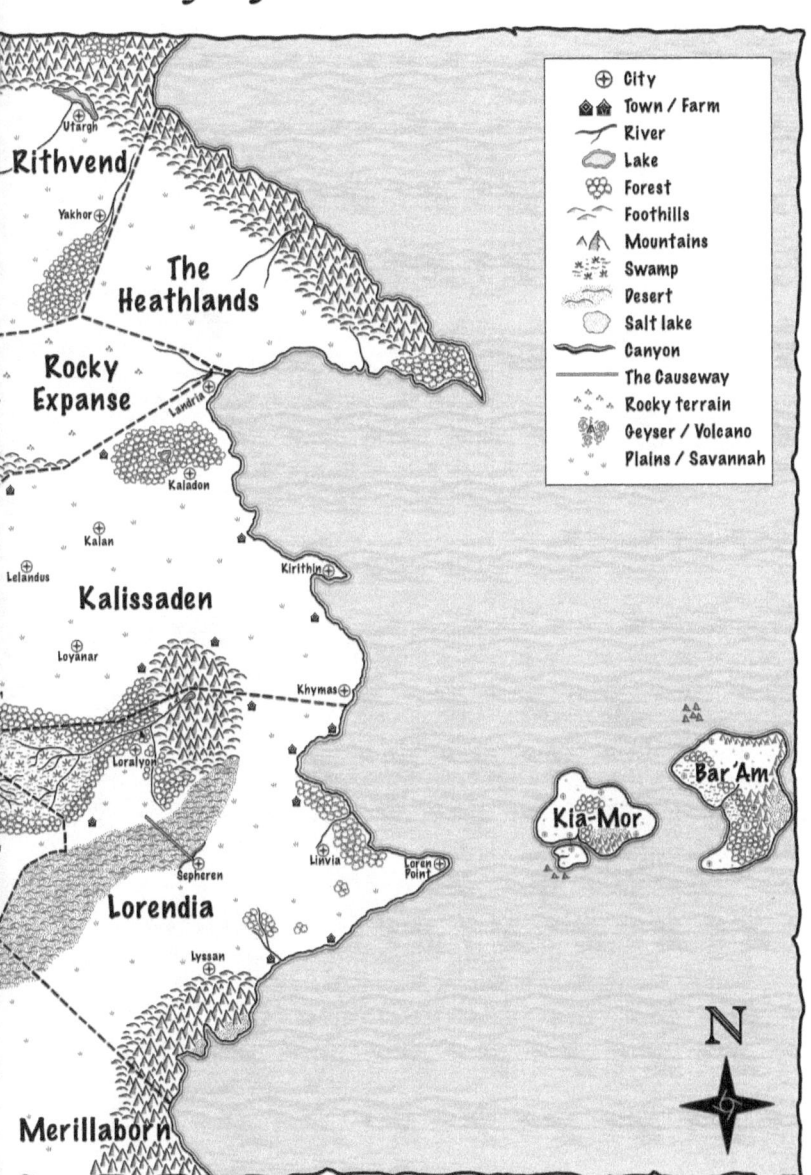

Legend:
- ⊕ City
- 🏠🏠 Town / Farm
- River
- Lake
- Forest
- Foothills
- ∧ Mountains
- Swamp
- Desert
- Salt lake
- Canyon
- The Causeway
- Rocky terrain
- Geyser / Volcano
- Plains / Savannah

Rithvend

Utargh

Yakhor ⊕

The Heathlands

Rocky Expanse

Landria

Kaladon

Kalan

Lelandus ⊕

Kalissaden

Loyanar ⊕

Kirithin ⊕

Khymas ⊕

Loralyon

Linvia

Loren Point ⊕

Sepheren

Kia-Mor

Bar 'Am

Lorendia

Lyssan

Merillaborn

N

PROLOGUE

The crack of a gunshot pierced the night, followed by a shrill scream. Nika cowered in the linen closet, trying not to make any noise. He could see shadows flickering in the light under the door and could hear yelling.

"I'm asking you one last time, Monique. Where's our money, bitch?"

Nika heard a sharp slap followed by a hiss.

"I already told you. We don't get paid until tomorrow. I'll pay you then," his mother spat back.

"We're going to need some collateral," a man said angrily. "Let's go get her kid."

"Nikolai!" she screeched, but Nika didn't move.

He heard some heavy footsteps rush past the closet, followed by the sound of his bedroom door being forced open. Cautiously, he peeked through a crack and could see the bad men in his room. Nika did what he was always told to do if something bad happened; he dashed from the closet and ran past his mother as fast as his little legs could carry him. She sat slumped over the coffee table; white powder and needles were scattered amongst empty beer cans and cigarette butts. Blood was oozing from the bullet wound in her shoulder.

The bad men shouted and Nika gasped; they'd spotted him. He pulled open the kitchen door and ran into the darkness. Terrified, he hid behind a burnt-out car in the abandoned lot across the road, and sucked in some deep breaths, his hands shaking. There was more yelling, then everything went quiet. After a long silence the bad men ran from the house.

"Where'd the little bastard go?" one of them growled.

"Don't worry about it. Let's get out of here."

They climbed into their car and sped off down the street, leaving Nika alone in his hiding place. He held back a sob, unsure what to do next. *Should I go and help Mother? Or should I wait in case the bad man come back? What if Father comes home?*

Thick black smoke started billowing from the kitchen. Nika heard the shatter of glass and watched in dismay as flames erupted from his bedroom window. *Oh no! Where will I sleep now?* His eyes were drawn back to the door, and he spotted his mother staggering from the burning house.

Nika took another nervous look around, then left his hiding place and ran back towards her. She sank to her knees and swayed for a moment, then collapsed. Her skin was turning blue and she started convulsing on the ground.

"Mother?" Nika asked, shaking her shoulder.

He felt sick and started to panic. She was making gurgling noises, and he didn't know how to help her. He knew that if his father came home and saw what was happening, Nika would be blamed and beaten half to death.

The wail of sirens sounded in the distance, growing louder, until a convoy of emergency vehicles screeched to a stop on the street, lighting up the driveway in red and blue hues. His mother was still, unmoving. Nika kept shaking her, trying to wake her up, but still she would not move.

Nika's seven-year-old mind couldn't comprehend what was going on. He'd seen his mother go still many times, but she always woke if he shook her hard enough. In his panic he didn't notice the people until he heard the crunch of a footstep behind him.

A lady in a uniform knelt down and wrapped him in a blanket. He gripped the blanket with shaking hands and tried not to cry, but the tears fell anyway.

"Hi, little buddy. What's your name?"

The lady reached towards him and Nika cowered, expecting to be beaten for crying.

"Hey, it's ok little buddy. I'm not going to hurt you," she said. "Is this your mummy?"

He nodded, looking at his feet.

"Is there anyone else still in the house?" she asked.

Nika shook his head, unable to speak.

"How about you come back to the ambulance with me, and I'll check that you're okay. My friend over there will try and help your mummy. Is that alright with you?"

Nika nodded and followed the nice ambulance lady. Firemen were spraying the fire with their hoses while police were unrolling tape around the house. Usually Nika was excited when he saw an ambulance or fire engine, but that night was everything but exciting. He paused and looked back at his mother to see if she was awake yet.

She lay on the ground, unmoving. Instead of helping her, a group of policemen were talking to one of the neighbors and pointing at the house, while someone was taking photographs of her. Her arms and legs had spasmed into unnatural angles, and her face was a ghastly blue. Even more terrifying was her eyes, wide open and staring into nothingness, her face twisted in a horrible expression. Nika felt the image burn into his brain and knew he would never forget that sight for as long as he lived.

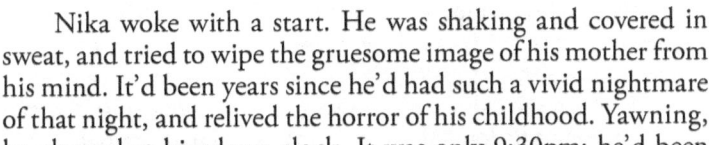

Nika woke with a start. He was shaking and covered in sweat, and tried to wipe the gruesome image of his mother from his mind. It'd been years since he'd had such a vivid nightmare of that night, and relived the horror of his childhood. Yawning, he glanced at his alarm clock. It was only 9:30pm; he'd been asleep for less than an hour.

Sitting up, he pulled on a pair of black pants, a white singlet, and a heavy black jacket. His garb suited his looks; dark black hair which sat just below his ears and fell across his grey eyes, and a face that rarely smiled. He wore a well-groomed goatee and was usually clean-shaven, but he hadn't shaved for two days and had a shadow of a beard growing on his face. Under his left eye was a very faint scar he received while fishing with his foster parents when he was ten. It was shaped similarly to the hook that caused the scar.

All his life, Nika kept to himself. An only child, he learnt to be self-reliant at a young age while his parents battled their addictions. He was neglected and beaten, and after the death of his mother, he was sent to foster care and never saw his father again.

Nika sat on the edge of his bed and pulled on his shoes. His body ached; three weeks of gruelling twelve-to-sixteen-hour shifts had left him feeling exhausted and tired. He was due to fly out early the next morning for shore leave and felt a pang of excitement. Two whole weeks of bars, women, and playing gigs in his favourite pubs for extra cash. He'd already packed, and his eyes landed on his bag sitting in the middle of the room with his guitar. Next to the door, his filthy coveralls lay in a crumpled heap ready to be sent to the laundry room.

With another yawn, Nika slipped on his hardhat and vest, then quietly left the accommodation block, pondering his nightmare. The cold wind hit him as soon as he opened the door, and he pulled his jacket tighter around him to ward off the chill.

Deep in thought, he made his way up to the helipad, sorting through all of the painful memories that his dream unearthed—his father drinking and hitting him, both parents arguing, and fights over drugs and money. Nika felt the bitterness rising and swallowed hard to suppress his emotions.

He walked slowly around the helipad. The night was much quieter than usual, almost too quiet. He jumped as an alarm sounded in the distance and roused him from his thoughts. Something wasn't right; he listened for a moment, then shrugged. *My shift is over. It's up to the night shift crew to respond, not me.*

As Nika turned to walk away, a *whooshing* sound made him freeze, and he looked up in time to see a massive ball of fire igniting and spreading across the deck below. The flames were followed by a deafening explosion and the rig shook violently. Nika was thrown through the air and his head collided with something hard. Thick black smoke bellowed towards him, and he started to choke on the toxic fumes. He tore off his vest and held it over his mouth and nose and tried to get up, but he couldn't; his head spun, and he could hardly breathe.

Nika crawled in the direction of where he thought the stairs were, desperate to find his way out of the thick smoke. He was dazed and confused, and had no idea where he was. Another fireball erupted from the lower deck and *whooshed* towards him, the heat so intense that Nika could feel his skin burn. The rig shuddered and the helipad tilted; he tumbled down the slanting deck, and fell.

Prologue

Nika's shocked mind hardly registered what was going on as he fell almost two hundred feet into the sea below. His life flashed before his eyes in an instant, and with a sense of dismay, he realised that his life was over. His dream of being a successful musician would never be. He hit the water feet first and felt his legs shatter on impact as he sank into the icy cold Northern Sea. In a panic, he tried to swim, but he had no strength left. Nika felt the last of his life drain from his body, and he sank to the depths of eternal darkness.

Part One
Kia-Mor

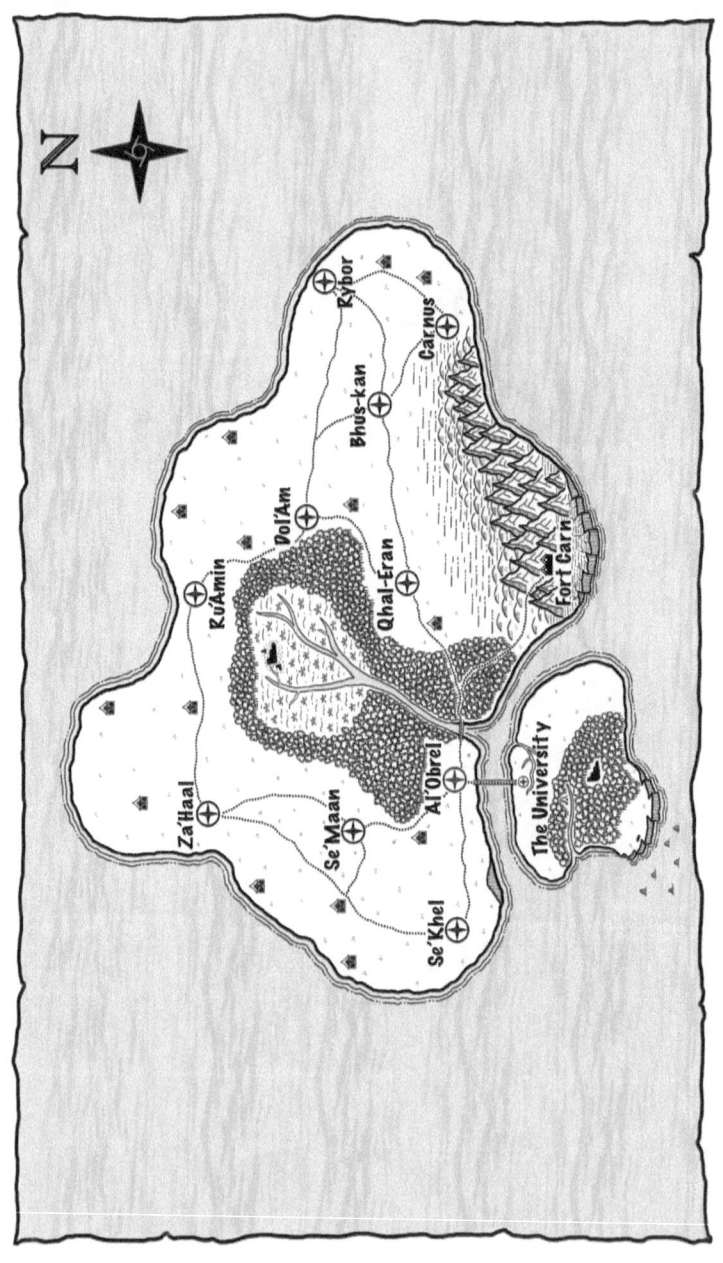

He floated through darkness, nothing but a mere consciousness being swept along by invisible tendrils. Something was pulling on the edge of his mind, dragging him forcefully from the comfort of his deep sleep and sending him hurtling through time and space. With a thud and a searing jolt of pain, he felt his body land on something cold and hard like stone.

His consciousness falteringly returned, and after a while he became aware that he was cold. He reached up weakly to rub his eyes, then opened them slowly and blinked. The sky was grey and dotted with clouds, the sun nowhere to be seen. He pushed himself up into sitting position and glanced around, at once confused.

He was sitting on an ancient altar which looked as though it had been neglected for centuries. Strange words and symbols were etched deeply into the stone in a wavy pattern on all sides, the writing hauntingly beautiful. Somewhere below him, waves crashed upon the cliffs. He became overwhelmed with confusion as nothing looked familiar.

Where am I? Who am I?

He could not remember.

With growing panic, he buried his head in his hands and tried to remember, but nothing came. For a brief moment he envisioned falling a great distance, but as quick as it appeared, it vanished from his mind.

Nika, he thought to himself. *Nikolai Mikhailov. Born... oh shit.*

A low rumble came from far out to sea, and for the first time he noticed the ominous clouds gathering in the distance. He could see that the storm was moving quickly and realised with a sinking feeling that it was moving towards him.

Oh, for fuck's sake. What do I do? Where do I go?

Nika swung his legs over the side of the altar and sat facing the forest. As his eyes swept the plateau, he spotted a majestic grey cat on the low stone wall that circled the altar, staring at him. A patch of white fur circled his neck, giving him the appearance of wearing a suit jacket, and on his forehead was a single white dot. The cat's gaze bore into Nika's eyes, almost as though he were trying to penetrate Nika's mind.

"Oh hi, kitty cat."

Nika clicked his fingers and patted his leg, but the cat flicked his tail almost disdainfully.

"There's no need to be insulting, human," a dry voice said inside his head.

He jumped and looked around to see who was talking.

"Who's there?" he called.

"Don't be foolish. One is right here in front of you. Now, if you don't wish to get wet, one suggests you find some cover." The cat leapt from the wall. *"And don't look at me like that. Haven't you ever seen a cat before?"*

"I-I'm sorry. I don't think I've ever spoken to a cat before," Nika stammered. "Am I dreaming?"

"Hardly. You're awake, aren't you?"

"Well, yeah. Cats can't talk, though."

"Says who? Just because you've never experienced something before doesn't mean it doesn't exist."

"Ok, if you say so."

He slid off the altar, and as his feet touched the ground, a shooting pain shot through both of his legs. Nika gasped and fell to his hands and knees.

"Ow! What the fuck?" he hissed.

"You have clearly sustained some sort of injury," the cat noted.

"No shit," Nika snapped.

He pulled himself up and sat with his back against the altar, breathing heavily. A tingling feeling ran up and down his weak and pained legs, and he sat there for a moment, regaining his breath while massaging his shins.

"A storm is approaching and one doesn't like to get wet. Farewell, human."

The cat turned and disappeared into the field of sea lavender that stretched from the cliffs all the way to the forest. Nika groaned and pulled himself up using the altar for support, then took a moment to get used to his weight on his aching legs. The cat was already gone.

"Hey!" Nika shouted.

"What is it, human?"

"I have no idea where I am. Can you at least help me?"

There was a rustle and the cat reappeared.

"How could one possibly help? Cats can't talk, remember?"

"Ok ok, I'm sorry. Are there any people nearby who may be able to help me? Please?"

"Very well. Follow me."

Nika took a few wobbly steps towards the cat until he was confident that he had the strength to walk properly.

"It's an hour-long walk to the forest for a human, but that's with strong and fit legs. It may take longer with you. To others, one is known as Arnie-Kyn. How shall one refer to you?"

"I'm Nika," he replied. "What is this place? And how did I get here? Do I live nearby?"

"One shall take you to some humans who may be able to help you. Perhaps when we reach our destination, you will learn more."

"Our destination is where, exactly?" Nika asked.

"You are just like a young whelp, so full of questions. Let's go before we get caught in that storm."

Nika grimaced and stumbled along in silence. The sky was growing darker as the storm clouds blew closer, and it wasn't long before the first drops of rain began to fall. The rumbling in the distance was growing louder and lasting longer, and an occasional flash of lightning lit up the sky.

They reached the cover of the forest just as the sky opened up. Lightning cracked overhead followed by loud claps of thunder, and icy gusts howled through the trees, snapping the branches and sending them plummeting to the ground.

Arnie led Nika deeper into the forest; it was growing darker by the minute, and the rain pounded through the canopy. Nika was soaked through to his skin and felt frozen to his core. His legs were burning and felt like they were ready to collapse.

"*We're almost there,*" Arnie-Kyn said.

Nika's mind was numb as he followed the cat through the forest. He saw something large and square in front of him, and as they drew closer, Nika realised it was the remnants of a stone building. As they walked, more gloomy ruins materialised out of the forest, melancholic in the dim light. He followed Arnie through the ruined streets, staggering as the pain flared with each step. *I'm so cold. I could really do with a nice warm fire.*

A light appeared in the window of one of the damaged houses. Arnie stopped abruptly and hissed, his hackles standing on end.

"*Wait here, human. Don't move.*"

Arnie stalked towards the house and leapt onto the windowsill before disappearing inside. Nika leaned against a broken pillar, too tired to argue.

"*There's no one here,*" Arnie said, returning to the window. "*This will be an adequate lodging for the night. Come on in.*"

Nika tried to open the door of the house, but it wouldn't budge. With a sigh, he clambered through the open window and landed in a lounge room. A welcoming fire burned in the fireplace, although it burned no wood.

"How...?" Nika started.

"*It must be a firestone,*" Arnie said. "*A stone that can ignite into flame at will. One believes they are very rare.*"

"How do they work?" Nika asked, a thousand questions popping into his head at once.

"*One is a cat, not a mancer.*"

"Mancer? What's that?"

"*Mancery is a type of magic that is performed by mancers. Now stay here and get dry, human. One shall return soon.*"

Arnie-Kyn disappeared out the window, leaving Nika alone with his unanswered questions. He took off his dripping wet clothes and hung them by the fire to dry, then sank exhaustedly onto a tattered rug in his singlet and underwear.

This has to be a dream, he thought, staring into the flames. *I'll wake up tomorrow and get on with my life. I probably won't even remember this in the morning.*

He sat, motionless, listening to nature and reading her signs. The trees whispered of a stranger upon the land, and the wind blew a foreboding warning of evil yet to come. Deep within his bones he could feel changes stirring within the land, and he felt a stab of fear at the thought of more evil in the already pained world.

Closing his eyes, he allowed himself to drift into the dreamy trance he so often sought comfort from, and listened ever closer to the voices of nature. At once, he realised that the stranger walked in *his* forest, but friend or foe he did not yet know. Strange voices were talking loudly in languages he could not understand; while many creatures were attuned to the voices of nature and could communicate through her channels, he'd never heard them so loud and distressed before.

With a grimace, he stood and slung his pack over his shoulder and turned to face the direction he knew the mysterious stranger would be. He'd never had intruders in his forest before, so while he was extremely curious, he knew better than to go blundering into the stranger's path.

He was a strange being, not quite human but not quite anything else. He lived a solo life in the forest and had forgotten his name many moons ago. In his opinion, names were unimportant. So long as he could listen to nature's musical voice and be with her, he was happy. He had dark black hair streaked with a hint of silvery grey, and the brownest of eyes. His beard and hair were long and scruffy from living in the wild for so long. He was slightly taller than average and was lean and strong. Years of solitude in the forest had granted him the stealth and agility required to survive off the land.

Swiftly and silently, he began his trek south. It was less than a day's walk to the edge of the forest, but the rain and approaching storm would surely hinder his journey. He made his way through the trees and stopped at a stream where he occasionally fished for food. A flash of lightning cracked through the sky, lighting up the bank for a split second. The resulting rumble of thunder was ominous, filled with warning.

The stream had swollen into a raging river from the downpour. Branches and debris were being swept along by the current. There was nowhere to cross safely. The ground was already turning to mud, and with a sigh of defeat, he turned and trudged upstream to where he knew was shelter.

I guess I'll just have to wait out this storm first. I don't think the stranger will be going far this day, either, he thought, walking as quickly as he could through the slippery mud. He was almost at the cave when the hair on the back of his neck stood on end. *Danger!*

He froze just in time as a feral pig emerged from the cave, sniffing the air. The wild pigs of the forest had terrible eyesight, but their heightened sense of smell made them dangerous. He edged slowly behind a tree then climbed it and crawled along a low branch. There was little doubt that the pig had already caught his scent; it grunted and chomped its jowls, its hackles standing on end.

The pig moved closer and circled the tree where he hid. A deep rumble of thunder made it tense and look up at the sky. *That's it, come closer,* he thought. *You will make a good meal.* He could sense its hunger, fuelled by the tasty scent on the wind and its need to defend its territory.

Lightning flashed and it was time to act. As the thunder rumbled once more, he drew his dagger from his boot and readied himself. The pig resumed its circling and moved directly below his hiding place.

It was the moment he'd been waiting for. Taking a deep breath, he leapt from the tree branch and landed on the startled pig's back. The animal squealed and tried to buck him off, but he held on tight with one arm and drove his dagger into the pig with the other. Hot sticky blood gushed from the wound and warmed his hand. Squealing and kicking, the pig tried to escape his grasp, but he kept it pinned under his bodyweight as its life bled from its body.

The pig's struggles grew weaker and weaker, until death took its final breath. He stood, breathing heavily, and glanced at the limp body at his feet. A deep sense of sadness came over him; to slay an innocent beast felt like a crime, whether or not the pigs were feral and wreaked havoc on the isle. With a tear in his eye, he knelt next to the dead body and prayed to his mother of nature, asking for her understanding and forgiveness.

I'm sorry. Your death will not be in vain.

Getting up, he retrieved his blade and went to the mouth

of the cave. It wasn't very deep, but it was dry and would be good cover to sit out the storm. A small pile of firewood was stacked neatly at the back from the last time he'd taken shelter there. He gathered some dry grass and twigs from the stockpile and lit a small fire just inside the opening.

The pig's body still lay where it had fallen, looking quite miserable in the mud. He cleaned his blade, then set to work. It took him over an hour to clean, skin, and gut the carcass, by which time he was cold, hungry, and tired.

Yawning, he returned to the cave and set up his spit to cook his dinner, while he disposed of the gizzards and cleaned his hands thoroughly. He hung his heavy cloak out to dry, then sat watching his dinner cook.

By the time the meat was done, he was ravenous, and ate more than his usual fill. Satisfied from his nourishing meal, he lay back against the wall and dozed off.

Darkness…running. Trees all around. Screams filled with terror. He couldn't see. He was blinded with fear, but he kept running. The smell of burning flesh growing stronger, an orange glow in the distance.

He knew he was too late, yet he kept running, trying to push himself to go faster, but it was no good. He reached the gates of the village, and heard the screams growing weaker. The once beautiful village lay burning and reduced to a slaughterhouse, mutilated bodies strewn around on the ground. He kept on. He had to.

He reached the remains of the village square and found the source of the screaming; at once he was violently ill.

"Freyne! Help me!"

She was on fire, staggering towards him, but there was nothing he could do. He stood frozen to the spot, watching as she slowed to a walk, then collapsed with a pleading hand held out towards him…

He woke with a start, trembling, still smelling the burnt flesh in his dream. The air was filled with rancid smoke, and he looked down to see that he'd forgotten to take the rest of the pig off the fire. With a groan, he got up and hurled the smoking leftovers out of the cave. The rain had eased, and the worst of the storm was over. An occasional rumble in the distance told him the storm had moved far away.

It was impossible to determine how long he'd slept. He retrieved the spit and waited for the smoke to clear, then put more wood on the fire. His mind racing, he sat back down and stared into the flickering flames. He could not recall having such a horrid dream before and was confused as to what it meant. Who was that woman, and how did she know his name?

His name, which he had not used for so long, was forgotten.

With a yawn, he settled next to the fire and bundled his cloak into a pillow. Lulled by the crackling fire and the flowing river, he soon drifted into an exhausted sleep.

2

Nika woke the next morning, exhausted and shivering. The air was frigid, and he could see his breath with each exhale. The only part of him that was warm was his legs which he'd covered with his jacket during the night. His body was stiff from lying on the ground, and he stood up, stretching. The rain was drizzling outside, and the sky was a cold miserable grey. Nika pulled on his now-dry clothes, and as he shook the dust from his jacket, he noticed a long rip under the arm which rendered it useless. As he stared at the tear it dawned on him; he wasn't dreaming at all.

"Oh, for fuck's sake!"

He kicked a broken piece of wood on the ground, then swore again when it sent a shock of pain up his leg. He was tired, hungry, scared, and alone. Breathing heavily, he ran his fingers through his hair and willed himself to calm down.

The firestone had gone out long ago, and Arnie-Kyn was nowhere to be seen. Nika picked up the stone and looked at it closely. It looked like a normal ironstone rock only a little redder, and it felt warm in his hand. A strong compulsion came over him and he slipped it into his pocket.

Nika glanced around the room and frowned. It was almost empty except for a broken bookcase, a few tattered books, and a wild vine that snaked through the window. He picked up one of the books and flicked through the pages. It was written in the same beautiful hand that he saw on the altar, and he longed to be able to read it. The other books were written in the same language, each as mysterious as the other.

His eyes landed on a smaller book with a black leather cover that had been shoved haphazardly onto a shelf. Unlike the other books, this one had tight sturdy binding and looked to be far superior in quality, and although he couldn't read the writing, Nika could tell that it was someone's journal. He flicked through the pages and saw some random drawings and notes. A warm shiver tingled down his spine, as though he had seen the small book before. He felt drawn to its owner and wondered if he knew them. Curious, he slipped the book into his pocket with the stone.

Next to the bookcase was a door. Nika pushed it open and stepped into a small windowless bedroom. He shivered; a feeling of despair resonated from the walls themselves, and without a doubt, he knew someone had died there tragically long ago. A single bed stood in one corner, and a wardrobe was pushed against the left wall, with one door slightly ajar.

Nika picked his way through the junk and debris that littered the floor and opened the wardrobe. Folded up neatly inside was a black cloak with long sleeves and a hood. He shook the dust off and held it up to the light. The cloak looked new and would fit him. He hesitated for a moment and weighed up his options; it felt wrong to steal, but he couldn't go out in the rain without adequate clothing. With a pang of guilt, he draped the cloak over his arm and left his jacket in its place.

In the other corner of the room, he spotted a side table strewn with a few cracked pieces of crockery and a fancy-looking knife in a sheath. Nika picked up the knife and felt a warm tingling feeling in his hand. He rubbed the dust off the hilt and saw that it was decorated with deep purple gemstones. As with the stone and the journal, he felt compelled to take it, and attached the sheath to his belt before returning to the lounge room.

There was just one more door, and when he opened it, a cold rush of air blew into the room. The rest of the house had crumbled away. He slipped on the cloak and felt warm at once. Pulling up the hood, he headed out into the rain.

A deep sadness hung over the ruins. Buildings that were once beautifully ornate lay crumbling and overgrown by vines and weeds. Nika couldn't help but feel bad for the people who died there. He circled around the house and found Arnie-Kyn sitting on the windowsill of the room he'd slept in.

"Are you ready to continue?" the cat asked.

Nika nodded.

"This rain is undesirable. One does not like to get wet." Arnie stood, his fur spiky from the rain.

"Err…would you like me to carry you?" Nika asked.

"What, and have you drop me or crush me? I think not."

"Fine. Get wet, then." Nika couldn't help but grin.

Arnie-Kyn jumped to the ground, and Nika could tell he was not happy. Still grinning, he bent down and picked up the wet cat, then gently stashed him beneath his cloak. Arnie resisted for a moment and dug his claws into Nika's skin, then finally gave up his struggle. Nika could feel his tail whipping around irritably.

"One feels most undignified!" Arnie said crossly.

"Beats getting wet though, doesn't it?" Nika countered.

Arnie didn't answer.

"Which way do we go?"

"Head north and you will see a track. Follow it."

After a few hours of walking through the forest, Nika's legs began to ache. He tried over and over to remember what had happened to make them so weak, but each time the memories remained elusive. Frustrated, he turned his attention instead to his surroundings. An occasional rabbit darted across the path, whilst birds chirped from the treetops, too wet to fly. Nika warily eyed something perched high up in the trees, watching him. He rubbed his eyes, but when he glanced back, it was gone.

The damp forest ended abruptly, and Nika stepped into a lush green field. The sun peeked out from behind a cloud to greet them, and there were patches of blue in the sky. They stood on top of a small hill, and Nika could see the sea all around them, albeit in the distance. They were on an island. Nika bent down and released the cat.

Right on the edge of the sea to the north was a dark smudge.

"What's over there?" Nika asked, pointing.

"That's the University. It's where we're going."

"Why are we going to a university? Wouldn't a doctor be better so I can get my memory back?"

"It's the *University*, not *a* university. People come from all*

over the world to study there in the vast libraries, some of which hold the rarest texts. There are people there who may be able to help you to get home."

"Whatever. Let's go, then."

They started making their way down the hill and into the sea of green dotted with tiny yellow flowers. With each step Nika's legs grew more painful until he could handle it no more. *Fuck this. I need to sit a moment,* he thought.

Arnie stopped walking and sat down.

"Don't be too long," he said.

"Wait, what? You can hear my thoughts, too?!"

"Of course not. Don't be ridiculous."

"Then how are we doing this? This doesn't make any sense!"

"Patience, young whelp. Sometimes, in order to make sense of things, we must first contemplate in silence. Calm yourself and it will become clear to you."

Nika grumbled and shook his head, his frustration once again mounting. He sat roughly and crossed his arms, frowning.

"What happened to the village back there?" he asked once he'd calmed down.

"Many years ago, a raiding party tried to attack the University, but they could not breach the wall. So, they travelled inland, found the village, and destroyed it instead," Arnie replied.

"Why would someone want to attack a university?"

"The University has existed for over a thousand years. It began as a simple monastery, and scholars would travel there to study the rare texts it held. Over the years, it grew rapidly, growing into a university and a small city. Around three hundred years after the original monastery was built, some of the monks were unhappy with the city's growth and the noises that came with it, so they ventured into the forest and built their own village. The founding monks had all taken wives, and over the years they built a small self-sufficient community. The village was peaceful and serene, and the community knew no hatred. Instead of building another monastery, they built that lone altar overlooking the ocean, and that was their place of worship. They were a beautiful people.

"When the raiders came, they killed all of the innocent people. No one escaped. It is said that someone, perhaps a god or a mancer, managed to cast a terrifying spell on the minds of the attackers.

They supposedly went mad and jumped off the cliff by the altar. No one knows what exactly happened, though. Unfortunately, there was no record of any survivors."

"*That's terrible.*"

Nika shuddered, and again he momentarily envisioned himself falling into water. He scratched his head, trying to remember, but still his memories would not come. The cat stood and shook himself off.

"*Come. We must continue before night falls.*"

The city loomed closer and closer, until finally they stood in the shadow of its wall. A wide flowing river separated them from the city. Arnie scratched around in the dirt on the edge of the bank, looking for something.

"*Here it is,*" he said.

He pressed his paw to something metal protruding from the ground. There was a slight *click*, and a section of wall swung down and landed with a *thud* on the bank.

"*This is a secret entry point. It was used by the villagers to attend the monastery and avoid the bustle of the city. Not many humans know about it,*" Arnie-Kyn said, covering up the button.

They crossed the bridge and entered a dark passageway, lit only by a faint green glow. The bridge drew itself up behind them, plunging them into darkness.

"*We are within the city wall itself. There are three other exits like the one we came through, all designed for discreet access to and from the city. This particular passage was only known to the monks who built it. One can move around the city from one point to another and no one would ever know. It is important that no one sees you use these hidden entrances, lest the city's security be compromised.*"

"*If it's such a big secret, why are you telling me?*" Nika asked, trying to make out the passage in the dim glow.

Arnie-Kyn said nothing and led the way along the passage to a steep flight of stairs.

"*Is there some sort of light down here?*" Nika asked.

"*One sometimes forgets the difference between our species. How horrible it must be, unable to see in the dark.*"

"It's not my fault," Nika objected. *"What about that stone I found? Can't we use it?"*

"Only if you want to burn your hand off. Only mancers can control them, and only if they are attuned to the stone. One doubts you have any magical ability whatsoever. It will be better to feel your way along. One will warn you of any hazards up ahead."

Nika grew annoyed and glared at Arnie in the darkness. *Once I get out of here, I'll ditch the cat and find a doctor,* he told himself. *I can't do anything until I have my memory back.*

Freyne crouched on a thick tree branch, watching the stranger and the feline walking through the forest below. He'd watched them for a few hours, slipping silently through the treetops and following their every move. He could sense a connection between the two, but try though he might, he could not penetrate the bond between them. Even in his meditative state, Freyne could not listen in. He continued to watch the odd pair intently as they left the forest and made their way into the field, heading towards the city.

I wonder what they're up to? he thought. He sat up on his branch and swung down, dropping easily to a lower limb, then glanced forward to make sure he hadn't been seen before dropping to the ground. As soon as he landed, he crouched and ran to the edge of the field, flopping to his belly and crawling forward into the weeds.

Moving carefully, he crawled stealthily through the flowery weeds until he reached the cover of a shallow ravine. He watched as the stranger and his companion made their way through the field towards the city.

Once the stranger reached the wall, Freyne watched in surprise as they opened a secret passageway and disappeared into the city's wall. He sat up and wiped off his dirty hands, his mind racing. The door looked familiar, yet he was sure he'd never seen it before. Frowning, he searched deep within himself for the memory, yet every time he came close it felt as if someone snatched it from his grasp.

A sudden jolt of energy coursed through him, and his consciousness slipped away, replaced by a vivid memory.

Large mosaiced windows, made up of countless pieces of coloured glass, reflected the dancing flames of the oil lanterns. Below, a white marble altar. There was a knock at the door, and he turned around slowly, sensing something strange.

Another loud knock, more desperate than the first. He strode past hundreds of wooden bench seats and opened the door. A young man barely in his twenties stood before him, dirty and caked in blood. He held out a bag of scrolls and parchments.

"Please help me, Brother. My life is in danger and I beg for sanctuary. I am of the seers to the north. My village has been destroyed and I am a lone survivor. Please."

Freyne heard himself gasp, and opened his eyes, his heart pounding in his chest. He knew not where the memory came from, but he knew without question it was his. Closing his eyes, he tried to remember more, but only a little came back to him. Who was the seer, and why should he care about a bag of muddy scrolls?

A strange sensation came over him, as though his mind was starting to awaken from a deep slumber. It felt like a veil was lifted, and at once it was clear to him. The signs he had been reading from nature about the changes swirling in the air, and the appearance of the stranger, could not be a coincidence. Friend or foe, Freyne had to find him; he had to know who the stranger was, and why he was there. And should he be the embodiment of evil, Freyne would kill him before he could unleash any more pain on the already damaged world.

⌐───────┘

Nika fumbled through the dark passageways, trying to feel his way along without falling or hitting his head. Despite Arnie-Kyn's warnings and directions, he felt blind and lost. His thoughts turned back to the firestone, and how it burst into flame in the fireplace back in the ruined house. *I wish it would start glowing again so I can see in the dark,* he thought.

The faintest light pierced the darkness, and Nika jumped, spinning around to see who was following them. The light moved as he moved, but there was no one in the tunnel. Perplexed, he looked down at his pocket and noticed a soft glow.

"What the…?"

He reached in his pocket and withdrew the glowing stone; it felt warm to touch, but not unpleasant. He turned it over and over in his hand, appreciating its warmth. *Turn off*, he thought, and once again the passage was plunged into darkness. *Turn back on.* The stone resumed its gentle glowing. Nika looked up to see Arnie watching him.

"Well now, that answers that question," Arnie's voice said inside his head.

"What question?" Nika asked.

"The question of who controls that stone. It would appear that it's attuned to you after all. Very interesting since you couldn't possibly be a mancer." The cat stood and continued his way along the passage.

"Why me?" Nika demanded. *"You said these things are rare, so why does one just happen to be lying around that just happens to work for us?"*

"Not us. You. Whoever put it there did so for a reason. Now hush and follow me, human."

Nika followed, his mind full of questions. He was pretty sure that the cat knew more than he was letting on. The tunnel branched abruptly to the right and they were met by a thick iron door. Arnie-Kyn sat and meowed loudly.

"Oh, so you're a cat now?"

"One said to hush, human. We all must set aside our dignity on occasion." His tail flicked with annoyance.

Nika could hear shuffling footsteps followed by several bolts being drawn back one by one. The door swung open, and a hooded figure wearing brown robes stood before them holding a torch. Nika shoved the stone in his pocket and willed it to stop glowing. The person eyed him up and down, then turned his gaze to Arnie.

"You're bringing living people to us now? I know I asked you to stop with the dead birds and mice, but this? This has gone too far."

Arnie-Kyn brushed past the man's legs and disappeared inside.

"Is that your cat?" Nika asked.

"He's just a stray who visits from time to time. He comes and goes as he pleases. More importantly, who are you and what are you doing here? This area is restricted. How in the gods did you get in?"

"Um. That cat brought me here. He said you might be able to help me find my way home."

"Oh, and now you think a cat can speak? I think your home must be at the asylum, friend." The man crossed his arms and tapped his foot.

"Look. I have no idea where I am or what's going on," Nika snapped. "I have no memory of anything in my life before yesterday, since waking up on that altar. I'm just trying to–"

"You what?"

"I've lost my memory–"

"No. What was that about an altar? Tell me everything, lad."

Nika frowned, then recounted his experience. The man pulled back his hood, revealing a shock of white hair and the bluest of eyes. He searched Nika's face for a moment, his gaze lingering on his scar.

"It would appear that Am has sent you to us. Come. I and my brethren will need to discuss this and see if we can help."

The man led him through a short passage and swung open a wooden door. As he passed through, Nika glanced back and saw that the door was disguised behind a loaded bookcase. They were in a library.

The library was dim, lit by just a few torches. The rows of shelves on either side of the walkway were loaded with ancient books, scrolls, and artefacts. After a while they reached the central area of the library which was dominated by a round desk encircling a spiral staircase, and five comfortable-looking chairs. From that round central area stretched four wings, each in line with a bronze compass design set in the ceiling above. Nika could see that they'd stepped from the south wing and a part of him wanted to explore the others.

The ornate iron staircase spiralled into the centre of the compass. The hooded man ushered Nika up the steps until he emerged in a sitting room. This room was a little brighter than the library; there were several couches scattered around a fireplace, some bookcases along one of the walls, a desk covered in scrolls and more books, and a small coffee table in front of the fire.

Arnie-Kyn leapt onto one of the couches and licked at one of his paws, looking every bit a real cat. Nika started to wonder if he was going crazy thinking Arnie could talk.

"Please wait here," the man said, locking the trapdoor at the top of the stairs. "I'll have some food prepared for you. Until then, make yourself comfortable. The latrine is through that door."

Nika nodded, too tired to argue. He sank onto the couch and yawned deeply. His body was stiff and sore, and his legs were aching from all the walking they'd done. The room was warm from the crackling fire, and as he looked into the flames, the image of a large fireball flashed before his eyes and disappeared. He sighed and shook his head. Lulled by the warmth of the fire, he fell into an exhausted sleep.

3

Freyne stood before the gates of the University, gazing upon the vast spires in the distance. The sun was starting to sink towards the horizon, causing the walls to cast long shadows over the city. The University had grown considerably since his last visit. What he remembered as a small shanty town camped just within the walls was now a vast sprawling district of derelict slums.

He scratched his cheek, frowning. *I only visited the city two or three years ago. How in the gods has the king allowed these slums to grow so quickly? And when were those new buildings built?*

The guard at the gates whistled and motioned him forward, looking him up and down disdainfully.

"What is your business here?" he demanded.

"I-I'm a merchant from Rybor, sir. My camp was attacked by bandits along the way, and they stole my horse and wagon. I plan to find an inn and clean myself up, then head to the market and hopefully find my friends."

Freyne's voice sounded dry and raspy from not talking for so long. It felt strange to hear his own voice after so many years of solitude. He pulled a jingling purse from his pocket that he'd pickpocketed from someone on the dock, and handed a single gold coin to the guard, who then smiled.

"Why thank you. You may pass. Take care through the slums; the scoundrels are growing more and more restless by the day."

The guard stepped aside, and Freyne ventured into the city. Dishevelled citizens lined the streets, begging passers-by for money. Much to Freyne's relief, none of them paid him any attention, and he hurried through the muddy streets until he reached the cobbled roads of the middle-class district.

He found an inn close to the market and purchased lodgings for the night. The room was tiny with a single bed and a basin, and no fireplace. A bad odour reached his nose, and he was not surprised to find it came from his own filthy body. With a sigh, he made his way to the bathhouse at the rear of the inn.

The building was lit dimly with torches, empty except for the attendant. To the left of the entrance was a hallway lined with doors, presumably each with a bathtub inside. To the right was the attendant's area, where a large cauldron sat boiling on a fire, and another cauldron was set up for washing clothes. The lady was folding towels into a neat pile on a bench.

"What can I do for you, sir?" she asked.

"I wish to bathe and shave, my lady," he said politely, producing another gold coin from his pouch and handing it to her. Her eyes widened a little at the sight of gold, and she quickly pocketed it.

"Of course, sir." She handed him a freshly folded towel and a clean bathrobe. "Bath three will be ready for you in a moment."

"Thank you."

The attendant poured some hot water into the bath, then brought Freyne a tray loaded with grooming products. She curtsied and quietly left the room.

Freyne stripped off his filthy clothes and slipped into the bath. He hadn't had a warm bath for as long as he could remember, and he closed his eyes, enjoying the warm water on his tight muscles. His bath usually consisted of a dip in the stream when it wasn't too cold. He took a rough bar of soap and lathered his body, then lathered his hair and beard, and dunked under the water.

Once he'd scrubbed himself clean, he gazed at his appearance in the mirror. He'd aged somewhat since he had last seen his reflection clearly; he now had a tinge of silver running through his hair and beard which had grown long and messy. The face staring back at him was barely recognisable anymore.

He climbed out of the bath and started cutting his hair off in clumps, then clipped his hair short at the sides and back, keeping a little length in the middle so he could comb it to one side. His attention then turned to shaving off his beard; again, he couldn't remember the last time he'd shaved. He rinsed off the loose hairs, then dried himself off and slipped on the bathrobe.

The temperature of the bathhouse had dropped considerably since he'd arrived; the only warmth came from the now dying fire under the cauldrons. Freyne handed his filthy clothes to the attendant, who looked surprised by his transformation.

"I'll bring your clothes to your room once they are dry, sir," she said politely. "Have a lovely evening."

He thanked her once more, then left the bathhouse feeling like a new man.

Nika had no idea how long he was kept in the sitting room. More of the hooded monks came and went, asking him abrupt questions almost to the point where Nika felt like he was being interrogated. They were rude, except for the kindly monk who greeted Nika on his arrival. To add to his frustration, Arnie-Kyn was nowhere to be seen.

Being cooped up for so long left Nika bored out of his mind. He craved a strong coffee and a steaming hot shower, but all he was offered was weak unsweetened tea, and cold running water from the tap over the basin. He was at least able to shave and groom his goatee, and he was grateful that the latrine was plumbed.

To keep himself from dwelling on his loss of memory and panicking, Nika spent the rest of his time flicking through books and sheets of parchment, pacing around the room, and playing with the firestone. He practised making it glow and change brightness at will and figured out how to make it burst into flame without burning him. *If these guys don't let me out soon, I'll burn their fucking library to the ground,* he thought darkly.

Finally, after what he assumed was a few days, Arnie-Kyn was let into the room by the kindly monk.

"What the hell is going on?" Nika stood and planted his hands on his hips.

"I'm sorry for keeping you for so long. We had to commune with our god and find out what to do with you. You are a stranger to this land, so we had much to discuss." The monk sat and gestured to Nika to sit back down. "We've decided to send you to meet with King To'Rel. Although we manage the royal archives, we are not privy to the information held within. Therefore, only the king will know if there is some way to send you home."

"Who's we?" Nika frowned, his insides squirming.

"We, the monks who run this library." He produced a sealed envelope from inside his robes and handed it to Nika. "Take this letter and make your way to Al'Obrel. We will pray that he can help you."

"I don't know who or where that is. I don't know where I am, and I can't remember anything to do with my life except for my name. How do you expect me to find some king?" Nika exploded.

"Your memory will come back. You probably just hit your head." The monk stood and crossed his arms. "King To'Rel may be the only one who can help you. I've offered you a way to get the help you need, but it's up to you whether or not you accept that help. Whatever you decide, you can't stay here."

Nika sighed and rubbed his eyes, his belly twisting painfully. "Fine. I'll do it. Is it far?"

"It isn't far at all. It's just a two-hour walk from here. We have packed you some lunch and some suitable attire for when you meet with His Majesty."

"And then what do I do?" Nika asked, accepting a pack from the monk.

"We've outlined everything in the letter. Just hand it to him and do whatever he asks of you."

The monk ushered Nika down the spiral staircase and led him along the north wing of the library.

"Are you coming too?" Nika asked Arnie-Kyn.

"Of course. One has felt caged up like an animal and yearns to hunt. The vermin are yet to replenish their numbers since my last visit here."

Nika did not have the energy to point out the obvious. He walked in silence, dwelling on his situation, until the monk stopped in front of an inconspicuous bookcase and swung it open, revealing another secret passage.

"Follow this corridor to the exit. It's the safest and fastest route. May you have the blessings of the gods on your journey, and forever hold Am in your heart."

The monk bowed. Nika followed Arnie through the door

and into the darkness. He withdrew his firestone and willed it to glow, eager to set off and escape the dank underground labyrinth.

"Lead the way," Nika said out loud. "Let's get this over and done with so I can get the hell out of here."

Freyne lay on the floor of his room with his hands under his head, staring at the ceiling. He'd managed to locate the stranger's aura and isolate him from the thousands of people in the city, but the stranger had been in one spot for three days, with minimal movement. All Freyne could do was wait until he moved into the open, and then he could once again follow him.

During the days of waiting, he'd visited the market and bought a few supplies and some new clothes, not knowing where his path would lead. He'd also scouted out the public areas of the University, but was deterred by the heavy presence of guards. He did not want to arouse suspicion or cause any trouble by being caught in a restricted area.

As he lay on the floor, he once again slipped into his trance, and sought out the now familiar aura. The stranger was finally on the move, heading towards the market. Freyne opened his eyes and stood up, his heart beating a little faster than usual. It was time to move. He collected his supplies off the bed, which he hadn't slept in, and hurried from the room.

The tunnel came abruptly to an end, with no door, just a dead end. Before Nika could grumble about how long they had been winding through the tunnel, Arnie-Kyn stretched up on his hind legs and pushed a protruding brick. The wall spun open, and Arnie led him into a narrow chamber. The door closed behind them and locked with a slight *click*. Nika eyed a steel ladder which disappeared into the darkness.

"I guess we're climbing then?" he asked.

"Inconveniently, yes." Arnie's tail was flicking angrily.

Without a word, Nika bent down and picked up the cat, and hoisted him onto his shoulder. Arnie hissed and dug his claws into Nika's skin.

"Ow! Just hold on and you'll be fine. Trust me."

Nika started climbing the narrow ladder effortlessly with Arnie clinging on for dear life. His tail was whipping about furiously, occasionally hitting Nika in the face. He grinned and kept climbing.

They reached the top which was covered by a steel plate. He clung onto the ladder and carefully wedged it aside. At once, Arnie-Kyn vaulted out of the shaft and disappeared. Nika sighed and pulled himself up, then replaced the cover and glanced around. He was in a narrow alleyway nestled between two buildings; one end of the alley was a dead end, and the other was shrouded by leafy bushes and shrubs. He peered through the branches and looked for Arnie-Kyn.

"One is over here, human."

Nika pushed his way through the garden and joined Arnie on the cobblestones.

"We'd better get moving if we wish to see the king today. It is late afternoon, and we must leave the city before nightfall."

Nika followed the cat along the cobbled road.

"Do those monks know that you're coming with me?"

"No. My whereabouts are no concern of theirs," Arnie replied.

"Why don't you talk to them like you talk to me?"

"You ask too many questions, young whelp."

They wove their way through the narrow streets, passing countless stone houses packed tightly together and with minimal decorations to distinguish one from the other. To Nika, it felt like they'd all been cloned all from one original house.

In the distance, he heard the buzz of a crowd, and his attention focused on the noise. The sound grew louder and louder, until he stepped from another alleyway and stood gaping at a great bustling market.

Arnie hissed and froze, his hackles standing on end. Nearby, a man who looked like a hunter stepped into view with six growling dogs roaming freely by his side. The man stopped to haggle with a trader about the price of a bow. Nika stooped and collected the cat, concealing him beneath his cloak. Arnie's claws pierced into his skin and made him flinch; Nika grimaced and moved hastily away from the dogs.

"Head north and don't talk to anyone."

The market was a bustling place of business; brightly

dressed merchants waved their products, trying to attract buyers for their wares. Nika noticed they wore symbols around their neck the size of a small saucer, and he couldn't contain his curiosity any longer.

"Merchants must wear an identifying symbol to show what type of wares they are selling, and they must sell only that. This minimises illegal trade, and makes inspections much easier for the authorities," Arnie explained.

"And does it minimise illegal trade?" Nika asked.

"Of course not; the merchants just get better at hiding it. One would bet one's paws that most of them have multiple permits under different names."

Nika could smell exotic foods being cooked around him, and his belly rumbled rudely. He craved a hot hearty meal; the food he'd eaten at the library was cold and bland. Nika picked up his pace, noting that his legs felt stronger and less painful.

The sky had filled with ominous dark clouds and was losing light rapidly. There was a chill in the air, and it felt like rain was on its way. By the time they reached the centre of the market, some of the merchants had already started packing away their wares, and the crowd was beginning to thin out.

Once they reached the edge of the market, Nika placed Arnie on the ground, and followed him towards a district of slums populated with crude hovels, tents, and abject poverty. The inhabitants were filthy and uncouth, and stared at him full of suspicion. A dishevelled man stepped in front of Nika, barring his path. His eyes looked wild, and his long hair was matted and dirty.

"Ey brother. Would yer have any spare change?" he asked, taking a step closer.

Nika took a step back.

"Sorry. I have no money at all," he replied, holding out both of his hands.

"Well then, I'll just 'ave ter cut it outta yer skin."

The man let out a crazy cackle and drew a rusty dagger, then lunged forward. Nika's instinct kicked in, and he grasped the man's outstretched arm and twisted, making him drop the blade. He brought his elbow around and connected with the man's face, knocking him to the ground. Before Nika could move, someone jumped him from behind, putting both arms around his neck in a chokehold. Nika stepped forward with the momentum and flung his attacker over his head and into the path of an incoming knife-wielding scumbag.

Another man appeared at Nika's side and managed to land a punch on his cheek. Nika spun around and slammed his fist into the man's face, knocking the few yellow teeth that were left into the air as the man fell. A few of the downed men's friends came to their aid, but Nika fought them off easily. He hadn't realised his strength before now, and the fighting came naturally to him. As quickly as he fended them off, though, more were stepping in, trying for a piece of the pie. Before he could make his retreat, he was surrounded; the scumbags kept coming.

Something hard cracked on Nika's head, and he fell to one knee, seeing stars. He looked up in time to see someone lunging at him with a rusty sword, but before he could dodge, the man with the sword suddenly screamed and fell to the ground, a dagger protruding from his throat. Nika shook his head, his eyesight blurry. Someone else had joined the fight and was downing the desperate scumbags quicker than they came.

Out of nowhere, a boot connected with his face, and Nika collapsed from the sudden pain. In the distance, the sound of a whistle blew, and many pairs of feet could be heard running their way. Nika could hear the remaining ruffians flee in a panic. He opened his eyes to see a man retrieving his daggers, before turning to peer down at him. The world spun as he lifted Nika over his shoulder, and everything went black.

Freyne carried the unconscious stranger through the slums and slipped out of the entrance without being spotted. He could hear the ruckus behind them as the guards came across the scene of the fight. Once he was out of sight from the gate, Freyne sat the stranger behind a pylon on the dock, and went in search of a boat to take them across the strait.

He'd shadowed the stranger from the moment he emerged from the secret passage, all through the market, and through the slums. He was impressed by the man's raw strength, and the ease at which he fended off the blows from his attackers.

Freyne found and paid the captain of a small ferryboat, then retrieved the stranger and hoisted him aboard. A low *meow* drew his attention, and he spotted the grey cat on the dock. Freyne whistled and beckoned it over. The cat obliged and leapt on board.

A pair of sailors helped Freyne to carry the stranger inside the cabin and laid him on a spare cot. The cat leapt onto the man's chest and fixed Freyne with an icy gaze. Freyne backed out of the cabin, and watched the sailors push out from shore. The boat slowly drifted into the strait, as the first drops of rain began to fall.

Nika drifted in and out of consciousness. Someone was carrying him, and then he heard voices discussing directions. When he came-to again, he was being laid on something soft and warm, comforting. He fell into a lucid sleep, and at once his memories flooded back, one after the other. He saw his entire life play out before him; his traumatic childhood, troubled upbringing, and his life on the oil rig. And finally, in gruesome detail, his death.

His eyes shot open and he tried to sit up, but something was on his chest, pinning him down. Pain shot through his body, and his head felt worse than any hangover he'd ever experienced. He groaned and felt the weight on his chest move a little. Nika raised his arm and touched his face. At once a sharp pain shot from a tender bump that made him see stars.

"Rest up, human known as Nika. You are safe."

A wave of exhaustion hit him, and Nika sank back into a restless sleep.

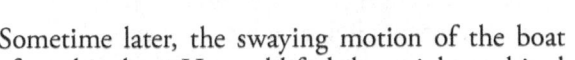

Sometime later, the swaying motion of the boat roused Nika from his sleep. He could feel the weight on his chest was gone, and Arnie curled up in a ball between his legs. Slowly and painfully, he opened his eyes and tried to see where he was.

He was in a dark cabin, with a single torch lit by the door. The room smelt dank and smoky. He could hear heavy rain on the roof and thunder rumbling in the distance.

The door of the cabin opened, and a man wearing a long dark cloak entered, glistening wet from the rain. He removed his cloak and hung it on a peg next to the door, then took a chair from the table and sat next to the cot.

Nika ran his gaze over the man, taking in his handsome features and his big brown eyes. At once he felt at ease; he could sense that the man was a gentle soul, a friend, and Nika felt drawn to him.

"How are you feeling?" the man asked. His voice was quiet and a little raspy, as though he hadn't spoken for a long time.

Nika groaned and held his hand to his head, wincing at the pain. The man wordlessly pulled a pouch from his pack and started mixing powders together in a tin cup. He added some water and stirred it.

"Drink this," he instructed.

He placed his hand gently under Nika's head and held the cup to his lips. Nika swallowed the substance and gagged.

"This should help with some of your pain. It will definitely help reduce the bruising in your face." The man took back the cup and sat it on the table. "My name is Freyne."

"I'm Nika. The cat's name is Arnie-Kyn."

"That was some fight you got yourself into back there."

"I've been in worse."

Nika's thoughts flashed back to the drunken pub brawls he'd survived in his past. With a frown, he pushed himself up to his elbow, and met with Freyne's calm gaze.

"Where are we?" he asked.

"We are in a boat crossing the strait towards Al'Obrel. The storm has swept us far off course, but we should hit land before nightfall tomorrow."

"Al'Obrel? I'm so confused."

"This isle is called Kia-Mor. We're to the far-east of Ayrillis."

Nika buried his face in his hands, momentarily feeling the panic return. The monk was telling the truth; wherever he was, it wasn't home.

"Why did you help me back there?" he asked, frowning.

"If I hadn't stepped in, you'd be dead, and that would be an innocent life on my conscience. You are a stranger to this land and would not survive here by yourself. You don't know our laws or customs."

"Can you please move?" Nika asked silently to Arnie.

The cat stood and stretched, then moved to one side, allowing Nika to sit up and swing his legs over the side of the cot. Arnie repositioned himself in the warm spot where Nika's body had been.

Nika looked down and saw that his cloak and shoes had been removed, along with his trousers. He covered his near-nakedness with a blanket, trying not to blush. A faint grin found Freyne's lips, and he took the dirty cup to rinse it in the washbasin in the far corner of the cabin. Nika looked down at his arms and noticed he was covered in scratches and bruises. The pain in his head had eased a little, though his cheek was aching and tender to touch.

"Are you hungry?" Freyne asked.

"Starving."

Freyne reached into his pack and pulled out some cured ham and a loaf of bread. He cut a thick chunk of ham and motioned to Nika to join him. Nika forced himself up, wrapping the blanket around his waist, and sat at the table. His head spun and was still hurting a little. Freyne tore the bread in half and started eating.

Nika took the knife and cut the bread into slices, then made himself a sandwich. Freyne watched him quizzically with a raised eyebrow.

"What?" Nika asked.

"I don't think I've ever seen someone cut bread before."

"Where I'm from, our bread is always sliced. We call this a sandwich," Nika mumbled.

"Where *are* you from?"

"Not from here, that's for sure. I-I think I'm from another world and I have no idea how to get back."

"How did you get here then?" Freyne asked.

"That's the part I don't understand." Nika frowned, trying to piece it all together. "The night that it happened. I woke up from a nightmare, so I went up to the helipad for some fresh air. There was an explosion, and I was thrown overboard. I died. We all died."

"Helipad?" Freyne asked.

"Oh, I worked on an oil rig. The helipad was the only way on and off the rig; that's where the chopper would land."

Nika saw Freyne's blank stare. After a pause, he went on to describe the rig in more detail.

"I worked in maintenance, so every time something broke down or malfunctioned, I fixed it. Gas and oil are extremely flammable, so it was a very dangerous job. If something wasn't fixed properly, it could spell disaster for the entire rig."

Freyne sat listening to Nika's words, enthralled.

"What a strange place," he marvelled. "What about the cat? I know that isn't just a normal cat."

"He was there when I woke up. He took me to the University, and now we're here." Nika shrugged.

"No, there is more to it than that," Freyne said in his quiet voice. "I know you two have been communicating. I have been watching you ever since I found you in the forest."

Nika looked at Arnie, and Arnie returned his gaze.

"Nature speaks in more ways than one. I have studied her for many years. I know the words of the birds and bees, flowers and trees. The bond between you two is very clear," Freyne said.

"Wait. You followed me all that way? I never saw you."

"I was mostly in the trees." Freyne shrugged. "I sensed your arrival and felt compelled to investigate. There are things afoot in this land. I had to make sure you were here for the benefit of good, not evil."

"You could have just asked me. It would have been nice having some extra company along the way." He shot a sideward glance at Arnie.

The corner of Freyne's mouth curled into a grin and his eyes twinkled for a moment, before turning serious again.

"Why are you going to Al'Obrel? Shouldn't you be trying to find a way back to your world?"

"Apparently the king may be the only one who can help me get back." Nika pulled the letter from his pocket and gazed at the seal, his stomach giving another lurch. "I hope he can help, otherwise I'm stuck here."

Freyne examined the seal and scratched his cheek.

"I've seen this seal before, but I can't remember when or what it means. It's like I'm missing half of my memory."

"I know how that feels," Nika said wryly.

"Well, since I'm here already, would you like me to escort you to Al'Obrel?"

"Are you sure?"

"Of course. It's not like I have any other pressing business." Freyne packed away their dinner items, then stretched and yawned. "It's late. I need to sleep."

Nika nodded in agreeance, and carefully settled back on the cot with Arnie-Kyn. He could tell the cat wasn't comfortable travelling by sea.

Freyne extinguished the torch, then lay on the floor next to Nika with his hands under his head. Nika looked at him over the edge of the cot.

"Why are you laying on the floor?" he asked.

"I'm used to sleeping in trees and on the hard ground. I don't need such luxuries."

Nika lay in his bed, mentally processing the events of the past few days. A stark realisation dawned on him; in his world, he was dead. Unless the king could somehow grant him a miracle, he was fairly certain that there was no way he could ever get back home.

The truth hit him harder than a punch to the stomach. He began to shake and his heart raced a little faster; he was stranded in a strange land, probably for the rest of his life, with nothing but a talking cat and an even stranger man for company.

He thought back on his plans for shore leave; had his rig not been destroyed, he would have been at his favourite bar, playing a gig before getting drunk and spending the night with whoever would take him home. He enjoyed his carefree single life, and chose to live without any ties or commitment to others in his pursuit for happiness.

Nika sighed miserably. He had one dream—to write and perform his own music, and one day to record an album. Making others happy through his music was his one passion in life, just as his favourite musicians had brought him happiness during his darkest nights. And now, all hope of that future was gone, buried at the bottom of the sea in a world to which he would never again return.

4

It was late afternoon when the ferryboat made its way into a tiny cove hidden along the shore. Nika stood on deck, his cloak pulled tight, watching the beach draw closer. Freyne silently joined him and leaned on the rail. The rain had steadied to a light drizzle, making the cove gloomy and uninviting.

The sailors dropped anchor, then pushed a rowboat into the water. Freyne handed their belongings to the sailor in the boat and thanked the captain, while Nika scooped up the begrudging cat and secured him under his cloak. He stepped carefully into the boat and sat in his seat, Arnie's sharp claws piercing his skin. Freyne slid into the seat next to him, and the sailor began rowing them towards the shore.

Instead of sand, the beach was covered in smooth round pebbles, and surrounding them on all sides were steep cliffs which were dotted with caves. The boat grounded, and the sailor climbed over the bow into freezing knee-deep water and pulled the boat onto the beach. Nika and Freyne climbed out.

"Thanks, friend," Freyne said, shaking his hand.

"Yer welcome." The sailor climbed back into the boat, and Nika pushed him into the swells.

He watched as the sailor rowed back to the ferryboat, then turned and walked with Freyne along the beach towards the cliffs. They were already losing daylight, and he was tired, sore, and hungry. Nika turned back to see the ferryboat had already disappeared.

Freyne paused and rested his hand on Nika's forearm. A warm tingle ran up his arm, and he halted, even as Freyne held his fingers to his lips to be quiet. His eyes took on a distant stare, his hand still on Nika's arm. The warmth of Freyne's hand was comforting, enough that Nika didn't feel the need to shy from his touch.

There was a faintest whisper in his mind, before Freyne's eyes came back into focus. He pointed towards a nearby cave, then once again held his finger to his lips. Nika nodded and made his way as quietly as he could to the cave and sat on a rock just inside the entrance. Arnie-Kyn made no effort to escape his hold, though his tail was twitching under the cloak. Nika suspected the cat was cold and in a surly mood. He waited in the growing darkness, the wind whistling around him, and jumped when a terrified squeal pierced the night. After what felt like forever, Freyne returned carrying a what looked like a skinned hare. He held it up for Nika to see, a triumphant grin on his face.

"I thought we could do with a hot meal."

"Oh good. I'm hungry." Nika's mouth started to water. He pulled his firestone from his pocket and willed it to emit a faint glow.

"What's that?" Freyne asked.

"What? Oh." Nika showed him the stone and told him what little he knew about it.

"I think I've heard of those. I'm surprised that you can use it, considering you're not from here."

"That makes two of us."

Freyne led Nika deeper into the cave, and they followed a narrow passage which eventually curved to the left, opening into a hidden campsite. It was small and cosy; basalt rock made up the rough walls, which offered natural seating to the cave's visitors, and there was a pile of driftwood stacked neatly to one side.

"How apt. It's a smugglers' cave," Freyne said, sitting the carcass on a rock. "I can only imagine what people are sneaking to and from Al'Obrel. Let's hope none of them decide to pay a visit while we're here."

"Is it safe?" Nika frowned. "I wouldn't want a group of smugglers to drop in while we're sleeping. They'd probably kill us if they're anything like the smugglers back home."

A sharp pang of homesickness hit him as he thought of his home, an entire world away.

"I'm sure we have nothing to worry about." He shot Nika a reassuring smile.

"Have you been to Al'Obrel before?" Nika asked.

"I don't remember ever leaving the island." Freyne shook his head. "I may have, long ago, but I just can't remember. I seem to be missing most or all of my early memories. It's so frustrating. I hardly know who I am anymore."

"I'm sure they will come back. Mine did."

Nika sat Arnie on a rock and stacked some wood into the fireplace. Freyne handed him a flint and steel, and they soon had a fire warming up the cave. Arnie-Kyn shook himself off, then disappeared into the darkness to hunt.

Freyne pulled some thin poles from his pack and slotted them together, making a spit. He threaded the hare into the middle and placed it over the fire to cook. Nika frowned as he remembered the lunch the monk packed for him. He opened his pack and felt his heart drop. Inside were some clothes, a towel, a map, a few medical supplies, an empty waterskin, and some dried beans.

"Why the fuck would they pack all of this crap if it's just a two-hour walk to Al'Obrel?" he demanded.

"It does sound strange." Freyne nodded his agreement. "Maybe they were just thinking ahead should you get lost. Can I see the map?"

Nika pulled out the map and unfolded it carefully, his heart dropping even more as his situation was further confirmed. On one half was the known world of Ayrillis, and the other half showed a zoomed-in section labelled the Eastern Isles. Freyne sat next to him, their shoulders touching, and studied the map on Nika's lap.

"This is where you started." He pointed to a tiny island, to a point marked by ruins. "This is where I started tracking you, and this is the University." He traced their path along the map. "This is where we boarded the boat, and we would have come aboard at the dock here—" he pointed to the icon of a city opposite the University, "—but we got swept all the way down to roughly here."

Nika looked closer at the map.

"How long will it take us to walk all the way back up to Al'Obrel?" he asked.

"Probably around three days of steady walking," Freyne estimated. "It was a bad storm. You're lucky you slept through it."

Nika started to fold the map, then stopped when he spotted a calendar on the back page. He held it up to the light and saw that there were ten months, each with forty-two days. Someone had marked in the seasons in different coloured inks, and *arrival* was written neatly on the 33rd day of Jalie, the sixth month of the year.

"Interesting," Freyne said. He counted on his fingers. "That's the date that you arrived here. I guess I wasn't the only one tracking you."

"Lucky me," Nika murmured.

"Tell me more about you and your world," Freyne said, leaning his back against the cave wall.

Nika leant back too, watching the hare sizzle on the spit, their shoulders and knees still lightly touching. Again, Nika felt comforted by Freyne's closeness, and didn't shy away.

"There's not much to tell, really," he said thoughtfully. "I'm just a regular guy. I'd work three weeks straight on the rig, then have two weeks off. It was hard work, but good money, and I enjoyed being away from people."

"Did you have a wife or family?" Freyne asked.

Nika shook his head.

"I fooled around a bit, but marriage was never my thing," he replied. "I just wanted to have fun while I was on leave, not be tied down to someone. I even sold my car when I started working on the rig so I didn't have to commit to payments while offshore."

"What's a car?"

Nika went on to tell Freyne all about cars, the different makes and models, colours, shapes, and sizes. Freyne listened to his every word, enthralled.

"You come from such a strange place," he said finally.

"Well, this place is just as strange to me," Nika pointed out. "I haven't met many people here yet so I can't really compare. But the people back home are more interested in themselves than helping others and turn a blind eye to those in need. Society also places expectations on everyone. You are expected to dress and act a certain way, get married and start a family. The man supports his wife and children and there's little room to deviate from that. It's stupid."

Freyne shook his head and stood up. He removed the spit from the fire, then pulled two metal plates and some cutlery from his pack. Nika's mouth watered as Freyne carved slithers of meat from the hare and loaded up each of the plates.

The meat was crispy and juicy, and as Nika chewed he closed his eyes, savouring the delicious meat. Arnie-Kyn returned soon after with a small rodent in his mouth, and sat by the fire, chewing noisily.

"This is so good," Nika murmured.

"Nothing beats freshly hunted game," Freyne agreed.

Once he was full, Nika yawned and rubbed his belly. He'd eaten too much, and felt a wave of exhaustion wash over him. The cave was warm, almost too warm, and made him feel sleepy. Freyne boiled some water in a small pot to wash the dishes, then made them each some tea. They sat sipping from their tin cups, watching the fire die down as Nika recounted more stories from his world, until it was time to sleep.

Freyne stretched out on the rocky ground next to the fire, and Nika joined him, using his cloak as a pillow. The ground was rough and uncomfortable, but Nika was so exhausted he almost immediately fell into a deep sleep.

Freyne woke early, feeling fresh and well rested. Nika was still sleeping, with Arnie-Kyn nestled into his neck. Freyne looked closely at the bruising on his face and was pleased to see the swelling had gone and the bruise was just a quarter of its original size. He couldn't help admiring Nika's striking features which were becoming more noticeable as his injuries healed. Arnie stirred and stretched, then sat up and started licking his paw.

With a sigh, Freyne gathered up the few things they'd strewn around the cave and redistributed the contents between his and Nika's packs. He wasn't too keen on having to walk for three days lugging his heavy pack by himself, so he was somewhat grateful that Nika's had plenty of room to spare.

Once he was satisfied, he headed outside. The rain clouds had broken up and blown away through the night. The rising sun made the sky a rippled pattern of orange and yellow; the wind still howled around the cliffs, but was not as icy as the night before. Freyne walked slowly along the beach, gathering his thoughts together.

In the few days he'd gotten to know Nika, he felt a firm friendship forming between them. He enjoyed hearing Nika's tales of his strange world, and in turn Nika always seemed to enjoy listening to some of his hunting stories. Whenever he tried to remember life outside of the forest, though, his memory was clouded, like there was a thick fog in the back of his mind. It was as though he'd been in a dream for a long time, and he was only just waking up.

For many years, he'd had no company, and never had he craved it. Yet now, he was enjoying having someone to talk to, no matter how strange the conversation. There was something different about Nika, and Freyne felt drawn to him.

The tide was out, exposing the rocks and reefs. Small crabs and creatures scurried around in the shallow pools as he passed. He sat on a raised rock, and watched the sunrise for a while, slipping into his familiar trance and feeling the land around him. The wind whispered of things afoot, and the waves sang of increased activity on her back. Most concerning, however, was the call of the earth itself; something was waking up, and the elements feared what would come.

"Trouble is rising. Prepare yourself," the winds whispered.

"Watch your step. There is evil hiding around every corner," the rocks warned.

"What should I do?" Freyne asked.

"Be careful, old friend. Trouble is coming."

Freyne pulled his mind back and sighed. The forces of nature were always being dramatic and warning of danger, but never told him what to look for. It was frustrating; he never knew if he should be worried or not. He did know that something big was coming, and suspected that Nika would somehow be involved, but still he had no idea what to expect.

Looking down, he caught sight of his reflection in one of the shimmering pools. He already had whiskers growing on his cheeks and needed to shave. Using the water as a mirror, Freyne pulled his dagger from its sheath and expertly shaved while still mulling over his thoughts. The splash of cold water over his face to rinse away the hairs was refreshing, and he stood, ready to face his day.

At the base of the cliffs to his right, he caught sight of Arnie-Kyn. The cat meowed, and Freyne felt compelled to go to him. As he approached, Arnie looked meaningfully up at the cliff, and Freyne followed his gaze. Rough stairs had been hacked into the cliff, giving them a way to leave the cove.

Freyne frowned and looked at the cat, who was gazing back at him. Curious, he pushed his mind forward, and was surprised when Arnie-Kyn joined with him.

"So this is how you've been communicating."

"You finally figured it out. One would have thought that someone so attuned to nature would have caught on sooner."

"What? Who are *you?"* Freyne demanded. *"How can you possibly know that?"*

"Don't be silly. One is just a cat."

"Why are you following Nika then?"

"One goes wherever one wishes to go. Right now, one finds the human compelling and is curious where his path will lead. Now, one suggests you go and wake him up so we can get moving, before we meet the occupants of that boat."

Freyne spun around and scanned the water. Sure enough, an ominous black dot in the distance was moving towards them. He groaned inwardly.

"Very well. I'll be right back."

Nika was tired and grumpy when he was woken and ushered out of the cave. He was stiff and sore from sleeping on the ground, and craving a coffee to help prepare him for the day. As they hurried along the beach, though, he caught a glimpse of the ship in the distance and felt a sense of foreboding that alerted him more than a strong coffee could.

"Do you think they're smugglers?" he asked.

"I doubt an honest sailor would come this way."

Nika climbed two steps, then paused when he noticed that Arnie wasn't following them.

"Are you coming?" he asked.

"Of course."

He waited, but the cat didn't move. Swearing under his breath, Nika bent down and picked him up, then hurried to catch up to Freyne.

They were almost at the top when the ship anchored and lowered two boats into the water. Freyne tugged on Nika's arm, and they crouched down low, watching over the edge of a rock. There were eight people in each of the row boats, all dressed in black robes.

"That's interesting," Freyne whispered.

"What is?"

"Whoever they are, I doubt they're smugglers. I wonder what they're up to."

Nika felt a shiver run down his spine.

"I really don't want to find out," he said, rubbing his head. "I've already met some of the unpleasant people from your land. Let's get out of here."

Nika couldn't help feeling anxious as they made their way towards Al'Obrel. They made good time, with minimal talking through the day and stopping only when necessary. At Freyne's insistence, they avoided the main road just in case the black-cloaked people had seen them leaving the cove. There was something ominous about the people from the boat, and after his skirmish in the slums, he didn't feel like meeting any more hostile people in his travels.

They set up camp each night in a secluded place, risking a small fire, and spent the nights sharing stories and relaxing. Nika enjoyed Freyne's company and looked forward to their evenings together. He felt a sense of familiarity, as though he'd known Freyne for much longer than just a few days. In a way, their budding friendship helped to keep Nika grounded whenever he grew scared about being trapped in the strange world.

As Freyne predicted, they arrived on the outskirts of Al'Obrel on the afternoon of the third day. As they drew closer, Freyne placed his hand on Nika's arm and pointed.

"There's a stream in the gully over there. Let's go and freshen up before we enter the city. It's considered rude to smell this bad in front of a king."

Nika sniffed his armpit and grimaced.

"Yeah, I stink."

Freyne led the way to the stream which was well-hidden from the road. Nika scratched his head and frowned.

"How did you know this was here?" he asked.

"The trees." Freyne pointed to the few lone trees that were dotted along the bank.

"Right." Nika had no idea what Freyne was talking about.

Freyne removed his cloak and shirt and hung them on a low tree branch, then reached down to undo his belt. Nika turned his back, feeling his face turn red; he'd never been naked around another man before. Even on the oil rig he chose to shower alone and avoid any embarrassment that could arise from such a situation. He heard a soft splash as Freyne slipped into the water.

"You can look now," Freyne called. Nika turned to see him in the water up to his neck. "The water's warm. Come on in."

Nika removed his cloak and shirt, then motioned to Freyne to turn around. He obliged; Nika stripped off naked and slid into the water. The spring was indeed warm and felt soothing on Nika's healing legs. He dunked his head under the water and held his breath for as long as he could before coming up for air. Wiping the water from his eyes, he watched Freyne lathering the soap all over his body. Their eyes locked for a split second; Nika blushed and quickly looked away. Freyne wordlessly handed him the soap and disappeared under the water for a few seconds.

A gentle *meow* drew Nika's attention, and he turned to see Arnie sitting on the bank, watching them bathe.

"What's up?" Nika asked silently.

"Are you prepared for your meeting with the king?"

"No, not really. I've never spoken to a king before. I wouldn't know what to say or do."

An odd sensation touched at the edge of Nika's mind, and he looked around uneasily.

"Perhaps he—" Arnie turned his head and nodded at Freyne, *"—can do the talking. One believes King To'Rel to be fair, but in this world, royalty must be respected and addressed appropriately."*

"How do we get to see him? Do we just walk in, or do we have to ask someone for permission first?" Nika asked.

"At the entrance to the castle, you will be met by guards. Show them the seal on the envelope, and say you bring word from the monks of the University. They should take you straight to His Majesty," Arnie replied.

"Sounds easy enough," Nika mused. He looked across at Freyne, who was returning his gaze with a raised eyebrow.

"Yes, I can do the talking. Although I can't remember it, I'm certain I've spoken to kings and queens before." Freyne's voice sounded in Nika's mind, making him jump.

"What, now you can read minds too?"

Freyne looked slyly at Arnie, then back at Nika.

"Your friend here showed me how to join our minds," he replied. *"I knew you two were communicating somehow. This is a useful skill to have."*

"Is nothing private here?"

"Relax. I can't read your thoughts any more than you can read mine."

Nika sighed and quickly finished washing himself. There was so much he didn't understand, and it was weighing heavily on him. *God, I hope the king can help me get home,* he thought.

Freyne offered him his razor, a piece of polished metal to use as a mirror, and some scissors. Nika studied his face in the mirror. The bruise had gone, and his goatee had grown into a short beard, disproportionate to the rest of the hair on his face. He was a mess. Being careful not to cut himself, he shaved and groomed his goatee back to his preferred length.

"How do I look?" he asked.

Freyne studied Nika's face, his eyes lingering for a little longer than necessary.

"Less like a delinquent and more like a noble man," he grinned. "I don't think either of us will offend the king now."

Freyne climbed out of the water and dried off, unperturbed by his nakedness. Nika covered himself as he emerged from the pool and quickly dried himself, then secured the towel around his waist and pulled out the clothes the monks had packed for him. To his dismay, they were hideous grey robes that looked way too big for him.

"There is no way in hell I'm wearing these!" Nika exploded. "What the fuck are those guys playing at?"

"They look terrible," Freyne agreed, a hint of a smirk on his face. "Don't worry. I have a spare set of clothes you can wear. It's a good thing I bought extra from the market."

5

The streets of Al'Obrel were congested with thick throngs of people. Merchants, farmers, and scholars all passing through on their way to and from the University, while the local inhabitants went about their daily business with an air of self-importance.

Nika walked with Freyne along the main cobbled road that spiralled around the city, winding its way up the hill towards the king's castle. He couldn't help but notice that some areas were run down and shabby on one side of the road whilst pristine on the other.

"The districts are sectioned depending on their status in society," Freyne explained quietly as they walked. "The poorest areas are on the outskirts, the farthest from the castle. Then you have the middle class which provides most of the workers for the trades and businesses. The wealthiest financial district circles the moat of the castle."

"That's not fair," Nika noted.

"I know. If the city was ever attacked, the poorer people would be the first to suffer, while the wealthiest would have the higher chance to survive. It's barbaric."

The streets of Al'Obrel were lined by narrow two or three-storey terraces made of dark granite, similar to the granite Nika saw back in the cave. The further up the hill they walked, the more elegant the buildings became. They passed inns and barbers, weapon smiths and tailors, all evenly spread out amongst the middle-class district.

After an hour of walking along the curved road, they found

a direct path that led up the hill to the castle. Nika's legs were aching from the constant incline, but he was determined not to let the pain stop him. *My ticket out of here is at the top of that hill,* he thought to himself. *Once I'm there, I can finally get out of this hell-hole.*

An elegant yet intimidating gate loomed over them, giving Nika the impression that it was more to deter people from entering than for actual security. It was manned by armed guards in polished armour; the plumes on their helms and the trims of their capes were purple, which matched the crests being flown from the king's castle. The wall was topped with sharp spikes and circled the entire financial district. Nika picked up Arnie and hid him under his cloak.

As they approached the gate, the guards stepped forward and drew their swords. Freyne stopped abruptly, and Nika bumped into him.

"What is your business here?" one of the guards demanded.

"We have come from the University and carry a letter for His Majesty, the king. We seek audience with him on a matter of great importance," Freyne said, bowing.

"Let me see the letter, and I will tell you if it is important or not," the guard snapped, eyeing them distastefully.

Nika rummaged in his pocket and withdrew the letter, then held it out. The guard snatched it with a snarl and glanced at the seal. His expression abruptly changed and his face paled.

"I beg your pardon, sir. I apologise most humbly for my rudeness. I'm Lieutenant Hisley. Please allow me to escort you directly to the king myself."

Lieutenant Hisley bowed deeply and handed Nika back the letter. The other guards sheathed their weapons and stood aside, allowing them to pass.

The financial district was clearly inhabited by the wealthiest citizens. Instead of drab stone, the houses were built from marble and rare, valuable materials. The houses each had their own walls and guarded gates, and the streets were lined with beautiful gardens and trees. Lords and ladies strolled along the streets and turned up their noses as Nika and Freyne passed.

Floating above the noises of the district came a tune from a single pipe instrument. Nika slowed and glanced around but he couldn't see where it came from. It was a slow and melancholic tune, and he could tell that whoever played it was a skilled musician. As he swept his glance back to the road, he spotted a group of black-cloaked people entering one of the villas. He frowned, then shrugged and hurried to catch up to Freyne.

The road continued to curve in its spiral motion away from the music, until they finally reached a drawbridge that spanned the moat. Nika could tell that it was man-made and felt sorry for whoever had to dig it out. The lieutenant led them across the bridge and nodded at the castle guards who let them pass without question.

King To'Rel's castle towered above them in all its glory. The castle itself was built from light grey stone, but was rendered on the external walls to make it look like shimmery quartz from a distance. They crossed a courtyard lined with garden beds and trees, then climbed a steep flight of steps that led to the entrance of the castle. A pair of heavy doors stood open, and Hisley ushered Nika and Freyne inside.

They were in an antechamber directly opposite the entrance to the court. Two guards in the same uniform as their escort stood to attention and saluted, then parted and allowed them to enter.

Nika felt his jaw drop and gaped around in wonder. The court was a large, brightly lit room, filled with lords and ladies milling around in their finery, gossiping and trying to make themselves look important. The king's purple crest hung at even intervals on the walls, alternating with torches hanging in fancy holders.

Directly opposite the entrance was a stage where the king sat on his throne overlooking the court. On the wall high above him was a round window which bathed him in natural light. King To'Rel was leaning on his elbow, listening to a dispute between a lord and a commoner.

"…and then he stole, killed, and ate my goat, Your Maj–"

"Stop. You are incredibly wealthy, Lord Lenier, am I correct?" The king spoke directly to the lord.

"Why, yes, Your Majesty," he replied, inclining his head.

"And you… which district did you say you are from?" the king asked, pointing at the poorer man.

"T-t-the northeast district, My Lord," the man stuttered.

"And am I to understand that, based on your lowest of status, you have no money to repay this lord for his goat?"

"That is correct, My King."

King To'Rel regarded the two men, then cleared his throat.

"Stealing is a crime punishable by law. But in this case, we have a lowly peasant who was merely trying to survive and feed his family. You, on the other hand, have plenty of money, and do not face such hardship. I hereby order you to employ this man into your service, and pay him fairly, so he may in turn afford to care for his family." The king's gaze landed on the lord, who looked furious.

"Your Majesty! This is outrag—" the lord started to protest.

"SILENCE!" he roared, sitting up straight in his throne. "My word is law, and if you break my law, you will be punished by death and your head placed on a pike in your own district square! Understood?"

"Yes, Your Majesty." The lord was visibly shaken and inclined his head.

"And should any harm come to this man, or if you do not treat him fairly, you will suffer the same consequence. Do you understood me?"

"Yes, Your Majesty."

"Good. Now get out of my sight." He waved towards the doors, and two guards stepped forward to escort the lord and peasant from the room.

The king looked wearily around the court, and his eyes fell on Nika and Freyne. He beckoned them forward and shot a questioning look at Hisley. The lieutenant bowed, then left without a word.

"What is your business here, gentlemen?" To'Rel asked, eyeing them intently.

Freyne took a step forward and bowed deeply.

"Your Majesty. I am Freyne and this is Nika. We bring you a letter from the University."

Nika felt Freyne's presence enter his mind.

"You need to bow," he said.

Nika blushed and bowed awkwardly.

"A letter could have been delivered to the mail room for

my later attention," the king said. "What's so important that you had to come and take up my time?"

Nika held out the letter, and a guard took it and handed it to the king. To'Rel glanced at the seal and flinched. He sighed and stood up.

"You two, follow me. Guards, send the rest of the civil matters away for today, and do not disturb me unless I call."

The king beckoned to Nika and Freyne to follow, then led them to a small office to the right of the stage. It was cosy, dotted with several lush red armchairs, which faced a carved wooden desk. Hanging on the wall behind it was a large tapestry map of the Isles.

King To'Rel took his seat behind the desk and motioned to Nika and Freyne to sit. Nika extracted Arnie from his cloak and sat him on his lap, his tail twitching. The king sat staring at the seal, then drew a small dagger and sliced it open. Nika felt awkward in the silence as To'Rel read the parchment, stroking his short brown beard and occasionally nodding his head. Finally, he put down the letter and leant forward to study the two men before him.

"This is grave news you have delivered," he said. "Do you know about the great prophecy?"

Nika and Freyne both shook their heads.

"It is not well known, except to a few curious individuals, world leaders, and the monks of the University. Let me tell you a story.

"It began in the year 1857 of the current calendar. The holy war was at its worst; it had been raging for forty years. The great leader of the Eastern Isles, King Za'Haal, was at his wits end. He was utterly despaired that his people were dying and decided to do something about it. He went on a secret pilgrimage to the place of the gods and made a pact with them. He offered them his own life in return for eternal protection of his people. The gods agreed, but at a higher price. It would take the sacrifice of his son and his sons' sons from there on, in order to keep the protection strong. And so, each leader made sure he had two sons, one to rule and one as a sacrifice, as only the blood from Za'Haal's direct line would suffice.

"Down the line, King Sa'Mel had just one son. His wife died shortly after giving birth, and in his grief Sa'Mel refused to breed with another. Instead, he invested everything into his only son, Ami'Khel. Enemies of the kingdom knew this would make him vulnerable, so Sa'Mel trained the boy in all types of combat and defence, in hopes to protect him until he could have sons of his own.

"Ami'Khel, however, grew into a selfish blood-hungry fighter. In 2372, at just nineteen years old, he murdered his father and took the throne for himself. Being an only son, and having no more family to contend for the throne, it was his by right.

"He ruled for seven years and had no son. The kingdom was failing, and in 2379, General Brint murdered him and took over the throne as regent. The pact was broken, and the people Za'Haal desperately wanted to protect were now once again vulnerable."

"Why did the general kill him if there was so much at stake?" Nika asked.

Freyne elbowed him gently and shot him a look, but To'Rel didn't seem to mind his question.

"Ami'Khel was evil in every sense of the word. He raised taxes just to make himself wealthy, and if the poor could not pay, he would send his army to terrorise their families. He decreed that those with outstanding debts would pay with their loved one's lives and dignity. I can only assume that General Brint was angry because it brought shame on Za'Haal's name and the army. He knew Ami'Khel was selfish and would never sacrifice himself like his ancestors did.

"As soon as Khel was dead, the protection that bound the people was ripped apart. The bloodline was no more, so there was no king to take the throne of the Eastern Isles. Civil war broke out, and the land divided into five separate kingdoms. Of course things have changed since then, but there is still a lot of corruption in these cities, as there is no one to govern the kings."

To'Rel leaned back in his chair and clasped his hands on his lap. An awkward silence filled the air.

"Er…with all due respect, Your Majesty. How will this help me to get home?"

"Home? The letter tells me that you are a wandering vagabond who agreed to help me on an urgent task I have."

Nika stared at the king open-mouthed, not believing his

ears. The monks had clearly lied to him, and the realisation made him sick to his gut.

"But—"

Freyne patted Nika's leg and cleared his throat.

"What would you have us do, Your Majesty?" he asked.

"There was no mention of you in the letter, but since you are here now, you will be going too. The great prophecy states that there is, in fact, a surviving descendant of Za'Haal's direct bloodline. I am sending you both to find this descendant, and you will escort him to the place of the gods to complete the sacrifice and restore peace to the Isles. If he does not willingly give his life to the gods, you must finish the task."

Freyne and Nika exchanged glances.

"We are just two nobodies, Your Majesty. Wouldn't such a task be better suited for people with more skills?" Freyne scratched his cheek, his confusion evident.

"This task is top secret. If my adversaries gather wind of this, it could affect me in devastating ways. I explicitly ordered the monks to send me a commoner with no ties or family who will blend in and not be missed should something happen. Plausible deniability, if you will. Now—"

A door burst open, startling Nika and making him jump. Arnie's claws dug into his legs. A frazzled servant hurried into the room and bowed hastily to King To'Rel.

"What is it, Deron?

"Pardon the interruption, My King. I have urgent news."

To'Rel beckoned him over, and the servant whispered something in his ear. At once To'Rel's face darkened.

"Notify housekeeping to prepare two rooms for my guests here. We will continue our conversation tomorrow."

"Yes, My King."

To'Rel swept from the room and slammed the door in his wake. The red-faced servant pulled on a cord, and shortly after a maid entered the office. They spoke in hushed tones for a moment, before the maid hurried off.

"What's going on?" Nika asked, feeling his stomach churn.

"I'm not at liberty to answer that. Please come with me, sir."

Deron led them through a maze of passageways and up two flights of stairs. As they walked along a hallway lined with doors, a group of around twenty guards ran past them. Nika stayed close to Freyne, not wanting to get separated from him.

"Here are your rooms, sirs. Please stay inside and do not roam the castle. Someone will be in soon to fill your baths and bring you your dinner."

Nika stepped into one of the rooms and waited for Freyne to follow, but Deron closed the door, leaving him alone with Arnie-Kyn and his dark thoughts. Nika wondered across to the window and gazed out at the city. Everything felt so strange, so foreign, and he couldn't remember ever feeling so lost in his entire life. With a deep sigh, he slid down the wall, hugging his knees to his chest. The monks were right about one thing. He *was* a vagabond, homeless, with nothing but the clothes on his back. *It's just like my nightmare, only this time, there's no foster family waiting to bail me out,* he thought miserably. *This time, I'm well and truly on my own.*

Freyne sat on the couch, his belly swollen from the rich hearty stew he'd eaten for dinner. He'd bathed already and was wrapped in a warm bath robe while his clothes were being laundered by the servants. Despite the comfort of his room, he was feeling unsettled, something he wasn't accustomed to. He'd grown so used to spending his evenings with Nika that he felt a pang of loneliness. He missed his friend's company, and more than anything, he wanted to check on Nika and make sure he was ok

He sat in silence for a while, growing edgier as time went by. His room was too quiet without bats and insects singing their melodies to lull him to sleep. The window was locked, so he couldn't even open it to let in the night air, and to make his night even worse, the bed was so soft he couldn't get comfortable.

Finally, he could stand it no longer. He opened his door and peeked out cautiously; two guards were leaning against the wall at the far end of the hall, too busy complaining about their late shifts to notice him sneaking from his room. He tip-toed down the hall and took a deep breath, then tapped lightly on Nika's door and waited.

The bath water was tepid by the time Nika was done. He dried himself off and had just slipped on a bath robe when he heard another tap at the door.

"What now?" Nika demanded.

He crossed his arms and frowned, expecting yet another servant to enter and bustle him around. To his surprise, Freyne entered instead, a gentle smile on his face. Relief washed over him and he felt his face twitch into a smile of his own.

"I'm sorry. I didn't mean to intrude," Freyne said. "Would you like some company?"

"I'd much rather you than those bloody servants," Nika said.

"They're just doing their job. At least we got to have a nice bath and a hot meal."

Nika sat on the bed and leaned against the back board while Freyne helped himself to the couch. He glanced around the room but couldn't see Arnie-Kyn anywhere.

"Are you alright?" Freyne asked after a pause.

"Not really. I feel like shit," Nika admitted. "Why would those monks lie and send me here?"

"I don't know. Something feels off about this whole thing."

"I'm stuck here, aren't I?"

"We don't know that for sure. Maybe if we do this thing for To'Rel, he might agree to help you."

"Why should we? Whatever it is, it's his problem, not ours." Nika pulled the blanket to his chin, more for comfort than for warmth. "Maybe I should go back to the monks and demand that they help me."

"No. In this world, the king's power is absolute. We must obey his every order, or we will be punished severely. And if we try to run, we'll be hunted down and put to death in a gruesome way."

"What are we going to do, then?" Nika asked, his hopes falling once more.

"When the king summons us, we will be expected to do as he asks. I don't think we have much of a choice."

"I'm so sorry I got you into this," Nika said sincerely.

"It's ok. I've already come this far with you, we may as well continue on together." Freyne's lips twisted into a grin.

"Besides, I think I'm much better company than the cat."

"Much better," Nika agreed. He frowned as another thought came to him. "Is it normal for cats to speak to humans here?"

"Hardly. I've studied nature for many years and have never seen anything like it. He seems harmless enough, though."

"Somehow I don't think he'd leave even if we asked him to." Nika sighed. "This is all so overwhelming. How are you coping with all of this and being away from your forest?"

"I've been roaming aimlessly for so long that a part of me is excited for an adventure. When was the last time you got to explore some place new and learn about a different culture?"

Nika mulled over Freyne's words for a moment, and as they sunk in, he realised his friend was right.

"You know, I've been working so hard since I finished school, I never got to go on any adventures except for a few camping trips here and there. Since I'm here, I may as well make the most of it I guess."

"There you go. Perspective is everything."

"Alright. I'll do it. What now?"

Freyne flashed him a warm smile.

"I'd really like to hear another one of your stories. Please, tell me more about your world."

6

Nika woke early, the sun still rising into the sky. It felt good to sleep in a proper bed for once, and were it not for the servants fussing over him, he would have gone back to sleep. With a groan, he rolled over and spotted Arnie-Kyn sitting on the windowsill, stalking and swiping at the birds fluttering by outside.

"Morning," Nika greeted him.

"Yes, it is," the cat replied.

Nika felt his face twist into a slight grin at the cat's response. There was a knock at the door, and Deron entered carrying an armful of new clothing.

"Excuse me, sir. Have you seen – oh, there you are." He sat the clothes on the bed and shot Freyne an irritated look.

Freyne yawned and stretched, then sat up on the couch.

"Is there a problem?" he asked.

"No. Not now, at least. His Majesty has sent for you both. Please dress and join me in the hallway as quickly as possible. His Majesty doesn't like to be kept waiting."

Nika sat up and looked across at his friend.

"Sleep well?" he asked.

"Not really. It was too quiet," Freyne replied. "At least the couch was comfortable. I'm not used to such luxuries."

Nika sorted through the pile of clothes and separated them into two outfits, one each for him and Freyne. He held up a long-sleeved shirt that was unlike anything he'd ever worn or even seen before.

"What on Earth is this?" he asked.

"It's an overshirt," Freyne explained, joining him. "Wear it over the undershirt – no, that one – and you can tighten those strings if you are cold. You might want to wear your belt with those trousers as they look rather loose."

The trousers were much softer than the pants of his world, clearly made by hand from finer fabrics. He turned his back to Freyne and quickly dressed, leaving the robe on the bed. Once he was ready, Nika turned back around. Freyne reached out and fixed Nika's collar, then winked. Arnie leapt off the windowsill, allowing Nika to hide the flush that crept into his cheeks from Freyne's attention.

Deron led them downstairs and through a maze of hallways and doors, until they finally arrived at the king's inner courtyard. They stepped into a magical garden hidden deep in the heart of the castle, the sky a perfect blue above them. A clear stream bubbled from a cluster of rocks in the corner and trickled its way around the garden to disappear underground. The castle walls were lined with lush flowering garden beds, and a cobbled path led to a wooden table with six chairs where the royal family were seated. The king motioned to Nika and Freyne to join them.

"Good morning, friends," To'Rel said, smiling. "This is my wife Nahal, and my daughter Iryna. This is Freyne and Nika who I was telling you about."

Nika followed Freyne's lead and made sure to incline his head when greeting the royal family. He nervously sat at the table, worried he'd say or do something to anger the king or embarrass himself. A host of servants filed into the courtyard carrying trays loaded with food for breakfast. There were eggs and ham, thick bread, pots of butter, as well as exotic fruits and grains he'd never seen before.

"Eat up, everyone," To'Rel said informally. "You too, Ur'Shad. I refuse to discuss important business on an empty stomach."

A burly guard sat in the remaining seat at the table next to Iryna and helped himself to the platters of food. Unlike the other guards, Ur'Shad's head was shaved completely bald, and he wore a formal cloak edged in the king's purple. He was only slightly taller than Nika, but built solid. Nika looked closer, his curiosity piqued, and saw that Ur'Shad's sword was much larger than the other guards, strapped across his back instead of dangling from his hip.

Just as he took a bite, Iryna pushed away her plate with a huff and crossed her arms over her chest. She wore a striking aqua gown and a short teal cloak that covered her shoulders. Her long golden hair was kept in place with a tiara, and her eyes flashed with anger.

"What is it now, daughter?" To'Rel snapped.

"I'm not hungry," she grumbled. "May I be excused?"

"You only just got here. Eat up, ungrateful child."

"I said I'm not hungry!" she screeched.

Iryna stood up abruptly, knocking her seat backwards. Ur'Shad sighed and stood also, shooting a longing glance at his breakfast. The princess stormed out of the courtyard and slammed the door in Ur'Shad's face. He wordlessly opened it and hurried after her. To'Rel rubbed his eyes and shook his head.

"I do apologise for my daughter. She is, in essence, a brat."

Nika took a deep drink of his tea to hide his awkwardness. They ate in silence until the king was done and cleared his throat.

"Deron," he called.

"Yes, My King?"

"Clear everyone out, then bring me Chardi and J'mai."

The servants whisked away the breakfast items, and Deron ushered the rest of the servants and guards from the courtyard. Shortly after, they were joined by two more guards who dropped to their knee before the king, their helms tucked under their left arms.

"Take a seat, you two," To'Rel said.

The two guards scrambled to their feet and quickly sat at the table. Nika shifted uncomfortably. They were dressed in the same armour as the rest of the guards, only they too wore their swords across their backs and looked to be of a higher rank than the others.

"Chardi and J'mai, this is Nika and Freyne. I'm sending you on a mission that's top secret. Here are your orders." To'Rel handed Chardi a folded piece of parchment and sat back in his chair.

Nika watched as Chardi read the parchment intently. His ginger hair was cut short and his beard neatly trimmed, whereas J'mai had long greasy black hair. Chardi frowned and handed the parchment to J'mai without a word.

"My King. Are you sure it's wise for me to leave after the attack yesterday?" Chardi asked.

"You are some of the few whom I still trust," To'Rel said, his expression stern. "Your elite team knows what they are doing, and your second-in-charge is more than qualified to step up during your absence. You two are my best fighters and are the most likely to succeed in this mission."

"Attack?" Nika asked, finding his voice.

"It's not important right now." To'Rel waved his hand. "You must find this blood descendant and finish what should have been done centuries ago."

"Where do you suggest we look?" Chardi asked.

"I've studied the prophecy and have spoken to the monks many times, but the passages still make no sense. There are two which may be relevant:

Filth and decay, abundance of life.
Pestilence, death and disease are rife.
The flesh will bleed dry and be left to rot.
Find truth beneath a mossy rock.

He walks among them like everyone else.
Nobody knows not even himself.
The battle of life and death must be fought,
but first many lessons have to be taught."

To'Rel pulled a map from somewhere under the table and gently unrolled it on the table. It showed the Eastern Isles in much more detail than Nika's map.

"It's referring to a cemetery or crypt," J'mai said at once. "Think about it. Death, decay, bleeding dry. It makes sense."

"You could be right," To'Rel mused. "Which one, though?"

"We could visit each of the major burial sites and inspect them," Chardi suggested.

"No."

Everyone turned to face Freyne.

"What do you mean, no?" To'Rel frowned, a hint of annoyance on his face.

"It's not talking about a burial ground. Filth and decay, abundance of life. It's talking about a swamp." Freyne shifted in his seat, his leg brushing against Nika's. "I know this sounds crazy, but I have a strong feeling that's where we have to go."

"Don't be ridiculous," J'mai scoffed. "There's not much that can survive in a swamp let alone a person. You want us to risk this mission based on a feeling?"

"There are insects, birds, animals, amphibians, trees, and all sorts of living creatures. Believe me, swamps are teeming with life, even if you do not deem those creatures worthy of being alive." Freyne crossed his arms and leaned back. "This isn't going to be some simple stroll to the next city, kidnap a person, and kill him in time for dinner. I think we're more likely to find a clue or something that will tell us where to look for him."

"What would you know–"

"That's enough," To'Rel said firmly. "I agree with Freyne. I think you should check the swamp to the north of here. If it's not there, scour the swamp that runs along the western coast of Bar'Am. This mission is not going to be a pleasant stroll through the garden."

J'mai scowled and shot Freyne a look filled with daggers.

"How are we going to recognise this descendant, My King?" Chardi asked.

"I honestly don't know. The monks say we should trust in Am to guide us, but I'm sure he'll have a mark or something that will allow us to identify him."

Nika sat only half-listening as the others discussed the ins and outs of the mission. He felt a soft brush against his mind tand turned to look at Freyne.

What do you think? Freyne's voice asked.

I think we're being sent on a wild goose-chase, Nika said.

A what?

A wild goose-chase, he repeated. *Haven't you ever heard of that saying before?*

No.

Oh. It means no one knows what they're doing and we're probably going to waste our time looking for something that isn't there. I don't like the look of J'mai, either.

Me either. I'll keep an eye on him.

Queen Nahal sat upright and cleared her throat.

"I've spoken to the head chef already. He's packed plenty of food and utensils for your journey," she said. "I've also spoken to the quartermaster. He has supplied some tents and equipment. Since you'll be venturing into the swamp, I'll organise a mule. A swamp is no place for horses."

"I'll give you some gold so you can buy horses later on if you need to," To'Rel added. "Any questions?"

"When do we leave?" Nika asked.

"Now." King To'Rel stood and took his Queen's hand, then strode towards the door. "This way, gentlemen."

To'Rel and Nahal led the way through the castle and emerged in a private courtyard lined with a small stable. Nika stood with Freyne to one side, watching as flustered staff ran about saddling a mule and buckling numerous packs to it. Chardi and J'mai disappeared, only to return dressed in plain clothes covering their chainmail. The servants took their packs and added them to the mule.

"Everything is ready, My King," one of them said, bowing.

"Thank you." To'Rel nodded and turned to Nika and Freyne. "If you are successful, you will be rewarded handsomely when you return. May the gods be with you on your journey. Good luck."

Nika followed Freyne's lead and shook To'Rel's hand, then hurried to follow Chardi away from the castle. It was much quicker and easier travelling down the hill; Chardi seemed to know every short-cut that kept them away from the main road.

As they passed through one of the more unsavoury districts, Freyne stopped abruptly and grabbed Nika's arm. His eyes had that faraway look for a moment.

"What's wrong?" Nika asked.

"I just sensed something. I'll catch up shortly," he said.

Before Nika could protest, Freyne slipped into a side street and disappeared. Nika hurried and caught up with the others, worrying that Freyne would get lost and not catch back up. *I hope he didn't just bail and leave me with these guys,* he thought.

As they made their way past a derelict inn, Freyne jumped

off the low roof and landed next to Nika, startling him.

"What the fuck?" Nika hissed, jumping.

"Hi." Freyne smirked.

He looked around to make sure no one saw his stunt, then Nika felt his presence join with his mind.

"Our friend from court yesterday, the one who lost his goat, is planning revenge on the king. He plans to kidnap Iryna," Freyne's voice said.

"Should we tell Chardi?" Nika asked.

"Let's just keep that to ourselves for the moment. The castle is well-guarded, and I doubt anyone will be able to get past her chaperone."

"Her what?"

"That guard, Ur'Shad. He was obviously her sworn protector. No one in their right mind would ever want to pick a fight with him. Besides, I saw something else that concerns me more."

"And what was that?"

"Remember those people we saw in the cove?"

Nika nodded and looked around uneasily.

"They were the ones talking with the goat lord." Freyne nodded his head towards Chardi and J'mai. *"If I tell them, they'll probably think I'm either in on it, crazy, or both. I don't think To'Rel would appreciate this mission being interrupted before we even reach the city gates."*

"One feels that there is more afoot here than meets the eye," Arnie chimed in. *"One advises caution and be careful who you trust."*

"Agreed," Freyne said. *"Once we get out of the city, we'll head straight for the deepest parts of the forest and stay out of sight."*

Nika was almost grateful when they passed through the gates and escaped from the spiral city. It was hot and humid, and he was already sweating from wearing so many layers. Once they reached the open road, a cool coastal breeze offered some relief. He was so preoccupied with himself that he didn't see Chardi stop. Nika collided with him and almost fell backwards.

"Hey!"

"Sorry," Nika mumbled, his cheeks flushing.

"What's the problem?" J'mai grumbled.

"Open your eyes and look," Chardi snapped.

He pointed to a man and two women wearing travelling cloaks with their hoods up. Nika watched on curiously as one of the women screamed at the man, stamping her foot and gesturing wildly.

"Gri'Ran's claws!" Chardi hissed and stormed towards them.

The woman stopped yelling abruptly and bolted towards the forest with the other woman.

"UR'SHAD!" Chardi roared. "GET YOUR ASS BACK HERE RIGHT NOW!"

Ur'Shad stopped mid-step and glanced between the fleeing princess and Chardi, then threw his hands up in defeat.

"Fine! You go and chase her, then!" Ur'Shad yelled back.

J'mai dropped the mule's reins and sprinted after her with Chardi close behind. Freyne picked them up and looked at Nika with a slight grin on his face.

"So much for the castle being well guarded," Nika murmured under his breath.

"I said that no one will be able to get in. That doesn't mean that no one can get out," Freyne said. "Come on. We'd better get out of sight."

They caught up with Iryna just a few feet into the forest, leaning against a tree and gasping for breath.

"What in the gods do you think you're doing?" Chardi exploded. "After all we did to keep you safe after the attack, this is how you repay us?"

"How DARE you speak to me like that!" Iryna gasped, still trying to catch her breath. "I'll have you hanged for this!"

"Iryna–" the other lady started.

"Lana! How could you allow her to talk you into this?" Chardi demanded, his eyes softening just a little. "You're supposed to be the sensible one."

"You know I had no choice." Lana crossed her arms, her long thick braid swaying lightly behind her.

"We need to get you back to the castle," J'mai said firmly.

"NO! I'm sick of being a prisoner in my own home just because my father is paranoid! I'm going to Qual-Eran to stay with King Lok and his family for a while. Now, you can either escort me there, or get going with whatever stupid mission my father has assigned you and leave us alone."

"I can't do that, princess, and you know it." Chardi groaned. "You know I'm bound to your father and must uphold my duty at all times."

"You're bound by that same duty, Ur'Shad, but here you are running away with your tail between your legs," J'mai sneered.

"Shut it!" Chardi snapped. "Go back to the road and keep watch. I'll handle this."

J'mai glared at him, then stalked back towards the road, swearing to himself and kicking piles of leaves as he went.

"Now, what's going on?" Chardi asked, his voice softening as he looked at Lana.

"I can't do anything without an escort, even when I'm inside the castle," Iryna said, lowering her voice at last. "I can't even use the latrine or bathe in private without someone having to be there all the time. It's stifling and I need to breathe. Please, don't try and send me back. I can't live like this anymore."

"It's for your protection. Had Ur'Shad not been with you when those fools attacked, you'd be dead."

"What is the point of living if I'm caged up like an animal?" Iryna retorted. "This is no life and you know it."

"Do you really think Lok will let you roam free once he finds out you've run away? He'll detain you and march you all the way back to Al'Obrel. Your father has probably already sent him a pigeon."

"Then let us come with you," Iryna pleaded, tears welling up in her eyes. "The safest place in the world is with you and Ur'Shad, and you know it. No one knows where you're headed, so we'll be fine. *Please?*"

Chardi walked away a few steps, scratching his head and swearing under his breath. When he returned, he crossed his arms and nodded at Ur'Shad.

"What's your view on this?" he asked finally.

"The castle isn't safe," Ur'Shad declared. "After that breech, I think she'll be much safer staying with Lok or in hiding. You know that I'll protect her with my own life, no matter what, but even I can only defend off so many fighters."

"Fine!" Chardi sighed and closed his eyes for a moment. "You both can deal with To'Rel when we get back. I don't want this to come back and bite me. I'll send J'mai back with a letter so your father doesn't send the entire army after us, and when we finish our task here, we'll head to Dol'Am and await his response. Got it?"

Iryna nodded and fluttered her eyelashes, but once Chardi turned away and began rummaging in the packs for some parchment, Nika spotted a smirk on her face. Freyne nudged him softly and winked.

Chardi scribbled a note and folded it into an intricate locked design, then whistled and beckoned to J'mai.

"Take this to To'Rel on the double," he ordered, handing it to J'mai. "Don't let anyone open it or he'll know it's been tampered with. Now go."

J'mai snatched the letter and stormed back towards the road and disappeared. Nika felt a wave of relief that he was gone, though he wasn't too excited for their new travelling companions, either.

"Well, what are you waiting for?" Iryna asked.

She started walking east, but Chardi didn't budge.

"We're going north, Your Highness," he called.

"North? It's nothing but swamp that way," she argued.

"Exactly. You wanted this, so you got it. Let's go, everyone."

7

They walked in silence through the coolness of the trees, following the arc of the sun and heading towards the north. Birds chirped in the canopy and wallabies bounced here and there, startled by the sudden presence of people. The floor of the forest was blanketed with twigs and bark from the trees, and ferns grew wildly around them. Wild flowers grew here and there, giving the forest the faintest hint of mauve and yellow amongst the shades of green. The trees were slender and tall, their bark peeling like torn paper and hanging off the trunks. In the distance, they could hear the steady flow of a river, and the occasional splash of water flowing over rapids. After several hours of walking, they came across a clearing with an upturned tree.

"Let's stop for lunch," Chardi called.

Nika sat on the felled tree and rubbed his legs, then glanced around. The princess sat too in a huff and removed her boots, clearly in pain.

"Are you okay?" Nika asked her.

She looked at him disdainfully.

"I'm fine," she snapped.

"If it's any consolation, after a few days of walking you won't feel it anymore," he said, indicating her sore feet.

"I said I'm fine!" she screeched.

Nika grimaced and backed off, feeling like he'd been slapped in the face. He got up and found Freyne sitting cross-legged on the ground leaning comfortably against a tree, and sat down next to his friend.

"It might pay to give Her Royal Highness a bit of space," Freyne warned. "She bites."

"I noticed." Nika said.

Freyne laughed, and after a moment Nika joined in. The sensation felt odd to him; he rarely laughed or smiled, unless he was drunk and having a good time. He wiped the tears from his eyes and continued to grin. Lana brought them their lunch, then hurried to sit with the miserable princess.

"Why do I get the feeling it's a bad idea to bring her along?" Nika asked.

"Because it *is* a bad idea," Freyne said. "She'll calm down soon enough. Who knows; this journey might actually be good for her and teach her something about the real world."

"I sure hope so," Nika agreed.

By the time the sun began its descent below the horizon, Freyne was already sick of the constant complaining and shrieking of the princess. He longed for it to be just him, Nika and Arnie-Kyn again; at least Nika's voice didn't hurt his ears. He took a deep breath and whistled to gain the attention of the party, then motioned for them to join him.

"We have under an hour left of daylight," he said. "I think we should set up camp here."

"Alright. Ur'Shad and I will set up the tents." Chardi nodded. "We only have three, so I guess we'll have to double up."

Iryna sat on a log and scowled. Freyne ignored her and busied himself with starting a fire, while Nika gathered extra firewood for the night. Lana set to work on preparing dinner. It didn't take long to have the campsite ready for the night.

"What's for dinner?" Ur'Shad asked.

"It looks like we'll be eating soup," Lana replied. "We have mostly dried ingredients."

Ur'Shad's expression clearly showed how he felt about soup, and he murmured something to Chardi under his breath.

After the day I've had, I'm not having soup, Freyne thought. *I need meat.* He slipped away from the campsite and into the trees, looking for signs of wildlife. His belly rumbled uncomfortably, and he hurried through the trees, driven by his hunger.

It didn't take long to track down some fresh rabbit warrens. He climbed a tree and scanned the scrub until he spotted some rabbits foraging a short distance away. Freyne slowly drew his dagger from the sheath in his boot and took aim, then expertly threw it at one of the rabbits. His aim was impeccable as always, and the rabbit was dead before it hit the ground. The others scattered, spooked. Freyne pulled the blade from his other boot and waited patiently. After some time had passed, another rabbit hopped into the clearing and sniffed the air, checking for danger. Freyne felled it before it could flee.

Satisfied with his hunt, Freyne climbed down the tree and quickly thanked his mother of nature for his dinner. The sun had almost completely disappeared, leaving him in velvety darkness. Freyne skinned and gutted the rabbits in the light of the rising moon, then headed back to camp.

Nika sat alone, sipping at his dinner and staring forlornly into his bowl. The soup was watery and bland, the chunks of potato and barley the only flavour. It did little to appease his hunger.

"Who wants some rabbit?"

Freyne emerged from the trees carrying two rabbits, a look of accomplishment on his face. Nika grinned and nodded, his mouth watering. Iryna crossed her arms and glared at Freyne, then deliberately turned her back on him.

"Barbaric," she hissed.

Ur'Shad, Chardi and Lana quickly declined the offer.

"All the more for us." Freyne winked then set up his spit.

The aroma of the roasting meat drifted across the clearing, and Nika caught the others casting wistful glances in their direction. Once the rabbits were cooked, he sat with Freyne away from the others so they could eat their dinner in peace.

"I ate too much," he mumbled, rubbing his belly.

"Me too," Freyne nodded.

They sat around in awkward silence for a while, until the princess abruptly shot to her feet.

"We're going to bed," she announced, gesturing at Lana.

"I think we all should," Chardi said. "Ur'Shad will take first watch. I'll take the other half."

"Very well," Freyne replied.

Nika followed Freyne to their tent and glanced inside. It was small, with two compartments that could fit two people per side. There was already a bedroll and blanket set up in each compartment, and Arnie-Kyn had already made himself comfortable on one of them. Nika crawled in next to the cat and removed his shoes. Freyne made his way into the left compartment and fastened the tent behind them.

"Isn't this a luxury," he murmured.

"Yeah," Nika replied.

The tent fell silent, and Nika felt awkward. He'd grown used to sleeping next to Freyne during their journey to Al'Obrel and sharing stories before falling asleep, but now there was a barrier between them, and he was no longer sure if their prior arrangement was still deemed appropriate.

He lay there quietly, unable to sleep. Every sound in the wild seemed too loud: the chirping of the crickets, screeches of bats and fluttering of wings high in the trees. He rolled over and faced the divider.

"Are you awake?" he whispered.

"Yes. You can't sleep either?" Freyne whispered back.

"No."

The tent fell silent again and Nika felt stupid.

"Would you like some company over there?" Freyne asked after more awkward silence.

"Yeah."

There was a rustle and the tent shook slightly. Freyne crawled around the divider into Nika's side dragging his bedroll. Nika moved over so there was enough room for two.

"Hi," Freyne said, covering himself with his blanket.

"Hi. I guess I got used to this before we were joined by the princess," Nika said, feeling a little embarrassed.

"So did I. You know, I lived alone for so many years and it never bothered me before. Now, though, I find myself looking forward to our evening conversations and your company."

Nika shifted and made himself comfortable while absentmindedly stroking Arnie's ears.

"Any luck on remembering where you lived before you went into the forest?" he asked.

"I still don't remember." Freyne sighed. "I've tried to recall my memories, but they just won't come. It's like they've been wiped from my mind. Although—" Freyne was thoughtful for a moment, "—the night you arrived, I had a vivid dream where I was running towards a village that was burning. By the time I got there it was destroyed. Everyone was dead. And then there was a woman…" Freyne's voice trailed off.

"A woman? Who was she?" Nika asked.

"I don't know." Freyne sighed again. "In the dream, she called my name, begging for help. Then she died right there. It was horrible."

"Sounds terrible," Nika empathised. "Was she your boo?"

"Boo?" Freyne asked.

"Oh, it's a pet name for a loved one, like a wife, girlfriend, boyfriend, whatever," Nika replied.

"Ah, I see." Freyne scratched his cheek. "I just don't know. If only I could remember more."

Nika's patience was waning more and more, and by the fourth day he was about ready to abandon To'Rel's mission altogether. The party walked mostly in silence through the day, trying not to trigger the princess' mood, but it seemed that no matter what they did, something would inevitably set her off.

After a second night of bland soup and being forced to watch Nika and Freyne eating a juicy boar, Iryna gave in and sampled Freyne's cooking, after which she begrudgingly agreed that meat would be welcome in their diet, and that Freyne would be the designated hunter. Nika looked forward to the hour or so after dinner that he and Freyne were free to sit by themselves and chat before bed.

The further they went, the more the terrain began to change. Slowly, the flowers and ferns gave way to prickly shrubs and bendy trees with low hanging vines. There were increasing swarms of bugs, and a nasty smell hung in the air.

On the afternoon of the fourth day, Freyne whistled and held up his hand, and beckoned the others to gather around. He was holding Nika's map and pointing to a fork in the river they'd been following.

"This is roughly where we are. From here on, we'll be in the swamp." He moved his finger along the western fork. "We'll need to find a point along here where we can safely cross with the mule."

"Cookie," the princess interjected.

"Excuse me?" Freyne asked politely.

"Cookie. Lana and I decided to give him a name," she said.

"Oh." Freyne chuckled, then continued. "Okay. We need to find a point in the river where Cookie can cross."

The princess looked pleased with herself.

"From here on, watch your step. There are all sorts of unsavoury creatures here, and you don't want to fall into the mud. Hopefully we'll find what To'Rel needs and be on our way."

Nika watched as Arnie-Kyn disappeared into the swamp, then set about gathering dry twigs and wood for a fire. Ur'Shad and Chardi started assembling one of the tents, talking between themselves.

Freyne handed Nika some tinder from his pocket.

"Hopefully there's something edible to hunt—" he broke off and froze, his eyes growing distant. After a moment, he refocused, and immediately drew both of his hunting knives. "Get ready, we're under attack!"

He dashed across the clearing and clambered easily up a tree. Nika glanced around, confused; he didn't see anything to cause concern. Behind him, Ur'Shad and Chardi drew their swords to the ready. Nika's stomach began to churn and he grew flustered. He armed himself with a club of wood from the pile and gave it a practise swing. It was a good weight in his hand.

"Stay with the women," Ur'Shad barked as a group of bandits came rushing out of the swamp.

Ur'Shad and Chardi cut down three of the attackers with ease, as one of the filthy bandits rushed towards Nika with a raised sword. Instinctively, he dodged and swung his club down hard on the man's arm, shattering the bone and making him drop the sword with a cry of pain. Nika moved with the momentum and swung his club at his opponent's head. There was a sickening cracking sound, and the man sank to the ground.

Two of the bandits veered towards Nika, waving their swords as they rushed to attack. Nika gripped his club, ready to crack more skulls. Before he could swing, though, Freyne leapt into the fray and landed lightly on his feet behind the two ruffians. He buried his blades in their necks and they sank to the ground in pools of their own blood.

A toothless man crept up behind the princess and pinned her arms to her sides. She screamed; Freyne spun and landed a knife between the man's eyes, the force making him let go and fall backwards. The princess stood frozen in fear.

Ur'Shad and Chardi had a pile of bodies growing at their feet as they fought back-to-back, dropping one after another. Freyne rushed two more bandits who were creeping up on the princess.

Out of the corner of his eye, Nika spotted movement, and spun around to see a lone scumbag stalking towards Cookie, poised to strike. With a grunt, Nika threw his club through the air as the man brought his sword down towards the terrified animal. The club collided with his hand and sent the sword falling to the ground. Enraged, the ruffian lunged at Nika with his fists.

Nika had been in many bar brawls and knew how to handle himself. His opponent swung his fists at Nika's head, but Nika side-stepped and the man missed completely. Nika tore off his cumbersome cloak and crouched, ready to fight.

The bandit swung his fists wildly, but Nika calmly blocked the punches with his arms. He caught the man lightly in the cheek with his right hand, then followed through with a powerful blow from his left fist. His opponent spun around and fell to his knees; he shook his head and scrambled hastily to his feet. He rushed at Nika again, who was ready. Nika pulled back his fist and slammed all the power he had into the man's face. The sheer force sent the man flying off his feet and into a tree. He slid to the ground, unmoving.

Nika scanned the clearing for his next opponent, but realised the fight was over. Across the clearing, he saw that Freyne was watching him, and when their eyes locked, Freyne winked. Nika blushed and quickly looked away.

The clearing was littered with around thirty corpses, some of whom were dressed in black robes. Ur'Shad and Chardi rummaged through the bodies, looking for clues and helping themselves to any gold and valuables.

"I found something." Chardi waved a piece of parchment. "It's ripped, but this part says, '...*the north. The reward for capturing the princess alive and delivering her to Carnus is 500 gold. Kill the rest of her associates. I'll be waiting for you at the usual spot. Lord L.'* Gri'Ran's claws! There are heaps of lords whose names start with L. It could be anyone."

"It's Lord Lenier," Freyne said.

"How do you know?" Chardi demanded. "We don't just accuse people without evidence."

"I overheard him back in Al'Obrel. He's plotting revenge on To'Rel by kidnapping Her Highness. We need to get as far away from here as possible."

"Alright. Let's get out of here." Chardi nodded.

Nika snatched up his cloak and slipped it back on, then helped Freyne to pack everything away as quickly as they could. His stomach didn't feel too good, and he tried to avert his eyes from the bodies. He told himself over and over that it was either them or him; he'd never killed anyone before and had no intention to in the first place. He pulled a sword and scabbard from the ground and fastened it around his waist, just in time to see Iryna faint.

Ur'Shad caught her and hoisted her easily over his shoulder. Chardi took his cue and collected Lana, who looked close to fainting as well, just as Arnie-Kyn bolted into the clearing.

"One has found a bridge that we can cross," he said. *"Hurry."*

The cat turned and ran back into the swamp.

"Everyone, follow me!" Nika barked.

Nobody argued; the party hastily left the clearing, leaving the dead bodies behind. The daylight was fading rapidly. Nika followed Arnie blindly, not knowing where they were going.

"Hold up! It's too dark," Ur'Shad called after a while. "It's too dangerous to keep going."

"One suggests you use the firestone," Arnie said. *"You should be able to isolate the light for those around you."*

Nika pulled out the firestone, and focused his mind on it, willing it to emit a very low light that only he could see. The stone glowed at his command.

"Can anyone see this light in my hand?" he asked.

"What light?" the guards asked in unison.

Nika took a deep breath and concentrated, this time willing it to glow only for him and Ur'Shad.

"How about now?" he asked.

"Now I do," Ur'Shad replied, but Chardi shook his head.

He focused hard on the stone and willed it to glow for the group. The stone flickered out a moment, and Nika broke into a sweat. Finally, the stone glowed again, and Nika breathed a sigh of relief. He was shaking from the effort of controlling it.

"What if someone's following us and sees the light?" Chardi hissed, shifting Lana gently to his other shoulder.

"Only we can see the light," Nika said.

Arnie meowed, drawing their attention back to their situation. He was sitting next to a bridge that was woven from trees. Nika hurried over and shook the viney handrail; the bridge swayed a little too freely for his liking. Below, he could hear splashes and growls of creatures in the river.

"We cross here," he declared. "It's not very sturdy. I think we should go across two at a time."

"You go first, Nika. That way we can see the light," Freyne said.

Nika nodded and edged across carefully, holding the firestone tightly in his left hand and gripping the handrail with his right. He reached the opposite bank and let out a deep breath. Ur'Shad was next to cross, still carrying the unconscious princess, followed by Chardi and Lana. Finally, it was time for Freyne to coax Cookie across. The mule resisted, eyeing the narrow walkway and the wide river with fear.

Freyne cupped his hands around Cookie's eyes, blocking his peripheral view so that all he could see was Freyne's face. Nika could sense the calmness he was projecting towards the terrified animal. Cookie took a hesitant step forward, and another, and soon Freyne had the mule following him across the bridge. Cookie's eyes were glued to Freyne's. Once they were across, Freyne removed his hands from Cookie's face. The mule glanced back at the bridge, then rubbed his head against Freyne's leg.

"Let's cut the vines so no one can follow," Freyne said to Nika. "Once we've done that, we should be alright to set up camp and tend to Lana and the princess."

Nika handed Freyne an axe, and they set about hacking at the woven trees that held the bridge in place. With a loud *creak,* the bridge fell free and splashed into the river below.

8

Nika sat alone in the dark, listening to the incessant calls of crickets and creatures of the night. It was his turn to keep watch, allowing Ur'Shad and Chardi to have a good night's sleep. He sat with his back against a tree, wrapped tightly in his cloak. The temperature had dropped considerably, and the first drops of rain were starting to fall. He sighed and pulled up his hood.

A slight movement caught his eye, and Nika turned to see Arnie-Kyn walking silently towards him.

"Are you well, human?" Arnie asked, sitting by Nika's feet.

"I'm fine. Just tired." Nika reached down and scratched behind the cat's ears. For once, Arnie-Kyn didn't object.

"One needs your help," he said.

"Sure, what's up?"

"Please follow me." Arnie said. *"You will need a spade and a light."*

Nika fetched a spade then followed Arnie through the swamp using the firestone for light. They walked for around a half hour, until Arnie stopped in front of a large flat rock covered in moss. Nika could see fresh scrapes in the moss and dirt by the rock, as though a small animal had been trying to dig; his eyes swept to Arnie's paws, which were covered in mud.

"One needs you to move this rock," Arnie said.

Nika bent and tried to shift the rock, but it wouldn't budge. He shrugged off his cloak and hung it on a branch, then positioned his feet firmly around the rock. Grunting, he heaved and heaved, using all of his strength, until the rock finally came free from the mud with a *squelch*. He rolled it out of the way then wiped the sweat from his brow.

"Now you must dig," Arnie instructed.

Curious, Nika took the spade and started digging where the rock had been. His clothes became covered in mud, but he continued, making the hole deeper and wider. It was as deep as Nika's hips when the spade hit something solid. He carefully extracted a small wooden box, sealed in wax, then climbed out of the muddy hole.

"Is this it?" Nika asked, showing Arnie his find.

"Well, obviously," Arnie replied.

"How did you know it's here?" Nika asked.

"You ask too many questions, human."

Nika sighed and sat the box carefully on the log. He filled in the hole and replaced the rock, just as the sky opened with a downpour. Arnie moved under the tree for cover, and Nika held up his arms, letting the rain wash the mud from his body.

"We should get back to camp," he said, shivering.

The cat stood up but didn't move. Nika slipped his cloak back on and patted his arms and chest dry, before picking up the box and cat, then marched grumpily back to camp.

When Nika returned, Freyne was lounging on a low branch, protected from the rain by the canopy of the tree. Nika eyed his friend, who was dry and clean, while he stood there muddy and soaking wet. They had no fire, having agreed earlier that it would be too risky.

"I don't think I'm game to ask," Freyne said quietly, his mouth curling into a grin as he looked Nika up and down.

"I've been doing favours for the cat," Nika grumbled.

He reached up and sat Arnie on the branch next to Freyne. Arnie shook himself, spraying Freyne with water, and Nika smirked. Freyne scowled, wiping his face. Arnie's fur was left spiky from the rain, and he sat licking his dirty paws.

"He led me to this," Nika added, showing Freyne the box. "Let's open it."

Freyne dropped quietly to the ground and offered him one of his daggers. Nika took it and carefully scored a line in the wax to break the seal, then pried off the lid with the tip of the blade. Inside the box lay three tightly rolled scrolls, a book, and a sheaf of parchment. Freyne picked up the book and flicked through the pages. Nika looked over his shoulder; the writing was the same beautiful hand as the book he'd found in the ruins. Freyne was tracing some of the characters with his finger, his mind far away.

"Can you read this?" Nika asked.

Freyne sat heavily on a log, his eyes sweeping over the symbols in the dim light. His hands started shaking. Nika sat down next to him, eyeing his friend and starting to feel a little concerned.

"Are you al—" Nika started to ask.

Freyne's hand shot out and grasped Nika's, his eyes growing distant once again. Nika felt his mind being pulled and his consciousness slipped away.

He was looking through eyes that weren't his own, in a body that wasn't his. There were three brown-robed monks sitting around a circular desk in a library. His eyes looked down; he, too, was sitting at the desk, and open in front of him was a small black leather-bound book, penned in that same beautiful language. A number of scrolls, open books, and sheets of parchment were scattered around the desk. His hands closed the book, and his view shifted to the three monks.

Just then, someone came scurrying down the spiral metal staircase.

"Brothers! I bring grave news. Our settlement to the south is under attack!" the man gasped.

Nika felt his hands turn into fists, and he brought them down hard on the desk, startling the other monks.

"My family! I must go at once." Freyne's voice uttered from his lips.

"No! You know your duty. You must stay here and prepare," one of the monks barked.

"Prepare for what? A prophecy that will never be fulfilled in our lifetime? No, my family needs me!"

He stood and stuffed the book into the pocket of his robe, then stormed past rows and rows of books. He was almost overcome with guilt, anger, and fear as he swung open a bookcase that concealed a door.

The viewpoint swirled and shifted, and Nika was running at full speed towards a burning village. The buildings looked strangely familiar. He ran to the village square, and stopped when he saw her.

"Freyne! Help me!"

She was on fire, running towards him, but there was nothing he could do. He stood frozen to the spot, watching as she slowed to a walk, then collapsed with a pleading hand held out towards him. He hurried to her side and used his robes to smother the fire, then took her hand and kissed it.

"Alira?"

He looked into her eyes, but her light was gone.

Nika felt Freyne's pain, the disbelief of what he was witnessing. He picked her up, wrapped in his robes, and carried her to a charred home. There were bodies strewn around the living room, all brutally slaughtered. His entire family, gone.

Freyne laid Alira's body next to his mother's, then flew into a rage, screaming and hurling things around the room. He swung a chair into the bookcase, breaking them both. In his fury, he hurled the small black book back on a shelf with the rest of the books, feeling nothing but raw contempt for the religious words it held inside. He stormed into his bedroom and threw all of his religious possessions onto his side table, then ran from the house. With a cry of despair, he fled into the forest without looking back.

Nika's consciousness slowly returned, and he realised he was back in his own body. His heart was pounding in his chest and his hands were shaking. He looked at Freyne, who had tears forming in his eyes, his hand shaking uncontrollably. Freyne's grip loosened and he pulled his hand free. He burst into tears, his shoulders heaving with each sob. Nika picked the book up off the ground and packed it back in the box, then gently rubbed Freyne's back to comfort him. Freyne lowered his head to Nika's chest; Nika bit his lip and pulled his friend into a tight hug and held him as Freyne's grief consumed him.

It wasn't until the sun started to rise that Freyne pulled away and wiped his tears. He sat upright, still visibly shaking.

"I-I'm sorry—"

"Shh. There's no need to apologise. We'll talk about it when you're ready. If you want to, that is."

The rain had settled to a light mist, and tendrils of fog wove its way through the gloomy swamp. Nika left Freyne on the log and set about making a hot breakfast for everyone.

Using his firestone to heat a large pot of porridge, he mixed in some sugar and dried fruit to make it more appetising, then made a pot of strong tea. He handed Freyne his breakfast and patted him on the shoulder, then went and woke the others.

"What's wrong with him?" Iryna asked, nodding at Freyne.

"Never mind," Nika said pointedly. He held up the waxed box and changed the subject. "I found what we came here to find."

The princess helped herself to a sheet of parchment and scanned the page, then shook her head and handed it to Ur'Shad.

"What in the gods is this?" she asked. "I've studied all of the main languages of Ayrillis but I've never seen this one before. Is it even real?"

"I have no idea," Nika admitted. "I think Freyne knows."

Chardi took the sheet from Ur'Shad and frowned.

"It looks like gibberish. How do we even know that it's relevant to our mission?" he asked.

"I think Freyne knows," Nika repeated. "I'll ask him later."

"What's the plan, then?" Ur'Shad asked.

Nika looked at Freyne for guidance, but he was staring at his feet, worlds away. Unsure of what to do, Nika pulled out his map and studied it for a moment.

"We may as well continue north," he said finally. "We're close to those ruins, so we may as well head there for the night. Hopefully we'll get there before dark."

"Ruins?" Chardi asked.

"The ruins of the swamp people," Nika explained, pointing to the icon on his map.

"That's strange. I've never seen those ruins on any map I've ever used," Chardi declared. "It's probably a mistake."

Nika shrugged.

"Or not. It sounds like the perfect place to find someone or something important. Let's eat up and get moving."

As the sun rose, so too did the humidity. Nika felt like he was melting and thought back to his days on the rig, where it was almost always cold and windy. He wasn't the only one suffering; Chardi and Ur'Shad were sweating profusely in their chainmail, grunting and cursing under their breath as they walked. The princess looked like a wilted flower, utterly defeated, but she kept up and didn't utter a word. Nika noticed that both she and Lana were jumpy, flinching at any sudden noises or movement. They walked in single file through the bog with Chardi in the lead and Nika at the rear leading Cookie.

Nika kept his watchful eye on Freyne who hadn't spoken a word all day. The further they walked, the marshier the swamp became. By the time they stopped for lunch, Nika was drenched in sweat and was convinced he stunk worse than the fetid swamp around them. He sat with Freyne away from the others, eating in silence. After a while, he felt Freyne's presence brush gently against his, and their minds joined.

"You saw it too?" Freyne asked.

"Yes," Nika said slowly.

"Did you recognise that village?"

"Was it the village near the University?"

"Yes. You were there, the first night you spent here."

"I've been in that library, too."

Freyne looked up sharply and their eyes locked. For a split second Nika became lost in Freyne's gaze and his cheeks flushed.

"Do you know what that library is?" Freyne asked.

"No? Just some old library?"

"That's not just some library. It's a secret library, built by monks to protect and study that prophecy. Very few people alive know it exists, and even fewer have ever been inside it. I doubt even To'Rel knows about it."

"How do you know about it then?"

"Many years ago, a seer turned up on the monastery steps begging for sanctuary. The seer had with him a prophecy and told us to protect it at all costs." Freyne went quiet for a moment. *"I was on the original board that was established to protect and study the prophecy. I was the one who greeted the seer and granted him sanctuary. I was a high priest of Am, utterly devoted to their service."*

His voice trailed off for a moment, and Nika sat quietly, trying to process what Freyne was telling him.

"Do you know how old I am?" Freyne asked abruptly.

Nika shook his head.

"No?"

"I'm just over a thousand years old." He gestured towards the box of scrolls that sat next to Nika's pack. *"I studied those texts for three hundred years, before my family were murdered. That means I spent seven hundred years in the forest!"*

"But…how?" Nika's mind boggled.

"My parents were amongst the founders of the village. When I was young, they sent me to the monastery to begin my training. I worked my way up through the ranks of monkhood, but unlike the others, I was elevated into priesthood and continued my studies.

"As a reward for our absolute devotion, Am extended the lifespans of those in my village and the high priests. For me, it meant that I could study for as long as I liked and not waste my knowledge by dying an early death.

"Once I'd become a high priest, it was decided by the elders that I must marry. I refused, of course. I had no desire to be with a woman let alone be wed to one, but my parents held that power and I was forced to marry.

"Alira was my wife. We were married for three years. She often begged me to leave the monastery and move to the village to be with her, but I refused. I never loved her. But she became my family, so I did love her for that."

"Did you have any children?" Nika asked.

Freyne shook his head.

"No. I wasn't interested. I was too wrapped up in my studies to care about anyone else. We fought over that several times and it always resulted in me storming back to the monastery. I'm so, so ashamed. I should have been a proper husband to her, despite my misgivings." Freyne sighed. *"I feel like a complete and utter idiot. Seven hundred years of my life wasted in that forest. I floated around like a wild animal with my head in the clouds, oblivious to everything, just listening to nature and learning to communicate with her. Then you came along and now I have no idea where I stand anymore."*

"I'm so sorry," Nika said.

"No. None of this is your fault, so don't you go and apologise. I'm just going to need a little time to myself to try and get my head around all of this. There's a lot I need to think about."

Emotionally, Freyne was broken. He walked in a daze, not knowing where to start or even how to begin unpacking his emotions. The guilt he felt for fleeing from the carnage in his village instead of laying his family to rest and mourning properly made him sick to his stomach. Shame for the way he'd lived, crazy and wild with little dignity. And fear, raw cold fear for not once praying to or even acknowledging his god in all that time. Had Am been punishing him, or was that yet to come?

What now? he thought, staring into nothingness. *I can't go back to that life. Surely if I were to return, I'd be exiled for turning my back on Am and my duties, or worse. By the gods, what am I going to do?*

A gentle hand landed on Freyne's shoulder and he jumped, startled. He turned to see Nika looking at him with a concerned look on his face, holding out a waterskin.

"Are you alright?" he asked.

Freyne shook his head and looked down at his feet, ignoring the proffered waterskin. More guilt twisted in his stomach, and he stopped abruptly, accepting the skin and taking a deep swig. Nika was the one person he felt like he could trust, who actually seemed to care about him, and was the only one Freyne could consider a true friend. With a stab of regret, he realised he'd never even had a friend in all of his long life. Instead of abandoning him or telling him to *be a man* like others had told him in the past, Nika stayed by his side and comforted him during his breakdown.

As he handed back the skin, their gaze locked for the briefest moment. Nika's striking grey eyes looked pained, more so than usual. At once, Freyne felt guilty for being so self-absorbed and not noticing that Nika was also going through something. He rested his hand on Nika's arm and his belly fluttered in a different way.

"What's troubling you?" he asked.

"I've never killed anyone before," Nika murmured. "I didn't mean to. I didn't want to. It just…happened."

Freyne gently rubbed Nika's arm in an attempt to comfort him, although he had to admit that it probably comforted himself more.

"I'm sorry. It's never easy the first time, and for good people like yourself, it won't be easy the next time, either. Or the next. We're not gods so we don't get to decide who lives and who dies. But in saying that, you are allowed to defend your own life when someone attacks you. Anyone who sets out to willingly murder someone has already lost themselves. It's a reflection of them, not you. Remember that."

***

The party continued their trek through the fetid swamp, which was growing more unpleasant the further they walked. Gases bubbled up from the bog around them, and swarms of bugs and mosquitoes fed on any skin that was exposed. It was late afternoon when Nika spied a pocket of fog emerging from the swamp ahead. He felt a strange compulsion to turn around and leave, that there was nothing ahead worth his while.

Chardi stopped abruptly and turned to face the group.

"There's nothing up ahead. Let's turn east and head to Dol'Am," he said.

Ur'Shad, Lana, and Iryna nodded their heads in agreeance.

"The fog is an illusion. It's an ancient defensive spell used to keep intruders away. Keep going," Freyne said.

Everyone looked at Freyne. It was the first time he'd spoken since the night before. Chardi shook his head, and Iryna started to walk back the way they'd come. Nika reached out and grasped her arm firmly, and she tried to wriggle free.

"Hey! Let me GO!" she shrieked.

Freyne closed his eyes and the fog started to shimmer.

"Forward," he said firmly, disappearing into the fog.

Nika followed him blindly, pulling the squirming princess with him. Ur'Shad and the others followed him, and together they stepped through the shimmering fog, away from the fetid muddy bog, and onto solid ground blanketed in soft lush grass. They were in a ruined village, which felt like an oasis in the middle of the swamp. The air smelt clean and fresh, and a crystal-clear stream trickled its way through the ruins. Overgrown garden beds flowered wildly in the yards of the crumbled houses, and tiny blue birds fluttered around the gardens, singing their happy tune. The setting sun was still warm, but the village was less humid than the swamp had been.

"What is this place?" Iryna asked, gazing around at the beautiful ruins that greeted them.

Nika quickly unhanded her and took a step back as Ur'Shad glared at him.

"These are the remains of the village of the swamp people," Freyne said quietly. "Not many people would know about it, which is why you won't find it on any maps. Someone's put an enchantment on this place to protect it from being discovered."

"It's beautiful," Lana breathed.

"Let's each find a place to sleep," Freyne suggested. "We're safe here, so let's rest up for an extra day. I don't think we'll need the tents."

Lana and Iryna linked their arms together and skipped away to find a room together, with Chardi and Ur'Shad in tow. Nika followed Freyne, and they walked in the opposite direction until they found a small cottage that was still mostly intact. They walked through the gap in the fence where a gate once stood, and passed through the overgrown garden to the front door, which had fallen off its hinges. Wild red roses grew up the side of the house and spread across the roof.

The living room was cosy and spacious with a welcoming fireplace. Several pieces of furniture were scattered about, and a thick rug lay on the floor. To their left were two doors, one which led to an empty bedroom, and the other which opened to what was once a kitchen, only its roof had caved in. Nika set up his bedroll next to Freyne's by the fireplace, then peeled off his cloak and draped it over a broken chair.

"I'm hungry," Nika mumbled, hearing his belly rumble.

"Let's head back and organise dinner." Freyne nodded.

They headed back to the others and saw that Ur'Shad and Chardi had already started a fire and placed some chairs around it. Lana was watching Iryna who was attempting to chop some vegetables.

"I can't wait to bathe in the stream tomorrow," Iryna said dreamily to no one in particular.

"Careful! You nearly cut your finger," Lana gasped.

"You do it, then!"

Iryna tossed the knife on the board and stomped over to the chair next to Ur'Shad. She sat and crossed her arms, her face as dark as a thunder cloud.

"I think we could all do with a bath," Nika agreed.

He wrinkled his nose at his muddied clothes and bad odour. When he looked up, he noticed that the princess was glaring at him.

"Not together, of course!" he added quickly.

Nika sat as far away as he could from Iryna and stared gloomily into the fire. He certainly wasn't in the mood for her to screech at him.

"Are you alright?"

Nika looked up as Freyne joined him, a hint of a smile playing on the corner of his mouth.

"Why did Chardi allow her to come with us?" Nika grumbled.

"Chardi is bound by his duty to the king and didn't really have a choice. If we returned her to the castle, To'Rel would have been furious and probably execute Ur'Shad and Lana for disobeying him. And if Chardi let them go, I'm sure To'Rel would have found out about it and execute him instead."

"This place is crazy."

"Don't even get me started. I have a feeling there's more going on here than meets the eye. We shall see."

Lana handed everyone a bowl of bland soup and sat with the sullen princess, her expression unreadable. Nika noticed that she didn't talk much, and spent most of her time catering to Iryna's every whim. The thought of being screeched at for trying to get to know Lana was enough to put Nika off trying to talk to her.

Once they finished eating their dinner, Chardi excused himself and returned holding up a flagon of liquor.

"Who's thirsty?" he grinned.

"Where'd you get that from?" Iryna demanded. "You know it's illegal for enlisted soldiers to have liquor!"

"I confiscated it from one of my men a few days before we left. Want some?"

The princess started to shake her head, then paused and reached out her hand. She took a sip and almost spat it out.

"Yuk!" she gasped.

Chardi laughed and passed the bottle around the circle. When it was Nika's turn, he sniffed curiously at the contents before taking a deep swig. The liquor was strong and fruity, similar to port, and left little aftertaste on his palate. Impressed, he passed the flagon to Freyne who also drank deeply. After just a few rounds, Nika was already feeling tipsy.

"I wonder how To'Rel reacted when he found out we gave him the slip," Ur'Shad mused some time later, his face flushed from the liquor.

"He didn't send his army after us to get you back, so I guess that's a good sign," Chardi grinned. "I can only assume that J'mai took the bait and delivered my letter."

"Bait?" Freyne asked.

Chardi laughed and took another swig from the flagon, then draped his arm over Ur'Shad's shoulders. Nika could see that they were both drunk, having guzzled most of the flagon between them.

"Well, the thing about being chief of To'Rel's elite guard, is I have spies *everywhere*. On the day before we left, some idiots stormed the castle and tried to snatch Iryna from her private courtyard. Of course they were no match for Ur'Shad here, and we had the castle locked down in no time. To'Rel refused to see reason that it was unsafe for her to stay, and instead sent me on this stupid manhunt where I'd be powerless to protect her..."

Chardi broke off and drank deeply, then handed the flagon back to Nika, who helped himself to another drink. Everything spun as he passed it to Freyne.

"So, you've successfully smuggled Her Highness away from Al'Obrel," Freyne said slowly. "What now? This mission could get dangerous. Is this really wise?"

"I can take care of myself!" Iryna snapped.

"Relax, Princess," Chardi grinned. "I encoded a message in my letter to To'Rel and let him know that I've apprehended you. I told him I'll escort you to Dol'Am once we've searched the swamp and will await further orders from him once we get there. Knowing your father, there's already a pigeon waiting for me at the garrison."

"I still don't appreciate being dragged around a stinking swamp," Iryna mumbled.

"It's better than being kept prisoner in the castle," Ur'Shad pointed out. "I think I prefer it out here."

"You know he's right." Lana nodded. "Even I was getting

sick of the castle. It's one thing having Ur'Shad around all the time, but when we're constantly surrounded by all those other guards, it's stifling."

"You know I'm only doing my job," Ur'Shad said defensively. "I will never let anyone harm either of you, ever."

"You're such a dolt." Iryna rolled her eyes and looked away, her cheeks flushed.

Nika sat in silence, listening to Chardi, Ur'Shad, Lana, and Iryna chatting amongst themselves. The flagon lay empty on its side at Chardi's feet. Nika looked at Freyne.

"Are you following anything they're saying?" he asked.

"Not really. Let's go and rinse our bowls in the stream and head back to the cottage. Your stories are much more entertaining than royal gossip."

Nika nodded his agreement, grateful to get away from the others. He knelt down at the edge of the stream and started rinsing his bowl, when Freyne came up behind him and shoved him into the water with a laugh. Caught by surprise, he tumbled into the cool water with a splash and flailed his arms around wildly. Once he was able to orient himself, he came up gasping for air, not believing what had just happened. Freyne continued to laugh uncontrollably.

"Really?" Nika spluttered.

He laughed even harder. Nika snatched the bowl that was bobbing on the surface and splashed him in the face. Freyne coughed and wiped his eyes, then leapt into the stream, showering Nika in a wave of water. Once he surfaced, Freyne shot Nika a grin while still trying to stifle his laughs.

"I'm sorry. I couldn't help myself."

Freyne snorted and undressed, throwing his sodden clothes on the bank. With another splash, he disappeared under the water, only to reappear moments later with his shoes and trousers. He threw them with the rest of his clothes, then splashed Nika playfully.

Nika cupped his hand and splashed him back, earning another round of laughter. Before Freyne could retaliate, Nika dived under the water and paddled back to the bank, then dragged himself out of the stream. For a moment he caught a hint of disappointment on Freyne's face. Warmed by the liquor, he peeled off his clothes and shoes, making sure the firestone was safe, then slipped back into the water.

The current washing over his exposed body was refreshing and felt calming. Still tipsy from the liquor, his inhibitions were washed away, and he no longer cared about being naked around Freyne. He zoned out, thinking back on the past few weeks since waking up on the altar, wondering if he'd ever see his own world again.

A wave of water splashed in Nika's face, startling him from his reverie. He fumbled and found his feet, then dived at Freyne under the water. Freyne dodged to one side, and when Nika surfaced, Freyne tackled him and pinned him against the far bank.

"That's not fair!" Nika gasped, trying to wriggle free.

He couldn't tell if it was deliberate or the current, but Freyne drifted closer, so close he was able to make out his features in the moonlight. Their eyes locked, and Nika sucked in a shallow breath, suddenly nervous. He stopped trying to escape Freyne's grasp and froze, his heart pounding, unable to look away. In slow motion, Freyne leant forward and planted a soft kiss on Nika's lips. A different type of warmth came over him, and for a moment nothing else existed in the world around them.

With a gasp, Freyne recoiled and let go of Nika's arms, looking suddenly flustered.

"I-I'm so sorry," he stuttered, sounding mortified with himself. His expression changed to embarrassment. "I—"

Nika's mind was spinning and not from the alcohol. Something was awakening deep inside him; that brief kiss offered a glimpse of what could be, and he needed more, so much more. Before Freyne could finish apologising, Nika waded closer until their bodies were almost touching. Freyne's eyes were downcast, his cheeks flushed. His expression softened as Nika tentatively reached out and ran his fingers down Freyne's cheek. With his hands slightly shaking, he leaned forward and brushed Freyne's lips with his own, then hovered, waiting for permission to proceed. Freyne remained unmoving, frozen in time, and for an agonising few seconds Nika feared that he was being rejected. He faltered, suddenly unsure as to what he should do next.

As he started to pull away, Freyne blinked and shook his head, no longer frozen. His hand shot out and grasped Nika's arm, startling him, and pulled him roughly into his arms. Freyne pressed his lips firmly to Nika's while holding him tight. Nika felt his insides melting and he parted his lips, deepening their kiss. Their tongues fought momentarily for dominance, until Nika relented. Little sprites of coloured light appeared before his vision, surrounding them both, which made everything feel even more magical.

Unlike the lust-filled kisses he'd shared with women, Freyne's kiss was so much more and made Nika's legs feel weak. He wrapped his arms around him and gently squeezed, delighting in the feel of their bodies pressing together while the water lapped around them. He'd never shared such an intimate moment in all his life and it consumed him. It felt so right, so perfect, and he never wanted it to end.

It wasn't until some time later when the sounds of the others went silent and they started to shiver from the water that they finally parted breathlessly. Freyne ran his wrinkled fingers down Nika's cheek and gazed into his eyes.

"Are you alright?" he whispered.

"Yeah." Nika nodded dreamily. "You?"

"I've never been better, although I am getting cold. Let's head back and dry off before we get sick. I think we'll have a few things to talk about, too."

They climbed out of the stream and gathered their sodden clothes together, then walked slowly back to the cottage. Freyne reached out and took Nika's hand and shot him a shy grin. They paused to drape their clothes over the fence, then headed inside. Nika sat his firestone in the hearth and willed it to emit a warm fire, while Freyne used the broken door to block the entryway. They towelled themselves off, then Freyne gestured to the bedrolls.

Nika couldn't help but feel nervous; where he was usually confident in the bedroom and always took the lead, he was no longer sure of himself. *What if it was just a mistake? What if he wants to take this further? What if...*

Freyne crawled into his bedroll and patted Nika's, a gentle expression on his face. Nika swallowed and joined him, his heart beating faster and his stomach fluttering. *What now? Is he going to kiss me again? Ugh, I feel like a bloody teenager.*

"I've never been with a man before," Nika blurted out.

"Neither have I, but I find myself drawn to you."

"Were you ever attracted to men?" Nika asked.

"Once or twice, yes. But society used to be so against any couplings that were not strictly between a man and woman, and we were told in the monastery that Am would strike down anyone who strayed from that. I'm still here, though, so I guess that wasn't true after all."

"I've been attracted to men, but only ever played with women," Nika said, blushing. "I was always too scared to pursue that side of myself. So, where do we go from here?"

"I don't exactly know," Freyne admitted. "A relationship between two men is frowned upon and punishable by law in these lands, or at least it was before I fled into the forest. If we do this, no one can know about us, especially the princess. Do you want to proceed, or pretend it never happened?"

"There is no way I can ever pretend it never happened. Let's see where we go with it."

"Okay. But let's take things slow. This is all new to the both of us."

9

Her Royal Highness, Princess Iryna of the bloodline Obrel, skipped through the ruins, her arm linked with Lana's. They'd braided each other's hair and pinned a myriad of flowers through the braids, which made Iryna feel extra beautiful. Lana's long thick black hair was braided all the way to her backside and swung like a pendulum with each skip. For the first time since leaving the castle, she felt like herself again, clean and fresh which was how a princess should be.

"Oh, look!" Lana stopped skipping and pointed ahead.

"What?" Iryna asked.

"Berries! Let's go and pick some. They'll make our porridge taste much better."

Iryna screwed up her face but followed Lana to the overgrown bush that grew wild across their path. Lana pulled up the hem of her dress to make a pouch and started picking the berries.

"Be careful of the thorns. They're sharp," she warned.

Iryna rolled her eyes and reached for a berry. She popped it in her mouth and crushed it between her tongue and teeth, and was rewarded by a burst of sweetness.

"Wow! These are so good!"

"Breakfast will be yummy tomorrow." Lana nodded.

Iryna helped her pick more of the berries while helping herself every few handfuls. She hated to admit that she was having fun; usually gardening of any sort was beneath her and she often scoffed at the peasants for caring so much for their crops. For the first time ever she understood why people bothered with it in the first place.

"What do you think about Nika and Freyne?" Lana asked.

"I don't know. They're just commoners. Why?"

"I was just curious. They're always so quiet and rarely talk to us, so I don't know what to think about them. And don't you think it's strange that they have that cat?"

"Am I supposed to care?" Iryna asked, crushing more of the berries in her mouth.

"You should care. They seem nice enough."

"Oh, so you have a crush on one of them?"

"Not at all." Lana shook her head. "I mean they're both really cute and they're physically strong and good fighters. I'm not interested, though. Hmm. If you had to choose from any of the men to be your future husband, who would you choose?"

Iryna frowned and thought for a moment.

"I don't get a choice. I have to marry whoever my father tells me. You know that." She sighed, feeling her former happiness wane. "If I *had* to choose...I don't like beards, so Chardi's out. Nika and Freyne are too strange, so they're out too."

"What about Ur'Shad?" Lana asked.

"That dolt?" Iryna looked away, feeling her cheeks flush.

"He's loyal and would never let you come to harm," Lana pointed out. "He's a nice man, too."

"No way. He works for my father and is too annoying. Besides, he isn't a noble so he'd never be considered." Iryna felt her mood sour and she threw the last of the berries she was holding into Lana's makeshift pouch. "I've had enough. Let's go back."

Nika was grateful for the extra day of rest, and spent the morning wrapped in Freyne's arms, making out like a pair of teens. It wasn't until they heard Chardi bellowing that lunch was ready that they reluctantly crawled out of bed, got dressed, and joined the others.

"Where have you been?" Chardi asked.

Nika felt his cheeks flush and quickly hid his face by sipping from a waterskin.

"We overslept." Freyne shrugged. "That liquor was potent."

"It can be for those who aren't seasoned drinkers." Chardi nodded, shooting a look in Ur'Shad's direction.

"That's not fair," Ur'Shad grumbled, wincing. "You know I'm rarely allowed to drink."

"Here you go," Lana said, handing Nika and Freyne a bowl of soup each.

"Thank you." Freyne smiled at her. "I'm going to go and sort through that box Nika found in the swamp and see if I can make sense of it. I'll see you later."

Freyne turned back towards the cottage and Nika hurried after him, trying not to spill his lunch. They sat together at a table with a wooden bench seat, their shoulders and knees touching, and ate their lunch in tranquil silence. It wasn't until they finished eating that Freyne took a closer look at the contents of the waxed box. His face was serious as he skimmed through the scrolls and the sheets of parchment. After a while he scratched his cheek, then sighed and tossed them back in the box, looking defeated.

"What's wrong?" Nika asked.

"These scrolls contain a lot of garbled small-town visions mixed in with the great prophecy. I used to have a journal where I'd copied the important passages to isolate them from the mess. I hardly need to focus on Mr Jokar's chickens getting eaten by foxes or his experience of forgiveness." Freyne rested his head in his left hand and looked sideways at Nika. "It was the little black book that you may have seen in our shared vision. It's probably been destroyed by now."

Nika thought back to Freyne's vision, and with a start he realised he'd seen that very book.

"Wait here a minute."

He dashed inside the cottage and rummaged around in his pack for the journal and dagger, then hurried back to Freyne.

"Is this it?" he asked, placing them on the table.

Freyne's jaw dropped open.

"Where did you find this?"

"I found it in the house I stayed in the first night I was here. I also found this." Nika placed the dagger on the table.

Freyne's eyes widened and the colour drained from his face.

"My family's home," he whispered.

"That was *your* house?" Nika asked incredulously.

Freyne nodded, his eyes far away. Nika looked down at his

cloak and immediately felt embarrassed.

"I guess this is yours then. I'm sorry. I only took it because mine was ripped and it was raining," he said.

"It doesn't matter. You keep it. I need to know, though. Were there…any remains?"

"No. Um. Is there a way for me to show you what I saw, like you showed me that time?" Nika asked.

Freyne took Nika's hand and he felt their minds join again.

"Just close your eyes and try your best to picture what you saw," Freyne's voice said quietly.

Nika closed his eyes and replayed his memory of the ruined house as best he could. He remembered in detail, climbing through the window, seeing the stone burning in the fireplace, the broken bookcase. Freyne broke off the connection and looked relieved.

"It looks like they received an appropriate burial after all," he said, still holding Nika's hand. "The monks must have come and taken care of everything. I can now rest knowing that their souls have been delivered safely to Am."

"Does that mean that the firestone is yours?" Nika asked.

"No. I have no idea where that came from."

Freyne picked up a sheet of parchment and scrutinised it, and after a moment his face lit up. He showed Nika a nautical chart and pointed at a small island to the north of Bar'Am. "Look at this. I think we have what we came here for. This must be where we have to take the blood descendant."

Nika placed his map on the table next to the chart and studied them side by side.

"Where do we find this descendant then?"

Freyne shook his head.

"I have no idea. I'll need to skim through my diary to refresh my memory and see what I can find. Remember, I haven't read this for seven hundred years."

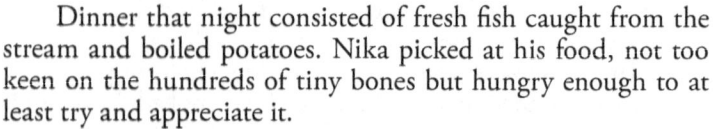

Dinner that night consisted of fresh fish caught from the stream and boiled potatoes. Nika picked at his food, not too keen on the hundreds of tiny bones but hungry enough to at least try and appreciate it.

"What's the plan for tomorrow?" Ur'Shad asked.

"We'll head east to Dol'Am and replenish our supplies," Freyne replied. "I'm still figuring out where to go next."

"You don't even know where we're going?" Iryna demanded. "What are we even doing?"

"There is some business that your father needs us to take care of," Freyne said delicately. "He has entrusted us to do it, so that's that. We're forbidden to speak of it."

"I am his daughter! You should be able to tell me." The princess grumbled. "Why do I even bother?"

"Orders are orders, princess," Ur'Shad said.

Nika finished eating quietly, sensing Iryna's declining mood. As he took his last bite of fish, Arnie-Kyn emerged from the ruins and sat at his feet.

"There you are," Nika said. *"Where have you been?"*

"One has been hunting and exploring," Arnie replied. *"We should resume our journey soon. Your quest is not yet over."*

"I know. We're leaving in the morning."

Lana collected their empty plates and set off with the princess to wash up by the stream. Nika bent down and picked up the cat and sat him on his lap. Arnie's claws pricked into his leg and his tail flicked irritably. Nika felt Freyne's mind once again join with his.

"You really need to teach me how to do that," Nika said.

"You've done it before without realising," Freyne said. *"I'll teach you properly later."*

"Are you ready for the next leg of the journey?" Arnie-Kyn asked.

"I'm not entirely sure," Freyne admitted. *"I just need to read through my journal and figure out the next step. I seem to recall reading about a golden relic, but that could be anything."*

"Would it be a small golden statue crafted in the likeness of Gri'Ran?" Arnie-Kyn asked.

"A golden statue? That does sound familiar." Freyne looked pointedly at Arnie-Kyn. *"How in the gods does a cat even know about this prophecy?"*

"The monks at the University spoke of little else." Arnie settled on Nika's lap and began to purr. *"They allowed me to come and go freely in exchange for my hunting abilities. One kept their mouse problem under control."*

"I know I've seen a golden statue before, but I can't remember where. Why is my memory so incomplete?" Freyne scratched his cheek, deep in thought.

"It will come back to you," Nika offered, patting his thigh without thinking.

"I sure hope so. I'm useless without it."

"Let's have an early night," Nika suggested. *"I'm not looking forward to going back out into that swamp tomorrow."*

"I hear you. Let's go."

Nika and Freyne excused themselves from the campfire and headed back to their cottage. Once they were out of sight from the others, Nika slipped his arm around Freyne's waist. Arnie trotted along behind them, seeming unbothered by their display of affection. The night was chilly, and Nika could smell rain coming. There was a flash and a rumble of thunder in the distance, and the first drops started to fall as they entered the cottage. Nika placed the firestone in the hearth and willed it to produce a warm flame.

"You're getting quite handy with the stone," Freyne noted, taking off his cloak and shirt.

"It's easy enough to control. I just think what I want it to do and it does it." Nika shrugged, kicking off his shoes.

Freyne swept Nika into his arms and hugged him tight. His grip was firm, unlike the delicate women he'd been with in the past. Nika held him back and nestled his face into Freyne's neck, inhaling his scent and getting used to the touch of another man. He was glad to finally be in private so he could show his growing affection without fear of repercussion.

"Are you even aware that you hold the gift of mancery?" Freyne asked, planting a kiss on his forehead.

"No? What's that?" Nika frowned.

"The force you use to control the stone is the same force used in mancery. Only a strong mancer can control those stones. Let's sit down and I'll show you."

Nika sat cross-legged on his bedroll and Freyne joined him.

"Mancery is the act of harnessing and manipulating the powers of the realm to do your bidding. To do so, you need to close out the physical world and enter the realm with your mind. With me so far?"

"I think so," Nika said, though he secretly felt confused.

"Take my hands and close your eyes. I want you to try and push your mind to join with mine."

Nika obeyed and took Freyne's sweaty hands in his. He tried a few times to reach out with his mind, but he couldn't find Freyne anywhere.

"Not quite," Freyne said. "You need to separate your mind completely from your body. Try again."

Nika closed his eyes again and concentrated. This time, he forced his mind to open up and he willed himself to separate from his body. He was standing in the lounge room, but everything was tinted with an off-beige, and when he looked back, he saw his body was still sitting upright on the bedroll, a pale pink aura surrounding him. Freyne was surrounded by a deep purple aura. Nika glanced around the room and spotted a similar light blue aura surrounding Arnie by the fire, and an orange glow for the firestone. He floated there for a moment, taking in the strange appearance of the realm. Everything felt and looked different; even his hands looked ghostly transparent. He regained his focus and found Freyne's aura again, then pushed his mind forward and joined with him.

"*There you are,*" Freyne said. "*The realms are shared by many different creatures, trees, beings of nature, and to a lesser extent, humans. Not everyone who uses it is friendly, so be careful.*"

"*Can anyone use it?*" Nika asked.

"*No. Only mancers can access and use the realm.*" Freyne replied. "*On that note, if we do meet a nosey or unfriendly mancer, you need to be able to defend yourself. You don't want to allow strangers into your mind.*"

"*How do I do that?*" Nika asked, already feeling overwhelmed.

"*Watch and I'll show you.*"

Freyne broke off their connection and summoned a shield around his aura, outlining the purple with light blue, similar to Arnie's colour. His method was slow and deliberate, which allowed Nika to see and understand how to do it. He followed Freyne's lead and summoned a wonky shield around his body, though his was nowhere near as strong. He felt his protection being penetrated and held it for as long as he could before it shattered into dazzling shards of light.

"*That was a strong shield for a first attempt. I'm impressed,*" Freyne said. "*That's enough for today.*"

Nika rejoined his body and at once noticed his hands were shaking and he felt weak.

"While you are in the realm, your body remains as is," Freyne explained. "Only enter the realm when your physical self is safe from harm. Otherwise, if someone attacks you, you cannot protect yourself."

"Why am I so tired all of a sudden?" Nika asked.

"The use of such power has a high physical cost," Freyne continued. "You'll need to increase your realm exposure a little each day until you can handle it. The more you're exposed, the longer you can stay in there. I'll help you practice."

There was a bright flash of light outside, followed by a loud rumble, and the sky opened up with a heavy downpour. Freyne wriggled out of his trousers and stretched out on his bedroll with his arms open. Nika pulled up the blankets and nestled into Freyne's arms. He felt weak and nauseous, and his head was spinning.

"Rest up and get some sleep," Freyne whispered. "You'll feel much better in the morning."

Nika's mood was sombre as they left the safety of the ruins and pushed through the fog barrier into the stinking swamp. The rain hadn't eased up, and they were already soaked and covered in mud. Arnie-Kyn led the way, walking slowly to ensure no one stepped into the bog. After an hour of trudging through the swamp, the rain eased up slightly, and Nika noticed that the terrain was slowly changing. The bog was beginning to thin out, giving way to more solid land, and by mid-afternoon they were in a thick forest.

"We should reach Dol'Am by sundown," Ur'Shad said, pausing to scratch his scalp. "We need to proceed with caution. Those bandits knew that we were in that swamp and that Iryna is no longer at Al'Obrel."

"Agreed." Chardi nodded. "I think we should split up and enter the city separately. Whoever those people are, they will probably have lookouts watching the gates for four men and two women travelling together. Ur'Shad and Iryna can go first, followed by Nika, Freyne and Lana. I'll go alone and drop by the garrison to see if we have a letter from To'Rel."

"Good idea," Freyne agreed. "Let's change our clothes here, then keep moving."

Nika ducked behind a tree and changed into a pair of deep blue pantaloons, a matching doublet, and a brimmed hat with a long blue feather tucked into the band. He looked over at Freyne, who was wearing the same outfit but in a dark green colour. Freyne winked, and they snuck a quick kiss before they made their way back to the group.

"Alright, let's go," Chardi said with a nod. "I'll meet you at the Red Rooster Inn in the centre of the city. Be careful."

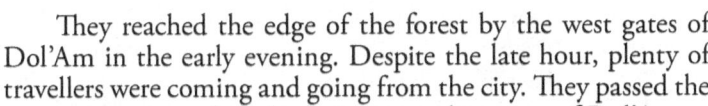

They reached the edge of the forest by the west gates of Dol'Am in the early evening. Despite the late hour, plenty of travellers were coming and going from the city. They passed the gates with ease and made their way to the centre of Dol'Am.

The inn was a squat stone building lined with windows on the upper floor. Nika followed Freyne and Lana inside and waited as he paid the innkeeper for their room. The murmur of many people came from the dining room, and Nika felt a pang of excitement that he would soon be eating a decent meal and may even get to have a drink. They took Arnie and their packs to their room, then headed back downstairs.

The dining room was quite large, hosting long rows of tables and benches. As it grew dark outside, tradesmen and farmers began flowing through the doors and filling the seats. Freyne disappeared to order dinner, and when he returned a server brought them a large steaming bowl of beef stew each, with a thick slice of hot bread dripping with butter on the side. Shortly after, a different server handed them a large tankard of black stout each. Nika tucked into his hot meal and guzzled his stout, already enjoying himself.

He glanced around the room and spotted Chardi and Lana not too far away. Iryna and Ur'Shad sat along the back wall at a small table by themselves, talking animatedly to each other. He turned back to face Freyne and saw that his tankard had been refilled.

The inn quickly filled with people, and at the far end of the room, a group of musicians started to play their instruments. Nika sat listening to the music, enthralled, and felt a pang of homesickness. Of all the things he left behind, he missed his music and guitar the most. His attention was drawn to one stringed instrument that looked and played like a guitar, only it was a little smaller. The melody was strange to Nika's ears, but not unpleasant. He continued to drink his stout and soon grew tipsy.

Much to his disappointment, after just a few tunes, the musicians stopped playing and left the stage. Shortly after, though, a different group clambered onto the stage and began to play, though the music was much worse.

"What's going on up there?" Nika asked Freyne, leaning in close so only he could hear.

"It's an open night. Anyone can go up and play a song," Freyne said. "It's been so many years since I've heard music."

"Ah," Nika replied, taking another deep swig. He stood up, a little wavy on his feet. "I need to take a piss. I'll be right back."

Freyne was feeling uncomfortable. Being surrounded by so many people after years of solitude left him feeling edgy. He was pleased that Nika was having a good time, though he was a little surprised by how many stouts he'd already consumed.

Nika stood up and excused himself; Freyne nodded and scanned the room for what seemed the hundredth time, keeping his eyes peeled for any kind of threat against Iryna. His gaze landed on the princess, and he watched her body language intently. She was lightly brushing Ur'Shad's hand as she was talking and making lots of eye contact, while her other hand was rested on his arm. Freyne felt his mouth twitch into a hint of a grin and lifted his tankard to his lips.

"Allow me to present you with a song from my homeland," a familiar voice called to the crowd.

Freyne spun around and spotted Nika on the stage, brandishing a cittern. He took off his hat with a flourish and bowed spectacularly. Several people in the crowd laughed and clapped. Freyne was pretty sure he was about to faint and took a long drink from his tankard to try and calm his nerves.

Nika began to strum the instrument in a way Freyne had never seen or heard before. He was stamping his foot in a steady rhythm and nodding his head in time with the beat. The crowd went silent, completely captivated. And then he began to sing.

"Baby I miss you, and all the things we used to do. Where did we go wrong…"

Freyne listened in awe, feeling his belly flutter and fill with warmth. He had no idea that Nika could sing, let alone play an instrument, and made a mental note to ask him about it later. As he sang, his voice held its pitch and tune perfectly. Freyne was pretty sure he could hear another instrument playing too, but Nika was the only one on the stage.

"…For I belong in your arms, and your arms alone. You are my temple, my goddess, my one true love…"

Nika's lyrics jolted Freyne upright, and he gasped as another memory clicked in his head. *The temple at Ner'Am! Of course! How could I forget about Gri'Ran's Gift? I delivered it there myself during my pilgrimage all those years ago. That's got to be it! Maybe the blood descendant is there, too.* He frowned and tried to remember the passage of the prophecy. *I'll check my journal tomorrow and re-read the passage as well…*

The crowd started cheering and Freyne realised that Nika's song had come to an end. Nika put down the cittern and bowed, then staggered to the side of the stage. Freyne stood up and hurried over to him, then caught him as he stumbled down the stairs and fell. He put Nika's arm around his neck and helped him back to their room.

"Did you like my shong?" Nika slurred. "I wrote it myshelf."

"It was unlike anything I've ever heard," Freyne said truthfully. "Honestly, I had no idea that you're a musician. Why didn't you tell me?"

"Because it wash my passion and the only thing I cared about in my world," Nika said. "Sinsh I came here, I doubt I'll ever get to live out my dreams. It hurts you know. Oh wow, I'm sho drunk. I'm shorry."

Freyne helped Nika into their bedroom and locked the door behind them. The room was tiny, dimly lit with a single candle by the fireplace. The only furnishing was the double bed. Freyne guided him onto the bed and sat next to him. Nika took Freyne's hat and threw it across the room with a laugh.

"You're cheeky tonight, aren't you?" Freyne grinned.

Nika pushed Freyne onto his back and straddled him, helping himself to the buttons of Freyne's doublet. Freyne felt his body responding to Nika in other ways, and he leaned forward to steal a kiss while fumbling with Nika's belt.

"It was definitely her," a man's voice said loudly on the other side of the door.

Freyne and Nika both froze and listened.

"It was the princess and the big guy. I'd bet my life on it."

"You're only telling me this now? We have to go find them! Where did they go?" another voice hissed.

"I don't know," the first man said. "I was watching that merchant sing, and when I looked back, they were gone."

"Idiot! We'd better go and wake up the men and station a team at each gate so they don't escape. We also need someone in the inn to trail her if she's still here."

"Relax. I already asked the barkeeper about them. He said that they're planning to leave for Qhal-Eran at sunrise. I've already organised an ambush just outside the southern gates so we'll capture them there. That gold is as good as ours and our lord will be pleased with us."

The voices moved past and two doors slammed at the far end of the hall. Freyne looked at Nika, his former excitement waning a little.

"Should we leave now?" Nika slurred.

"No. She'll be okay. We'll meet with the others in the morning and see what To'Rel's message says, then decide what to do from there. She'll probably receive a royal escort home."

A warm smile lit up Nika's face and Freyne felt his belly flutter again. His former excitement returned as Nika resumed fumbling with the buttons on his doublet.

"Now," Nika said, his smile widening. "Where were we?"

Nika woke with sun in his eyes and flinched. His head was pounding, and his tongue felt like cardboard. He groaned and patted the bed next to him, but it was empty. With a start, he sat up and glanced around the room. Freyne was sitting at the end of the bed, dressed in his travelling clothes and his mouth curled into a smirk.

"Sleep well?" he asked.

Nika groaned again. Freyne handed him a waterskin and he took a long drink.

"Thanks," he said, his voice sounding raspy. "That stout is much stronger than I'm used to. Are the others up?"

"They're downstairs waiting for us," Freyne said.

Nika slid his legs out of bed, feeling groggy and nauseous.

"What about those guys we heard last night?" he asked.

"Er, we have a change of plans," Freyne said. "Iryna, Ur'Shad and Lana have been ordered to come with us—"

"WHAT?!"

"Shh! Calm down. To'Rel heard about the attack in the swamp and decided that she would be safer with us. He also decided that he wants Iryna to witness the outcome of our mission to add credibility should things pan out right and shine in his favour."

"This is bullshit!" Nika grumbled. "I never should have gone to meet him. What's the plan for today, then?"

"Chardi's sent one of the guards to take Cookie back to Al'Obrel with a message for To'Rel. I've already organised some horses and supplies, and we'll be heading straight to Rybor. All I could get were Rarn mountain horses, so we'll be riding two apiece. Have you ridden before?"

"No."

"Don't worry. I'll help you. You'll get the hang of it in no time."

Freyne shook a pair of trousers and knelt to help Nika slide them on, then paused, staring below his naval. Nika followed his gaze and saw that Freyne had noticed his tattoo. A five-point star was inked into his lower abdomen, with a pair of wings spread out below his belly. Wordlessly, Freyne helped him to dress, then carried their packs downstairs. Nika followed him slowly, holding onto the wall for support so he didn't fall.

Arnie-Kyn was waiting for the party by the stable, his tail

twitching. The horses were much larger than those Nika was used to seeing and he couldn't help but feel intimidated by their size. The saddles were made for two riders instead of one. Nika had never ridden before and wasn't too keen on riding such a large horse while suffering a hangover. Ur'Shad helped Iryna mount one of the horses then turned to help Chardi with the packs.

Nika swallowed and tried to mount and swing his leg over the saddle, but the horse moved and he fell roughly to the ground. Iryna and Lana giggled at him. His cheeks burning, he picked himself up and tried again, and only just managed to pull himself into the saddle. Freyne picked up Arnie-Kyn and handed him to Nika to hold and shot him a wink.

"Where are the rest of the horses?" Iryna asked, glancing around. "We're two short."

"We're riding two-apiece, princess," Ur'Shad said.

"What? Did you fall and hit your head while you were drunk and stupid last night?" Her voice grew louder and more shrill. "I WILL NOT BE RIDING WITH YOU!"

"Hey! There she is!"

Nika spun around and spotted a group of people dressed as guards running towards them, their swords drawn. He swore under his breath and clung on to the saddle as the horse shifted.

"Now look what you've done!" he snapped.

Iryna drew herself up, her face flashing with anger.

"Who do you think you're talking to?" she exploded. "I'll have you hung for this!"

Ur'Shad and Chardi drew their blades and ran to head off the approaching attackers. Nika winced with each clang of steel on steel, and gasped when he spotted another of the black robed figures lurking by the stable. Like lightning, Freyne pulled a dagger from his boot and threw it; the robed figure made a gurgling sound and sunk to the ground, clutching at the dagger protruding from their throat. By the time Freyne retrieved his dagger, Ur'Shad and Chardi were done cutting down their attackers.

"Go go go!" Chardi bellowed.

He leapt into the saddle behind Lana and wheeled the horse around, kicking up a cloud of dust. Freyne mounted behind Nika and snatched the reins, then kicked the horse into a gallop, following Ur'Shad and Chardi through the streets of Dol'Am. Nika clutched onto the saddle for dear life, his stomach heaving. *That bloody princess!* he thought angrily. *I hope those fuckers don't follow us all the way to Rybor! I can't take much more of this.*

10

Nika felt seedy for most of the day, and as they rode, he concentrated on keeping his nausea under control. The ride was rough and jarring; at Chardi's insistence, they avoided the main road in case they were being followed. He sipped quietly from a waterskin, feeling embarrassed for letting himself get out of control the night before. *I was so stupid. I hope Freyne doesn't feel any less of me.*

His thoughts turned to Freyne and their budding romance. There was no denying the feelings that were growing between them each day. Unlike the flings of his past, he knew his feelings towards Freyne were not based on lust, but a deeper connection they shared. *What if I'm just clinging onto him because he's my only friend here?* he wondered, taking another sip of water. *Oh, get a grip of yourself. He's so obviously into me as much as I'm into him, and he is the only person here whom I can trust. I just wish this world wasn't so fucking weird...*

"Are you alright?" Freyne whispered in his ear.

"I feel like shit," Nika grumbled. "I shouldn't have drank so much. I haven't been this hungover in years."

"It'll be ok. I'll mix you up something when we stop."

"Did I make a complete fool of myself last night?" Nika asked, cringing inside.

"Quite the opposite, actually. The crowd really loved you."

"No, they didn't."

"Yes, they did. I will not lie to you, ever. Your song was amazing; it was unlike any music I have ever heard. And your voice..."

Nika blushed and looked away.

"This world is so strange!" he blurted out. "Everything is so different here. I'm different, and I'm not sure where I fit in anymore. I shouldn't even be here!"

Freyne slipped his arms around Nika's waist and pulled him back against his chest. Nika let go of the saddle and interlocked his fingers with Freyne's, and closed his eyes. Everything about him felt so right.

"You're here for a reason, and whatever that reason is, it's brought us together. You know, my life has completely changed too since you arrived."

"I'm sorry," Nika said.

"I've already told you not to apologise. I'm glad you're here and I wouldn't have it any other way."

"What happens when all of this is over?"

"Who knows?" Freyne shrugged. "Anything could happen between now and then."

"I mean, will you go back to living in the forest?"

"I think after seven hundred years of living in the trees, I'm ready to build a nice little cottage somewhere, settle down, and enjoy life as a free man," he said, chuckling. "One can dream, right?"

⎍⎍⎍

Chardi led the party to a cluster of trees hidden at the bottom of a shallow gully. The trees provided plenty of cover, and they agreed that it would be safe enough to light a fire. The leaves were turning yellow and deep shades of orange, announcing the arrival of autumn. As soon as they stopped, Freyne slipped off the horse and helped Nika clumsily dismount.

Nika's legs were stiff and sore after riding for so long. He stretched, grateful to be on solid ground again, then watched as Freyne mixed several powders together into a liquid.

"Drink this," he instructed, handing Nika the cup.

Nika tilted his head back and downed the liquid in one go, the taste making him splutter.

"Horrid!" he gasped, reaching for a waterskin.

"Horrid, yes, but you'll feel amazing in no time," Freyne said. "I'll go and hunt us some dinner."

116

Sure enough, it wasn't long before Nika started to feel much better. He wandered amongst the trees and gathered some sticks and branches for a fire, then cut them into manageable lengths with the axe. Once it was lit and he had a decent pile of wood, Nika sat by himself, poring over the map and tracing how far they'd come with his finger. They'd made good time despite riding over rough terrain.

Ur'Shad and Chardi were busy setting up the tents, while Lana and Iryna were talking quietly by the horses. Nika ignored them and stared into the flames until Freyne finally returned carrying the carcass of a large boar over his shoulder, and his cloak in his free hand.

"Nice catch," Nika said.

"Thanks." Freyne grinned and looked sideways at the fire. "This one almost outsmarted me. I'm going to enjoy eating it."

Nika helped him thread the boar onto the spit and place it over the fire, then sat back and stretched out his aching legs. His body was sore all over from riding all day. He looked across the fire, and noticed that Iryna was sitting closer than usual to Ur'Shad, and Lana was chatting quietly to Chardi. Freyne sat next to Nika and stretched.

"Are you feeling any better?" he asked.

"Much better." Nika smiled at him. "Can you teach me more of that realm stuff?"

"Sure, why not. It'll give us something to do before dinner." Freyne nodded and returned his smile. "Do you remember how to enter the realm?"

Nika nodded and concentrated on separating from his body. He felt his mind enter the trance that he'd seen Freyne enter so many times and glanced around the realm. Freyne's aura was still a vibrant shade of purple, but when he looked down at himself, he noticed that his own aura had changed to a deep shade of magenta. Nika stepped away from his body and stood gazing at his glowing silhouette. Freyne's mind joined with his and at once their auras became hazy and blurred like they were fusing together. Nika frowned and scratched his ethereal head.

"Why has my aura changed colour?" he asked.

"Hmm. That's strange," Freyne said. *"I think auras can*

*change once we enter the realm for the first time, but this isn't your
first time. I like your new colour, though."*

"Me too. What do the colours mean, anyway?"

*"The yellow that you can see around the others means that
they are neutral and aren't aggressive or violent. When we get
angry or emotional it changes colour."*

"Why are we different colours, then?" Nika interrupted.

*"We're mancers, which means the forces of the realms flow
through us. I don't know if the colours mean anything."*

Nika turned and looked at their companions opposite the
fire. Instead of the beige tinge to his vision, everything looked
purplish instead. All four auras were a light yellow colour. Nika
took a step towards them, then stopped when Freyne appeared
ghostily by his side.

"Ah, you've figured out how to travel," he noted.

"What's that?" Nika asked.

*"It's a form of projection. It's where you step out of your body
and project yourself into the realm. You can move around freely in
this form, which is handy for hunting or scouting because people
outside the realm have no idea that we're there."*

Nika walked around the fire to where Iryna and Ur'Shad
were sitting, their arms and knees touching, and noticed their
auras were slightly hazy and fused together also. He reached
out and touched her shoulder but his hand went through her
and she didn't react.

*"It's a good thing she didn't feel that. We'd never hear the end
of it."* Freyne chuckled. *"How are you feeling?"*

"Much better. Your hangover cure really helped."

*"Good. I noticed some people were setting up camp nearby
while I was hunting. Let's go and take a look."*

Freyne held out his spectral hand and Nika took it.
His hand felt different in the realm, soft and tingly, but not
unpleasant. With Freyne's help, Nika figured out how to drift
through the realm, and together they ghosted towards the other
campsite. Everything looked much brighter with the purple hue
and allowed him to see details that he wouldn't normally see.

The camp was much larger than Nika expected and was
dominated by two fires, each surrounded by around a dozen
people. Their auras varied from yellow to red. Freyne stopped a

short distance from the camp and summoned a shield around them both, surrounding them with a shimmering blue.

"*Don't go any closer,*" he warned. "*The red auras means that they're feeling aggressive.*"

"*But they can't see us in the realm, can they?*"

"*You're right; those people over there are just normal people. But if you look just past the left fire, you'll see a hint of a brown one. Look closer and you'll see it.*"

Nika squinted and could just make out a dark brown aura in the distance. A feeling of unease tingled down his neck and he shivered.

"*Are they a mancer too?*"

"*More than likely.*" Freyne nodded. "*I don't like this one bit.*"

A hint of movement caught Nika's eye, and he turned back to see someone standing up abruptly from the fire, his aura a deep red. He could just make out that he was wearing long black robes with his hood up.

"*Do you think they're the ones who're after Iryna?*"

"*I don't know, boo. I can't tell from here and if we get too close, that mancer will detect us. We'd better be careful just in case.*"

Nika smiled at Freyne's choice of endearment and moved closer to him. Freyne hovered, still watching the campers, when Nika felt a wave of exhaustion wash over him, and the realm turned hazy before his eyes.

"*I-I think I need to go back,*" he said.

Freyne nodded, and they ghosted back towards their own camp. As they approached, he saw Chardi's outline standing in front of his body, waving his hand in front of Nika's face. He rejoined his body and felt his consciousness return with a fresh wave of nausea.

"Hello? Anybody in there?" Chardi was asking.

Nika shook his head and blinked.

"What?" he grumbled, his stomach churning worse than when he was hungover.

"Gri'Ran's claws!" Chardi swore. "You scared me!"

"Is something wrong?" Nika asked.

"Oh. I was just letting you know that dinner looks ready," Chardi replied a little sheepishly. "Are you two okay?"

"We're fine," Freyne said. "There's a campsite around six miles from here, with potential for trouble. They may not have anything to do with us but be on alert just in case."

"How do you know?" Chardi asked.

Freyne winked but said nothing. He stood and hurried over to inspect their dinner. Nika's head was spinning worse than any hangover he'd ever experienced. His head felt clouded, leaving him confused and disoriented. The contents of his stomach shifted, and the burning taste of bile greeted the back of his throat. Nika rolled shakily onto his hands and knees and crawled away from the clearing into the darkness. The whole world began to spiral out of control, and the nausea overtook him. His stomach heaved, and he threw up what was left of his lunch. Everything lurched sideways and he fell, tumbling down a steep slope into oblivion.

The smell of the roasting boar made Freyne's mouth water. He carved it into thick slices and stacked it onto a plate for everyone. After being in the realm for so long, he was hungry and felt weakened. He had to admit that his tolerance to exposure wasn't as high as it once was.

"Where's Nika?" the princess asked.

"He's just over there." Freyne turned and pointed, but Nika was gone. "He was a moment ago."

"He's probably watering a tree," Ur'Shad suggested.

A faint whisper came from the within realm, startling him. *"Your lover is in trouble! Go to him!"* the trees called. They sounded worried. *"Hurry!"*

An overwhelming sense of dread welled in his gut. Freyne shoved the tray of meat into Ur'Shad's hands, then ran from the clearing as fast as his legs could take him. He used his senses rather than his eyes and quickly found where Nika had fallen. Freyne slid down the slope and found Nika's body sprawled at the bottom of the gully. He shook Nika's shoulder, but he didn't move; his breathing was shallow and his pulse was weak. There was a flash of light and a muffled grunt behind him, and Ur'Shad and Chardi slid down the hill, panting. Nika's face looked deathly white in the torch light.

"Help me carry him back to camp," Freyne ordered.

He could hear the panic in his own voice. Ur'Shad

fumbled with the torch and picked Nika up under the arms, while Chardi took hold of his feet, and together they carried him back up the slope.

"Take him to our tent. He needs urgent care."

Freyne led the way back to camp, then held open the tent flap for Ur'Shad and Chardi. They lowered Nika onto the bedroll, then shuffled out of the way.

"Anything we can do?" Ur'Shad asked.

"Not at the moment. Please, leave us be."

Iryna sat with Lana by the fire, worried and confused about Nika. Her empathy surprised her; usually she only cared about herself. She had no idea what was going on. Ur'Shad and Chardi emerged from the tent and joined them by the fire.

"There's something different about those two," Chardi said quietly. "They remind me of the royal mancers back home; you know how they zone out all the time?"

"I always thought they were just being dramatic." Ur'Shad shrugged. "What about it?"

"I've seen Freyne do it a few times since we left Al'Obrel. Then tonight, both of them were doing it," Chardi said. "When they came back, Freyne said that there's a camp six miles away that could be trouble."

"You think they're both mancers?" Iryna asked.

"I think so." Chardi nodded.

"But mancers are required by law to be registered. I've never seen either of them on duty at court." Iryna frowned and tossed her hair. "If they are practising illegally, I'll have no choice but to inform my father."

"What exactly *are* mancers?" Lana asked. "I never really understood it."

"I'm not sure exactly. It's some kind of magic, I think," Chardi said. "The king's mancers supposedly screen the court and warns your father if anyone is dangerous, but come to think of it, I don't think they've ever actually caught anyone. That's all I know."

"There's more going on here than meets the eye, isn't there?" Ur'Shad asked slowly. "What are you not telling us?"

Iryna levelled her gaze at Chardi, who looked down at his feet, defeated. He sighed and nodded his head.

"It has everything to do with the great prophecy. Your father sent us to find some blood descendant who supposedly exists and to fix whatever it was that Ami'Khel broke."

The princess frowned as she mulled over Chardi's words. She knew the story well, and she also knew of the prophecy and her father's obsession with it. It all made sense to her.

"I think I heard my father saying the time of fulfilment is near, but I never believed him. If that's the case, though, we need to do everything in our power to get this done right. The fate of everything hinges on this."

"If it's so important, why did he just send you and two nobodies instead of his army or something?" Ur'Shad asked.

"For secrecy, mostly," Chardi said.

"If any of my father's enemies knew about this, they could try and interfere. Although, I still don't understand why he ordered us to go along instead of returning home."

"Do you think that was his aim all along?" Lana asked.

"No? Why would he want me travelling all over the Isles in the company of all these men? He wouldn't even let me roam the castle without an escort."

"If he asked or ordered you straight up to go, though, would you?" Lana asked pointedly.

Iryna glared at her handmaiden, and for a moment she felt as though she were about to explode. She bit her tongue as she mulled over Lana's words, then sighed.

"You're probably right," she grumbled. "I bet this was all just some elaborate plan. I'm so sick of being the pawn of my father's politics!"

"Well, you're away from him now," Lana said, smiling. "He can't control you while you're away. I think you should make the most of it and enjoy it while you can. This is probably the only opportunity you'll ever get to travel afar without a royal escort hounding you."

"Speaking of secrecy, I can tell that Freyne knows a lot more than he's letting on," Chardi added, glancing towards the tent he shared with Nika. "I think it's time he comes clean and tells us what he knows. We're going to need to work together on this."

"Let's all head to bed and have an early night. I'll take first watch," Ur'Shad said.

Iryna stood and hovered for a moment; once Lana and Chardi's backs were turned, she leant over and kissed Ur'Shad on the cheek. He startled and shot her a puzzled look.

"Er. Good night," she said quickly, then hurried after Lana to hide her blush.

A wave of excitement washed over her, along with a sense of freedom she'd never felt before. Lana was right; for the first time in her life, she was on an adventure without being surrounded by royal guards or her overbearing father. *This is my time to live like a normal person and see what it's like to be free,* she mused as she crawled into the tent. *I may as well make the most of it before this journey is over and I'm married off to some random royal man-pig."*

Freyne covered Nika with both of their blankets and placed his hand on his forehead; his skin was cold and clammy, and his breathing was shallow. Once Ur'Shad and Chardi were gone, he buried his face in his hands and began to weep. *I can't believe I was so stupid,* he berated himself. *What in the gods was I thinking? Me of all people should know that he wasn't ready for projection yet. It's way too soon and I don't even know the extent of his abilities yet! I've put his life at risk and this is all my fault.*

He stayed by Nika's side, holding his cold hand, monitoring his pulse and breathing. Even though they'd only known each other for the shortest time, Freyne couldn't bear to lose him.

"What's wrong with the human now?"

Freyne jumped and looked up to see Arnie-Kyn sitting just inside the tent flap.

"I pushed him too hard," Freyne wept, a fresh wave of tears springing from his eyes. *"I just wasn't thinking. My memory isn't what it used to be. I've probably killed him."*

"Don't be dramatic." Arnie padded softly across the bedding and settled next to Nika's neck. *"He'll be fine."*

"How would you know?" Freyne demanded, his grief turning to anger. *"You're just a—"*

Nika's fingers twitched and a groan escaped his lips.

Freyne's heart almost leapt from his chest, and with a gasp, he leaned closer to inspect Nika's face. A hint of colour was creeping into his cheeks, and his breathing was steadier. Even his pulse was stronger. Freyne reached down and stroked Nika's cheek, tears once again forming in his eyes. He slipped into the realm; sure enough, Nika's aura was pulsating between magenta and a soft healing mauve. He was going to be alright after all.

"F-Freyne?" Nika whispered.

"I'm here, boo."

"I'm so fucking hot."

Freyne wiped his eyes and removed one of the blankets. Nika squirmed and rolled onto his side, then reached out and tugged weakly at his sleeve. Freyne nestled down beside him and pulled him protectively into his arms.

"Get some sleep, the both of you," Arnie-Kyn said, purring. *"You are both safe now."*

He stood before a dark tower which stretched into the sky, growing thinner towards the top like a giant spike. The tower had large double wooden doors, edged in gold leaf, and he yearned to step forward and open them. Lightning cracked overhead, and in the darkness, something with large wings fluttered through the air, but he couldn't make out what it was. He looked back at the door, longing to open it, and reached out a shaking hand towards the handle…

Nika woke with a start, shaking, and had no idea where he was. He could feel someone's strong arms wrapped around him, and he felt safe in those arms. As his memories slowly returned, he remembered waking through the night and seeing Freyne upset. He frowned and opened his eyes slowly; his face was pressed into Freyne's chest, who was snoring softly. Nika's body was stiff and sore. With a yawn, he tried to roll onto his back to stretch, but Freyne's grip was too tight. Nika shook his shoulder and Freyne's eyes shot open. At once, he could sense Freyne's overwhelming emotions, especially guilt and worry.

"Oh boo, you're awake."

Freyne brushed a strand of hair from Nika's face. The

gesture was usually gentle and caring, but instead it felt like a sharp jolt of electricity when their skin touched. Nika flinched from their contact, confused.

"What happened?" he croaked.

"I thought I'd lost you," Freyne whispered with a sob. "I was so careless. I'm so, so sorry."

"What do you mean? I'm so lost."

"I pushed you too far. We were in the realm for too long, and the effort drained so much of your energy that you barely had enough to keep your heart beating. I never should have allowed you to travel so soon let alone so far for your first time. I almost killed you."

"You never told me that this realm shit is dangerous."

"Anything we do in life is dangerous if we're not careful. The same applies for mancery. I guess I'd better start teaching you properly so we don't have any more accidents. I could never forgive myself if I was responsible for your death."

"It's not the first time I've died, and it's bound to happen again someday," Nika said wryly.

"Just shush. Are you hungry?"

"I'm too exhausted to eat. I just want to sleep."

"Well, I'm hungry. Stay here and rest up. I'll go and organise breakfast."

The morning was cold and the sun was only just beginning to rise. Freyne stirred up the coals in the fire and busied himself with making a pot of strong tea. He poured some for himself then set about making breakfast. The worry of the night before weighed heavily on him, and he tried to rub the fatigue from his eyes.

"Morning," Chardi said, emerging from the trees. "Sleep well?"

"Eventually. Any movement from that other camp?"

"No." Chardi shook his head. "I've been a soldier for long enough that if something did happen, you'd already know about it."

Freyne handed him some tea and took a sip of his own

"I'm sorry. I didn't mean to question your skills. How long have you been a soldier?"

Chardi stared into the fire and took a deep swig from his tea, looking deep in thought.

"When I was fifteen, my parents became sick and they both died. I had the choice of being a homeless street urchin or joining the army. The idea of fighting for and defending my king was much more desirable than living on the streets, so I marched into the local garrison in Ru'Amin and joined up.

"After a few years of training I was sent to Al'Obrel for an exercise. I saw the elite guards training and I knew that that was what I wanted to do. I was already skilled with a sword and knew there was more to my life than being just a regular soldier. So, I put in my request to join and was accepted. Over the past 16 years I've worked my way up through the ranks until I eventually became the chief of the guard."

"No wonder To'Rel selected you for this task, then." Freyne gave the porridge a final stir and reached for the bowls. "Breakfast is ready."

Chardi went to wake the others, then returned to warm his backside on the fire. The princess, Lana, and Ur'Shad emerged from their tents one by one and joined them.

"You're up early," Ur'Shad noted, accepting a mug of tea. "Is Nika alright?"

"He's awake now. The worst is out of the way."

"What happened to him?" Iryna asked.

"He hit his head when he fell," Freyne fibbed.

"No, he didn't. You can tell us the truth."

Freyne shook his head, unwilling to give anything away.

"We know about the prophecy, and we know that you're both mancers," she said firmly. "We're all in this together, so at least be honest with us."

Freyne closed his eyes and sighed.

"Alright then, it's true. Nika is an untrained mancer, so I've been teaching him a little here and there. Last night we took it a bit far. It happens."

"You seem to know a lot more about this prophecy than you're letting on," Chardi said. "Care to bring us up to speed?"

Freyne avoided Chardi's gaze and started dishing up their breakfast. He wasn't ready nor willing to talk about his time and position at the monastery. He'd been enjoying living his life as a common man instead of having to play the part of a high priest for once.

"I've read it before, a long time ago. There's a copy of it in that box we found in the swamp, so I'm going to re-read it and refresh my memory. Bits and pieces are slowly starting to come back to me."

"So where are we going to find the blood descendant?" Ur'Shad asked. "He could be anywhere."

"I'm not sure yet. Hopefully we'll get more clues when we reach Ner'Am. The priests should be able to help us."

"That's not much to go on," Chardi said.

"It's more than we had when we left Al'Obrel. Now, if you'll excuse me, I need to go and check on Nika."

Freyne placed his and Nika's breakfast on a tray with their tea and made his way back to their tent. Nika was sitting up in bed, topless, his face still a little pale. His hair was messy and he had dark patches under his eyes. Arnie was sitting on his lap while Nika scratched behind his ears.

"How are you feeling?" Freyne asked.

He knelt and rested the tray on his bedroll, then sat and tucked in to his breakfast, suddenly ravenous.

"I feel like I've been hit by a Mack truck, to be honest."

Freyne stared at him, confused.

"I mean…like I've been run over by a stampede of horses," Nika corrected himself. "My whole body is sore, I'm exhausted, and I feel like shit."

Freyne reached out to brush Nika's hair behind his ear, but as his fingers touched Nika's face, he flinched in obvious discomfort. The guilt stabbed at Freyne's gut, and for a moment he feared that Nika was mad at him.

"I-I'm so sorry," Freyne said.

"No, don't be sorry. It's not your fault." Nika frowned. "Everything feels different somehow. It's like every sense has been magnified and it hurts. I don't like it."

Freyne studied Nika's face for a moment, deep in thought. He frowned and concentrated, trying to force his brain to yield the answers he needed. A thin layer of sweat formed on his brow, and just as he was about to throw up his hands in frustration, something clicked, and his memories came flooding back. There were so many things he'd forgotten that he sat there, bewildered, until the answer finally came to him.

"Close your eyes and listen for a moment. Tell me what you can hear," he said softly.

Nika closed his eyes and frowned.

"I can hear the princess and Lana whispering about Ur'Shad and Chardi. There's a swarm of wasps buzzing around in a log somewhere nearby, a flock of birds flying over that way, and I can hear riders on the main road. I can smell the rust on Ur'Shad or Chardi's chainmail, the water in the stream, and the faintest hint of honey. I can even smell the body of the boar lingering on the clothes you wore yesterday."

Freyne's eyes widened as he realised what happened.

"No wonder you got so sick," he whispered. "You didn't just enter the middle realm last night like I first thought. You somehow managed to enter the lowest realm instead. This changes everything."

"The lowest realm?" Nika asked.

Freyne nodded.

"I can't believe I forgot all about this. Do you remember how I said that one's aura can change when we enter the realm for the first time?"

"Yeah," Nika replied.

"There's actually three realms. Most mancers can only ever enter the middle realm, which is by far the easiest to access. It's where everyone starts. The highest realm is used mostly by trees and creatures of nature to communicate. Mancers seldom use it, as they cannot understand the languages. The lowest realm, though…" Freyne paused and took a sip of his tea. "The lowest realm can only be entered by the most powerful mancers and creatures. It has been documented in the literature that some mancers have gone mad just from trying to access it. I'm astounded that you've entered it at all, let alone with so little training. Your senses, aura, everything, has changed because you entered that realm."

Nika rubbed his forehead and looked overwhelmed by what Freyne was telling him.

"Is this going to be a blessing or a burden?" he asked.

"It's a blessing," Freyne assured him. "Everything should settle down in a day or two."

"None of this makes any fucking sense to me."

"We'll talk more about it later when you're feeling better. I'll go and tell the others that we'll spend another night here."

"No. I should be ok," Nika murmured.

"You're unwell. You need to rest."

"I'll be fine," he argued.

"You're so stubborn. Eat up, then. You're going to need all your strength to fully recover."

Kia-Mor

A cold breeze blew in from the north, rustling the yellowed leaves on the trees in the gully. Nika still felt weakened and sick in his belly and had to be helped onto the horse. Freyne sat to the front of the saddle with Arnie, and Nika clung on to Freyne's waist for support. He really didn't want to spend the day riding, but he knew he had no choice.

He dozed on and off as they rode, resting his head on Freyne's back, drawing comfort from his warmth. His newly heightened senses were overwhelming; the thundering of the horses' hooves, the sounds of stones being kicked along the ground, and the creaking of the leather on their saddles were all loud and gave him a headache after just a few miles. Nika wished he could drown out the noises, but he was too weak to even try.

Adding to his discomfort were the intense smells wafting seemingly from all around him. He could smell the bad breath of the horses, Ur'Shad and Chardi's sweat and body odour, and, somewhere, a dead animal lay decaying in the grass. The only scent that wasn't too offensive was Freyne. Nika focused on that one familiar scent that anchored his troubled mind to sanity, and soon drifted into an exhausted doze.

After a few more days of non-stop riding, they topped a hill and could see the sea in the distance. The port city of Rybor stretched for miles in front of them; a smoky haze hung over the city like an ominous cloud. From their vantage point, Nika could just make out the dots that were ships drifting through the sea. Along the main road to their right, a long caravan of merchants and their wagons were crawling towards Rybor. The sky was grey and threatening to rain, and the wind that blew from the sea was icy cold.

Nika still felt overwhelmed by his new senses and was drained from the constant noises and smells. He knew it was only going to get worse once they entered the city.

"Do you think we could stop here for lunch?" Nika asked quietly in Freyne's ear.

"I don't see why not," Freyne replied. "Are you okay?"

"I need your help with something before we reach the city."

Freyne nodded and nudged their horse forward.

"Let's head over to that gully and stop for lunch," he called to Ur'Shad and Chardi, pointing.

Before they could argue, Freyne spurred the horse into a gallop and led the way. The ravine was just deep enough to conceal them from the road. A crystal-clear stream bubbled from an underground spring and wound its way through a cluster of trees. Where Nika would usually enjoy such a tranquil place, the noises and smells were more than he could handle.

"We're just going to check something," Freyne said, passing the reins to Chardi. "We'll be back shortly."

Nika sat Arnie on the ground and pulled his cloak tighter, then walked in silence with Freyne. The gully curved to the right, and they found a secluded place under a lone tree. Nika pulled Freyne into a tight hug and closed his eyes, feeling comforted by Freyne's closeness. They held each other for a moment, then let go and sat side by side under the tree.

"What's troubling you?" Freyne asked.

Nika bit his lip and was quiet for a moment.

"How do I make it stop?" he asked finally.

"Make what stop?"

"The sounds and smells. They're all so overwhelming and I can't take it anymore."

"They're still troubling you?" Freyne sounded surprised.

"We wouldn't be here otherwise."

"I'm sorry, boo. I didn't realise. You should have told me sooner."

"I have no idea what's going on anymore." Nika shifted uncomfortably. "I do know that I can't keep going like this."

Freyne scratched his shadowed cheek thoughtfully; Nika clenched his teeth at the rasping sound, feeling his patience wane.

"There is a way to silence them, but to do so, we must enter the realm again. Do you feel strong enough?"

"Physically strong, but mentally drained," Nika replied.

Freyne took Nika's hand, sending a sharp jolt up his arm. Nika flinched, and it took all of his self control to not pull away.

"This is advanced mancery, so you need to know from the start that you might not get it right at first," Freyne began. "To put it simply, you need to enter the realm and separate your senses from your physical state. Not all, though; you still need to be able to hear and smell."

"Will that remove them permanently?"

Freyne shook his head.

"You can never remove them, as they are part of you. You will be able to adjust your senses when you need to use them. Sometimes, increasing your hearing or sense of smell can be useful, especially for hunting. In a way, the realm acts like a storage place for them."

"Is this going to make me sick again?" Nika asked.

"Not if we're careful. I'll guide you in to the correct realm so we don't have any more mishaps."

"Is there anything else I should know before I try this?"

"Know that I am here and I won't let you come to any harm," Freyne replied.

He leant over and kissed Nika on the forehead; Nika once again felt that thrilling jolt, and momentarily they were surrounded by the shiny pinpricks of light.

"Ready?"

Nika nodded and the specks of light disappeared.

"Ok. Wait for me to guide you in."

Freyne's eyes grew distant, and a few seconds passed before Nika felt a soft tugging on the edge of his consciousness. He pushed his mind towards it, and Freyne pulled him into the realm. His view was tinted with beige, and Freyne's familiar aura was next to him. The sounds and smells were gone, and for the first time in days, Nika felt at peace.

"This is the middle realm," Freyne explained. *"It should feel different compared to the lowest realm."*

"It looks different, too," Nika replied.

In the distance he could see the very faint outlines of their party's auras, and along the main road, a large group of people were riding past. Nika shivered; one of the auras was the same brown he'd seen the night he became sick.

"Do you think they're the people from that campsite?"

"More than likely." Freyne paused and watched as they rode past. *"They didn't see us. It's probably a good thing we came for lunch when we did. I have a bad feeling about them."*

"Me too."

"Alright, let's get this done while we can. I need you to focus on one sense and one sense only."

Nika focused on his hearing and became aware of the noises around him.

"Look deep into yourself and visualise the sense. You need to isolate a small portion of it, then shift it outside of your body. Adjust it a little each time, until you get the level right."

Nika did as he was instructed and was able to see all sorts of colours and patterns swirling around his body. He instinctively found his hearing and isolated half of it.

"How do I know if it is enough or too little?" he asked.

"Leave the realm and we'll test it," Freyne replied.

It took Nika a few tries to get his hearing back to a tolerable level; he adjusted it slightly above his usual range and was finally satisfied. Freyne looked impressed.

"That's enough for today," he said, smiling. "Let's—"

A cold shiver ran up Nika's spine and the hairs prickled on his arms. Freyne froze, and Nika heard a faint whisper in his mind. He instinctively re-entered the middle realm to see what was going on, and at once he saw that the group of riders had turned around and were heading towards the gully. Several of the auras were turning red and the brown aura was nowhere to be seen.

"Nika!"

Nika pulled his mind back, his heart racing. Freyne snatched his arm and half-dragged him until Nika found his feet and began to run. Ur'Shad and Chardi looked up as Nika and Freyne raced towards them, gasping for air and clutching at their sides.

"What's wrong?" Chardi demanded.

"We have to go *now!*" Freyne barked.

Without hesitation, Ur'Shad hoisted Iryna onto their horse

and leapt up behind her. Lana fumbled to stuff the food back in the pack, but her hands were shaking so much that she dropped it.

"Oh, no," she said, stooping to pick it up.

"Leave it," Freyne said, mounting.

Nika scooped up Arnie-Kyn and passed him to Freyne, then mounted and held on tightly to Freyne's waist. Chardi reached down and pulled Lana onto the saddle in front of him and looked across at Freyne.

"We're all ready," he said.

"This way."

Freyne kicked their horse into a gallop and led the way along the bottom of the gully, past the lone tree, and up the shallow incline back to level ground. Nika slipped back into the realm and immediately spotted the other riders pouring into the area by the trees where they had just been moments before.

"They're right behind us," he reported. *"I can't see the mancer."*

"He's shielding himself," Freyne said, urging the horse towards the road. *"They're obviously tracking our auras. I'm going to need you to shield us and keep an eye on them. Hopefully we can hide amongst one of those caravans."*

"Ok."

Nika carefully re-entered the realm and concentrated on summoning a shield around himself and Freyne. Once he was sure it was strong enough, he slipped from his body and ghosted into the air, surveying the area around them. Chardi and Ur'Shad were close behind them, following Freyne towards the road. Their pursuers were still milling around the trees, looking for them, and Nika's skin crawled when he spotted a man in a black cloak holding up Lana's discarded pack. The man pointed towards the far end of the gully and yelled to the others to follow.

By the time Nika rejoined his body, Freyne had almost reached the caravan. Two riders drew their swords and broke away to head them off.

"Whatta ya want?" one of them demanded.

"We got cut off from our load a few miles back and are being chased by around twenty bandits," Freyne called. "Can we join you? We are no match for them."

"Where ya comin' from?"

"The University."

"Alrigh'. But if yer try anythin' funny, yer dead. Gottit?"

"You have our word."

Nika's hands were sweaty and his stomach twisted painfully. Much to his relief, the riders sheathed their swords and returned to their defensive positions. One of the wagon drivers slowed enough to allow them through a gap and waved for them to join him.

"Thank you, friend," Freyne called.

"It's my pleasure. I'm Jora from Qhal'Eran." The driver tipped his hat then pointed at a cloud of dust in the distance. "Is tha' them?"

"Yeah," Nika said, nodding.

"Where's yer crew?" Jora asked.

"We don't know," Freyne fibbed. "They've probably rejoined the caravan somewhere back there. We'll find them once we get to the port."

"Yer welcome ter ride with us ter the docks. No one in their right mind would attack us. As yer saw, we 'ave our own mercenaries ter defend us."

Nika calmed his breathing and dared to enter the realm again. This time, he saw the mancer's brown aura in amongst the other riders, who had stopped by the edge of the gully

"They've stopped," Nika reported. *"Do you think they will keep trying to follow us?"*

"They've followed us this far. I don't think they will stop," Freyne said grimly. *"You did well back there."*

"I didn't do much. Where—"

Nika broke off as a sharp stab tried to penetrate his shield. He gasped at the pain as the attack grew stronger and almost shattered his defence.

"Oh, no you don't!"

Freyne's presence surrounded Nika's shield, strengthening it tenfold. Nika could feel Freyne drawing from the realm, and as another attack came as suddenly as the first, Freyne released and targeted the other mancer with an attack of his own. Nika heard a scream within the realm and his blood turned to ice.

"Did you just kill him?"

"No. I sent him a warning to leave us alone. If he tries again,

though, I'll have no choice but to kill him," Freyne said. *"Are you ok?"*

"I'm fine."

"That was a good shield. I'll take over for a while so you can have a break. We will take turns in short intervals so neither of us end up sick like the other night. When we get out to sea, I'll teach you how to defend yourself and fight back, and as much as I can about mancery. Ok?"

"Ok."

The ride through the narrow streets of Rybor was a journey in itself. Unlike the neatly organised streets and districts of Al'Obrel and Dol'Am, Rybor consisted of sprawling stone shanties built with no thought for roads or structure. The road weaved in and out of the rough buildings, sometimes forcing the caravan to halt and pass through in single file. Many of the dwellings had tent fabric stretched over crumbled sections of the roofs, giving Nika the impression that no one planned to repair the damage.

As they wove deeper into the city, Nika spotted a tall building that was built from stone much darker than the shanties around them. The architecture was different, too. A balcony circled the uppermost level, and he could see guards wearing red spread along evenly, watching the streets below.

"What's that over there?" Nika asked.

"That's the port authority, though it's more like a barracks." Jora explained. "The bottom two levels house the militia. The top level is where the gov'nor an' his cronies monitor the imports an' exports to an' from the city."

"Isn't this place ruled by a king?" Nika asked.

"No. Rybor, Fraal, an' Fiz'Am all make up the Independent District. The kings 'ave no power 'ere. Is this yer firs' time haulin' goods?"

"Yeah," Nika replied. "I'm not from these parts."

"We all gotta start somewhere."

"This is one of the most corrupt cities on the Isles," Freyne added silently. *"Keep your guard up. I don't think we're being followed, but I doubt they've given up on us, either."*

The dock was teeming with sailors and dock hands who

were loading and unloading countless ships and wagons. The overwhelming stench of rotting fish hung in the air, forcing Nika to cover his nose to stop himself from gagging. The caravan quickly dispersed as the merchants made their way to their ships. Freyne, Ur'Shad and Chardi all shook Jora's hand and thanked him for his help.

"It's my pleasure," he smiled. "Charter boats are up tha' way. Yer best chance o' findin' a way across is with decent coin. I hope yer find yer crew intact."

Once Jora was gone, Freyne dismounted and motioned to the others to gather around.

"I'll go and hire us a ship," he said. "Wait here and keep your eyes open. We don't want any trouble here of all places."

"Alright." Chardi nodded.

Freyne turned and disappeared into the crowd. Nika readjusted his shield and ensured it was strong, then carefully dismounted.

"You're getting better at that." Iryna smirked as she slid gracefully off the horse she shared with Ur'Shad.

"I can also mount by myself now, *without* making a fool of myself," Nika said proudly.

"I'm not so sure of that." She crossed her arms, still smirking.

"Oh, don't be mean," Lana chided her. "I'm sure he'll be an excellent rider at some point. We all have to start somewhere."

Nika's cheeks flushed with embarrassment, and he turned his back abruptly, swearing to himself. *I should have just kept my mouth shut,* he thought. *Hurry up, Freyne.*

By the time Freyne returned, the sun was beginning to set. The moment Nika spotted him emerging from the crowd, he felt his mouth curl into a smile, and it took all of his self-control not to run to him.

"I found us a ship," Freyne announced. "We can't leave until tomorrow when the tide turns, but the captain is happy to load us up now. We can also stay on board for the night."

"Lana and I…um…need some supplies for the voyage," Iryna piped up, her cheeks flushing red. "Can we go to the market? It isn't far from here."

Freyne looked thoughtful for a moment.

"I suppose Nika and I can take the horses and get them loaded up." He nodded.

"But what if that mancer is watching us?" Nika asked.

"They won't be able to tell who's who in a busy market. Remember, all neutral auras look the same. So long as they are careful and don't get separated from Ur'Shad and Chardi, they'll be fine." He turned to Chardi. "Our ship is on dock seven, bay twelve."

Chardi nodded, and without a word they pushed their way through the crowd and disappeared.

"Do you think you can ride by yourself?" Freyne asked, turning his attention to Nika.

He nodded, feeling confident despite Iryna and Lana's earlier comments. Being careful not to drop or crush Arnie, he remounted and took the reins of the packhorse, then rode next to Freyne towards dock seven.

Their ship was smaller than many of the vessels in the port, but to Nika it was still quite large. Several sailors wearing crisp white uniforms were loading barrels of goods into the cargo hold via a wide gangway. A loud boisterous voice hollered from above, and Nika looked up to see a buxom woman with deep burgundy hair waving down at them.

"Ahoy there! Come on up!"

Freyne waved back and motioned to Nika to dismount. The sailors hurried over and took the reins, then loaded the horses straight into the hold. Another sailor beckoned them to follow and led them through the ship to the upper deck.

"Welcome aboard the Scruffy Mongrel!" the woman's voice boomed. She crossed the deck and shook both Nika and Freyne's hands. "Please, call me Maple."

"I'm Nika."

"You're a cutey." She winked at him suggestively. "Feel free to come and join me in my quarters for a drink later."

Freyne coughed slightly and Nika blushed, suddenly feeling very uncomfortable.

"The rest of our party should be here soon," Freyne said. "Would you mind showing us the way to our quarters?"

Maple turned to a nearby sailor.

"Oi! Take these two to their berth," she bellowed, then turned back to Nika and pointed. "My quarters are over there. I'll see you around, sweetie."

She winked again; Nika turned and hurried after the sailor, his cheeks burning. They went below deck and made their way to the guest berth. There were four rooms and a closed door opposite the entryway.

"These are your quarters, sirs. The door in front of us is the latrine and washhouse. It's sea water, so don't drink it. Fresh water is available from the kitchen but is limited for drinking and cooking. Now, to get to the mess and kitchen, go back down this hall and turn to your left, then follow all the way to the very end. You can't miss it."

"Thanks," Nika said.

The sailor nodded and hurried off. Freyne led the way to the room on the far left. It was small, with two hammocks hanging on the left and right walls. A plush rug covered the floor, and along the far wall was a small table and chairs and some storage cupboards. Nika placed Arnie-Kyn gently on the rug and stretched. Arnie's tail swished back and forth as he looked around the room.

"One shall stay in here for the duration of the voyage," he announced. *"The sea is no place for a cat."*

"Would you like us to bring you food?" Nika asked.

"Yes. One does not desire to hunt here."

"I'll go and get our things from the horses," Freyne said softly. "I'm not a fan of hammocks."

"Would you like some help?" Nika offered.

"It's okay. I won't be long."

Freyne gently brushed his fingers against Nika's cheek then slipped out of the room. Nika sat on the rug next to Arnie and scratched the cat's favourite spot behind his ears.

"I'm tempted to stay in here for the duration of the trip, too," he said, recalling Maple's unwanted advances with a shudder.

"Why is that?" Arnie-Kyn asked.

"I'm not too keen on our captain. She was coming onto me and I don't like it."

"Is she a female of breeding age?" Arnie asked.

"What?!" Nika said out loud, shaking his head. *"Humans*

140

don't just breed for the sake of breeding. There's so much more to it than that," he added silently.

"Breeding for the continuation of one's species is a deeply ingrained instinct, even in humans," Arnie countered. *"Surely you have already considered mating?"*

"I'm not interested," Nika said flatly.

"One does not understand your reasoning."

He sighed and wished he'd said nothing.

"Humans don't just bond for breeding purposes," he tried to explain. *"We bond through emotion, connection, trust. We call it love, and that forms the basis of a relationship. Mating, as you call it, is not the sole reason."*

"The difference between our species is interesting." Arnie began to purr. *"Is it common for two male folk to bond in that way?"*

"What? I...of course." Nika felt his cheeks burning once more. *"Like I said, we bond for love."*

"One does not understand your coupling concepts, but a bond is a bond nonetheless."

"Does that mean we have your almighty approval?" Nika asked sarcastically.

"You do not need my approval. One shares the mind of a pack, so as your companion, one is satisfied that each of you fulfil your duties within our pack. Although, one does not care to witness you in the act of mating."

Nika's face grew hotter. Despite their nightly exploration of each other's bodies, he and Freyne were yet to have the privacy needed to take that step. He jumped when he heard a light *thud* outside the door, then let out a deep breath when Freyne entered, laden with their packs. As he sat them by the door, Arnie brushed past him and left the room. Freyne wordlessly retrieved the bedrolls from the hall, then came to a stop when he noticed Nika's flaming cheeks.

"What's wrong?" he asked.

"I've just been forced to explain the dynamics of human bonding and relationships to a cat," Nika replied, still blushing.

"Oh dear."

Freyne chuckled and locked the door, then kicked off his shoes and helped to set up their beds. Nika removed his cloak and shoes, then laid back and stretched.

"How long do you think the others will be?" he asked.

"Given what we know of the princess, I think we can expect them to be gone for over an hour." Freyne dropped to his knees and crawled his way seductively between Nika's legs and along his body until their faces were level. "I finally get to have you all to myself."

Nika grinned and reached down to undo Freyne's belt, then pulled his shirt over his head. Freyne sat back and freed himself from the sleeves and his trousers, then helped Nika to undress. Once they were naked, he lay on his side and pulled Nika against his body, then kissed him hungrily. At once, the sprites of coloured light appeared in Nika's vision and swirled around them both, tinting everything in a purple hue. Nika parted their kiss and gazed around in wonder; the sprites stopped and hovered around them, twinkling like stars. Freyne kissed him again, deeper and with more intent, and the sprites resumed their dazzling show.

"I need you," he murmured, running his hand across Nika's backside while nuzzling at his neck. "I'm so ready for this."

"Me too."

Nika was no stranger to sex. It was a given while on shore leave, but those encounters were usually fuelled by lust and liquor, a quick release after a long and gruelling stint at sea. Freyne was as magical as the world Nika had been thrusted into. A euphoria entwined amongst them as they guided each other like the waves lapping around them; slow and peaceful with sudden moments of shift in the tide as the storm raged on between them, then cumulating together until they crashed upon the shores in a frothy clash of riptides.

They lay together for an eternity, their breathing and heartbeats in sync as the tide receded and left them shivering and exposed. The tiny pinpricks of light had disappeared long ago, though Nika could still feel the magic that had formed between them.

"You're amazing," Freyne whispered.

"So are you." Nika trailed his fingers over Freyne's sweat-covered body, unwilling to part their contact. "It's never been like that before. I can't describe it."

"I know what you mean, boo."

"Tell me something. You've experienced all three realms, right?"

Freyne nodded.

"Did your senses go crazy like mine did?"

"Only when I stumbled into the highest realm, and even then, it wasn't a sudden overload like yours," Freyne explained. "My senses calmed down on their own after a few days. Maybe it's because I was trained in the other realms at the monastery under very controlled conditions, so I was used to exposure at the time. Remember, I didn't visit and learn the highest realm until after I fled to the forest."

"So what are those little specks of light that I see every time we kiss, then? Do you see them too?"

"Light?" Freyne sounded puzzled. "I thought I saw a few white orbs on the edge of my vision, but I was a little preoccupied at the time."

"It was like I could feel everything you were feeling as well as what I was feeling. Is that normal here? I've never experienced anything like this before."

"No. It's never felt like that for me before, either." Freyne kissed Nika's forehead. "Did you notice you slipped into the lowest realm while we were...you know?"

"No?"

"You did, and you pulled me in, too. I think that's why we shared everything." Freyne gazed at Nika and brushed his fingers across his cheek. The action no longer caused him pain, but instead a warm tingling in his belly. "I think you have a special gift there. You seem to have the ability to push half of your mind into the realm while remaining present here. I've never heard of other mancers being able to do that."

"What's so special about the lowest realm, anyway?"

"That's the realm where you can manipulate the reality of the physical world," Freyne explained. "The lowest realm is where you can perform the most dangerous mancery, and if not careful, you can unintentionally harm others or yourself."

"This all sounds so scary," Nika admitted.

"You'll be ok," Freyne said gently. "I won't let anything bad happen to you. Now, let's go and have a quick wash, then see if the others are back yet."

By the time they'd washed and dressed, Nika's belly was rumbling. He followed Freyne through the ship to the cargo hold, a warm glow radiating through him as he thought back to the magical time they'd just spent together. Lana and the princess strolled up the gangplank arm-in-arm looking pleased with themselves, followed by Chardi and Ur'Shad, who were struggling to carry all of their purchases.

"Ur'Shad! You mongrel, who let you off the leash?"

Maple's voice roared from behind him, making Nika jump.

"Maple, you crazy wench!" Ur'Shad roared back. He dumped his goods on the ground and opened his arms, sweeping her into a big hug. "What are you doing here?"

"Loading my ship, obviously," she replied with a hearty laugh, planting a big wet kiss on his cheek.

"Your ship?" he asked, letting go and taking a step back. "What happened to the captain?"

"That fool decided to go for a swim with the sharks," she said slyly. "Everyone knows better than to cheat at my table."

Ur'Shad and Maple roared with laughter. The princess was glaring at the two of them with her arms crossed.

"Come and have a drink with me later, all of you! Now, go make yourselves comfortable while I finish up here. Dinner should be ready soon."

Nika helped Ur'Shad pick up the dropped items while Freyne took some of Chardi's, then led the way through the ship to their quarters. Iryna pushed past Nika and stormed into the room opposite his and Freyne's, then slammed the door loudly behind her. Ur'Shad scratched his head in obvious confusion.

"I wonder what's wrong with her? She was fine before."

"Um. I'll go and talk to her." Lana frowned, then hurried after the princess.

"Who knows." Chardi peered into another of the empty rooms and grunted. "Hammocks. You and I may as well bunk in here together. That way we can use the other room for our packs. I don't feel comfortable leaving them in the hold."

"Good idea." Freyne nodded.

"I'm hungry," Ur'Shad mumbled, shooting a look towards Iryna's door. "Let's get ourselves sorted then head off to dinner. Maple only hires the best cooks."

The mess hall was well lit and spacious, boasting four large tables which could comfortably fit eight people at each. At the head of the room was the captain's table. Maple waved and beckoned to the group to join her. The room was filled with laughing sailors and crew, enjoying their last night in port before setting sail. Many were already well on their way to getting drunk. Ur'Shad sat on the bench next to Maple and wrapped his arm around her. They laughed and reminisced, their voices drowning out the noise of the sailors. Nika tried to sit as far away from her as he could, but Maple saw him first.

"Come over here, sweetie," she called.

Nika cringed, but did as he was told, not wanting to cause a scene. Freyne sat beside him and discreetly rubbed his knee under the table. Iryna slid onto the bench opposite Freyne with her arms crossed, her face darker than a thunder cloud.

"So, you big oaf. How on earth did you manage to get away from that dank castle?" Maple asked Ur'Shad. "Don't tell me you left the king's service?"

Ur'Shad eyed the angry princess then lowered his voice.

"We're actually on official business for the king," he said. "Top secret, of course."

"Of course." Maple laughed. "How's his brat of a daughter? Still spoilt and obnoxious?"

Iryna sprung to her feet.

"I HATE YOU!" she screamed at Ur'Shad. The princess turned and ran from the mess hall.

The room went quiet for a moment as the sailors watched her flee, then settled back into the rowdy chatter as though nothing had happened. Ur'Shad looked like he'd been slapped in the face, but Maple laughed even harder.

"I guess that's her?"

"Yes, that's Iryna." He sighed, his former happiness gone.

The kitchen staff bustled into the mess carrying platters of food and barrels of liquor. Each table received a small roasted boar, already carved into easy to eat portions, a platter of roasted vegetables, and a pitcher of rich gravy.

"Eat and drink up, everyone!" Maple bellowed.

The sailors cheered and got stuck in to their meal. Nika's mouth was watering as he loaded up his plate and poured himself a generous helping of gravy. Freyne filled their tankards from one of the barrels and passed Nika a dark stout.

"Thank you." Nika shot him a smile and took a sip.

"You're welcome, boo. Ur'Shad was right about the food."

"Yeah. I still prefer your cooking, though."

Lana looked uncomfortable as she ate her dinner in silence. Once she was finished, she excused herself politely and took a small plate of food for the princess. Maple took a deep swig from her tankard and let out a loud belch, then put her heavy arm around Nika's shoulders.

"Hello, handsome," she purred. "How's the food? Are you having a good time?"

Nika wanted to die.

"I-I guess," he stammered, feeling his face flush red.

"Don't be shy, sweetie. My offer still stands. Come by my quarters for a chat some time." She laughed and drained the rest of her tankard, then turned her attention back to Ur'Shad.

"How embarrassing," Nika said.

"I'm sorry she's making you feel uncomfortable," Freyne said. *"If she doesn't back off, you might have to have a word with her."*

"What, and have her throw me overboard?"

"She can try. Don't worry, boo. I'll be there to help you."

Once they finished eating, Freyne thanked Maple for dinner and said goodnight to the others. Maple shot Nika another wink, and he turned abruptly and hurried from the mess with Freyne.

"I wonder what's wrong with the princess," Nika said as they made their way down the hall.

"She and Ur'Shad need to have a good long talk, I think," Freyne replied. "Her Royal Highness is starting to realise that in the real world, if she wants something, she has to ask nicely for it, and the answer will not always be yes."

Iryna sat at the table in her room, crying her heart out into her arms. Although Lana tried to console her, the princess was too distraught and ignored her efforts. She was hurt, a feeling she'd never had to feel, and she didn't like it at all.

Ever since she was a child, Iryna knew that one day her father would choose her a worthy husband, and she would have little or no say in the matter. At first she didn't care; the life of a royal princess and eventually a queen was lavish and she would be well-cared for. Since she left the castle, though, Iryna was starting to see just how precious life was, and realised that she truly was a spoilt obnoxious brat.

Her thoughts turned to Ur'Shad and the captain and a fresh wave of sobbing overtook her. Her newfound freedom had turned into hope; hope that perhaps she could have a relationship with someone she actually loved before she was forced into a life of misery.

Iryna secretly adored Ur'Shad, but hid her true feelings by being curt and unkind to him. She'd told herself over and over that it was for both of their own good, and hated herself for treating him so poorly. He had, after all, taken an oath to protect her from harm, and had saved her life more than once. The princess continued to sob, feeling her heart break. She was a fool. Ur'Shad would *never* want to be with her; he clearly preferred larger and rougher women.

The door opened and closed, and she heard heavy footsteps approach. Two strong arms wrapped around her, startling her. Iryna tried to wriggle free, but Ur'Shad's grip was too strong. She gave up, too miserable to try and fight him.

"Princess, please don't cry," Ur'Shad said gently in her ear.

He wiped the tears from her eyes and stroked her hair until she stopped sobbing. His tenderness surprised her enough to calm her down and listen.

"That woman. Maple. Her real name is Mar'hea and she's a good person. She has known your father for as long as I have, *and* she has known *of you* for as long as I have," Ur'Shad said quietly. "Why are you so upset?"

"You love her, don't you?" Iryna sniffed.

"As a matter of fact, I do. Do you know who she is?"

The princess shook her head, unable to look at him.

"Mar'hea is my sister."

He stood before the dark tower, gazing at its tip high up in the sky. Lightning cracked overhead, and in the darkness, the winged beast fluttered through the air. He turned his attention back to the door and reached out his shaking hand to open it. With a sense of dismay, he realised it was locked. He needed a key...

Nika woke with a start, his heart racing and his body drenched in sweat. It took him a moment to realise that he was no longer outside the tower but on board the Scruffy Mongrel, laying next to Freyne who was still sleeping peacefully. He pushed himself up and noticed that his hands were still shaking.

Being careful not to wake Freyne and Arnie, he slipped out of bed and dressed, then made his way to the upper deck. It was still dark outside, and the icy wind stung at Nika's face. On the far horizon he could see a faint glimmer of orange from the approaching sun. He made his way to the port side and leaned over the rail, watching the bustling city that never slept. The dock hands and sailors spoke in quiet murmurs as they went about their tasks in the early hours of the morning.

Nika's dream troubled him. It felt so real, and deep down he yearned to open the mysterious door. It was calling to him and he had to know what was inside.

"What's troubling you, sweetie?" Maple's voice came to him from behind, somewhat subdued in the early morning light.

"Oh, nothing. Just a bad dream," Nika said, not wanting to be disturbed.

Maple joined him at the rail and followed his gaze.

"It's nothing but a cesspool," she said, her voice quiet for once. "This is the most corrupt city you will ever have the displeasure of visiting."

"Why are you here, then?" Nika asked.

"I'd just offloaded a valuable cargo of linens from H'Rak and was planning to go straight back to sea. But then your friend came and offered me a very nice price to take your group across." She chuckled softly. "I had no idea that my brother was with you, otherwise I may have given you a discount."

"Your brother?" Nika frowned and studied her face for a moment. "Oh. Ur'Shad!"

"Well obviously I was blessed with the better looks."

She made a silly face and Nika couldn't help but laugh.

"You lot have come a long way. Where's your wife?"

"I'm not married," Nika said, then regretted it immediately.

"Not married? Are you betrothed then?"

Nika looked down at the water below and grew flustered. Maple gently took him by the chin and turned his face to hers, her gaze boring into his.

"Hmmm. I see a deep love in your eyes, but it's not for a woman."

"So? What's it to you?" Nika asked defensively.

"Sweetie. I am the only woman aboard a ship of over thirty men. When one is at sea for weeks or months at a time, one starts to notice things. Some men have needs that cannot be satisfied by a woman. You have nothing to worry about whilst on board this ship, and you are safe to express yourself, too."

She smiled warmly, and for the first time Nika noticed a gentle beauty in her features. She looked a few years older than Ur'Shad and he could finally see the resemblance.

"You had me scared earlier," he admitted. "I thought you were coming on to me."

"I was only joking around. Most of my passengers love it when I flirt with them, but I realised last night that there's something between you and Freyne. I'm sorry for making you feel uncomfortable."

"Once upon a time I probably would have flirted back and tried to take things further. Now, though, I only care for him. I've never felt like this before."

"I know what you mean, sweetie. I was deeply in love once, too." Maple's expression was overcome with a hint of sadness.

"*Was?* What happened?"

"We were young and in love, or at least I was. Her family is wealthy, so we would sneak out to one of their barns to be with each other as much as we could. After Ur'Shad was accepted into the king's service, I asked her to run away with me so we could start building a life together. To my surprise, she refused. She didn't want to give up her lavish lifestyle or her guarantee of a hefty inheritance, so I left and found work on a ship as a cook. I worked my way up from there, and now I'm the captain of that same ship."

"I'm so sorry," Nika said.

"What's happened cannot be undone. I still miss her sometimes, but the important thing is I moved on and made my own life. As much as I loved her, she loved her money more. It's a shame since I have my own wealth now."

"So why do you flirt with men if you're into women?"

"The loud boisterous me you have seen is really just an act. It hides the soft me. A captain can't afford to be seen as weak."

"Does your crew know?" Nika asked.

"Of course they do, and they accept me as much as I accept them. As for you, sweetie. I can see that you're scared of what your friends might think if they find out. Remember, you are who you are, and love doesn't lie. If your friends don't accept that, then they aren't really your friends. Got it?"

Nika nodded. The sun was finally peeking above the horizon, spreading orange and yellow ripples through the sky. The sunrise was beautiful, and Nika realised that Freyne was right; Maple was a good person and wouldn't be a problem. He felt a newfound respect for her and was glad for their talk.

As he turned back towards the city, he spotted a group of red-clad soldiers marching along the dock, accompanied by several people wearing black cloaks with their hoods up. A shiver ran down Nika's spine as he felt a soft breeze against his mind. He slipped into the realm and immediately spotted the familiar brown aura amongst the soldiers.

"Maple!" Nika tore his mind back from the realm. "We need to go, now!"

"Why? What's wrong?" she asked.

"They're the ones who have been dogging us all the way from Al'Obrel." He pointed.

"Militia." She snorted and turned to face the few sailors who were milling around on the deck. "Oi! Get everyone up! We're leaving now!"

Nika's stomach twisted uncomfortably as the soldiers stopped marching. The mancer raised his arm and pointed in their direction; the soldiers shouted and broke into a run, charging towards the Scruffy Mongrel.

Oh shit! Our shield is gone! Nika panicked and tried to re-enter the realm, but as he did, a sharp pain stabbed at his mind. He gasped and fell to his knees, clinging on to the rail for support. Terrified, he tried to stand back up, but another attack much stronger than the first struck. Nika yelled in pain and collapsed, clutching at his head while writhing in pain. He could feel the other mancer drawing power from the realm and could sense that he was readying to strike one final time. At once he saw and understood what the mancer was doing. Without thinking, Nika pushed his mind back towards his attacker while drawing from the lowest realm and lashed out. There was a deafening roar in his mind followed by a shrill scream. A groan escaped from Nika's lips as the realm became silent. The hold over his mind was released, and he sank back on the deck, his consciousness wavering.

"Nika!"

Someone was shaking his shoulder. He opened his eyes and saw Freyne above him, his face creased in worry.

"W-What happened?"

"That mancer won't be troubling us anymore," Freyne said grimly. "How did you know to do that?"

"Do what?"

He pulled Nika to his feet and helped him back to the rail. The Scruffy Mongrel was already drifting away from the dock which was swarming with militia and the people dressed in black. Nika looked closer at their persuers and could see they wore bronze chestplates and pointed helms over their red doublets. A deep sense of forboding emanated from them.

"Drop the sail!" Maple hollered.

The sailors scrambled to unfurl the sail, and as the wind caught hold, it made a loud *boom*. The ship jolted then sped towards the open water. Freyne pulled Nika into a brief hug.

"Are you alright?" he demanded.

"I-I think so. Lucky you came when you did."

"I didn't do anything, boo. That was all you."

"But…how?"

"I can only assume that it was your survival instinct stepping in. This is my fault. I should have started training you sooner. There's so much you need to learn."

"It's a bit hard when we're constantly riding and only stop properly at night." Nika looked down at the water and sighed. His head was throbbing and his body hurt. "Life was so much simpler back in my world. Why couldn't To'Rel just send me back? It's not like I'll be any help here."

"Who knows?"

Freyne leaned on the rail and grew silent. The faintest of whispers came from within the realm and, feeling curious, Nika closed his eyes and followed it. Freyne was sweeping their surrounds, ensuring they were safe.

"No one's following us," Freyne said finally. "Let's go and have some breakfast. I'm famished."

Iryna, Ur'Shad, Lana, and Chardi were already sitting at one of the tables talking quietly amongst themselves. Only around half of the sailors were there, and the ones who were looked hung over.

"Morning," Nika said, sitting next to Lana.

"We thought you were still asleep," Chardi said.

"We've been up for a while," Freyne replied. "There was a little bit of drama before we left."

"What happened?" Chardi asked.

Nika recounted the incident on the dock. As he spoke, he noticed that the princess' face was still puffy from crying the night before, and Ur'Shad had his hand resting on her leg under the table. The kitchen staff brought out bowls of porridge and a large platter of hot bread and butter. Nika's belly rumbled as he helped himself to a piece of the buttery bread.

"Now that the mancer is dead, do you think they will try and follow us across?" Ur'Shad asked.

"Who knows?" Freyne scratched his cheek. "They've followed us all this way from Al'Obrel, so something tells me they won't give up now. We should be safe while we're at sea, though. Nika and I will be able to detect any approaching ships long before they're even visible."

"They must really want you, Princess," Ur'Shad said. "I hope everything is ok back home."

"How long will it take us to cross the sea?" Lana asked.

"Usually around two or three weeks, depending on the weather and the power of the ship," Chardi replied.

"Two weeks? Whatever shall we do on a ship for two weeks?"

"We'll be focusing on Nika's training," Freyne said, indicating himself and Nika. "We all need to sit down at some point and plan the next leg of our journey, too."

"That sounds boring." Lana sighed.

"There's plenty of things to do." Chardi shot her a warm smile. "I can teach you how to fish if you like."

"This is my first time on a boat," she said. "If I knew we were coming this far, I would have brought some books to read."

"It's not so bad," Nika said. "I used to live and work on a platform in the middle of the ocean for weeks at a time. It's quite peaceful out here."

"Were you on one of those fishing platforms off the Kalissaden coast ?" Chardi asked.

"Er...something like that."

"The closest I ever got to the sea was crossing over the University bridge with Iryna," Lana explained. "I grew up in a small farming village north of Al'Obrel. We didn't even have a lake there."

"How did you come to work for Iryna?" Freyne asked.

"When I was fifteen, my family's farm was struggling. The crops failed two years in a row and we didn't have the food or money to survive," she said sadly. "My two older sisters were married off to farmers in other villages. My parents tried to marry me off as well, but I refused. The man was much older, and so, so horrible. I ran away to the city and lived on the streets for a while, until I was caught trying to steal some food.

"I was captured and taken to receive my punishment from

the king. I told him my story, and he said that my punishment was to enter his service as Iryna's handmaiden. I would tend to her every need without question in return for meals and a bed.

"I never saw it as a punishment, though. I had food, a home, and finally a purpose other than being forced to be a man's slave and baby-maker. I found out years later that the king had been sending a small monthly payment for my services to my family which saved them from having to sell the farm."

"And what about you, Ur'Shad?" Freyne asked.

Ur'Shad shot Iryna a look then shrugged.

"I was a member of To'Rel's elite guard with Chardi. Not long after Lana arrived, the king opened applications to be Iryna's bodyguard. Most of the elites saw the role as beneath them, especially since one of the requirements was seen as... *lewd*. I had to undergo some background checks and prove myself as trustworthy. Since then I've sworn an oath to protect her with my life and will do so until the day I die."

"Lewd?" Nika asked, confused.

Lana giggled and Iryna's cheeks flushed. Nika frowned.

"Chastity." Ur'Shad shifted uncomfortably. "There are many rules which I must follow and obey, which includes being locked away, if you know what I mean. And, I'm honestly fine with that. I'm happy with my life."

Nika's curiosity was piqued, but as he opened his mouth to form his next question, the princess drew herself up and gestured at him. He held his breath, half expecting her to tell him off and to mind his own business.

"That time you sang at Dol'Am. I enjoyed it," she declared. "No one told me you're a musician."

"Er...thank you," he said, surprised at her sincerity.

"Close your eyes and put out your hands," she ordered.

Nika felt awkward but obeyed and rested his hands on the table. Something smooth and wooden landed in them. He opened his eyes and saw that he was holding a cittern made from a dark polished wood.

"Wow."

He sucked in a deep breath, admiring the fine craftsmanship.

"We found it at the market and hoped that you would play for us again," she said.

He glanced at Freyne and saw that he too was smiling.

Nika blushed and plucked at a single string, eager to play.

"Thank you," he said. "I'll be happy to, but only after I've had a stout or two to warm me up."

⌐──────┐

The voyage across the Independent Sea was smooth and mostly uneventful. Nika spent his days sitting with Freyne on the stern, where he could look out over the grey swells and watch the sea birds gliding over the waves catching fish in the ship's wake. He felt at peace on the open waters and was feeling a sense of happiness and belonging, something he'd never experienced before waking up on the Isles. Arnie-Kyn stayed in the room and would spend his days curled up on Nika's blanket or hiding in the cupboard. Nika was worried about him, but the cat always insisted he was fine.

In the week or so they'd been sailing, Nika felt that he was finally becoming friends with the others, including Iryna and Maple. Ever since the first night on board, Iryna seemed to be a different person and was actually pleasant to be around. Ur'Shad and Lana traded rooms, and judging by Iryna's blushing and furtive looks towards Maple, Nika was pretty sure that Ur'Shad was no longer wearing his chastity device.

But most of all, Nika came to accept himself for who he was. He no longer shied away from Freyne when others were around, and a few times he openly took Freyne's hand in front of his friends. He was pretty sure they all knew their secret, but no one seemed to mind which made Nika appreciate his new friends so much more.

As his knowledge of the realm grew, so too did his closeness with Freyne. He felt a great bond forming between them, as each day they spent longer and longer exploring the middle realm and its uses. In just a week, Nika had mastered most of the basics of that realm, which, Freyne reminded him, usually took mancers many years to learn.

"I think it's time we start on the lowest realm," Freyne said one morning as they made their way from the mess hall to their usual spot on the stern.

"Ok. I don't feel so scared of it now," Nika admitted.

"I won't let anything bad happen to you."

As Nika opened the door to the deck, a cold gust of wind slapped him in the face. It was icy and spitting with rain. They made their way to the stern and huddled in their usual corner out of the wind with their hoods pulled up.

"Using the lowest realm is a little different to using the middle," Freyne began. "You'll recall that the middle realm is mostly for passive and protection purposes. The lowest realm is used for manipulation of our surrounds and can be used in both a defensive and offensive manner."

"Okay." Nika nodded.

Freyne held out his hand and conjured a small ball of fire in his palm, then held it up for Nika to see.

"I don't think I need to remind you that the lowest realm can be dangerous," Freyne cautioned. "This fire looks harmless enough, but if not done correctly, you can burn yourself. Not only that, remember that anything we do has a physical cost."

Nika nodded again, giving Freyne his full attention as always and absorbing every word.

"To do this, you need to visualise the fire in your mind. Picture it exactly the size you need it, then focus the force of the realm into that image. Essentially, you are drawing the power from inside the realm and channelling it into the physical world, making your image a solid thing. Does that make sense?" he asked.

"Surprisingly, it does," Nika replied.

"Hold out your hand and visualise a small cold fire. Make sure it's cold, or you'll burn your hand," Freyne instructed.

Nika visualised a small fire in his hand and concentrated to make sure his image was as accurate as possible. It took him a while to get the flames to look like proper fire.

"Once you have the image in your mind, enter the lowest realm and reconstruct that image. Then, you need to kind of push it into the physical world. It's a little like when you separated your senses that time."

Nika slipped into lowest realm and recognised the purple tint immediately. He recalled his image of the cold fire in his hand, then feeling creative, he made his fire a deep shade of blue. He looked at his spectral palm and pushed the image of his fire from the realm. At once, the fire flickered and came to life. He retreated from the realm and held up his fire proudly, admiring the blue flickering flames. It felt cold as the flames licked around his fingers.

"Why blue?" Freyne asked.

"Something a bit different." Nika shrugged. He held up his left hand and transferred the flame from his right. "It's a bit like using the firestone, only instead of controlling the stone I'm controlling the forces from the realm. If I wanted to start an actual fire, I'm guessing I'd go about it the same way?"

"That's correct," Freyne replied, sounding impressed. "You'd visualise a hot fire on the kindling though, not in your hand."

Nika played with his blue flame for a moment, letting it pass from hand to hand and getting used to the feel of it.

"When you conjure a cold fire, it's your energy that is keeping it alight," Freyne explained. "Whereas if you conjure a hot fire, the heat will spread to the kindling and the fire will eventually sustain itself. The longer you sustain it, the more of your energy it will take from you. Be careful."

Freyne stood and motioned to Nika to join him.

"Now for something fun." He grinned, then pulled back his arm and hurled his fireball towards the waves. It disappeared into the water with a puff of smoke. "As you throw it, give it a little push from the realm to release it, otherwise it will cling to your hand."

It took Nika a few goes before he figured out how to throw his fireball into the water, and he couldn't help grinning as it was quickly engulfed in the waves.

"That *was* fun," he admitted. "Can we use this as an attack?"

"Yes. Fire, water, wind, balls of pure energy. Anything in the physical world can potentially be used for attack." Freyne nodded. "Practice with that for a little bit. I'll be back shortly."

Freyne turned and hurried below deck. Nika focused on his fireballs, making a range of different colours and hurling them into the sea. The more he made, the quicker he got at summoning and releasing them.

When Freyne returned he was carrying a wooden barrel tied to a long length of rope. He sat it down and watched as Nika's purple fireball flew through the air and disintegrated into the swells.

"Maple was kind enough to lend us this to practice on," Freyne said, gesturing at the barrel. "It's a little dangerous to be lighting real fires on a wooden ship. Besides, this is a good way to get some target practice."

Nika grinned.

"Conjuring a flame or fireball with the intention of burning something is a lot harder and more dangerous." Freyne leaned on the rail next to Nika, their sides touching. "For this, you start with cold flame much like before. The trick is to will it to burn *after* it leaves your hand. When you get the hang of it, you won't need to physically draw back your arm since you're really throwing it with your mind. Using your arm looks more dramatic, so do it the way you feel comfortable."

He held up his hand and summoned another fireball, then effortlessly hurled it into the water. Nika could hear a faint *hiss* when it landed. Freyne tied the end of the rope to the rail, then tossed the barrel into the water. It trailed along in the ship's wake, bobbing in the waves. Nika fired a few cold practise shots at the barrel, perfecting his aim, until he felt ready to try with heat. Freyne gave him an encouraging smile.

"Okay, here goes," Nika said, focusing.

On his first try he missed the barrel completely and sent the ball of flame a few feet to the left. He tried again, this time setting fire to the sleeve of his cloak.

"Concentrate," Freyne said, stifling a laugh.

Nika drew himself up and blocked out his surrounds, focusing his mind on nothing but the barrel. When he was ready, he reached into the lowest realm with only half of his mind, maintaining his focus in the physical world. He felt the power flowing into him and braced; he formed the image in his mind and willed the flame to flow forth. Reaching out with his right hand, a large ball of fire exploded from his palm. Nika directed it towards the barrel and channelled the power he'd harnessed from the realm into the flames, willing it to burn.

His aim was absolute. The fireball hit the barrel and exploded it into chunks of timber and metal. Nika was flung backwards from the force and landed roughly against a wooden crate. He slid to the ground, dazed.

"Fuck me!" he gasped.

Dazzling stars twinkled before his eyes and he felt drained of all his remaining energy.

"Are you alright?" Freyne asked sounding worried yet awed at the same time.

"I think I'm done for the day," Nika said, feeling shaken. "Is the barrel okay?"

Freyne helped Nika back to their bed, then lay down next to him, brushing the hair from his eyes. He could see that Nika was exhausted and ready for sleep.

"You did really well today," he said, smiling. "Your fireball was so powerful. I'm so proud of you, boo."

"I'm not that good," Nika said sleepily. "I'm sure anyone can do that."

"No, they can't," Freyne replied. "Mancers who draw from the middle realm are uncommon. Those of us who can draw from the lowest realm are rare. And those who can draw from all three, well, I'm not sure if anyone has been able to other than myself."

Nika mumbled something incoherently. Freyne kissed him gently on the forehead and brushed a stray strand of hair from his face.

"Sleep, my love," he whispered.

Nika fell into a deep sleep. Freyne lay by his side for a while, watching over him and ensuring he didn't have a repeat episode of realm sickness. He was astounded by the strength of Nika's fireball and the vast amount of power that he was drawing from the realm. At first, he was terrified that Nika would get distracted and have a serious accident. But he didn't. Nika had funnelled the power with deadly accuracy and destroyed the barrel with ease. Freyne had never seen anything like it.

"What ails the human this time?" Arnie asked.

The cat helped himself to the space between Freyne and Nika's chests, his gaze boring into Freyne's eyes.

"He's alright this time. He is excelling at his training."

"That's good. He has an important role to play in the prophecy and he won't make it without your guidance. You are good for him."

"I've studied the prophecy for years and I still don't see how he fits in," Freyne said.

"The prophecy you studied is an abridged version," Arnie said.

"The three scrolls recovered from the swamp contain additional passages. However, this is where you must make a choice."

"What choice?" Freyne asked.

"You already swore an oath to your god that you will not intervene with the course of the prophecy. If you choose to go ahead and read the missing passages, you must uphold your oath and not try to change the outcome." Arnie was holding Freyne's gaze, unblinking, his tail weaving slowly from side to side.

"How can you possibly know that?" Freyne demanded.

"One knows what one must know. That will be a discussion for another day, and until then, don't ask."

"What's the other choice, then?" Freyne asked.

"If you feel you cannot uphold your oath, you must leave the group as soon as we hit land, and not seek to follow us."

"What? Why? Who are you?!"

Freyne felt their connection severed abruptly. Arnie meowed and snuggled into Nika's chest, purring. Irritated, Freyne stood up and fished around in their belongings for the waxed box, then tiptoed from the room. He slipped into the spare room and lit the torch above the table. His mind was racing; in the three hundred years he'd spent studying the prophecy, it never occurred to him that it might be incomplete.

He upended the box and sifted through the sheets of parchment. Many of the pages were scribbled notes, maps, or sketches; he sorted them into piles of relevant and irrelevant, then placed the irrelevant sheets back in the box. With a sigh, he flipped open the book and started to read.

The book was a handwritten children's tale which spoke of a great winged beast with the head of an eagle and body of a lion. The tale described the gryphon as the guardian of a magical castle ruled by a great king and his queen forever more. He read the obscure book twice, hardly making sense of it. Freyne was so frustrated that he almost threw the book at the wall.

He heard footsteps and there was a light knock at the door.

"Come in," he called.

"Oh, there you are." Lana smiled. "We haven't seen you all day, so I told the others I'd come and look for you. Where's Nika?"

Freyne leaned back in his chair and stretched, feeling his back crack in several places.

"He's resting. He overdid it a bit earlier."

"Is he okay?" she asked.

"He's fine. He had a bit of an argument with a barrel."

"Well, dinner's about to be served. Will you be joining us?"

"Dinner already?" He frowned, realising he'd spent at least six hours studying the stupid book.

"Like I said, we haven't seen you all day. I was starting to think you'd abandoned ship."

"Alright. I'll quickly go and check on him first," Freyne said, standing up and stretching again.

Nika was still in a deep sleep, snoring gently.

"It looks like he'll be sleeping for a while yet. Let's go."

Only a few sailors were sitting around the hall and having a quiet drink with their dinner, and Maple was nowhere to be seen. Ur'Shad, Iryna, and Chardi sat at a table by the door and looked up as Freyne and Lana joined them.

"There you are. We were beginning to think you'd fallen overboard." Ur'Shad grinned. "Where's your shadow?"

"My shadow?" Freyne asked. His head was still foggy from hours of reading in dim light.

"Nika. You two are never apart. Where there's one there's always the other," Ur'Shad said.

"Oh." Freyne spied a half-drunk tankard sitting in front of the burly guard. "He's sleeping."

"One of the sailors said they saw some sort of explosion earlier," Chardi said, narrowing his eyes. "That wouldn't have anything to do with you two, would it?"

Freyne thought back to the barrel exploding and Nika flying backwards. He tried to keep a straight face, but instead he burst out laughing. Tears of mirth sprang to his eyes and he snorted, triggering another round of uncontrollable laughter.

"I'm sorry," he said, trying to supress his laughter. "I told him to try and set fire to a floating barrel. Instead, he blew it to oblivion. The poor thing got thrown three feet backwards and was a bit dazed. He'll be fine."

Everyone laughed and it took Freyne some time to bring his laughter under control. One by one they went around the table sharing stories about their day as a simple dinner of soup and bread was served.

"What was the book I saw you reading?" Lana asked.

"Oh. It's some children's story about a gryphon and a castle. It was in the box that we found in the swamp."

"Is it the one where the princess marries a great king, and they live together in a castle in the sky with the gryphon as their guardian?" Iryna asked.

"Sounds like it." Freyne nodded. "You've heard of it, then?"

"It's a common tale. Most little girls have heard it. My mother used to read it to me all the time."

"Ah." Freyne sighed. He'd wasted a day reading a fairy tale.

"Tell me something," Chardi said to Freyne. "Why have you been lighting fires the normal way for all this time if you could have just clicked your fingers and had one instantly?"

Freyne chuckled.

"First of all, anything we do has a great physical cost. You'll recall the night that Nika got sick when we were between Dol'Am and Rybor, and again today with him needing to rest. Just because we can do it, it doesn't mean that we should." He paused and took a sip of his stout. "Second, I think you all would have been freaked out if we started hurling fireballs around when we first met you. And third, people with our skills are rare and are often forced into service as slaves. Therefore, we need to be careful who sees us use those skills."

"That's horrible," Lana said. "I think the mancers back home are paid for their service."

"They are." Iryna nodded.

"I've also heard stories of some mancers using their powers for greed by offering their services for a hefty price, no matter how nefarious the job. We've already had one chasing us, so we need to be careful."

"Is there a chance we'll come up against more of them on our journey?" Ur'Shad asked.

"There's always a chance," Freyne replied. "Nika and I are prepared to handle it should it happen again."

A faint whisper came from within the realm. Freyne looked down at his empty bowl for a moment and checked Nika's aura. He was beginning to stir.

"Speaking of Nika, he's about to wake up. I should go and check on him," Freyne said, standing up. "See you tomorrow."

The others nodded and murmured their farewells. Freyne made a quick stop at the kitchen to get Nika and Arnie-Kyn some dinner, then hurried back to the berth.

Nika was still asleep when Freyne tiptoed inside. He placed Nika's dinner on the table and could just make out his silhouette in the darkness, tossing and turning and mumbling in his sleep. Arnie was nowhere to be seen. Freyne knelt and rested his hand on Nika's shoulder. His eyes opened slowly; in the dim light Freyne could see that he was confused.

"Hello, sleepy," he said softly, brushing the hair from Nika's face as he always did. "It's dinner time."

Nika yawned and rubbed his eyes.

"Come here," he grumbled, tugging on Freyne's arm.

Freyne lay down and gently pulled Nika into his arms.

"I missed you," Freyne whispered. "The others called you my shadow at dinner because we're always together."

Nika managed a chuckle.

"I brought you and Arnie some food," he added. "You should try and eat. It will help you get your strength back quicker."

"In a minute." Nika cuddled into him. "Do you think the others know about us?"

"Possibly. We haven't exactly been hiding it lately."

"I'm at a point where I don't care if they do find out," Nika said. "It's not like Iryna and Ur'Shad are allowed to be together, so if they can get away with it, so can we. And besides, I feel like they're our friends now. I trust them."

"I feel the same way. Besides, I think we have more things to worry about than who's shagging who." He bent his head and kissed Nika gently on his forehead. "Let's get you sitting up before your dinner gets too cold."

Freyne helped Nika to sit up, then passed him the bowl of soup. He found Arnie hiding in the cupboard and placed the fish in front of the cat.

"Thank you," Arnie purred.

"You're welcome."

"Are we doing more training tomorrow?" Nika asked.

"I think you could do with a day off, boo," Freyne replied. "I've been pushing you hard ever since we left Rybor. Besides, I think I need a day to just lay here and snuggle with you."

"You know what?"
"What?"
"That sounds like the best idea you've had all day. "

Part Two

Bar'Am

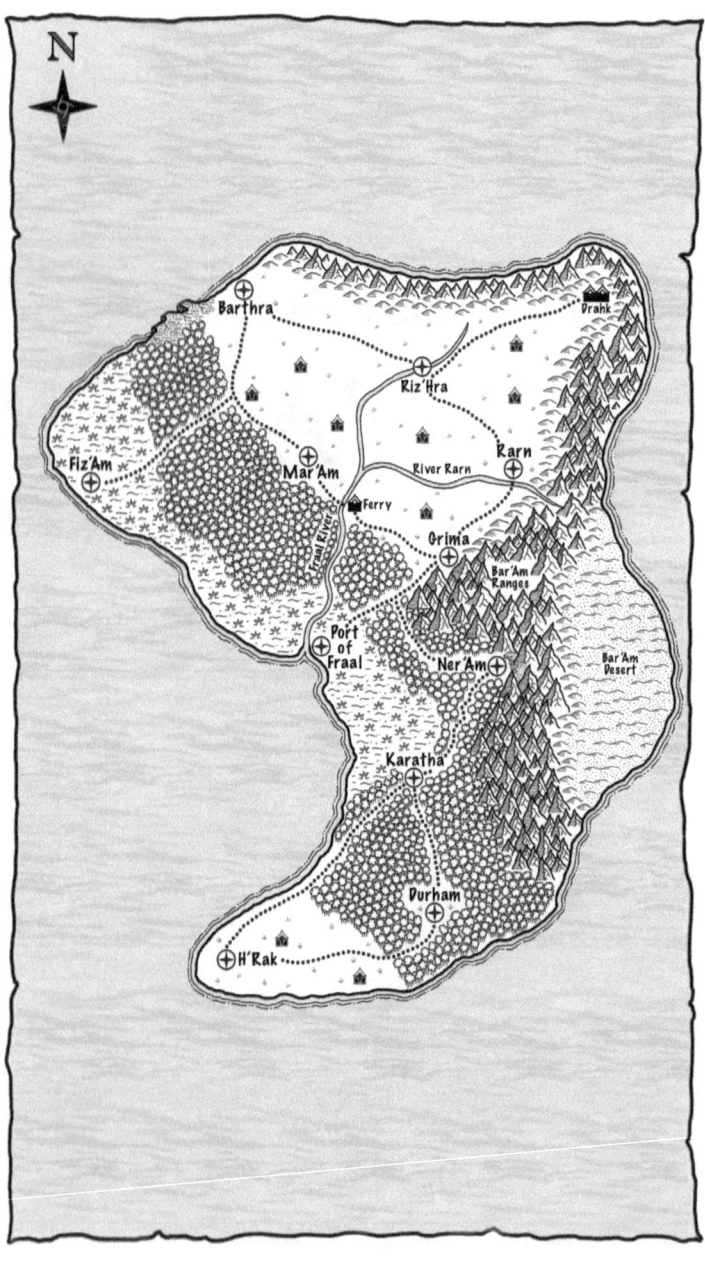

13

Nika stood with Freyne at the bow of the ship, eyeing a pinprick of land in the distance. After three weeks on the open water, he was glad to see land again, and was looking forward to both a decent bath and to sleep in a proper bed. He heard footsteps behind him and half-turned to see Maple approaching. She wedged herself between them and draped an arm around each of their shoulders.

"How are you two doing?" she asked with a smile.

"Okay," they replied in unison.

Maple chuckled.

"We'll reach the port just before daylight, so tonight is our last night at sea. Are you coming downstairs for the feast and a final drink together?"

"Sure, why not." Freyne nodded.

"Come on, then."

Maple steered them across the deck and down to the mess hall.

"Where are you sailing to next?" Nika asked, sliding onto the bench beside her.

"I think I'll take the Scruffy Mongrel to the maintenance dock and look into some upgrades and repairs. That'll give the crew a month of shore leave. We've been at sea for almost a year, so they deserve a rest."

"That's fair," Nika said. "You've earned it."

"Thanks, sweetie." Maple pinched his cheek. "Are you going to sing for us tonight? Iryna and Lana said that you're really good. I'd love to hear you play."

"I suppose. I'll need a few drinks first, though."

He'd only played the cittern a few times during their voyage, and only on the rare occasion that he was by himself. It took him a little while to tune it to his satisfaction, and a while longer to get the hang of the extra two strings, but overall he was happy and excited to play. He looked at Freyne and grinned.

"I'll behave myself this time, I promise."

"Sure, sure." Freyne chuckled.

There were more sailors in the mess than usual. Nika assumed that the calmer water meant less crew were needed up on deck. They were rowdy, and their uniforms were looking tattered and messy from the long voyage. Once they were joined by Ur'Shad, Iryna, Chardi and Lana, Maple called for a fresh round of drinks. The kitchen staff handed everyone a tankard brimming with the dark stout Nika had grown to enjoy.

"Cheers!" Maple thrusted her tankard into the air and spilt some over the table.

"Cheers!" the sailors echoed.

Nika took a modest swig of his stout, then watched as Iryna and Lana both took a sip from their tankards. He couldn't help but grin as they screwed up their faces and pushed the offending drinks away. Maple laughed and spoke to one of her crew, who promptly returned with a bottle of wine and two goblets. The princess looked much happier and poured herself and Lana a drink.

The kitchen staff returned and began serving dinner. Nika's mouth watered when an individual dish topped with crispy brown pastry was placed in front of him. The pies contained thick chunks of meat, gravy, and root vegetables, and were seasoned with exotic herbs. Nika enjoyed every bite and used a piece of bread to mop up the leftover gravy in his dish, then sat back and rubbed his full belly.

As he took another sip of his stout, Nika saw that Freyne had already drained his tankard and was refilling it from the pitcher on the table. He discreetly placed his hand on Freyne's knee, who shifted slightly closer so their bodies were touching. Freyne topped up Nika's and passed the pitcher to Chardi.

"I'm going to – what do you call it – take a piss," Freyne said, staggering to his feet.

"Alright. I'll go and get the cittern and meet you back here."

By the time Freyne stumbled back to the mess, Ur'Shad and Chardi were already well on their way to getting drunk. Iryna sat with her arms crossed, watching Ur'Shad with a disapproving glare, while Chardi and Lana were talking animatedly about something. Freyne spotted Nika sitting next to the captain and sat heavily beside him. The room spun, and he grabbed Nika's arm to steady himself. Nika looked at him questioningly, and it took all of Freyne's self control to not lean over and help himself to his lips.

"Are you going to play that thing or not?" Maple's voice boomed out over the noise of the sailors.

Nika grinned and reached for the cittern. Freyne watched as he took the instrument and placed the strap over his shoulder, then plucked at the strings and tuned it to his liking. A tingle of excitement travelled down his spine; he loved hearing Nika sing and wished he would do so more often. Nika stood and placed his left leg up on the bench seat, then turned his body slightly towards Freyne.

The hall fell silent, and Nika started to play. Freyne rested his elbow on the table and took a deep drink of his stout. He couldn't remember ever being drunk before and wasn't expecting the room to spin as much as it did. Apart from the occasional ceremonial sip of wine during certain religious events, the priests were forbidden to drink. Freyne wanted to let go of his past and try and have some fun.

Nika began plucking at the strings of the cittern, creating a melancholic tune. Once again Freyne was struck by his talent. Nika's music was so unlike any of the music Freyne had ever heard in his thousand or so years of life.

> "...I feel the darkness stir inside of me
> It's throbbing within my soul
> Am I even alive?
> Or am I under someone else's control..."

Even the words of the song were foreign to his ears, and as Nika sang them beautifully, Freyne felt himself being drawn in, the words resonating with him. His life at the monastery flashed before his eyes, followed by the destruction of his village.

"…I'm surrounded by the ghosts of my past,
My future, my shame
They speak to me,
I hear them calling my name…"

Tears sprung to his eyes, and he brushed them away on his sleeve. There were still ghosts of his past that he had to face, and he wasn't ready for that.

"…Just hold me fucking tight, I can't do this by myself.
I can't do this alone…"

As Nika's song came to an end, Freyne glanced around and saw that he wasn't the only one to become emotional. Several sailors were also wiping their eyes, and one of them was bawling his heart out. Someone handed Nika his stout and he downed the rest of it in one long swig.

"Sing us another song!" a burly sailor called.

"More!" another sailor yelled, thumping the table with his fist.

Soon most of them were chanting for more. Freyne took another swig from his tankard. He'd lost count on how many he'd consumed. Nika grinned and removed his overshirt, revealing his singlet tucked into his trousers. He clambered up onto the table amongst a round of cheering, then started playing a different song.

Freyne recognised the tune as the one he'd played at Dol'Am and tapped his foot in time to Nika's beat. Once again he could hear several instruments playing along, their sounds projected by Nika's mind. He thought back on his studies and tried to remember what he'd learnt about sound projection, but he was too drunk to gather his thoughts.

The room was spinning faster each time he turned his head, making him dizzy. He rested his head in his hand and gazed up at Nika, running his eyes over his sexy body. The desire to take him back to their room and ravish him was almost unbearable. He shifted uncomfortably and waited.

Nika finished his song and managed to bow with a flourish. He turned and clambered off the table amidst cheers and applause from the crowd. Laughing and clearly enjoying himself, Nika sat on Freyne's lap and threw his arm around his neck; Maple and Ur'Shad were belting the table like drums and the girls were squealing with delight. Before Freyne's foggy brain knew what was happening, Nika bent his head and planted a big sloppy kiss on Freyne's lips.

"I need you so bad right now," Freyne said silently.

"I need you more. Let's get out of here."

Nika was woken abruptly with a kick to his stomach. He drew his knees to his chest, gasping for breath. Several torches lit up the cabin, the bright light burning his eyes. He squinted until they came into focus, only to see the tip of a sword weaving just inches in front of his face. Nika froze and realised he was surrounded by soldiers who were wearing the bronze chest plates and red doublets of the militia.

A soldier with a long black moustache and greasy hair sticking out from under his pointed helm pushed his way into the room. Some of the soldiers scrambled out of his way and saluted sharply.

"Disgusting abomination," he snarled at Nika. He turned to his men. "Take them!"

Two of the soldiers pulled Nika roughly to his feet and bound his hands behind his back. His stomach heaved and he was overcome with nausea. Someone punched him in his mouth, making him see stars and taste blood. A commotion broke out behind him, and Nika turned to see Freyne struggling to break free. His captor hit him hard over the head, knocking him senseless to the ground.

"Hey!"

Nika tried to go to him, but was dragged from the room and into the corridor. Ur'Shad and Iryna stood under guard, swords held to their necks, their hands also bound. Blood was trickling from Ur'Shad's nose and he was swaying on his feet. Iryna looked terrified.

As Nika was pinned against the wall, Chardi and Lana were shoved into the passage. A long cut across Chardi's bare chest was dripping with blood. Nika started shaking as fear overcame him.

"Move it out," someone barked.

Nika was shoved roughly from behind. He tried to look over his shoulder to see where Freyne was, but his captor hit him again, almost making him fall. They were marched in single file through the ship and down the gangplank. The few sailors who were on duty were being held at sword point by more of the militia. Nika managed to catch a glimpse of Freyne being carried by two of the men before he was shoved forward again. They were met by more of the militia on the dock, and the captain's voice floated to him on the wind.

"Take the princess to my office and triple the guard, but she is not to be harmed. There is a lord who will pay quite handsomely for her. As for the others, take them to the deepest level of the dungeon and leave them there to rot."

As the order was passed along the line, Nika was shoved forward. His heart was racing and he felt sick to his stomach. The militia formed a tight ring around them and herded them away from the dock. The sun had still not risen; they marched by torchlight along the waterfront, sailors and deckhands scrambling out of their way and eyeing the prisoners wearily. They marched up a steep hill towards a menacing stone building which overlooked the dock like a dark sentinel.

The militia pushed Nika and his friends inside and dragged them through a maze of corridors. They entered a dank passage that smelled of stale sweat and body odour. Nika figured they were walking through a barracks; only a few torches were lit, casting dark flickering shadows on the walls as they passed. They came to a stop by a large heavy door that was guarded by two more of the militia.

"Halt," a harsh voice commanded. "Take that one to the captain's office immediately. Throw the rest of them in the lowest level and leave them there to rot."

The soldier behind Nika reefed on the ropes binding his hands, forcing him to stop abruptly. Pain shot through his wrists as the rope chafed his skin. Four soldiers broke away dragging Iryna roughly by her hair and disappeared around a corner. Nika listened as her screams faded to a mere echo.

"I'll kill them for this," Ur'Shad whispered just loud enough for Nika to hear. "We need to free her before—"

"Shut it!"

Ur'Shad grunted as one of the guards punched him in the face. Nika stole a glance over his shoulder and saw that Freyne was still out cold, unmoving. An overwhelming sense of dread came over Nika as the seriousness of their situation sunk in. The air suddenly seemed so thick that he struggled to take a deep breath. There was a *clunk*, and with an eerie creak the door swung open.

One of the militia forced him down a steep flight of stairs following Ur'Shad and Chardi. Somewhere behind him he could hear Lana's muffled sobs. The top level of the dungeon was well lit. Nika could see rows and rows of bleak cells with barred doors and nothing but a stone slab for a bed. The place smelt like vomit and urine, and locked in a cell to their left was a lone man in the tattered uniform of the militia. His gut heaved and he forced himself to breathe through his mouth so he wouldn't throw up from the smell.

As they passed, the prisoner woke up and scrambled off the stone slab.

"Let me out, yer bastards!" he shouted angrily.

The soldier holding Ur'Shad's bonds spat in his face.

"Shut it, Slavin. You'd better hope that I'm not the one floggin' ya later," he sneered.

Nika's gut heaved violently and his mouth filled with bile. He spat it out on the floor, earning another shove. It took everything to keep himself grounded. His breaths came in short gasps, and his palms were sweaty and shaking. He wanted to run, but he was trapped, doomed to a horrible death. His legs felt like jelly, and he would have collapsed if it weren't for the guard behind him, who pulled him to his feet and shoved him painfully in his back.

They reached the bottom level of the dungeon which was unlit except for their captors' torches. Rats and roaches scurried away from the light, and a foul stench reached Nika's nostrils that made him gag. Unlike the open spacious cells above, the cells on the bottom level were small and fully enclosed. The soldiers pulled open a solid steel door and tossed Freyne inside, locking it behind him.

Nika started towards Freyne's cell, but was jerked backwards and dragged deeper into the bowels of the dungeon by two of the militia. They hurled him through a door with such force that he lost his footing and slammed into the far wall. Nika fell roughly on the cold grimy floor, and out of nowhere a boot drove into his gut. The pain blinded him, and he squirmed around on the ground, winded, gasping for breath.

"Let's see if any of them are still alive in a month," one of the soldiers snorted.

"I doubt any of them will last longer than a week," the other laughed.

The voices trailed off, and the dungeon fell silent except for the scurrying of rodents and distant echoes. Nika managed to draw a rasping breath and awkwardly pushed himself upright. It was so dark that he couldn't see a thing. For a moment he felt his panic return, and he frantically tried to free his hands from the rope. At once a burning pain shot from his wrists, forcing him to give up.

Calm down, he thought, fighting back his terror. *You're the only one who can get us out of here. Now concentrate, or we're all dead. You've got to get to Freyne and see if he's ok.* Nika entered the lowest realm and glanced around his cell. Although tinted in purple, he could at least see his surroundings and felt much calmer for it. He stepped away from his body and noted the bruises already forming on his chest and face.

The skin around his wrists was red from the chafing, and a trickle of blood dripped from his left hand. He untied the rope and watched, bemused, as his hands came free and fell by his sides. *That wasn't so hard. Now for the door.* It didn't take long for him to figure out how to pick the lock using the realm. With a satisfying *click,* he returned to his body and picked himself up off the floor.

Whispers and footsteps echoed through the dungeon from the guards patrolling the hallways. There was a faint hint of light that allowed Nika to see as he crept from cell to cell, looking for his friends. Out of the darkness came an eerie laugh as six guards stepped into the hallway. Nika dashed into one of the empty cells and hid behind the door until they passed, his heart racing. *That was close. Too close. I need to be more careful.*

Once the guards were gone, Nika peeked out into the hall, then tiptoed to Chardi's cell. There was a faint ticking sound in the back of his mind like the hands of a clock. He frowned and shook his head to regain his focus. Using the realm, he unlocked the door. Chardi's head whipped around as it swung open with a soft *creak*.

"Shh," Nika whispered.

"Nika?" Chardi sounded surprised.

"Yeah. Come on."

He untied the rope around Chardi's hands, then scouted out the dungeon to find the others. There were several groups of guards patrolling the lowest floor, too many to fight. Nika slipped his mind half-way into the realm, then led the way to Lana's cell. She was curled up on the floor, sobbing quietly.

"Lana," Nika whispered. "It's okay. Let's get out of here."

"How did you..."

"We'll talk about it later. We need to go quickly. Come on."

He helped her up and guided her into the hall. She fell into Chardi's arms and they hugged each other tightly. Nika beckoned, then turned and continued on his way. As they rounded another corner, Nika gasped and stopped abruptly. A larger patrol of twelve guards were just two cells away. Chardi pulled him backwards and into one of the cells.

"What was that?" one of the guards asked sharply.

"What was what?" another asked.

"I thought I heard something back there."

"You're imagining things again. Aint nothin down here except for rats and mice."

"Shut it, you two," a third voice growled. "Let's go and check it out just in case. We don't want no prisoners escaping on our watch or we'll be flogged. Let's go!"

Nika held his breath as the guards marched by their cell, murmuring and grumbling amongst themselves. His hands were shaking but he fought to remain calm. Once the hall was clear, Nika beckoned and hurried to Ur'Shad's cell. He unlocked the door and crept inside.

Ur'Shad spun around with his fists raised and lunged towards him. He'd managed to free his hands and had a look of murder on his face. Nika dodged out of the way just in time.

"Relax. It's me!" he breathed. "Let's go."

Ur'Shad lowered his hands, looking sheepish. Nika led

him from the cell and joined him with the others, then guided them to Freyne's cell, his heart racing. *I swear, if they've harmed him, I'll level this place to the fucking ground,* he thought darkly as he unlocked the door.

Freyne was sprawled on the grimy floor, unmoving but alive. His body was bruised and covered in cuts and scratches. Nika knelt down and brushed his fingers across Freyne's cheeks, then bent down and kissed his forehead.

"Wake up. We have to go," he whispered urgently.

Freyne's eyes flickered open and he groaned.

"Shh." Nika held his finger to his lips.

Chardi pulled Freyne to his feet, then caught him as his legs buckled under his weight. Freyne's head drooped, barely conscious. With a grunt, Chardi hoisted him over his shoulder.

"Follow me," Nika whispered.

They tiptoed through the hallways, hiding in the open cells when guards came too close. Nika was on edge, expecting to be caught at any moment. *Did I close the doors to our cells? What if a guard checks and we're not there? What if Iryna's been taken away from here?* The higher they climbed, the more nervous he became. He swallowed and tried to maintain his focus.

As they stepped into the top level of the dungeon, Freyne groaned and squirmed. Chardi lowered him to the floor, then steadied him.

"Where—"

"Shh!" Chardi hissed.

Nika hurried to Freyne's side and pulled his arm around his shoulders. Freyne leaned on him, still groggy, and glanced around with confusion. Below them came the sound of many pairs of boots climbing the stairs. The hairs stood on Nika's neck, and he ushered his friends into another hallway.

The top level was lit by torches throughout, and with the open cells, there were few places to hide. More footsteps reached his ears, then stopped abruptly. Nika pulled Freyne into one of the darker cells and strained to listen.

"The prisoners are secure, sir."

"Good. Double the guard and I want hourly reports. Our Lord wishes to inspect them and will be here soon. Now move it out."

"Yes, sir."

Nika listened as the guards dispersed and readied himself to move. He took a peek into the hallway and a loud shout made his blood turn to ice.

"Hey! HALT!"

Ten guards ran towards them, their swords drawn. Chardi and Ur'Shad moved forward to fend them off, though they were weaponless. Nika's panic returned with a vengeance. He lowered Freyne onto a stone slab and ran into the hallway. Chardi and Ur'Shad were standing defensively, waiting for the guards to reach them.

The ticking sound in Nika's mind grew louder and faster, although time itself seemed to slow down. A wave of calm settled over him. *I have to do something. We don't stand a chance!*

The guards were almost upon Ur'Shad and Chardi, spreading out in the hallway, ready to attack. Nika pushed half of his mind into the lowest realm and summoned a wall of energy around his friends. They guards leapt forward and collided with the invisible barrier and fell backwards. Ur'Shad and Chardi looked confused for a moment, but sprung into action and snatched a sword each from the dazed militia. They quickly disposed of the threat, their swords dripping with blood.

Another shout echoed through the dungeon, and more guards poured into the hallway from both ends, trapping them. Nika turned and faced the soldiers, his concentration absolute. He summoned a ball of energy and hurled it at the nearest guard, who collapsed with a gurgle. One by one he downed them, until the few remaining soldiers faltered and turned to flee. Nika summoned three more balls of energy and downed them in one attack. Behind him, Ur'Shad and Chardi were locked in bloody combat. Nika leapt into the fray and picked off more of the guards one at a time. Soon there was only one soldier left, who Ur'Shad finished with a single stroke.

"Hey! Get *off* me!"

Nika spun around to see Lana struggling with a soldier trying to pin her arms behind her back. Without warning, she slipped from his grasp and elbowed him in the groin, then rolled out of his way and snatched a dagger from the ground.

The guard roared and limped after her; Nika watched in disbelief as she sprang to her feet and drove the dagger into his exposed abdomen. The man screamed and sank to the ground in a pool of blood.

"Gri'Ran's claws!" Chardi cursed and hurried over to her. "Are you alright?"

"I'm sick of people grabbing me like I'm their property," Lana exploded, still gripping the dagger. "Why are you looking at me like that?"

"Like what?"

"Never mind."

She wiped her bloody hand and the dagger on the sleeve of a dead guard. Chardi's face was a mix of awe and surprise.

"I hate to break this up, but we need to find Iryna," Ur'Shad said pointedly.

Freyne staggered from the cell, still unsteady on his feet. Nika caught him just as his legs almost collapsed.

"Which way?" Chardi asked.

Nika beckoned and led the way through the dungeon to the final flight of stairs. As he prepared to help Freyne up the steps, he heard a whispered exchange behind them. He spun around in time to see Ur'Shad pluck the dagger from Lana's hand and stalk towards the prisoner they'd seen earlier.

"Give me a hand with this," Ur'Shad growled.

The ticking sound grew a little louder and faster in Nika's mind. He focused on the cell and unpicked the lock. Ur'Shad stormed inside and pulled the sleeping Slavin to his feet, holding the blade of the dagger along his exposed throat.

"What the—"

"Shut up or you're dead," Ur'Shad hissed. "Do exactly as I say and I'll let you live. Got it?"

The prisoner nodded, his eyes wide and bulging. Ur'Shad manoeuvred him from the cell and guided him to where Nika was standing.

"You're going to take us to the captain's office. One wrong move or sound and you won't see the light of day ever again. Now, which way do we go?"

Slavin pointed to the top of the stairs then made a curving gesture to the right. Chardi nodded and brushed past Nika to take the lead, his sword at the ready. They clambered up the stairs to the heavy door.

"Open it," Ur'Shad said, lowering the knife just a little.

"I – it's locked from the outside. I don't have a key, I swear!" Slavin whimpered.

Nika was growing impatient. The ticking sound was grating on him and he wanted nothing more than to get it to stop. He unfurled Freyne's arm from his shoulder and transferred him to Lana.

"Stand back."

His voice felt oddly detached from his body. The strange calmness settled over him again, silencing his fears and nerves. As soon as his friends had retreated a few steps, Nika turned his full focus to the door and began to draw from the lowest realm. He funnelled the forces into a ball of energy and directed it at the centre of the door while shielding himself and the others. The door exploded outwards in a deafening roar and the shockwave made him stagger backwards.

Once the dust cleared, Nika spotted four guards writhing around on the floor. They were covered in debris and groaning. Chardi rushed forward and finished them off. Nika turned back to Lana, who looked like she was struggling under Freyne's weight. Still feeling that strange sense of calm, he hoisted Freyne over his shoulder, who felt oddly weightless.

"We have to hurry," Chardi said, glancing nervously down the hall. "There's no way that no one heard that."

Ur'Shad pulled Slavin into the hall and led the way to the captain's office. The barracks was eerily quiet, not a guard in sight.

"This' it," Slavin said, indicating the door at the end of the passage. "Can I go now?"

"Open it," Ur'Shad ordered.

Slavin reached out a shaking hand and rattled the knob.

"It's locked."

"Stand back," Nika said quietly.

His patience was once again waning. Nika summoned a smaller ball of energy and directed it at the lock. The mechanism shattered into pieces. Ur'Shad let go of Slavin and barged inside. Several shouts rang out followed by a loud crash. Nika hurried inside followed by Chardi and Lana.

Iryna was tied to a chair in the corner, her head bowed and unmoving. Two uniformed guards and a cloaked figure were standing by the window, their swords at the ready. In the middle of the room, Ur'Shad was scrambling up off the floor. Towering over him was a hulking figure with long greasy black hair. The man turned and sneered, and Nika's jaw dropped.

"You traitor!" Chardi roared.

J'mai drew his sword just in time to parry Chardi's blow. The sound of steel on steel rang in Nika's ears, fuelling his anger. Enraged, Ur'Shad disposed of the remaining guards in the room, leaving little chance for them to defend themselves. Lana retrieved her dagger off the floor and cut the ropes binding Iryna to the chair.

There was a smash as J'mai tumbled into the plush mahogany chair behind the desk. The chair splintered and he fell roughly to the floor. Chardi aimed his sword tip in front of J'mai's face.

"To'Rel trusted you. We *all* trusted you. How could you betray our king?"

"You're all fools," J'mai hissed. "I am loyal only to My Lord, and I will die happily for him. So, save your breath and get this over with."

"You aligned yourself with that pompous Lord Lenier?" Chardi asked incredulously. "You betrayed your king over a stinking goat?"

"Intelligence was never your strong point, Chardi. Lenier is nothing but a pawn in the great plan. Now go ahead and kill me. My Lord has been summoned and you will not escape alive."

Chardi growled and ran his sword through J'mai's throat. Nika watched the life drain from his eyes, too detached to be horrified. He could feel his own blood beginning to boil as he was filled with rage that wasn't his own. The voices in the room seemed muted to his ears as the ticking sound came back with a vengeance. His skin prickled and he sensed someone powerful approaching amidst the footsteps of dozens of soldiers; he looked towards the door and spotted countless auras despite not being in the realm. Amongst them was the pulsating aura of a powerful mancer.

"We have to go *now!*"

Without waiting, Nika sent a wave of energy at the window. The glass shattered outwards along with a section of the wall. Iryna and Lana gasped as the door slammed open.

"Go!" Nika shouted.

He spun around and sent another wave at the soldiers flooding into the office. They flew backwards and slammed into the wall, but more soldiers forced their way inside. Nika staggered backwards, with Freyne still over his shoulder, and levelled a blast at the roof. The floor shook and half of the roof collapsed, trapping the soldiers beneath it. Nika turned and leapt through the hole in the wall just in time for the rest of the roof to collapse.

"Nika!" Chardi yelled.

They were in a courtyard at the rear of the building lined with training dummies and stands of wooden swords. Soldiers were pouring in from both directions, trapping them between the barracks and the wall. Nika gritted his teeth and blasted a hole in the wall. His energy was starting to drain, but he had to keep going; his life and his friends depended on him.

As they ran back towards the dock, Nika sensed a sudden overpowering flash of rage emanating from the realm. He instinctively summoned a shield around he and his friends and kept running. The air was thick and humid, making him sweat and gasp for breath. Freyne was growing heavier with each step.

The docks were already packed with sailors and merchants. Chardi drew his sword and charged into the crowd, opening up a narrow gap for them to pass through. Nika felt relieved when he spotted The Scruffy Mongrel up ahead. As they hurried along the pier, though, he realised the ship was already drifting back to sea.

"Maple!" Ur'Shad bellowed at the top of his lungs, coming to a halt next to the bollard.

Nika looked back and saw around fifty soldiers running towards them, pushing people out of their way and yelling to stop the prisoners.

Maple's head appeared from above, and she started yelling orders to her crew. They lowered two rope ladders down the side of the ship, and waved for them to jump across the widening gap.

Lana and Iryna jumped across first and scrambled up the ladders as fast as they could. Nika waved to Ur'Shad and Chardi to go next, the gap between the ship and the dock growing wider with each passing second.

The soldiers were so close that Nika could hear their laboured breathing and grunts. He took a few steps back, and took a running jump across the widening gap, pushing off his right leg with all of his strength. As he flew through the air towards the ship, Nika aimed his spare arm at the space between two rungs and caught the side of the ladder. A searing pain shot through his shoulder, but he clung on with all of his remaining strength. One of the soldiers attempted to jump across the gap, but the ship had drifted too far, and the soldier fell into the harbour with a splash, spraying Nika with water.

The soldiers milled around on the dock, watching their bounty escape. Nika's arm was aching from holding both his and Freyne's body weight, and he could feel his grip starting to slip. Ur'Shad, Chardi, and some of the burly sailors carefully pulled the ladder up to the rail. Several pairs of strong hands reached down and pulled them to safety. Nika was breathing heavily and could feel the last of his strength draining from his body. After a final glimpse to to ensure they were out of danger, he dropped to his knees and crawled across to where Freyne's motionless body lay, and collapsed.

"Fireballs were flying everywhere, and then he blew the door right open," a man's voice was saying excitedly. "We went and found the princess, and he collapsed a section of the roof on half of the barracks and blew their wall to smithereens. I've never seen anything like it!"

"I knew he was a mancer but didn't realise he was so talented," a woman's voice said.

"It was like he was in a trance and his eyes were glowing, too," the first voice added.

"Remind me to never mess with him," a second man's voice said with awe.

"More like, don't ever mess with his lover," the first man said. "I had a feeling there was something going on between those two."

"That's enough, you two," the woman said firmly. "Their relationship is no one's business but their own. Now behave, or I'll pull every whisker out of your faces, one by one."

"Sheesh, we were only joking," the first man said. "We have no problem with it. They're our friends."

Nika reached out his hand, feeling beside him for Freyne. A gentle hand slipped into his, filling him with warmth.

"He's waking up," a soft voice said.

Nika knew the voice and felt his heart swell. He tried to open his eyes, but couldn't. He squeezed Freyne's hand instead.

"Rest up, boo. We're safe," Freyne whispered.

"He still looks out of it," the woman said.

"Where are we going now?" another woman's voice asked.

"I'm taking you down the coast to the edge of the swamp. I know a small smugglers' cove where we can safely offload the horses. You'll be able to continue your journey from there," the first woman said. "I don't think we're being followed, but once we drop you off, we'll sail further south just in case."

One of the men made a hissing sound.

"Sit still," the other man said.

"You try having straight whiskey poured all over your cuts," the man sulked.

"I already did and you didn't hear me carry on," the other voice said. "A little sting now is better than the pain of infection and possible death."

Nika finally managed to open his eyes and recognised Maple's dimly lit private quarters. Freyne was sitting on a chair next to the bed, holding his hand. He slowly turned his head and spotted Ur'Shad and Chardi sitting on chairs against the wall, who were being fussed over by Iryna and Lana as they treated the men's wounds. Nika tilted his head back and could see Maple sitting at the table. He looked back at Freyne and tugged weakly on his hand. Freyne looked down and flashed Nika a warm smile. His handsome face was bruised and scratched, but his smiling face showed no sign of pain.

"Hello, sleepy," he said.

Nika managed to curl his lip into a grin, and Freyne reached down, brushing a strand of hair from Nika's eyes.

"Your face," Nika whispered, still feeling weak. "Are you ok?"

"You're alive, I'm alive, our friends are alive. That's all that matters," Freyne replied.

Maple pulled her chair over next to the bed and smiled.

"You've been busy, haven't you?" she said, pinching him gently on the cheek.

"What happened?" he asked Freyne. "How did they know we were on this ship?"

"We were so drunk we must have lowered our defenses."

"Those soldiers would have been from Rybor. I bet they left before us so they they could plan an ambush." Nika frowned, then tried to push himself up. "They must have been J'mai's cronies. Did the others tell you–"

"Calm down, boo. You need to rest. Ur'Shad and Chardi filled me in. We'll talk about it later."

Nika sank back down onto the bed when a horrible thought came to him. He tried to sit up again, but Freyne gently held him down and shook his head.

"You're so stubborn." He sighed.

"Where's Arnie?" Nika demanded. "Is he ok?"

Freyne bent down and returned with Arnie-Kyn in his arms. He placed the cat onto the bed next to Nika.

"You mean this pain in the backside?"

Nika pulled the cat into his arms and scratched his ears. *"Are you alright?"*

"Not so close, human." Arnie's tail swished, showing his annoyance. *"One was fine until a sailor chased me up the mast. One was most grateful that your mate was able to help me down."*

Nika frowned and looked at Freyne.

"How long have I been out of it?" he asked.

"At least an hour or two, maybe a little longer," Freyne replied. "It's well past lunch time."

"I'm hungry," Nika grumbled. "We didn't get breakfast *or* lunch, and I still have the worst hangover."

"I have my cooks making a light lunch for you all. Rest up while I go and check on them," Maple said.

She bent over and gently pinched his cheek then left the room. Nika sank back into the pillow, his mind racing with questions and thoughts about their capture and J'mai's betrayal. His head hurt and he wanted to drift back to sleep, when Iryna's face appeared above him.

"Thank you for saving me – us," she said with a smile.

"You're welcome," Nika replied. "Are you okay, though? Did they hurt you?"

"A little, but nothing that won't heal in time. We're all okay thanks to you."

She bent down and kissed him lightly on the cheek, shot him another smile, then turned and hurried back to Ur'Shad's side.

14

Saying goodbye to Maple and the Scruffy Mongrel was hard, and as he watched the small ship drifting back to sea, Nika couldn't help but feel sad. He'd enjoyed his time on the open water, during which he'd developed a close friendship with the rowdy captain and some of the crew. His friends sat on their horses two a piece, watching the ship as it sailed away. Nika could sense that he wasn't the only one who was feeling forlorn.

After a while he sighed to himself and turned away from the sea. Surrounding them was nothing but desolate swamp. Swarms of gnats and mosquitoes were already feasting on his exposed skin, and he was pretty sure there were leeches lurking in the mud. It was hot and steamy, and Nika could feel the sweat chafing in uncomfortable places on his body.

"Where do we go?" Chardi asked.

Freyne pulled the map from his pocket and studied it for a moment, frowning.

"We'll head south-east and replenish our supplies at Karatha. It should only take us four or five days. From there, we'll head north to Ner'Am, which will take us another week."

"Alright." Chardi nodded. "When we get to Karatha, we'll find an inn that has a bathhouse so we can freshen up."

Iryna's eyes lit up.

"We're going to have to be very careful," Freyne cautioned. "We can expect to find patrols in every city and along the roads looking for us. I'm also concerned about that mancer who was at the barracks. We're going to have to take extra precautions."

"What do you suggest?" Nika asked.

Freyne scratched his cheek.

"The militia are searching for a group of six people, so I think our tactic to split up at Dol'Am will work well. In addition to that, Nika and I will take in turns holding up the shield. Half a day and half a night each. We'll stay off the main roads and try not to be seen."

"Good ideas." Ur'Shad glanced around at the others with a frown. "The only other suggestions I have is that we cover our hair and faces as best as possible so that we aren't recognised. Knowing J'mai, he probably had someone sketch us in detail. We also need a cover story, and a way to get a message to To'Rel to warn him of J'mai's betrayal."

"I have some scarves from the market that should cover Iryna and I," Lana offered.

"We'll work out the finer details as soon as we get out of this fetid swamp. Let's keep the breaks to an absolute minimum and aim to get there in two or three days." Freyne nodded and turned the horse towards Karatha, nudging her into a trot.

Nika could tell she was happy to be free from the hold of the ship; Freyne had to pull the reins several times to slow her down. Even Arnie-Kyn seemed happy for once, purring and kneading Nika's inner thigh with his claws. Nika reached down and scratched his favourite spot behind his ear.

"Are you alright, furball?"

"One is glad to be off the ship. One will be gladder once you and your mate bathe. You both stink."

Over the next few days, the swamp gradually changed from a stinking bog to a beautiful marsh that felt like another world altogether. The trees were thick with black bark, and on either side of their path were large bodies of water covered with green algae. Various species of water birds fluttered around the bushes and scrub, occasionally startling as the horses got too close. Nika spotted a coot paddling through the algae, leaving a black trail in its wake. A short distance away, a white egret stood in the water, watching them as they passed.

Giant salamanders were resting on the banks, and as the

party rode by, they scurried into the water and disappeared with a splash. Nika felt a great sense of peace and tranquillity.

"There's so much life here," he said dreamily.

"In places like this, you get to witness the true beauty of nature," Freyne replied. "Each species of plant and creature is dependent on each other, whether they are the predator or prey. There is great balance here."

"I hope people don't come along and destroy it," Nika said.

"I've been talking to the trees. They rarely see humans come through here. Usually, people take the smuggler's track from that cove, which takes them back to Fraal."

"What do you mean, you've been talking to the trees?"

"I find solace in the highest realm. I go there to meditate, and sometimes the trees talk to me. It's hard to explain. Would you like me to show you?"

"Is it going to change my aura again or make my body do more weird things?" Nika asked warily.

"I don't think so." Freyne half-turned and rubbed Nika's thigh. "Follow me in. I have a feeling you'll be able to enter."

"What do you mean?" Nika frowned.

"Not everyone can access all three realms, remember?"

"Oh, right."

Nika felt Freyne's mind join with his and followed the familiar tugging towards the realm. He pushed his mind forward, and after a moment of poking around, he found and entered the highest realm. The swamp came to life before his eyes; each critter and creature had their own bright sprites of energy, darting around in his green-tinged vision. He looked up at the trees and could see the life energy flowing between the leaves and branches, whispering to each other on the wind. That same energy encircled Freyne, glittering like specks of gold.

"Nika?"

Strange voices were talking to one another in languages he'd never heard. Nearby, a swarm of bees were busy working in their hive, their collective consciousness content in knowing their queen was safe. Somewhere in the distance, a branch snapped and fell crashing to the ground; Nika could feel the tree screaming in pain. Miles below his feet, the ancient rocks groaned, and deeper still he could sense the planet's magnetic field.

And then he felt it; ever so subtle, a ticking sound, like time herself was watching on with bated breath. He sensed that time was rushing towards a great climax, and that time would be very soon. With a start he realised it was the same ticking sound he'd heard in the dungeon.

"*Nika!*" Freyne's voice snapped him from his reverie.

"*Sorry! I'm here,*" he said quickly.

"*You had me worried,*" Freyne said. "*What do you see?*"

"*Everything,*" Nika replied, eager to get back to exploring. "*The trees, the wind, time itself…*"

"*I think that's enough for the moment,*" Freyne said.

"*Can't we stay a little longer?*"

"*No. Out you come,*" Freyne said firmly.

Nika reluctantly withdrew from the cool serenity of the realm and at once was back on the horse in the soupy humidity.

"That was unlike anything I've ever seen," he breathed.

"It's a wondrous place, but you need to be careful in there, just as you would with the other two realms. It's easy to lose oneself in there."

"I never knew that trees can feel pain," Nika said.

"Every living thing experiences life and death. Some feel pain; some cause pain. It's all a part of the balance of nature. It took me seven hundred years to learn that balance is the ultimate goal of nature. We are living in a world that is unbalanced and will remain that way until the prophecy is fulfilled."

"This is what I don't understand. How did this prophecy even come about?"

"Alright. Nature needed a way to restore balance, so she created seers. The seers wrote down and collated their visions, which when put together, created the prophecy. By fulfilling that prophecy, the balance *should* be restored to how it's supposed to be, and the world *should* return to its stable state."

"Should? But if someone's written down these visions, wouldn't that mean they've seen the outcome, too?"

Freyne shifted slightly in the saddle.

"Not exactly. Humans are unpredictable and mess things up all the time. The prophecy is merely a guide that tells us what needs to be done, not how or when. So many variables then come into play which can skew the outcome. Therefore, there is every chance that something might happen to throw us off-course. For instance, if we can't find that relic, we could fail. If we can't find the blood descendant or if he dies before the time is right, we will fail."

"So, what happens if we fail then?" Nika asked curiously.

"If what I'm hearing in the highest realm is true and not just exaggeration, failure will bring about the destruction of humankind, and maybe even the world itself. I – I think Am meant for me to be a part of this, too. I'm scared, boo."

———

As they reached the edge of the marsh, the lakes of water gave way to solid land, and the trees began to grow thicker and closer together. The temperature dropped steadily while they rode, and soon they were in a lush green forest. By late afternoon, dark ominous clouds filled the sky. They reached the edge of the forest just as the sun was setting, and in the distance, Nika thought he heard a low rumble of thunder. Freyne reined in and waved to the others to join them.

"The city is just beyond those trees over there," he said, pointing. "Let's redistribute the packs and get changed into our disguises, then split up."

"What's the plan?" Ur'Shad asked.

"Nika, Chardi, and Lana will enter from the west gate. You, Iryna, and myself will skirt around and enter from the east gate. Chardi can find an inn, and we will meet you there."

"How will we know where to find them?" Iryna asked.

"I'll know." Freyne winked.

Nika dismounted and changed into his merchant outfit, then helped Chardi with the packs. Iryna and Lana busied themselves with wrapping scarves around their hair and dressed in plain brown peasant dresses.

"Do you think the gates will be guarded?" Ur'Shad asked.

"I'll have a look." Freyne's eyes went distant for a moment. "There's only six guards at each gate. It's nothing we can't handle."

"It didn't take us long to get here by boat," Nika said thoughtfully, scratching his goatee. "We didn't see any other ships following us, either. Can we be safe in assuming that these guards haven't been briefed yet?"

"It's possible. It's a two-to-three week ride from the port to here." Chardi said. "If the militia is anything like King To'Rel, though, they'll have a pigeon network or enchanted messenger birds. We can't assume anything."

"Let's just assume they do know and make sure we cover our tracks," Ur'Shad said. "We don't want any more rude-awakenings or to ride into a trap."

"Alright. Let's get moving before the storm hits." Freyne mounted the spare horse and waved to Ur'Shad to follow.

Nika made sure Arnie was safely hidden in his cloak, then gently nudged the horse into a trot. Chardi and Lana rode beside him in silence. By the time they reached the west gate it was almost dark, and the thunder was growing louder. Nika slowed his horse to a walk and approached the guards cautiously. They wore the same red doublets and bronze armour of the militia which filled him with unease.

"State your business," one of them demanded.

"We're travelling north for a wedding and seek an inn for the evening," Chardi replied.

The guard eyed them suspiciously.

"Who's wedding?"

"My wife's sister who lives in Ner'Am."

"And him?" he asked, nodding at Nika.

"He's the bard who'll be playing at the wedding."

Nika reached back and unhooked the cittern that was hanging with his pack and gave the strings a strum.

"Would you like me to play you a tune?" he asked.

"Move along," the guard snapped, waving them through.

Karatha was unlike any of the other cities Nika had visited. While Al'Obrel and Dol'Am had been teeming with welcoming merchants and residents, the few people who roamed the streets of Karatha eyed Nika, Lana, and Chardi with suspicion bordering on hostility. He felt uncomfortable and unwelcome.

The city was very old. The buildings were slender two-storey terraces built from bluestone and decorated with ornate iron trimmings, squished together along the narrow streets. They rode slowly along the bluestone road towards the middle of the city where a dark building loomed before them. As they drew closer, Nika made out four ornate spires that reached towards the night sky and realised it was a temple. The stained-glass windows glowed warmly, flickering from the winds that were growing stronger. Nika's breath caught in his throat; the temple was beautiful. A gentle yet powerful presence beckoned to him, inviting him inside.

"There's an inn."

Chardi pointed down the curved road and jolted Nika from his thoughts. He followed Chardi's finger and spotted a squat building a short distance away.

"Perfect," Nika said.

He steered the horse away from the temple and followed Chardi, trying to ignore the urge to turn back and follow the presence. They reached the entrance of the inn and dismounted. The door swung open and they were greeted by the innkeeper.

"Good evening, my friends," he said pleasantly with a bow. "I'm your host, Ronol. What can I do for ya?"

"Good evening," Chardi echoed. "Do you have any rooms available?"

"I do indeed. How many do ya need?"

"Three, please."

"Very well. Gather ya things and I'll have my lad take ya horses to the stables."

Ronol tugged on a bell pull and a young man scurried outside. Nika unbuckled his pack and handed him the reins then followed Ronol inside. Chardi promptly paid for the rooms, earning a warm smile from their host.

"Thank you. This way, please."

Ronol led them up a flight of stairs to the second level and stopped in front of a door.

"I'll have ya meals brought up to ya rooms shortly. Foreigners aren't treated too kindly here, so you'll wanna avoid the bar and dining areas."

"Why are you so welcoming, then?" Chardi asked.

"I need the money." Ronol's expression changed to despair. "Business has been slow with the drop in travellers. I can't afford to turn paying customers away, can I? Now, is there anything else ya want?"

"Do you have baths here?" Lana piped up.

"Of course we do, my lady. My inn boasts a bath and latrine in every room. I'll send the servants to fill them immediately."

"Thank you," she smiled. "I could soak for a week."

"Me too." Nika nodded his agreement.

Ronol bowed and disappeared down the stairs. Nika slipped into one of the rooms and released Arnie-Kyn from his cloak and glanced around. Opposite the door was a small table with two chairs, a comfortable looking couch, and to his left, an empty fireplace. To his right was a luxurious four-poster bed. Nika peeked into the bathroom and was excited to see a bath that would easily fit two people. Two long black bathrobes and towels hung on pegs, and another door led to the latrine.

The air was chilly, and every now and then the windows rattled from the wind. Nika rummaged around in his pack for the firestone and sat it in the hearth, willing it to emit a warm welcoming flame. He sat on the couch next to Arnie, then closed his eyes and projected himself into the realm. It felt good to be free from his aching body which was still healing from their escape just days ago. He ghosted his way to the front entrance of the inn, floating effortlessly through the closed doors, and headed towards the east gate of the city. It didn't take long for him to spot Freyne's aura. Nika floated to the middle of the road and pushed his mind forward to join with him.

"Hello, you," Freyne's voice said. *"Where are you?"*

"I'm right here in front of you," Nika replied.

Freyne reined in his horse sharply and motioned to Ur'Shad to stop. Nika watched as Freyne's ghostly figure joined him, then poked out his tongue.

"Now you're just showing off," Freyne said.

"Me? Never!" Nika grinned and wriggled his backside suggestively. *"Follow me. Our bath is ready."*

Ur'Shad drew his horse alongside Freyne's as he returned to his body. Nika ghosted closer to them.

"Is everything alright?" Ur'Shad asked.

"What? Oh, fine. Nika's taking us to the inn. He said our baths are ready."

"Nika? I don't see him anywhere."

"I can see him all right, and he's going to get a smack when I get there."

Nika was the face of innocence when Freyne entered the room. He stood next to the bed with his hands clasped behind his back, trying to keep a straight face. Freyne eyed him up and down, then wordlessly closed and locked the door. He removed his cloak and hung it on a peg by the door, then without warning, rushed at Nika and shoved him onto the bed, landing on top of him. Nika burst out laughing.

"I'll show you what you can do with that tongue in a minute," Freyne said with a raised eyebrow.

"Oh yeah?"

Before Freyne could reply, Nika latched onto him and rolled him over, switching positions. He leant down and ran his tongue along the full length of Freyne's cheek. Freyne put his hand over his eyes and shook his head, laughing. Nika rolled off and collapsed next to him, laughing so hard that tears ran down his cheeks.

"I can't believe you just did that." Freyne snorted. "In all my thousand years..."

Nika wiped the tears from his eyes, trying hard to stop laughing, and pushed himself up.

"Would you like a hand to the bath, pops?" he asked with another fit of laughter.

Freyne shook his head in defeat. Nika stood and helped himself to Freyne's belt, then pulled off his shoes, trousers, and undergarments. Before he could stare and admire his handywork, Freyne sat up and pulled Nika roughly towards him. Nika snorted a giggle as Freyne undid the buckle and let his trousers and underwear fall to the floor.

"You never did tell me about that," Freyne said slyly, pointing at Nika's tattoo.

He traced the outline of the tattoo with his fingers, his touch waking Nika's body.

"This is the result of too much drinking whilst on shore leave one time," Nika replied. "I'd been working on the platform for four weeks straight. It was brutal. When I got back to shore, I headed to a bar with some of the guys from work. We were so drunk, possibly the drunkest I've ever been, and one of the guys dared me to get a tattoo. It seemed like a good idea at the time, so I dragged them to the nearest tattoo parlour and that's all I can remember. I woke up with this and a hangover."

"Your world is so strange," Freyne said, shaking his head.

Nika pulled him to his feet and they quickly removed each other's shirts. As Nika lowered his arm, a shooting pain shot up his shoulder. He grimaced and hesitated, then took Freyne's hand and led him to the bathroom.

The bath was full and inviting, hot enough that it would last for a long soak, but not too hot as to burn them. As Nika climbed in, Freyne spanked his backside, earning another round of laughter. He sank down into the steaming water to his chin, then leaned back and tried to relax.

Freyne reached for a bar of soap and started lathering his hair, chest, and arms. He disappeared under the water for a moment, then resurfaced and wiped his eyes.

"Come here," he ordered.

Nika begrudgingly sat up and manoeuvred between his legs. Freyne ran the soap gently over Nika's back and neck, but as he rubbed it across his shoulder, Nika flinched from the sudden pain.

"Are you okay?"

"Yeah. Just a bit sore still from the other day, that's all."

"You should have told me," Freyne scolded him. He put down the soap and gently prodded Nika's shoulder. "No wonder you're in pain. You have a tight knot right here. Try and relax."

Nika closed his eyes and focused on Freyne's magic touch. Several contented sighs and groans escaped him as Freyne gently worked the knots and kinks from his back and shoulder. After a while, Freyne leant forward and started kissing his way along Nika's neck. Nika turned his head and pulled Freyne's lips to his. The moment their lips came together, a whirl of colourful sprites and swirls exploded in his mind, dazzling him.

"I want to make love to you…" Freyne murmured.

"You want to fuck me," Nika corrected him.

"Huh?"

"That's how we say it in *my* language. Go on, try it."

"I want to fuck you." Freyne pursed his lips. "You know, that sounds much spicier than making love."

"I know. Now shut up and fuck me."

It was only much later, after their bath and dinner, that Nika and Freyne crawled onto the bed and snuggled into one another. Nika was warm and content, still basking in the afterglow of their earlier tryst.

"What will we do when we get to Ner'Am?" he murmured.

"We need to go to the temple of Am. The monks will hopefully have the artefact we need," Freyne replied, running his fingers across Nika's cheek.

"Do you know what we're looking for?"

"Yes. It's a small golden statue known as Gri'Ran's gift."

"What's it for?"

"I'm not too sure," Freyne admitted. "I never understood this part of the prophecy. Apparently, the copy I studied for all those years at the monastery was an abridged version. Those scrolls you found in the swamp are supposedly the full version."

"Why were you made to study it for so long if it wasn't the real thing?" Nika asked.

"I honestly don't know, boo. It feels like I just wasted my time for all those years. Back then, I was so invested and believed that I'd prepared sufficiently for this day. But all of that groundwork I did, like ensuring that Gri'Ran's Gift was safe at Ner'Am, seems to have been for nothing."

Nika tenderly touched the back of his hand to Freyne's cheek. He closed his eyes and leaned into Nika's hand.

"I should have started reading this copy while we were at sea, but…I'm scared, boo. There is a lot from my past that I'm not ready to face or even talk about yet. There are days when my thoughts and memories don't even feel like my own; it's like someone is moving me like a puppet. Do you know what I mean?"

"Yeah."

A flash of lightning lit up the windows, followed by a low rumble of thunder. Nika could hear the wind growing stronger outside and the rain pounded against the glass. They slid under the blankets and lay together in silence for a while, listening to the storm overhead.

"Who's Gri'Ran?" Nika asked finally.

"Gri'Ran is one of two gods who came to our world.

When compared to Am, Gri'Ran had a very powerful physical presence, and their power was absolute. Their followers believed that they were superior to all else and were quite arrogant. That was never Gri'Ran's intention, but as I said the other day, humans are unpredictable and often reckless. Eventually, Gri'Ran decided to return to the Crystal Heavens and left their high priests in charge of their temples.

"Over time, many of their followers became corrupt and spread hatred through the world. The priests twisted Gri'Ran's words to their own will until the original teachings were unheard of. Eventually, they declared war against Am's people, who were deemed unworthy of living in Ayrillis for simply worshipping a different god. They were told to either worship Gri'Ran or die. This became known as the Holy War.

"When Za'Haal made his pact, Gri'Ran returned and banished their priests to exile and destroyed their temples. They punished those followers who spoke against their will, which all but decimated their remaining followers. The war ended, and the world was once again at peace.

"That is, until Ami'Khel broke the pact and caused havoc. Gri'Ran finally had enough and left this world for good, or until such time as humankind can prove that they deserve such a powerful god.

"Not all of Gri'Ran's followers were corrupt. There was one temple which never strayed from the true teachings. Those priests were spared and lived the remainder of their lives in peace. As their numbers started to diminish, one of the high priests of Gri'Ran made a small golden statue and delivered it to the priests of Am as a gift, a symbol of unity and solidarity. That gift was also supposed to be a reminder that we should appreciate what we have and take nothing for granted, lest it be abused and taken away…"

Freyne's voice trailed off, and he sat in silence, stroking Nika's hair. Nika felt his eyes droop, and he drifted into a sleep plagued by unsettling dreams.

…He stood before the door again, utterly despaired that he couldn't open it. He frantically searched his pockets but they were empty. In desperation he reached up to bang his fist on the door…

Someone shook him awake and the image of the door vanished from his mind. Thunder rumbled overhead, and rain lashed at the windows. He sat up with a start; he was in a strange place and didn't know where he was.

And then Freyne was there, his strong arms wrapped around him. He pulled Nika against his body and held him protectively. At once Nika felt safe; he fell back into a deep and peaceful sleep.

Freyne lay in the darkness, listening to the storm while Nika slept in his arms. Talking about Gri'Ran had unearthed a number of memories and feelings that he wasn't ready to deal with. He was inwardly dreading their visit to Ner'Am. He'd not reached out to Am in prayer since his awakening from the forest, and he was worried that he would no longer be welcome to step foot in the temple. Freyne knew that Am was usually loving and forgiving, but he'd turned his back on Am the day he fled from his village. According to his teachings, such an act was unforgivable and would incur banishment or death for punishment.

The biggest worry for Freyne was his relationship with Nika. He'd always been taught that Am would smite any priest who took another man for a lover. That fear had pushed him into an unhappy marriage with his wife whom he never loved. But now that he had Nika and a taste of love and joy, there was no way he could return to his former misery. How could any god deny their people from experiencing something so beautiful?

The rain continued throughout the night and into the morning. Nika was woken by a loud knock at the door. He opened his eyes to see Freyne opening the door in his bathrobe.

"Morning," he said.

"Morning. We weren't sure if you were awake yet," Chardi's voice said from the hall.

"Nika's still asleep but I've been awake for a while. Come on in," Freyne replied.

He stood aside and allowed Ur'Shad, Iryna, Chardi, and Lana inside. They were already dressed in their travelling clothes and carried their cloaks over their arms. Nika quickly pulled the covers up over his bare chest, leaving only his and Arnie's heads poking out.

"Oh look, he *is* awake." Chardi chuckled.

Nika grunted.

"We were just talking to Ronol," Iryna said, sitting on the couch with Ur'Shad's arm around her shoulders. "He told us where to find the market, so we thought we'd take the horses and replenish our supplies."

Freyne sat on the edge of the bed and scratched his cheek.

"I need to do a few things before we leave, too. How about we split up after breakfast and meet up at the east gate?"

"Alright." Chardi nodded. "Hurry up and get dressed. Breakfast will be here shortly. We're hungry."

***

After they'd eaten, Nika and Freyne left the inn on foot and trudged through the sodden streets, trying their best to avoid the puddles. It was cold, but having Arnie under his cloak offered Nika a little warmth. They walked in silence until they reached the temple he'd seen the night before. He stopped and gazed up at the tall spires, momentarily forgetting their busy schedule.

"It's a temple of Am," Freyne mumbled.

"It's so beautiful."

"Am is a beautiful god."

"You keep saying 'them'. Are there more than one?"

"Am is neither male nor female. Gods have no need for gender. Am is the god I served at the monastery for all those years and dedicated my life to."

He nudged Nika and drew him abruptly away from the temple, leading him towards another road.

"Had? Do you no longer serve them?" Nika asked.

Freyne shrugged and looked away.

"I don't want to talk about it."

There was a hint of finality in his voice, a tone Nika had never heard from him before. He couldn't help but feel taken aback by Freyne's shortness. They walked through the sodden streets in silence, until Freyne finally stopped outside a building. The sign above the door was painted orange with a white book and quill in the centre.

Freyne wordlessly pulled back his hood as he entered and Nika followed suit. The room was warmed by a crackling fire to his right, and shelves lined the rest of the walls, laden with heavy-bound books, sheafs of parchment, and writing tools. Nika stood by the fire and warmed himself while glancing around in awe.

"What do you want?" the shopkeeper demanded.

She eyed them up and down with disdain. Nika felt uncomfortable and wanted to leave, but Freyne didn't budge.

"My lady." Freyne bowed his head respectfully. "I'm sorry to intrude. I merely wish to purchase a new journal and some writing instruments and then we'll be on our way."

"You have coin?"

"Of course, my lady."

The woman emerged from behind the counter, her hand hovering over the hilt of a dagger that was buckled to her belt. She led the way to a shelf that contained leatherbound journals of all shapes and sizes.

"What size do you need?" she asked, gesturing at the shelf.

"Oh, about so big." Freyne held up his hands to demonstrate.

"Parchment or vellum?" she asked.

"Parchment is fine."

She plucked a small book from the shelf and handed it to Freyne to inspect. He ran his fingers over the cover and flicked through the pages, testing the stitching of the binding.

"Your quality is very fine," he said. "I'll take this one."

"It's rare that foreigners appreciate a properly bound journal," she said. "Where are you from and why are you here?"

"We're from Kia-Mor and we're heading to a wedding in Ner'Am. We were supposed to sail to Fraal and travel from there, but our ship was swept off course by a storm. It would have taken too long to sail all the way back up the coast, so we decided to come ashore nearby and head to Ner'Am via Karatha."

"I see."

"What's going on here? I don't remember Karatha ever being so hostile. Is everything ok?"

She studied his face for a moment, then glanced at Nika.

"Alright. There's been lots of foreigners passing through over the last year or so who are nothing but trouble. Just five months ago, some bandits attacked the temple and attempted to destroy it. We Karathans are deeply religious and our temple is sacred to us, so when it happened, my people fought back and defeated the bandits. The city's folk are still pretty shaken from it, so now we trust very few foreigners who visit the city."

"How could anyone attack a house of Am?" Freyne choked.

"Filthy heathens." Her nostrils flared as she shook her head. "Even the militia are acting strange. There must be someone new in charge or something. Patrols are everywhere. If you run into them on the roads, they demand to know who you are, your reason for travel, and even your family line. And if you refuse, they arrest you. It's scary."

"We'll definitely be careful then. Thank you for your help."

"You're welcome. Is there anything else you would like?"

It was almost noon by the time Nika and Freyne went in search of the others. The rain had eased to a light mist, though it was still bitterly cold. As they walked towards the eastern gate, Nika heard a low whistle and turned to see Chardi waving them into an alleyway.

"Is there a problem?" Freyne asked.

"We were just questioned by the militia," Chardi said quietly, nodding. "Our cover story held, but it was intense. Thankfully they didn't seem to recognise us. Still, we don't want to be questioned again."

"Many of the merchants refused to trade with us, too," Ur'Shad added. "They really don't like foreigners here."

Nika helped Freyne pack away the things they'd bought, then mounted to the front of the saddle. Freyne leapt up behind him while filling the others in on what they'd learnt.

"Alright, let's go. It's definitely not safe here."

A shiver ran down Nika's spine. He nudged the horse into a walk and followed Chardi towards the gates. As they turned onto the main boulevard, he heard an angry shout.

"Get out of here, foreigners!" An angry old woman threw

a rock at them, narrowly missing Lana's face. "Be gone! Your type aren't welcome here!"

Nika's heart started racing. Several people ran to the woman's side and joined her, shaking their fists and yelling obscenities. Something hard collided with Nika's shoulder; he gasped as the rock fell to the ground with a clatter.

"Let's go!" he shouted.

They spurred their horses into a gallop and sped from the city, the taunts and curses of the Karathans warning them to never return.

15

Ner'Am sat nestled at the base of the Bar'Am Ranges, bordered by steep mountain peaks and jagged cliffs. A lone waterfall cascaded from the mountains and disappeared somewhere behind the city. Nika gazed at the picturesque scene and became lost in the tranquillity. He could sense the same presence he felt outside the temple at Karatha. Ner'Am had no wall or gate, and for the first time since he awoke in Ayrillis, Nika felt like he was home.

"It's beautiful, isn't it?" Freyne whispered in his ear.

Nika nodded, unable to take his eyes off the city. He reached behind and pulled Freyne's arms around his waist.

"Why does it feel like we're home?" he asked.

"This was where Am used to dwell in their physical form. It feels like home because we are Am's children. They wanted it to be a place where anyone could come and commune, regardless of one's status in society. Am loves all of their children, whether they are peasants or kings."

"Have you ever met them?" Nika asked.

"Only once."

"Are we good to go?" Ur'Shad called.

Freyne sucked in a deep breath and sighed just loud enough for Nika to hear. Nika could tell he was anxious and could feel him trembling. He shook the reins and gently urged the horse forward. Freyne did not let go of Nika's waist, and as they descended the hill and drew closer to the city, a strong sense of fear began to radiate from him. Something about Ner'Am had Freyne on edge, but still he would not talk about it.

The buildings of Ner'Am were constructed from the same bluestone that Nika saw at Karatha, only the buildings were much older and more beautiful. Most of the terraces had private balconies which were decorated with ornate iron lattice and supported by spiralling marble pillars. Neatly pruned roses of different colours grew on vines from the tiny front gardens, reminding Nika of the wild roses they saw in the ruins of the swamp people. The residual energy of countless generations of souls resonated from the walls themselves.

Very few people were out and about, but those who were gave them a wide berth and scurried away. *They seem to be more shaken than the Karathans,* Nika thought as he rode slowly, taking in his surrounds. In the back of his mind, he again heard the quiet ticking sound. *What is that?* he wondered, frowning. *It must be another weird thing from entering the realms. How annoying. I hope that's not here to stay.*

The deeper into the city they rode, the stronger the presence became. It was powerful yet welcoming, and filled him with warmth and love. Nika rode towards it, allowing his instinct to guide him. As they passed the final row of houses, the road sloped downwards into a pristine basin, an oasis on the outer edge of the city. The temple of Am sat on an island in the middle of the lake which was fed by the waterfall.

Freyne gasped and stiffened behind him. Nika frowned and glanced back at the temple, then he too gasped. The once beautiful building had been destroyed, a mere burnt-out husk that was abandoned and at risk of collapse. Much of the grand spires had tumbled into the lake and jutted out of the water at odd angles. The stone bridge that spanned the water was still intact, but it too was blackened by fire.

Again, Nika heard the ticking sound and grimaced. He followed Ur'Shad down the hill and dismounted next to the bridge. Freyne hesitated before joining him, a dark scowl etched into his features. Nika reached out and tried to join with him, but to his surprise Freyne's mind was closed off.

"You may as well take the horses for a drink," Nika said, handing his reins to Ur'Shad. "I'm not sure how long we'll be."

"We'll go and wait over there." Ur'Shad pointed to a grassy knoll by the lake, nestled amongst some tall pine trees.

Nika nodded and placed Arnie-Kyn on the ground. He firmly took Freyne's hand and guided him across the bridge. Each step they took, Freyne's shaking grew more pronounced, and as they reached the ruined entrance, he stopped and snatched back his hand.

"I can't go in there," he choked.

"Babe, what's wrong?"

Freyne shook his head.

"You go. I'll wait for you."

Arnie brushed past Nika's legs and leapt over the crumbled section of wall, disappearing into the temple. Nika placed the back of his hand tenderly on Freyne's tear-streaked face for a moment, feeling the fear and inner torment radiating from him. He realised that nothing he could say or do would be able to coax Freyne along. Nika turned and hurried to follow Arnie-Kyn inside.

A deep sadness resonated from the very walls of the charred temple. The rays of light shining through the collapsed sections of the roof showed a trail of destruction. Nika carefully stepped over and around the burnt remains of what were once long bench seats. As his eyes adjusted to the gloom, he was able to see the remnants of a blackened marble altar on a raised dais at the far end of the temple. Arnie-Kyn was sitting at the bottom of the dais, gazing up at something Nika couldn't see. He wordlessly joined the cat, unsure of what to do next.

There was an eerie *creak* as a charred statue set in the wall beside the altar swung open revealing a hidden passageway. A monk in brown robes appeared in the doorway, his face hidden beneath his hood.

"Come."

He beckoned for Nika to follow. Arnie-Kyn trotted towards him and Nika followed warily. The monk turned and led them down a steep flight of stairs into a dimly lit chamber, furnished with nothing but a small bed and two chairs. The monk gestured for Nika to sit, then sat in the opposite chair and pulled back his hood.

"You are a long way from home," he said softly. His voice was kind and gentle, which helped Nika feel at ease. "My name is Orison. I am the last of Am's followers here."

"What happened?" Nika asked.

"Just a few months ago, our beautiful temple was attacked and destroyed," Orison said sadly. "Mercenaries driven by hatred, nothing more. I am the only survivor."

"Why are you still here then?"

"My god gave me a task to perform and I will not break my oath," Orison replied. "I have waited many years for this exact moment in time."

Nika heard the ticking sound yet again. It was a little faster and growing louder, almost like there was a sense of urgency. He frowned and turned his attention back to the monk.

"I know why you're here and I have what you seek," Orison continued. "I must ask, though. Where is your companion?"

"He's waiting for me outside."

"I see. Your companion is deeply conflicted. He holds Am deeply in his heart but is no longer sure of his place in this life. He needs you more than ever. Do not let him lose sight of his task, and do not let him give up."

"What's his task?" Nika asked.

"He needs to hurry and decipher the original scrolls," Orison replied. "He's studied his version for long enough that the originals will become clear to him in time."

"And what's my role in all of this?" Nika asked. "I'm sure I'm not here just for To'Rel's plausible deniability. Do *you* know how I can get back to my world?"

"Alas, I cannot help you," Orison said. "You must obey the king's orders. Your role will become clear when the time is right. Am will be there to guide you."

"So why are we here, then?" Nika asked, starting to feel frustrated. "Freyne seems to think we need to search for something important. Can you at least help us with that?"

"Of course that's why you're here. Come with me and I will give you what you seek."

Orison pushed the bed away from the wall and opened a hidden trapdoor. He picked up a lantern and led Nika down a small flight of stairs and into a narrow stone passage. It was stuffy and dark, and Nika had to stoop to avoid hitting his head on the ceiling.

"This way, please. We need to hurry."

Freyne stood by the entrance of the destroyed temple, tears streaming down his cheeks as he took in the scene of devastation. The most sacred of Am's houses was nothing but a crumbled ruin. He stood glued to the spot, his fear threatening to turn into panic. Closing his eyes, he took several deep breaths to try and calm himself. He vividly remembered his first visit to Ner'Am; the fresh smell of pine in the air, the excitement of the people lining the streets, cheering at him and the other priests who were making their pilgrimage. The temple was once the heart of the city, and now it was gone.

The destruction of the building wasn't the only thing upsetting him, though. Wiping his eyes, he took another deep breath and reached out with his shaking hand. As his fingers brushed the stone wall he flinched, expecting to be struck down or hurled backwards through the air in contempt. Instead, he felt a warm pulse flow through his fingers and spread throughout his body. Am's familiar presence flooded through and around him, so strong that Freyne almost choked.

"Come to me, my son."

It was an order he dared not disobey. Freyne staggered inside and slowly made his way along the trail of debris to the place where Nika had stood only moments before. He was shaking and felt like he wanted to be sick.

The presence grew stronger. Freyne fell to his knees, absolutely terrified. A small slither of light appeared in front of the altar and began to swirl, growing first into a ball, then ebbed and grew until it resembled the shape of a being. Freyne prostrated himself, trembling, his face pressed to the floor. The spectral being took a step forward.

"My son."

Am's voice was soft and gentle, yet powerful and commanding at the same time. Freyne stayed where he was, unable to move. His chest swelled with guilt and his emotions ran free. Am knelt on one shimmering knee and gently took Freyne by his shoulders, guiding him upright.

"My son. Why do you weep?" Am asked.

"I have forsaken you." Freyne sobbed. "I – I turned my back on you for seven hundred years. Not once have I reached out to you in prayer since I started this journey with Nika. And now I defy you even more."

Am sank to their knees, resting their hands on Freyne's shoulders and looking him in the eye.

"I do not see one single point in time where you have failed me," they said softly. "You have been my most loyal follower of all time. Why do you feel you have defied me?"

Am reached out and brushed away Freyne's tears.

"I have taken a man for my lover," he wept. "That in itself is enough to be banished from your house. I'm not willing to abandon him. Not now, not ever."

"What does the passage of my laws state regarding love?"

"A man who feels true love may be wed within a house of Am," Freyne quoted without hesitation.

"Does that passage say that he must be wed to a woman?"

"I...No?"

"Love is love, whether it's between a man and a woman, two men, two women, or any other combination. I am deeply saddened and angered that my words have once again been twisted to push someone else's agenda. Things in this world are far worse than I believed."

"When I was an acolyte, two young men were caught holding hands in the Sanctuary during a Kharung celebration. The high priests denounced and humiliated them in front of all those people, then banished them from the monastery and told them never to return to any of your temples. That's the only reason I agreed to marry Alira."

"We will address this soon, my son. Unfortunately, we have graver issues at hand which we must focus on for the moment." Am stood and helped Freyne to his feet. "You must get that prophecy translated as quickly as possible. That task is yours alone. Time is running out."

"I will, My God." Freyne wiped his eyes. "Are we on the right path to finding the blood descendant?"

"Yes, you are. At this very moment, Brother Orison is taking your Nikolai to fetch Gri'Ran's gift. Protect both of them with your life. You will be facing great danger very soon, so tread carefully."

"Yes, My God."

"One more thing. You are going to face a major crossroads which will challenge you and your beliefs. Remember your oath and trust in me, no matter what. Everything is happening for a reason." Am's energy began to shimmer. "So long as you hold me in your heart, I will always be here for you. Remember, I'm only a prayer away. I love you, my son."

Am's glowing energy began to fade and they disappeared, leaving Freyne in the gloomy darkness, alone.

Beneath the temple were sprawling catacombs that spread out below the lake. Orison led Nika through a maze of passages until they reached a reinforced door with seven locks. One by one, the monk fumbled with a ring of keys and unlocked them. The door swung open to reveal a tiny cubical with nothing but a single bookcase and a locked cabinet mounted on the wall. Orison selected another key, then unlocked the cabinet and extracted something golden.

"Here is the idol you seek." He held out a tiny statue of a gryphon that fit snugly in his palm. "Without it, it will be impossible to fulfil the prophecy. Keep it with you at all times and don't lose it. Humanity is counting on you."

Orison placed it in Nika's hand, and at once he felt an odd tingling in his palm. Warmth spread up his arm and to the rest of his body, and the image of the door from his dreams flashed into his mind.

"It's the key from my dream!" he gasped.

"You should keep that information to yourself," Orison said, a look of concern crossing his face. "When things are made clear just for you, it's for a reason."

"Oh."

Orison locked the cabinet and the door, then led Nika back through the catacombs. Once they reached the bed chamber, the monk paused and listened, then frowned.

"It would appear that our time together has been cut short," he said. "Take your companions to the waterfall by the lake. Behind the water's flow is a hidden cave that leads to the mountains. This will enable you to avoid capture. Go quickly."

Orison put out his hand and Nika shook it firmly.

"Be careful. I have been sensing an evil lurking around here of late. Now go. Blessings to you and your friends, and may you forever hold Am in your heart."

Sensing Orison's urgency, Nika raced up the stairs two at a time. Freyne looked startled as Nika emerged from the hidden passage and hurried down the dais steps to join him. To his surprise, Freyne pulled him close and kissed him deeply and with what Nika could tell was all of his love. His belly fluttered and for a moment he forgot where they were. As their lips parted, the hairs went up on the back of Nika's arms and neck, and he remembered Orison's warning.

"We need to go," he said urgently. "They're coming."

Nika scooped Arnie into his arms and ran from the temple as fast as he could with Freyne by his side. The cat's claws dug into his skin and his side ached. Up ahead, he caught sight of the others quickly stuffing their things away and mounting their horses. Ur'Shad held out the reins for Nika and Freyne, and they quickly mounted.

"Thanks. Let's go. This way," Nika panted.

He urged the horse towards the waterfall and carefully led the others to the cave behind the flowing water. As soon as they were hidden, Nika held up his hand to stop and quickly entered the realm. He separated from his body and ghosted across the lake to try and make sense of what Orison was talking about.

Riding down the slope towards the temple were around thirty soldiers wearing the red and bronze uniforms of the militia. The rider at the head of the unit wore a full set of spiked armour and looked quite intimidating, and flanking him were two people dressed in black robes. They stopped at the bridge and two of the soldiers disappeared inside the temple. Shortly after, they returned and remounted, and the patrol galloped away. Nika returned to his body and let out a deep breath.

"They didn't see us," he reported. "Orison said to follow this cave into the mountains."

"Orison?" Chardi asked.

"It's a long story." Nika held up the golden statue for all to see. "I got what we needed. Let's get out of here."

The mountain passage was narrow and stifling. Ur'Shad and Chardi each carried lit torches to brighten their path, which hissed and spluttered while casting flickering shadows around them. No one spoke; the only other sounds were the horses' hooves echoing loudly off the walls and the distant burble of gushing water.

Freyne rode behind Nika, replaying Am's visit over and over in his mind. A part of him felt elated knowing that Am was not disappointed in him, but the rest of him still felt guilty. He knew he'd snapped at Nika more than once and had been standoffish since Karatha, and Nika didn't deserve that. Freyne leant forward and slipped his arms around Nika's waist and pulled him back against his chest. He felt a tentative probe from Nika's mind and quickly joined with him.

"Hello, you," Nika said silently, interlocking the fingers of his free hand with Freyne's. *"Are you okay?"*

"I'm better now," Freyne replied. *"I owe you an apology. I'm sorry for being so moody lately."*

"It's okay."

"No, it's not. You don't deserve to be snapped at, especially if you've done nothing wrong. I was being – what do you call it – a jerk?"

Nika shrugged.

"I was scared," Freyne continued. *"I spent my entire life at the monastery, worshipping Am and doing my best to be a loyal follower. It was taught that to turn our back on the monastery, we would be turning our back on Am and therefore punished severely. I was also taught, amongst other things, that for a man to take another man as his lover, the punishment is banishment into exile."*

"That's horrible," Nika replied.

"Religion is a complex thing. People twist the words of the gods to mean whatever they want them to mean. While you were with Brother Orison, I had a visitor."

"A visitor? Who?"

"Am."

"Wow. What's it like to meet a god?"

"It's hard to explain. They are powerful and commanding and deserve our absolute respect at all times. Given my former position and the fact that I haven't reached out in prayer since getting my memory back, I feared they were angry with me. Instead

215

they showed me love and understanding. All of my fears were unfounded. Am is happy with me even though I left the monastery, I'm not being banished, and we have their blessing to be together."

Nika gently squeezed his hands and nodded.

"Am used a different name for you," Freyne added. *"Nikolai."*

"Ugh."

"Why ugh?"

"My full name is Nikolai Mikhailov. I hate it. I've always preferred Nika."

"I like it. Why do you hate your name?" Freyne asked.

"It reminds me of my father. He was a complete arsehole."

"I'm sorry," Freyne said.

"Don't be. He used to beat me. Sometimes he'd lock me up for days at a time with no food. He deserved every bit of what he got."

"He may have been a horrible person, but you are better than him in every way, regardless of what your name is. You are your own person, boo."

Freyne kissed Nika's cheek and cuddled into him, drawing comfort from their closeness.

"Wait a minute. How does Am know my full name?" Nika asked. *"I haven't told anyone since I came here."*

"Your name is set deeply in your core and is a part of who you are," Freyne explained. *"As we know, Ayrillis isn't the only world in existence. The gods choose which worlds to visit and claim as their own. Maybe Am or Gri'Ran have already been to your world, or your god has been here."*

"I doubt it," Nika said.

"I don't. How is it that we speak the same language? And how else would you explain that the humans of your world and the humans of this world have both evolved to the same level of sophistication? It's no coincidence."

Nika sucked the air in through his teeth, then turned to look at Freyne over his shoulder, his grey eyes reflecting the torch light.

"I never even gave that a thought," he admitted. *"In my world we call this language English, which has existed for thousands of years. I always thought the language evolved along with humans."*

"And yet, here we are, two people from completely different worlds with different histories, conversing easily with the same

language." Freyne felt his face crease into a smile as a tinge of excitement dawned on him. *"I think we've just proven that language* does *come from the gods and didn't evolve from growls and grunts to begin with. How fascinating! This is why I love studying so much."*

"What about your writing, though? It looks nothing like ours."

"That's different again. It's a codified cipher that has no spoken translation. It was developed during the Holy War by the followers of Am. You cannot speak a language if it has no words."

"It must be difficult to learn."

"Incredibly difficult. It's the main language used in our religious literature though, so I had no choice but to learn it. Now, however, whenever I read or write with it, I find that I can actually translate it into what we're speaking now."

Nika sat upright and stretched, breaking Freyne's hold. Freyne settled back and pondered his revelation on the origin of language and it wasn't until the cave opened into a spacious cavern that he returned his focus to his surroundings. A pristine stream trickled through a groove in the stone that was formed over eons of constant flow. The roof was laced with stalactites which shone like crystals and the veins of quartz reflected the shine in dazzling arrays of rainbow.

Freyne closed his eyes, feeling a sense of timeless patience pulsating across the millennia. He could feel the pressure of the mountains pressing down upon the stones deep below his feet, and the slow drips running along the stalactites, calcifying and forever growing.

"...Pressure, time, weight disrupted.
Nature aches, her creations corrupted..."

"Let's stop here for lunch," Ur'Shad said loudly.

Freyne jumped, startled. Ur'Shad's voice echoed around the walls of the cave, silencing the cries of the earth. He frowned and tried to hear nature's call, but it was gone.

"Oh good. I'm hungry," Chardi said.

"You're always hungry." Ur'Shad smirked.

Iryna and Lana giggled and dismounted. Freyne wandered across to the stream and knelt down, watching the crystal-clear water tumbling gently over the timeworn pebbles. He splashed some on his face and rubbed his eyes; his reflection stared back at him, mirroring his fatigue.

"...*Ebbs and flows, souls abducted.*
Evil grows, its anger erupted..."

Freyne froze and strained to hear the whispered words, but once uttered they were gone. He scratched his cheek, perplexed. *What's going on? I'd better write this in my journal. I've never heard the voices speak like this before.*

Lunch was plain and bland. Freyne sat next to Nika chewing on a thick chunk of almost-stale bread, wishing he was outside where he could hunt for some decent food. He looked wistfully at Arnie who sat at Nika's feet devouring a small rodent.

"So, where are we going now?" Chardi asked.

"Once we get out of this cave system, we'll follow the mountain path for a while until we can find a safe way down," Freyne said. "We don't want to be in the mountains when it starts to snow."

"Do we even know where we're going?" Iryna asked.

"North, towards Riz'Hra," Freyne said.

"Let's hope the militia have given up looking for us," Ur'Shad said darkly.

"I don't think they'll ever stop." Chardi shook his head.

"Unless..." Lana said slowly.

Everyone looked at Lana and a wicked grin spread across her face as she ran her fingers over the sheath of her dagger.

"Iryna. Your father and the king of Riz'Hra are strong allies," she said. "Since we are heading in that direction anyways, why don't we drop by and visit King Kaiton? I'm sure he'll happily send out some of his royal army to put those scum back in their place."

"You know, that could work." Iryna nodded. "We need to send a letter to my father to let him know what's going on. King Kaiton has enchanted messenger birds, so it only takes around a day for the letter to reach Al'Obrel."

"I like it," Chardi agreed. "He needs to know about J'mai and take all of the appropriate security measures. J'mai had lots of friends, so I'm worried that there's more of those crazies still roaming the castle."

"I'm sure your parents are anxious to know that you're ok too, princess." Ur'Shad added. "Is this ok with the rest of you?"

"Of course." Freyne nodded. "I think it's time To'Rel took this prophecy seriously and not as a political manoeuvre. If you don't mind, I'll have some questions to ask him, too. There's a few things I need to know and he's the only person alive who can answer them."

There was no way of telling how long they rode through the caves. Nika was beginning to feel claustrophobic from the constant darkness, especially when they had to dismount to lead the horses through the narrower sections. After a while, he felt a gentle breeze brush against his cheek and sat up straight, eager to escape into the open.

The tunnel stopped abruptly and opened into an enormous cavern dominated by a large still lake. A stone bridge stretched across the water, and in the distance, he could just make out a patch of velvety black sky filled with twinkling stars.

Nika sighed with relief. He could feel the air growing cooler as they rode across the bridge. The cavern was so large that he couldn't see the walls in the torchlight. They rode in silence, the only sound the echoing of the horses hooves. It wasn't until they stepped onto the soft sand on the lake's edge that Ur'Shad stopped and held his torch higher, revealing a wide sandy area.

"How about we set up camp here?" he asked.

"It looks like a good spot." Freyne nodded. "Nika and I will go and hunt. We could all do with a decent meal."

Nika dismounted and stretched, then quickly adjusted his sight so he could see better in the dark. He'd never been invited to hunt before. Freyne took his hand and lead him through the ferns and mossy stones, and up the natural steps that stretched towards the entrance.

The wind was icy cold and bit at Nika's exposed skin. Freyne stopped and pulled Nika into his arms, their bodies pressed tightly together. Nika buried his face in Freyne's neck, inhaling his scent and relishing in their closeness.

"I've been wanting to do this all day," Freyne said.

"I've been wanting to do this, as well." Nika reached up

and helped himself to Freyne's lips. At once, the sprites of light came to life in a dazzling show of colour in his mind's eye.

"There's something else I want to do, but it will have to wait." Freyne parted their kiss and ran his fingers down Nika's cheek. *"We'd better organise dinner first, though. It's already well past our usual bed time."*

"Yeah. I'm so hungry."

He heard a whisper as Freyne entered the highest realm. Nika waited a little awkwardly, unsure what he was supposed to be doing.

"I've spotted a mountain goat," Freyne said after a while. *"Wait here. I won't be long."*

Nika sat on a rock and rubbed his arms in an attempt to stay warm. The wind whistled in the mouth of the cave, it's melancholic song a testament to an eon of erosion and constant change. He could almost feel the weight of the rocks diminishing around him as the dust blew away in the breeze.

A distant squeal broke his reverie and he jumped, startled. Soon after he heard the crunch of gravel and Freyne returned with his prey. Nika stood, allowing Freyne to lay the goat on the rock. He watched in awe as Freyne set to work skinning and gutting the animal.

"Did you learn how to do that before you went to live in the forest, or after?" Nika asked.

"After. I had to learn how to hunt from scratch, and I found out pretty quickly that if I couldn't catch something, I'd go hungry. Starvation is a good teacher."

"At least you've had seven hundred years to hone your technique." Nika smirked.

Freyne sighed and rolled his eyes, though Nika could see his grin in the dim light. Freyne's hand flashed as he worked, stopping only to fling the offcuts over the side of the mountain.

"We don't want to attract the local wildlife," he explained in response to Nika's frown. "Usually I bury it, but it's a bit hard when the ground is rock–"

Freyne broke off and froze. The hairs stood on the back of Nika's neck and for a moment he sensed danger on the wind.

"What *was* that?" he asked.

"I'm not sure." Freyne shivered and glanced around.

"Are we in danger?"

"I don't think so. Whatever that is, or was, is a long way from here. We should be fine. Can you give me a hand with this?"

Freyne grasped the back leg stubs and nodded for Nika to take the front. Together, they carried the goat back to the entrance and carefully descended back into the warmth of the cave. The glow of the fire lit the way like a welcoming beacon.

Lana's eyes lit up when she saw the goat and hurried forward to help. Chardi and Ur'Shad were a short distance from the fire, swinging their swords in what Nika assumed was practice. Once the goat was secure on the spit, he followed Freyne down to the lake and washed his hands in the freezing cold water.

"Winter is closer than I thought," Freyne announced as they returned to the fire. "We're going to get ice and the first snow within a week or two."

"It snowed every winter back in my wor – homeland," Nika said. "So long as we have warm clothes, we should be ok."

"I'm not used to the colder climate," Freyne said ruefully, massaging his fingers. "Maybe I'm just getting old."

"Just maybe?"

"Oh hush, you." Freyne shook his head in defeat.

Iryna disappeared into one of the tents and returned carrying one of the packs. She called out to Ur'Shad and Chardi to join them, then opened it and handed everyone a cap and long-sleeved shirt, each made from the softest wool and fur.

"We got these from the market at Karatha. The farmers are predicting a cold winter this year," Iryna explained. "We're not used to extreme cold, either."

"Good idea," Nika said. "We don't want anyone to get sick."

"Will the horses be ok in the cold?" Lana asked.

"Of course they will. This is their natural habitat, so the cold won't bother them," Freyne said. "These mountain horses were bred in Rarn. They're naturally bigger and stronger than standard horse breeds which is why they can handle two riders instead of one. Smaller horses might struggle in the cold."

"They're such beautiful animals." Lana sighed. "Before I ran away, I used to go for long rides on our horse. It broke my heart when we had to sell him so we could buy food."

"I wonder how Cookie is," Iryna said.

"Wow. It feels like forever ago that we were at Dol'Am."

"And Al'Obrel," Chardi added.

Iryna's smile left her face.

"I don't want to go home."

"Why not?" Nika asked.

"This journey has already taught me so much," she replied. "As a royal princess, there was always a servant nearby to cater to my every whim. My life was never my own and soon I will be forced to marry and bear children to a man that I don't love. At least out here I have some freedom. I guess this is what it feels like to be a normal person who wasn't born into royalty."

"A forced marriage? That's horrible." Nika frowned. "Is there any way to get out of it?"

"No. I've known about this since I was a little girl and I've come to accept is as a trade-off for a life of luxury. I could even be a queen someday."

"If you do become a queen, can't you change that rule for future princesses?"

"It doesn't work like that." Iryna laughed softly. "Queens don't hold any power. We make heirs and ensure the king's bloodline will be preserved."

"Wait. I don't understand." Nika scratched his head. "If your father passes away, who takes over the rule of Al'Obrel?"

"Seriously. Don't you have a king where you're from?" Iryna rolled her eyes.

"No, I don't," Nika retorted.

"King To'Rel has nominated a regent to rule in the event of his death or in such an occasion where he is unable to rule," Ur'Shad explained. "Since Iryna is an only child, the throne would go to the regent who will run the kingdom until a new king is selected."

"Or, if Iryna were to marry a prince from another kingdom and have a son, that son would become the heir since he is of the direct bloodline," Chardi added. "This ties the prince to our kingdom and rends him ineligible to rule in his own kingdom."

"So why doesn't the prince become the heir?" Nika's mind was boggling. "I'm sorry. None of this makes any sense to me. Surely he would be better than having a regent?"

"Because he isn't from the bloodline." Iryna drew herself up and shook her hair. "Blood is everything here. My future prince husband won't have my father's blood, but our child will. Therefore, that child will be eligible to rule. In our case, though, my father has two brothers. If Father and I were to die now, the regent would step in and guide the process to select one of my uncles or cousins to become king."

"I couldn't imagine ever being married to someone I didn't love," Lana said sadly.

Iryna shrugged and crossed her arms. Ur'Shad put his arm around her shoulders and squeezed her gently.

"Just take each day as it comes, princess," he said wisely. "I can always slaughter your future husband so I can keep you all to myself."

Iryna's face dropped and she stared forlornly into the fire. Nika excused himself and took a large pot down to the lake to fill with water, then sat it in the coals next to the spit. The entire mood of the campsite was melancholic after the reality of Iryna's future set in. *I can't believe I actually feel sorry for her,* he thought to himself. *No one should ever be forced to marry or have children. I'm glad I'm not royalty so I can be with whomever the hell I want.*

By the time dinner was ready, Nika's belly was rumbling. He guessed it was almost midnight and struggled to stifle his yawns. The cave was filled with the smells of roasted meat and the vegetables Iryna cooked. Nika felt tired and drained, and he could see that he was not alone. One by one, they finished their dinner, washed their plates in the pot of boiled water, and drifted off to bed.

Nika and Freyne were the last to go to bed. Once they'd stored the leftover meat properly, Nika followed Freyne to their tent and noticed that the bedrolls had been put together instead of in separate compartments. A small bump under his blanket showed that Arnie was already curled up and sleeping in a ball. Nika carefully manoeuvred himself under the blankets so he didn't wake the cat, then yawned.

"Goodnight, boo," Freyne said sleepily.

Nika reached out and took Freyne's hand, then fell into an exhausted sleep.

He stood before the dark tower, gazing at its tip high up in the sky. Lightning cracked overhead, and in the darkness, the winged beast fluttered through the air. He turned his attention back to the door and reached into his pocket. His fingers closed around the golden gryphon statue. With his hands shaking, he placed it in a notch in the door.

Click.

As the door swung open, his vision swirled and shifted.

He stood alone on a mountain path, a light dusting of snow on the ground, and the sky above a miserable grey. There was a darkness behind him, a being of pure evil. He started to run, but it followed him, hunting him, hungry for his flesh and blood.

Nika looked over his shoulder, but the beast was nowhere to be seen. He slowed to a walk, sure he was no longer being followed, then turned his head back towards the path.

The beast lay before him, an enormous serpent three times his length, its body thicker than a person's. Its eyes were black and soulless, it's skin mottling like it'd been cut with a razor all over its body. It drew back its head and hissed, a long, pointed tongue protruding from between its sharp fangs.

The snake drew back its head, then darted forward towards Nika's face...

"Argh!" Nika yelled and jolted upright.

Arnie hissed and dug his claws into Nika's leg. He swore loudly and wiped the sweat from his face. His hands and legs were shaking uncontrollably, and his heart was pounding as though he really had been running through the mountains. He tried to take deep breaths to calm down but it wasn't helping.

Something landed on his shoulder and startled him again. He tried to slap it away; it took him a moment to realise it was Freyne's hand.

"What the fuck?" Nika gasped.

"Calm down, boo." Freyne said grumpily, yawning. "It was just a python. I doubt it was venomous."

"It nearly fucking killed me!"

"It was nowhere near you."

Nika buried his face in his hands and tried to calm himself. Everything felt so real and he was sure the snake was still lurking somewhere nearby. Freyne pulled him roughly into his arms and held him tight.

"It's ok, boo. You're safe. I'm here with you," he whispered. "Everything's going to be alright."

"I fucking hate snakes. More than anything in the world. Just keep them away from me."

"It's ok," Freyne repeated. "You've got nothing to worry about. It was just a bad dream."

16

Nika woke with a pounding headache. He opened his eyes to see Freyne sitting cross-legged next to him, reading intently and writing in his new journal. Arnie was nestled between them, purring softly. He yawned and stretched, then grimaced from the throbbing pain.

"Morning, boo." Freyne smiled.

Nika grunted and massaged his temples.

"Did I sleep in?"

"No. The others are still asleep."

"I wish I was," Nika grumbled.

"You were restless last night. You somehow managed to project your dream onto me."

"Sorry."

"You never told me that you're afraid of snakes." Freyne looked at him with his eyebrow raised.

"Yeah, well. We all have fears."

Nika dressed irritably and crawled out of the tent. Both of his dreams were disconcerting. The snake, the tower, and even the key, all felt so real that he wondered if he were actually there. *None of this makes any sense. Are these memories? What the fuck is–* Nika stopped dead in his tracks as he noticed for the first time the beauty of the cave. He sucked in a deep breath and gazed around in wonder, his sour mood diminishing at once. Various species of lush green ferns grew wildly, interspersed with flowering bushes. Ivy snaked its way around the trunks of the taller ferns, choking them in its quest to reach the sky. Shimmering rays of sunlight filtered through the entrance and lit up the cavern, dazzling the still surface of the lake. A soft yet icy breeze ruffled the leaves and chilled Nika's exposed skin.

He tore his gaze away and stirred up the fire which had died down to coals overnight, then warmed some water and had a quick wash and shave. As he dried himself off, two strong arms wrapped around his waist and squeezed gently. Nika startled; he'd been so self-absorbed that he hadn't even sensed Freyne's presence.

"Are you okay, grumpy?" he asked.

Nika sighed and leaned into him.

"I'm sorry. My head is aching and that dream got to me. I've always been afraid of snakes. I can't stand to be around them and I can't stand look at them."

"There's nothing wrong with that," Freyne offered. "What is it that you find so unsettling about them?"

"There's some shit from my past that I'm still not ready to face, and my fear of snakes is one of them. Sorry, babe."

He was saved by Lana emerging from her tent, a bright smile lighting up her face.

"Morning, you two," she greeted them. "Have you started breakfast yet? I'm hungry this morning."

Nika shook his head.

"I was just about to."

"Oh, good. I'll go and wake the others."

It wasn't until after Nika had finished his breakfast and downed two cups of tea that he felt his pain ease and his mood lighten. He sat cross-legged on the sand and leaning slightly against Freyne when Arnie-Kyn appeared and sat next to him.

"How are you doing?" Nika asked, scratching his ears.

"One is cold, but alright," Arnie replied.

"You certainly know where to find the warmest spots in bed."

"One is resourceful."

Nika reached over and picked him up, then roughed up the fur on his head. Arnie's tail whipped around irritably.

"Must you?" he asked curtly.

"Yes, I must." Nika grinned for the first time that day.

"You humans are incorrigible." The cat wriggled free and stalked off towards the ferns.

"Am I the only one who isn't grumpy today?" Freyne asked.

The sky was a perfect blue that morning. Although the sun shone brightly, the breeze that whistled around the rocks and peaks was bitterly cold. In the distance, Nika spotted a pair of birds circling in the air, eyeing their prey far below. He was surprised at how high they'd climbed through the caves. Surrounding them were mountains in every direction, some tipped with snow and others dotted with trees or rocky outcrops. Nika had donned his fleece shirt and hat under his cloak, and much to the cat's dislike, had wrapped Arnie gently in one of his old shirts for warmth. He had Arnie resting between his legs as they rode, shielding him from the wind.

"It's freezing up here," Iryna complained.

"It's only going to get worse," Freyne said. "It hasn't started snowing this low yet, but it will soon."

"Don't worry, princess. I'll keep you warm."

Ur'Shad grinned and wrapped his arms around her, earning a scowl. Iryna shrugged and tried to escape his grasp, but Ur'Shad held her firm. She stopped struggling and mumbled something under her breath.

"Body heat can save your life in the snow," Nika pointed out.

"Oh, shut up."

Chardi chuckled and urged his horse forward, taking the lead. They rode slowly and carefully along the meandering mountain path in silence. Nika felt insignificant amongst the tall peaks surrounding him, as though he could be squished like an ant at any time. Behind him, Freyne sat quietly, reading one of the scrolls and writing in his journal, using Nika's back to lean on. It was almost lunch time when his skin prickled and jolted him upright. He sensed danger, similar to what he felt above Ner'Am, only it was stronger and felt much closer. Freyne stopped writing and looked around.

"*What* is *that?*" Nika asked.

"*I don't know, boo. It feels like it's coming from somewhere up ahead. Whatever it is, I don't like it. Let's take turns in holding the shield up and proceed with caution. Who knows what could be lurking in these mountains.*"

Freyne woke early, shivering. The winter chill was seeping into his bones, making his joints ache. His bladder was uncomfortably full, and he groaned inwardly at the thought of having to go outside to empty it. Nika was still asleep, snoring softly. Freyne sighed and quickly dressed, then hurried outside. There was a gentle crunch under his shoes, and he could just make out a thin dusting of snow on the ground. Freyne hurried a short distance away from the camp and relieved himself behind a dead tree, the cold biting at his exposed skin. The faintest hint of light brushed the tip of the peaks, signalling the coming of dawn. Freyne closed his eyes, feeling the forces of nature flowing around him.

"...Swarms, crowds, lives affected.
Manifestations, only one defected..."

He startled and glanced around to see where the whisper was coming from, but he was all alone. For a moment he was tempted to enter the highest realm and investigate, but he was cold and tired and craved the warmth of Nika's body. He tucked himself away and hurried back to camp.

They'd been riding through the mountains for almost two weeks, and already Freyne was looking forward to getting back to the lowlands. He'd been making good progress on the prophecy until it became too cold for his fingers to grip his pencil. The only chance he had to work on it was in the evenings by the warmth of the fire, when he was usually too tired to concentrate.

Nika stirred and rolled over. Freyne snuggled into him, relishing in their closeness and listening to his gentle breathing. He reflected on their journey and tried linking it to what he knew of the prophecy, and his thoughts turned back to their meeting with King To'Rel.

Why is To'Rel so invested with this? he wondered. *He of all people should know that the prophecy will be triggered for fulfilment only when the time is right, not when he desires a political advantage. And why would he be ok with Iryna travelling abroad with four men instead of a royal escort? Unless he really did intend for her to come. I'd better read through what I've translated so far and see if I've missed something.*

Freyne sighed. Everything he thought he knew about the prophecy was no longer clear. *All those years I spent studying the abridged prophecy was a waste of time. What was the point? This full version is an absolute mess. Am I even cut out for this? Why me and not Darius or one of the other high priests?*

He closed his eyes, lulled by Nika's warmth, and was drifting back to sleep when something tugged softly on the edge of his mind. Whoever or whatever it was pulled him from consciousness and into a dream.

He walked through the snow, following a winding path on the edge of a steep hill. The wind was bitterly cold and whipped about him. By the time he reached the peak, his lungs were burning from exertion. He took several deep gasping breaths and glanced around; a short distance away, a cloaked figure was standing with their hands clasped behind their back. As he approached, the figure turned to face him. There was a dark void where their face would be, but at once he knew who it was and fell to his knees in the freezing snow.

"Stand, my child. We don't have time for formalities." Am reached out and guided Freyne to his feet.

"My God. Is this real or a dream?" Freyne asked.

"One being's reality is another's dream. You know I do not appear in people's dreams in the form of imagination, so I think we can agree that this conversation is indeed a reality. However you choose to treat what we are about to witness is up to you, though."

"Very well. Why have you summoned me, My God?"

"I've been sensing your worry and felt that it was time to talk to you in person. Spectral form is draining and limits our time together, so I thought I'd bring you to me," they said. *"Rest assured, your years at the monastery were not in vain."*

"This version of the prophecy is completely different to the one I've studied. The passages are strange and make no sense at all. I have no idea what I'm doing or if we're even close to finding this blood descendant."

"You are much closer than you think, my son." Am reached out and patted Freyne's shoulder. *"You are on the right path, and you are doing well in your task. Continue to translate the prophecy and soon you will be able to understand it."*

Freyne nodded and looked past his god for the first time. Below them was a sprawling city engulfed in flames. His stomach turned at the thought of all the people who might be caught in the devastation, dead or dying.

"What happened down there?" he choked.

"War, greed, and failure to respect me as their god." Am guided Freyne closer to the edge so they could see better. "This world is about to be destroyed by humanity's own hand. I am here to deliver the few remaining faithful souls into the afterlife before everything – the people, animals, nature – is wiped out for good and this place ceases to exist. Tis a heartbreaking day that will echo throughout the heavens for millennia to come."

A terrifying explosion lit up the sky beyond the doomed city. The ground shook and for the first time he noticed a vast battle was waging beneath them. Bright beams of colour flashed from their strange weapons that surely had to be powered by some sort of magic; whenever the light hit someone they were instantly killed. The bile rose in his throat, and before he could take more than two steps, he threw up what was left in his stomach.

"Why don't you save them?" he demanded.

"Everything that happens does so for a reason. Sometimes we must sacrifice those we love in order to fulfil a destiny," Am explained. "As a god, I am responsible for my worlds and my people. However, sometimes humanity diverges from its path and I must step in. It brings me great sadness, but sometimes even I must admit I have failed and let humanity run its course. Even if that leads to their ultimate destruction."

"Are you saying that you've destroyed this world?" Freyne asked incredulously.

"No, my son. You misunderstand me. This world is far more advanced than yours. The technology they created to sustain their lives has failed, leading to a desperate struggle for food and resources. This war is the last hope for those people. Little do they know, they have set off a chain of events that cannot be stopped, even by me, and is about to destroy everything they know."

"But surely you can do something, My God? I don't understand."

"My power is determined by how many faithful followers I have. In your world, my power is moderate, though slowly fading as more people turn their backs on me. Here in this world, I have

very little. Once those few have died, I will only have the strength to carry their souls back to the afterlife. There is nothing I can do to save them, and yes, my grief will be profound."

"I was devastated to lose my village. I could never imagine how it feels to lose my entire world," Freyne said, his heart breaking for the desperate people below them.

Am turned and faced Freyne, their head bowed.

"My beloved son. You must know that I did try to save your village. Please understand, there was an anomaly which prevented me from knowing what was happening until it was too late." They paused and wiped an invisible tear. *"It was I who sent those murderers insane and forced them to jump from the cliffs to their death. I was enraged, and rarely do I lose myself to my emotions. Your village was never meant to fall and it spawned many problems not only for me, but for all of Ayrillis."*

Another explosion erupted in the middle of the battlefield, making Freyne jump. Something large and metal glided overhead like a bird, only its wings didn't move. Freyne watched as the armies on both sides retreated and regrouped.

"It was I who sent you into the forest," they continued. *"It was all I could do to protect you and save your life. Without the safety of the village, I had to do something to shield you until it was time. It was the only way I could teach you the highest realm without your grief taking hold and sending you mad. I am so, so sorry, my son."*

Am's words hit Freyne hard, and he stared across the battle as he tried to process what he'd just heard. His eyes brimmed with tears, not only for the loss of his family, but for the love and protection of his god who so clearly cared for him.

Another explosion lit up the sky as the flying metal bird was shot down and crashed into the army below it. Freyne's mind baulked at the senseless carnage and death. In the distance, beyond the great battle, a bright blue flash lit up the sky, and something exploded with even more force than the mightiest volcano. Freyne gasped and shielded his eyes, and when he looked back, he spotted a blue beam of light shooting into the sky from something that was on fire. A few seconds after, a wave of energy knocked him backwards into the snow, followed by a deafening boom.

"It is time. Go back to your Nikolai and get some rest. I love you, my son."

Freyne felt his body jolt and jerked himself awake, the vivid dream still fresh in his mind. His ears were ringing and he could feel his hands shaking. A hint of bile was still on his tongue, and for a moment he thought he was still on the hill with Am. He glanced around frantically, confused, until he realised Nika was sleeping peacefully in his arms. He was safe.

A different warmth came over him, one which could only mean that Am's visit was not just a dream. His fear and confusion settled and dissipated, leaving only Am's calming presence and reassurance. Why they decided to show him such a terrifying scene, though, he didn't know or understand. The only comfort for Freyne was the feeling of closure for the loss of his village and his people.

Seven hundred years of my life, gone, just because my home wasn't supposed to be destroyed. What would have come of me if it hadn't? Would I still have met Nika? Freyne cuddled into him and closed his eyes. *This hurts my head. I'll write it down in my journal tomorrow and come back to it when I'm ready.*

"Wake up, you two!" Ur'Shad's bellow jolted Nika from his sleep. "Breakfast is ready!"

"We'll be out there soon!" Nika barked, shaken from his rude awakening.

Freyne grumbled and rolled over, his eyes scrunched into a frown. Nika yawned and sat up, then stretched his aching back. Freyne grimaced, then with a sigh, he too pushed himself up. His eyes looked weary with dark patches underneath.

"You look like you haven't slept," Nika said, concerned. "Are you alright?"

"I had a bad night."

"What happened?"

"Nothing, boo. Just a bad dream. I'm frozen and could really do with a nice strong tea."

"I'll go and make you one."

Nika leant over and kissed him on the cheek, then quickly dressed and crawled out of the tent. The sky was a miserable grey, reflected by the freshly fallen snow, and the wind was bitterly cold. He pulled his cloak tighter around him and hurried across to the fire where he warmed himself, his breath visible in the air.

"Nice of you to join us." Chardi grinned. "Ur'Shad was about to eat your breakfast."

"Oi! No I wasn't."

Chardi laughed and slapped him on the shoulder. Nika ignored them and busied himself with making a stronger pot of tea. He too was frozen and sick of riding through the mountains, and would kill for a real coffee.

Freyne was quiet when he joined them at the fire and sat staring at a page in his journal while he sipped his tea. Nika could sense his frustration and confusion and fought to keep his curiosity to himself. After a while, Freyne sighed and slammed the book closed.

"What's wrong?" Nika asked.

"This just doesn't make sense! Have a look at this."

He reopened his journal and handed it to Nika. His translation was beautifully penned, unlike Nika's rough scribbles whenever he had to write something down.

A battle will rage, so close to the gods.
Stabbing, bleeding, death to the squads.

New friendships are forged, one of the (food?),
And one almost lost, an unfortunate shove.

A sacred hermit will (give you?) love
Bring him along the path(?)

"That third passage," Freyne said, pointing. *"No matter how many times I try and translate it, it just doesn't seem to work or fit. The words seem to change and dance around every time I do it. It's so frustrating."*

"That entire thing looks confusing to me," Nika admitted. "I'm sorry. I'm not much help."

"It's ok, boo. I think I'll just move on for a while and come back to it when my mind is fresh."

They'd been riding for a few hours when Nika felt the hairs prick up on the back of his neck. Freyne roused himself and sat up, then whistled to Ur'Shad and Chardi to stop. Nika heard a whisper as Freyne slipped into the realm.

"There's trouble up ahead," he reported, pointing to the north. "It looks like some people need our help. Nika, Iryna, Lana; wait here while we check it out."

"But why?" Iryna asked.

"Bloodshed is no place for a royal princess. Take the pack horse with you."

Nika picked up Arnie and dismounted, his stomach churning with nerves. He took the reins of the pack horse and hurried out of the way with Iryna and Lana.

"Be careful," Nika said silently.

Freyne shot him a wink.

Ur'Shad and Chardi drew their swords and urged their horses forward and out of sight. Nika turned back to the ladies, noticing that Lana had also drawn the dagger she'd taken from the dungeon at Fraal.

"Come on. Let's find a place to hide," Nika said quietly.

Not far from the track, they found a cave hidden behind a boulder that was just big enough to squeeze them and the horse. Nika pulled the firestone from his pocket and willed it to glow softly and emit some warmth.

"We should be safe here," he said, sitting Arnie on a rock next to the firestone. "Wait here. I'll go and keep watch."

He took a step towards the opening and heard a hurried step behind him. Turning, he spotted Lana following with a fierce look on her face.

"What are you doing?" he asked.

"I'm coming too."

Nika eyed her for a moment, then glanced at the princess who looked shaken. He chewed his lip for a moment, unsure of what to do. Lana met his gaze; he could sense her determination and stubbornness and knew there was no way of changing her mind.

"Alright." He nodded. "But don't go looking for trouble. Stay out of sight. That knife is for defence only. Got it?"

A plume of smoke billowed from just over the rise and several screams and shouts rang out. Freyne drew his dagger and glanced at Ur'Shad and Chardi to check that they were ready. They both nodded, their swords drawn. Freyne signalled to attack, and together they kicked their horses and charged over the hill, startling a patrol of militia.

Several bodies littered the clearing and a wagon was engulfed in flames. The soldiers were caught off-guard and froze. Ur'Shad leapt from his saddle and expertly cut down two before the rest sprang into action. Chardi easily lopped off several heads and sent them flying before he too jumped to the ground. The sound of steel on steel echoed around the mountains as they fought in bloody battle.

Freyne sharply reined in his horse, causing her to rear up on her hind legs; he clung on tightly, and as she landed, he threw one of his daggers directly at the face of a soldier who was wrestling with a frantic woman. The soldier screamed as the knife landed between his eyes, and he crumpled to the ground, twitching and convulsing.

Drawing his second dagger from his boot, Freyne wheeled his horse around and surveyed the scene of carnage. Chardi was locked in combat and parried a blow just in time. As he drew back his arm to strike, another soldier bounded closer and ran his sword into Chardi's side, the blade passing through the seam of his chainmail.

Chardi bellowed in pain. Freyne hurled his dagger with all of his strength and landed it in the soldier's neck. The soldier collapsed, pulling the sword free as he fell in a pool of blood. Chardi blocked a blow from another attacker and finished him off, then sank to his knees with his hand on the gash in his side.

Ur'Shad roared and finished off his final opponent, then rushed to his friend's side. Chardi's shaking hand was covered in blood. Freyne tore some fabric from one of the bodies and pressed it to the bloody gash as best he could.

"Press on this firmly," he instructed. "Can you walk?"

"I think so." Chardi winced as Ur'Shad helped him to his feet.

"Take him back down to that clearing we saw, then get Nika and the others," Freyne instructed. "I'll make sure we finished everyone off and check for survivors."

Ur'Shad nodded and half-carried, half-dragged his friend back in the direction of Nika. Freyne turned and surveyed the gruesome sight, then picked his way through the carnage, retrieving his daggers and looking for survivors. He saw a slight movement out of the corner of his eye and spun around, expecting another fight.

"Stay your hand!" a voice called.

"Show yourself!" Freyne shouted back.

An older woman emerged from behind a rock, her hands in the air and a steely look on her face. Her grey hair was pinned in a tight bun, and she wore a bloody white dress and apron. Freyne lowered his weapon and stood up straight. The woman strode towards him seemingly unperturbed by the death around them.

"Are there any other survivors?" he asked.

She shook her head.

"No. But three soldiers took off that way." She pointed back in the direction where Nika and the others were waiting.

"They've probably already been dealt with. Are you a healer?"

"Well, obviously."

"Our friend has been injured. Can you help us?"

"I can. What do you plan to do with all these bodies, though? They'll stink up the mountain and attract the wolves if you leave them."

"We'll take care of them after you help our friend. Please, we need to hurry."

Nika watched as a lone soldier sprinted along the mountain track that was just a few feet from his hiding place, looking over his shoulder in apparent fright as he ran. Following close behind were two more of the militia, their swords drawn.

"There he is! Get him!" one of them shouted, pointing.

Nika snatched Lana's dagger and edged closer to the road, being careful to stay hidden. As they drew closer, he sprang from his hiding place and buried his blade into the armpit of the nearest soldier. The man screamed and tripped over his own feet before tumbling along the rocky ground. Still running, the other soldier fell over his friend's body and dropped his sword.

He swore loudly and scrambled to his feet, drawing a small knife. His eyes darted wildly around, then settled on Nika, full of hatred.

Nika crouched low with his arms out wide, eyeing his opponent with a steely glare. The soldier feinted with his blade, but Nika didn't fall for it. He could sense his fury mixed with desperation. Nika stalked around the soldier, his body tensed like a tightly wound coil ready to snap. For a moment he was back in a dingy bar, facing a drunken lout who was wielding a broken glass bottle.

The soldier lunged. Nika twisted his body to the side and caught the soldier's arm with both of his hands. The man lost his balance and stumbled forwards, pulling Nika with him. The knife clattered to the ground as Nika and his opponent scrambled to their feet.

Nika clenched his fists and flashed him a wicked grin, the rush of the fight filling him with renewed prowess. The soldier no longer looked sure of himself, and lunged blindly with his fists flailing. Nika dodged him easily and landed his left fist in the soldier's jaw, loosening several teeth. The soldier reeled from the blow and paused to steady himself, then spat a glob of blood on the ground.

"Death to you and your family!" he bellowed and charged.

Nika dodged and landed his right fist in the soldier's face, this time shattering his nose. Blood spurted from his face and the soldier staggered back, momentarily dazed. For a moment Nika thought he was going to try again, but instead he turned and fled. Just as Nika was about to chase him, the first soldier who had bolted past earlier leapt from behind a rock and swung his sword at the running soldier's neck. His head flew through the air and fell to the ground with a sickening splat while the rest of his body tumbled forward and collapsed in a heap.

"Please, don't kill me!" the remaining soldier threw down his sword and held up his hands. "I'm not like them. Please, you've got to believe me!"

Nika tensed and eyed him up and down.

"Why should I believe you?" he hissed.

"I'm unarmed. You can check if you like." The man parted his legs and kept his hands in the air.

Nika patted him down cautiously. There were no weapons.

"Lana," he called, pinning the man's arms behind his back. "Bring me some rope, quick."

Lana scrambled back to the cave and returned with a length of rope. Nika started to tie his captive's hands when he spotted Ur'Shad half-dragging Chardi down the hill who was covered in blood.

"Help us!" Ur'Shad yelled.

"Just go!" Nika snapped, shoving the man away.

Ur'Shad lowered Chardi to the ground. He was pale and his skin was clammy. The cloth that was pressed into the hole in his chainmail was soaked in blood. Lana gasped and fell to her knees beside him, tears running down her cheeks.

"IRYNA!" Ur'Shad bellowed at the top of his lungs.

The princess hurried from the cave leading the pack horse. When she spotted Chardi, her bottom lip started to tremble. At the top of the hill, Freyne and an older woman were running towards them.

"Out of the way, all of you," the woman barked.

Ur'Shad pulled Iryna away and held her as the woman knelt and regarded the wound. Nika reached out and petted Lana on the shoulder, unsure what to do.

"His armour needs to come off. Does anyone have anything we can use to cut it?"

"It's chain mail. Nothing can cut it," Ur'Shad growled.

"Well clearly a sword already cut through it. It's the only way I can save your friend."

"I-I can help."

All eyes turned to the lone soldier. Instead of leaving as Nika had ordered, he'd inched forward and was watching them with curiosity etched on his face. Ur'Shad shoved Iryna behind him and drew his sword.

"I ought to kill you right now," he yelled. "If not for being one of the scum who hurt my friend, but for the audacity of intruding. How dare you!"

"He's a deserter." The woman laughed. "If you want to kill someone who might be able to help you, then go ahead. While you're at it, you may as well kill me too."

Ur'Shad scowled but didn't lower his sword.

"Do what you must. But try anything funny and I'll kill you."

The soldier reached up and undid the buckles on his chest plate, then tossed it on the ground. He knelt down and inspected the chainmail.

"Do you have any tools?" he asked the woman.

She rummaged around in her bag, then held out a number of gruesome implements. He gingerly selected one and began pulling apart the rings one by one. Soon he had a hole wide enough to allow her to start treating Chardi's wound.

"Standing around and watching isn't going to help our situation," Freyne said quietly to Nika. "We may as well set up camp and get a fire going. We're going to have to go back and take care of the bodies up on the hill, too."

Nika and Freyne set up camp while Chardi's wound was treated and wrapped in a swath of bandages. Under the woman's strict instructions, they built a litter and carried Chardi into one of the tents.

"I think some introductions are in order," Ur'Shad said finally, a dark look on his face.

"I'll start. My name's Gaitan. I never wanted to be in the militia, but I was forced into service without a choice."

"So why were you attacking innocent civilians?" he shouted.

"*I* wasn't. I wanted no part of it."

"Either you start talking or I'll kill you," Ur'Shad growled.

"Fine. My platoon was dispatched from the Fraal garrison a few weeks ago and stationed at Grima. I kept to myself, but the rest of the platoon were bored. Early this morning, we stopped a group of people to search them for some fugitives we're after, but it wasn't them. A few of the guys decided to rough them up and have some fun. I objected and they threatened to kill me if I tried to stop them.

"The people escaped and fled into the mountains. We chased them for a few hours and finally caught up to them. The other guys went crazy and started killing them all. I tried to intervene and stop them, but then they turned on me. That's when you showed up."

"That's at least true," the woman said. "I'm Priye, a healer from Mar'Am. Our group travels between the poorer villages and aids the sick and poor. Gaitan did try to help us."

Freyne looked at Gaitan with a raised eyebrow.

241

"Tell me. What is the description of the fugitives?"

"A woman with blonde hair, a woman with black hair, two big guys, and two other guys," Gaitan said with a shrug.

Lana removed her soft fleece cap and shook out her hair, then nudged Iryna to do the same.

"You mean us?" Lana asked.

Gaitan's eyes widened as he glanced around the circle.

"It's you!" he gasped.

"So? What are you going to do about it?" Ur'Shad demanded, cracking his knuckles.

"You saved my life, so of course I'm not going to try and turn you in," he said quickly. "I can't go back to the garrison, either, or I'll be flogged to within an inch of my life. Can I tag along with you?"

"Are you kidding me?" Ur'Shad laughed incredulously.

"I can help you get through any militia checkpoints we encounter. And I can fight."

"Not very well." Ur'Shad snarled.

"That's not all. Before I was forced into the militia, I was an artisan. I can craft anything," Gaitan added with desperation in his voice. "I just need help to get away from Fraal and Grima, then I'll happily go on my way."

"Having a skilled artisan might be useful," Freyne mused. "Besides, if we do get hounded by more militia, it will be handy to have someone with us who knows their ways."

"Where are you going?" Priye asked.

"Riz'Hra," Iryna said, tossing her hair.

"May I ride with you also? It is not safe for a woman to travel alone. I'll need to go to the hospital at Rarn to report this. I can help take care of your friend along the way, too."

"I don't mind either way." Nika shrugged.

Ur'Shad looked grumpy, but nodded.

"Okay, next issue. There are roughly twenty bodies up there. We can't bury them, so we'll have to burn them." Freyne looked at Priye. "Did your companions worship a god?"

"I think Borgen worshipped Am, but most of us follow science."

"Very well. We'll go and take care of things." Freyne stood up and motioned to Ur'Shad, Gaitan, and Nika to follow him.

"I'll come too. I need to retrieve my medical supplies."

"I hardly think a lady should see such gore." Ur'Shad said.

Priye looked him in the eyes in a no-nonsense way.

"I have seen more death than all of you put together. There is nothing on that hill that will shock me," she said firmly. "I've delivered so many babies that even blood doesn't bother me any more. So don't give me that nonsense."

"Sheesh. Fine." Ur'Shad sighed.

Gaitan led the way up the hill with Ur'Shad close behind, watching his every move. Nika slipped his hand into Freyne's, earning a kiss on his forehead. As they reached the top of the hill, though, Nika's stomach turned. He was unprepared for the carnage waiting for them. Rigor mortis had already started to set in, and Nika felt sick to his stomach. He'd never seen so much death before. Priye walked through the bodies as though she was walking down a garden path, unperturbed by the gore around them. She rounded up the two horses which hadn't bolted and started rummaging around in the packs.

"Let's make two pyres," Freyne said. "One for Priye's friends, and one for the scourge. Also, search the bodies for any money and valuables. We may need it along the way."

It took them a few hours to gather enough sticks and wood for the two pyres. Once they were stacked high enough, Nika helped to place the bodies on the piles. The stench was palpable as the sun shone and melted the snow around them.

Nika wiped the sweat from his forehead, then stood back to inspect the pyres.

"Is that everything?" he asked.

"Let's hold off lighting them until we leave," Freyne suggested. "We don't want to be smelling burning bodies all night, or to announce that we're here."

"What now, then?" Gaitan asked.

"We're going to heat some water and have a wash, for starters," Freyne said. "We smell like death."

They walked back to the camp in silence. Nika's body was aching and he was tired. To his relief, Chardi was awake when they returned.

"Well there's an ugly sight," he said weakly to Ur'Shad.

"Stop looking in the mirror, then." Ur'Shad retorted. "How are you feeling?"

"Wonderful," Chardi said sarcastically.

Iryna wrinkled her nose.

"You stink," she complained.

"I know. We're going to bathe shortly," Freyne said.

Nika shook the waterskins but they were empty.

"I'll go and fill these up and get the water on," he called.

"Alright. I'll go and hunt, then. After the day we've had, we all need a good hearty meal. I'll be back soon."

The sun was setting by the time Freyne returned to camp with a wild goat. Nika moved quickly to help him thread it on the spit and place it over the fire, just as Gaitan returned from his wash wearing some of Nika's spare clothes.

"I feel like a new person," he said, joining them by the fire. "Whoever's next will need more hot water."

Freyne wordlessly lifted a pot of hot water from the fire. Nika scooped up a folded pile of towels and clean clothes and followed him to the cave. It was bitterly cold away from the fire, but the cave offered ample protection from the wind. Nika sat the towels and clean clothes next to the firestone and stripped off his putrid ones. Freyne undressed and they washed their bodies in silence. Nika could tell that Freyne was as tired as he was.

"You smell much better now," Freyne said once they were done. He leant over and kissed Nika on his forehead.

"I'd never smelt death before today," Nika said, shuddering as the gruesome scene flashed before his eyes.

"It's never pleasant," Freyne said. "Thanks for your help, boo. I know it's something you weren't exposed to in your world."

Nika shrugged.

"It had to be done. Bodies don't move themselves."

Freyne chuckled and reached for a towel. They dried off and dressed, then washed their clothes in what was left of the hot water. Nika could smell their dinner wafting through the cave and his belly rumbled with hunger.

Gaitan was sitting by himself when they returned to the fire. Nika sat purposefully next to the young man as Freyne checked on dinner.

"So, um, thanks for not killing me today," Gaitan said.

"There's always tomorrow," Nika said with a shrug.

"Hey," Gaitan objected. "That's not fair."

Nika grinned and put out his hand. Gaitan stared at it for a moment, then shook it.

"What made you join that awful army?" Nika asked.

"I may as well tell you the full story. I grew up in a small village, and when I became of age, I started learning the artisan trade. Everything was fine until my master, um, caught me with his daughter. I was forced out of my village, and if I ever go back, they'll kill me."

"Where are you from?" Freyne asked, sitting on his other side.

"A small village near H'Rak," Gaitan replied. "When I left, I travelled all the way to Riz'Hra, trying to find a master craftsman to complete my training. None would take me in, so I applied to join the King's Army.

"My application was denied. I had no idea where to go from there, so I made my way down to Fraal. I had no gold, so I thought I'd try and stow away on a ship and try my luck in Kia-Mor. Instead, I ran into a patrol and the militia threatened to arrest me for being vagrant. They gave me the option to either enlist or rot in their dungeon. Of course I opted to enlist."

"Couldn't you just leave?" Nika asked.

"The only way to leave is in a corpse-carrier." He snorted and shook his head. "If they find out that I've deserted, they'll do worse than kill me."

"They already tried the dungeon option with us," Freyne said. "They didn't get very far."

Gaitan looked at Freyne, then Nika, and back to Freyne.

"Are you the ones who broke out of the garrison dungeon?" he asked in disbelief.

Freyne nodded with a slight grin.

"Wow. So many soldiers were flogged as punishment for letting you escape," Gaitan said incredulously. "I was lucky. I was on patrol elsewhere so I didn't get the whip."

"How far out are they patrolling for us?" Freyne asked.

"All the way to the River Rarn, along that border, and as far down as H'Rak. They know better than to cross the border into Kaiton's territory. He would see it as an invasion and wipe them out for good."

Freyne scratched his cheek.

"Surely a princess isn't worth all of that effort," he mused.

"At first, the orders were just to capture the princess. They changed not long ago," Gaitan replied.

"What do you mean?" Nika asked.

"After you escaped, she was no longer the priority. The focus is now on the man who helped the princess and other prisoners escape. He's wanted on charges of high treason, murder, unauthorised mancery, destruction of the Authority's property, and sodomy." Gaitan pointed at Ur'Shad. "Was it that big guy over there?"

Nika started laughing and Freyne joined in. Gaitan looked taken aback and frowned.

"That would be me." Nika snorted. "And Freyne, if you want to count the sodomy charge."

"So…you two?" Gaitan glanced from Nika to Freyne, then blushed. "Oh. *Oh!* Right!"

17

The alpine winds howled through the peaks and tore at the tents, threatening to rip them from their mores and hurl them over the edge of the mountain. Unable to sleep, Nika wrapped himself in his cloak and a blanket and went outside. It was still dark with a hint of a pink glow on the horizon. The fire had been doused overnight, leaving the campsite cold and unwelcoming. He fetched some dry wood from the pile and used the realm to light a fire, then sat and stared gloomily into the flames.

"You're up early."

Nika startled and spotted Lana approaching the fire.

"I couldn't sleep." He shrugged.

"Me either. It's too windy and Chardi was in pain."

Lana's eyes were sunken and tinged with red, accompanied by dark shadows. He could sense her worry and sadness, along with something else that surprised him.

"You love him, don't you?" he blurted without thinking.

"What?" Lana's head whipped around. "How could you possibly know that? Did Iryna tell you? She'd better not!"

"No, no she didn't," Nika said quickly. "I'm sorry. I just noticed how much you seem to care about him and kind of made an assumption."

Lana sighed and looked down at her feet.

"I've always cared deeply for him, but he's just a really good friend, nothing more."

"Why, though? Does he not feel that way about you?"

"I really don't know."

"But what if he falls for someone else?" Nika asked.

"Honestly, the thought of that happening tears me up inside. I don't think I could handle it."

"You really need to talk to him and see if he feels the same."

"But what if he doesn't?" Lana tugged on her long braid.

"At least you'll know and be able to move on with things."

Nika heard a rustle and turned to see Priye emerging from Chardi's tent. She seemed unpurturbed by the cold.

"How is he?" Lana asked.

"He was moaning a lot," Priye said.

"Oh, no!"

"What? That's a good thing. If he's moaning it means he's alive." She moved to warm herself by the fire.

"Is-is he going to be alright?"

"He's lost a lot of blood, but he should be okay. Our main concern now is internal bleeding and infection. We won't be able to move him for a day or two or we risk doing more harm."

"Thank you," Lana said, her eyes misty.

"Don't worry. I'm sure your lover will be fine."

Lana shot her a look then glanced back at Nika.

"N-no. We're just friends."

"If you say so, dear."

Priye's face twisted into her usual smirk and she headed back to Chardi's tent. Lana threw her hands up in exasperation.

"Fine! I'll talk to him when he gets better and is up for it. I'm going to go and sit with him."

Nika shrugged and made himself some strong tea, then settled back down and watched the sun slowly rise. As it peeked above the horizon and spread pink ripples through the sky, the winds became calmer and a quiet tranquillity spread throughout the mountains.

One by one, his friends joined him by the fire, speaking in hushed tones until everyone was up. To Nika's surprise, Ur'Shad sat next to Gaitan and started chatting to him, all signs of his former hostility gone.

"Yesterday, you said that you rode up here from Grima," he was saying. "How long would it take for us to ride down there to replenish our food and supplies?"

"Grima's only around an hour's ride from here," Gaitan said.

"It's not that far at all. The only reason it took us so long the other day is because…er, we were chasing Priye's people."

"You're going to need some more clothes, and we need to ask around to find out what's going on with the militia," Ur'Shad continued. "Can you show us the way?"

"Sure." Gaitan nodded. "My unit were the only ones who were dispatched to Grima so it should be clear."

"We need to know what could be up ahead, too. For all we know, Grima could have been reinforced by now. We don't want to blunder into a mess."

"I don't suppose you could try and get us some eggs while you're there?" Nika asked hopefully.

"That's a good idea." Iryna nodded. "I'm so sick of porridge."

"Me too." He scooped up some runny oats and let them dribble from his spoon.

"Are you two coming with us?" Ur'Shad asked.

Nika looked at Freyne, then shook his head.

"No. I need a break from riding. I'll stay here and cut some more wood for the fire, fill the waterskins, and whatever else needs doing."

"I'll stay as well. I have some work to do," Freyne said.

"Suit yourselves."

Once Ur'Shad, Iryna, and Gaitan left for Grima, Freyne pulled out his journal and sat by the fire, frowning at one of the pages. Knowing how important it was for him to finish, Nika let him be and busied himself with gathering and chopping wood. Although he was pleased to have a break from the saddle, he was still feeling edgy and a need to keep moving. He refilled the water skins from the stream and heated some for a wash and shave, and still he felt restless.

"I'm bored," he said, stretching. "I might go for a walk and see what's up over that rise."

Freyne stood up and pulled Nika into a tight hug, then planted a long lingering kiss on his lips. Nika grew warm and for a moment he was tempted to drag Freyne with him for some alone time. To his disappointment, though, Freyne pulled back and released his grip.

"I'll see you when you get back. Be careful, boo." He brushed Nika's hair from his eyes and shot him a smile.

Nika placed the back of his hand on Freyne's cheek for a moment, then set off for his walk. The sky was a dark and threatening grey and promised more snow or rain during the day. Nika pulled up his hood and retracted his hands inside the sleeves of his cloak. He followed the stream until he came to a small waterfall. Curious, Nika climbed the edge of the embankment to see where the water was coming from.

Before him stretched a still lake nestled within a deep crater. The water was crystal clear with patches of ice forming here and there along the bank. Nika could see the pebbles on the bottom of the shallower areas and tiny fish darting about. He sat on a fallen log and took in the beauty surrounding him. The tips of the peaks around the lake were all blanketed in snow, but here and there were patches of green, as though the grass itself was defying winter's cold breath.

Nika sat there for some time, enjoying the calm and tranquillity. It wasn't until he spotted a cabin nestled in some trees on the far side of the lake that he felt it. The hairs on his neck and arms stood on end, the same sense of danger he'd first felt above Ner'Am. He startled and instinctively slipped back down the embankment, where he crouched behind a large rock.

Everything went eerily quiet; not even the birds chirped. *Something doesn't feel right. Fuck this, I'm going back to camp.* As he stood, he felt that same prickling feeling that he'd felt in the garrison office in Fraal. A strong mind began drawing power from the realm, preparing to attack. Nika gasped and realised he'd wandered beyond the range of Freyne's protective shield and quickly summoned one for himself. He could feel the hostile mancer probing around, looking for him, until it finally retreated back across the lake. Nika's heart was racing; once he calmed himself, he stepped out of his body and scanned the lake.

A deep red aura was standing by the hut, so incensed that Nika could feel their anger from where he stood. Ever so carefully, he slipped back into his body, strengthened his shield, and crept slowly back down the hill. As soon as he was sure he was out of earshot, he ran as fast as he could through the mushy snow and headed back to camp.

Freyne watched Nika walk away, then sighed and turned back towards the fire. He wished he could go too, but he needed to take advantage of the break in travel and get as much of the prophecy translated as possible. Out of the corner of his eye, he spotted Priye watching him, her mouth twisted into a grin.

"They're right. You two *are* a cute couple," she said.

Freyne raised an eyebrow and returned her gaze.

"They?" he asked. "I assume you're referring to a certain princess and her lady?"

Priye laughed and walked around the fire to his side.

"Nobles love to gossip," she said. "I'm too old for that nonsense. What are you doing?"

"I'm just transcribing some old poetry," Freyne fibbed.

"Chardi's sitting up, so he should be able to ride tomorrow."

"Good. We need to get out of these mountains before we get snowed in." Freyne nodded.

"I have a good remedy for that."

Priye pulled a small flask from her pocket and offered it to him.

"No, thank you," Freyne said politely, shaking his head.

"Suit yourself." She smirked and took a swig from the flask. "Enjoy your poetry."

Priye returned to the tent with Lana and Chardi and Freyne sighed again. *Enough distractions. Now focus.* He carefully unrolled the scroll and started piecing together more snippets of prophecy, sipping at his tea and re-reading what he'd already translated.

> *A battle will rage, so close to the gods.*
> *Stabbing, bleeding, death to the squads.*
>
> *New friendships forged, one of the blood,*
> *And one almost lost, an unfortunate shove.*
>
> *A hermit so vile, knows only his hatred,*
> *Culls all in his path, nothing is sacred.*
>
> *Don't go! Go back! Be warned he's destructive!*
> *There's nothing that way that isn't obstructive!*
>
> *Go after your love and bring him back safe!*
> *There's nothing but madness and death in that place!*

Freyne blinked his eyes and read the passage again; words which moments before made no sense at all were suddenly as clear as day. Looking up in the direction Nika had gone, he felt a wave of dread wash over him. He quickly scanned the realm for Nika's aura but he was nowhere to be seen. Freyne pocketed his journal and placed the scroll back in the wax box, then set out to find him. He followed the stream past the pyres and followed Nika's muddy footprints. Rounding a bend, he gasped as he almost collided with Nika who was running towards him. Nika skidded to a stop and Freyne caught him.

"Are you okay?" he demanded.

Nika pulled away and bent over, panting.

"I followed the stream over that way and found a lake," he said between gasping breaths. "There's a strong mancer up there who definitely isn't friendly."

"Did he see you?"

"Yeah." Nika nodded. "I shielded just in time. We'd better make sure we keep ours up and don't go that way."

Freyne pulled Nika into his arms and held him tight.

"Are you alright?" Nika asked. "You're shaking."

"I am now. You had me worried. Look at this."

He reached into his pocket and extracted his journal, then read the passage out loud. Nika's eyes widened.

"Does that first part refer to Chardi or Gaitan?" he asked.

"Gaitan. Wait…by the gods, he must be the blood descendant! *New friendships forged, one of the blood.* We've found him!" Freyne wanted to jump for joy.

"That's everything we need then, isn't it?"

"I think so. We just have to convince him to stay with us and not leave when we get to Rarn." Freyne glanced around furtively then grinned. "I think I've earned a little break. There's only one more thing I need."

"Oh? What else?"

Freyne pulled him closer and kissed him suggestively, nibbling his lip and trailing his fingers along Nika's neck. Nika ran his fingers down Freyne's chest and gently rubbed him through his trousers, teasing him awake. He longed to be intimate again, just he and Nika entwined in their sheets, not having to worry about being too loud or being discovered.

Nika pulled him off balance and fell backwards onto a clump snow. Freyne landed on top of him and pinned Nika's hands above his head. He could feel Nika's body quivering beneath him and leant down, kissing him hungrily despite the cold from the snow melting beneath them.

The clatter of horses' hooves nearby made them both gasp and scramble to their feet. Freyne was hot and flustered and quickly helped to brush the snow from Nika's back.

"How did they get back here so soon?" Freyne grumbled.

Nika swore and looked as frustrated as Freyne felt.

"I guess we'll have to go for another walk a bit later if it doesn't get any colder." Nika sighed. "The others are going to pay for interrupting us. Follow me."

Iryna was riding alone on the pack horse, following Ur'Shad and Gaitan and not paying attention to where they were going. There was no need; they were almost back at camp, and Ur'Shad was leading the way. Nothing would or could happen to them.

Out of nowhere, something hit Ur'Shad in the face. He cursed and reined in sharply, looking confused. Iryna drew herself up and glanced around, but failed to spot any danger. Gaitan drew his sword with a steely hiss, ready to fight.

"What was—" he started, when something hit him in the back of his head.

Ur'Shad dismounted and drew his sword, while Gaitan leapt from his horse and scrambled behind a rock. Iryna sat where she was, amused, when a ball of snow exploded in Gaitan's face. Raucous laughter drifted from behind a rock. Nika's head popped up and he hurled another ball of snow at Gaitan, but missed.

"Hey! I saw that!"

Gaitan sheathed his sword and gathered some muddy snow into a ball, looking around wildly for a target. Iryna watched on as the men became immersed in their snowy battle, forgetting that she even existed. They were so focused on their pretend war that no one noticed her dismount to round up the horses. Nika leapt out from behind his rock and planted another snowball in Gaitan's face, then ran off up the track, laughing. Ur'Shad chased him, only to be ambushed by Freyne.

"Alright, alright, that's enough," Iryna called, riding into the middle of the battlefield.

She drew alongside Nika and scowled at him. Nika's grin left his face and for a moment he looked disappointed. With perfect aim, Iryna smashed a snowball into his face.

"Who's that and where's Iryna?" Ur'Shad asked.

Iryna laughed and rode off, leaving them stranded in the snow. By the time the soggy men trudged back to camp, she and Lana had already finished cooking lunch.

"Looking a bit wet there, boys," she sniggered.

"Gee, I wonder why," Ur'Shad said.

He picked her up and spun her around and around so fast that she became dizzy and nauseous.

"Stop!" she squealed.

Ur'Shad lowered her to the ground but kept his arms around her. Iryna swayed for a moment until the world settled, then smiled and cuddled into him for warmth.

"Where did you go in such a hurry?" Priye asked Freyne.

"Oh, I thought I heard something up on the hill."

Iryna frowned and pursed her lips. She knew Freyne well enough to know when he was telling a fib.

"Did you find anything, or was it just us?" Ur'Shad asked.

"There's a crazy hermit further up on the hill," Nika said, pointing. "We can't go that way."

"Why not? Surely he won't try and attack a group of us?" Priye asked. "Besides. He out-numbered."

"He's a mancer," Nika replied. "He could easily take us all."

"Oh." Priye frowned. "Come to think of it, I've tried to treat a few people for insanity who supposedly had a run in with a mancer a few years ago. It's never pretty."

"Can they be cured?" Nika asked.

Priye shook her head.

"All we can do is admit them to the asylum and make them comfortable. The mind is fragile. I've never seen anyone recover from this."

Iryna shuddered at the thought and tightened her grip around Ur'Shad.

"We saw a path down lower that leads through the foothills," Gaitan said. "Maybe we could go that way?"

"There's no snow down that low either," Iryna said quickly.

"We do need to hurry and get below the snowline," Freyne said, scratching his cheek. "We've been lucky the snow's held off for this long. The first heavy snow is due to fall any day now and it will be too dangerous if we get caught in a blizzard. We'll also need to be careful. Gaitan's militia will still be searching for us. Nika and I will take watch tonight in case that mancer decides to try anything."

Iryna swallowed, suddenly nervous. Ur'Shad could protect her from anything in the world except for magic and unpredictable wild weather. For the first time since sneaking away from Al'Obrel, she realised just how dangerous their mission really was. *I need to be more careful,* she thought to herself. *I don't think I could ever live with myself should any of these people – my friends – get harmed because of me. A blizzard won't miss me just because I have royal blood. By the gods, I'd better pull my head in.*

Nika sat by the fire, watching the sunrise paint beautiful yellow, orange, and red hues through the sky. The sun peeked above the horizon, slowly bathing the campsite in light. Although it he was tired from being on watch for half of the night, seeing the sun rise for the second morning in a row was reinvigorating. Yawning, he set a pan on the fire and began making breakfast. He cut some thin slices of ham and fried them, hoping it would resemble the bacon from his world, and fried up some duck eggs to go with it. His belly rumbled as the smells reached his nose. Something brushed against his leg, and when he looked down he spotted Arnie-Kyn.

"Morning," Nika greeted him.

"Well obviously," Arnie said.

Nika scratched the cat's ears, suppressing his grin. Even after all the weeks they'd been travelling together, Arnie still did not comprehend human greetings.

"Are you going to hunt before we leave?" he asked.

"It's too cold to hunt. One shall wait until we're out of the snow."

"Try some ham. Maybe you will like it."

He reached down and offered him a small piece. Arnie sniffed it, then took the ham and chewed noisily.

"It's horrible, but better than going hungry," Arnie said.

Nika cut some more ham and sat it on the ground for the cat. As he yawned and stretched, he spotted Gaitan leave his tent and dash away from camp to relieve himself. Nika shrugged and prepared a fresh pot of tea.

"Morning," Gaitan said once he returned, washing his hands. "Breakfast smells so good. I'm starved."

"Yeah," Nika said with a grin. "We're all so sick of porridge so I thought I'd cook up a treat before we head off."

"Anything is better than what we had in the militia. The food was horrible, even at the garrison."

"At least you don't have to go back there," Nika pointed out. "What will you do when we get to Rarn?"

"I really want to get back into my trade. I miss working with my hands and making things."

"What did you say your trade was again?" Nika asked.

"Artisan. I can craft nearly anything, but jewellery is my specialty." Gaitan narrowed his eyes and shot Nika a sly look. "I also learnt to locksmith, so I can pick any lock no matter how complex it is. It's saved my life once or twice."

"That's a handy skill to have."

"It sure is. What's your trade?"

"I was a mechanic," Nika replied, choosing his words carefully. "I worked in maintenance and fixed machines when they broke down."

"Oh, like steam engines?"

"Similar," Nika replied. "Breakfast is almost ready. Would you mind waking the others?"

One by one, the sleepy companions joined Nika around the fire. Their eyes lit up as he handed everyone a plate of buttery toasted bread, eggs, and ham. With the help of Priye and Lana, even Chardi managed to hobble from his tent and join them. Freyne was the last to wake and Nika could tell that he was tired. He handed him his breakfast and felt Freyne's mind join with his.

"Hello, you," he said silently. *"Did you get much sleep?"*

"Not really," Freyne replied. *"It was too cold without you. Arnie only warms so much. How was your watch?"*

"I felt some movement in the realm about an hour ago, but nothing to worry about."

"Good. We have enough people chasing us for the time being."

After breakfast, everyone pitched in to break camp, and finally it was time to leave. Under stern guidance from Priye, Ur'Shad helped Chardi mount his horse. Nika could see that he was still in pain and felt bad for him.

"Let's go and light those pyres and get out of here," Freyne called. "The smoke is likely to attract attention that we don't want to be the centre of."

Once they were lit, Nika followed Gaitan down the mountain path and into the foothills. The remaining patches of snow had turned into slush on the ground, making the path slippery and muddy. The sky was dark and grey, threatening them with more rain or snow.

Nika was glad to be leaving the mountains. As they descended below the snowline, the sky opened up and it started to rain. He pulled up his hood and soon fell into a light doze, his head on Freyne's back and arms around his waist. His energy was already depleted from his watch the night before, and he craved a decent sleep.

After a few hours of riding he was woken by a powerful surge from within the realm. Freyne reined the horse in sharply and Nika felt their minds join. Instinctively, he followed Freyne into the middle realm.

"What was that?" Nika asked, still groggy from sleep.

"I'm not sure. Let's go and check it out."

Nika projected himself and took Freyne's spectral hand. Together they flew back along the path and up the mountainside they'd traversed just hours ago. The pyres were still burning despite the heavy rain.

Just past the pyres, a squad of around twenty militia stood rooted to the spot, a look of terror on their faces. There was another surge from the realm, and the men began to scream, tearing at their faces with their fingernails. Blood started to drip from their eyes and ears, and they fell to the ground in agony, still screaming and clawing at themselves. The horses bolted, trampling some of the soldiers underfoot. Nika watched, horrified, as some of the struggling soldiers began ripping the skin from their own cheeks, while others pulled out their hair in thick clumps.

The realm shimmered and the incensed hermit's projection appeared nearby, watching his victims writhe about in agony with a cruel grin on his face. The mancer turned slowly and his spectral eyes bore into Nika's, and for a second he felt like his remaining strength was being drained from his body. In one swift movement, the hermit summoned a ball of energy and hurled it at them. Nika tensed, caught off-guard, but Freyne deflected it just in time and formed a shield around them. The energy sizzled and made Nika's hair stand on end.

Freyne tugged urgently at his hand. Nika shook his head and allowed Freyne to pull him back down the mountain to their horse. As soon as he left the realm, a strong wave of nausea washed over him. Nika dismounted and dashed behind a tree where he was violently ill. He was dizzy and weak, and held onto the tree for support as another wave of nausea shook his body. Freyne landed a comforting hand on his shoulder and passed him a towel.

"Thanks," Nika croaked. "I don't feel so good."

"Drink this," Freyne instructed, handing him a small vial.

Nika did as he was told and downed the liquid in one gulp. He grimaced and handed it back.

"That should help settle the nausea. It's also going to help you sleep so you don't succumb to aftersickness again. We can't afford any more mishaps while that mancer is loose."

At once Nika started to feel woozy. Freyne stooped and picked up Arnie-Kyn, then leapt back into the saddle. Nika clambered up behind him, then clung onto his waist, his belly still churning. Freyne urged the horse forward, and Nika fell into a deep sleep.

"Is everything okay?" Ur'Shad asked when Freyne caught up.

Freyne shifted uncomfortably with Nika's weight pressing against him, then described the carnage back on the mountain. Gaitan's eyes widened with fear.

"This place must be crawling with militia. They'll never give up until they find us. If they do, we're worse than dead."

"Keep your wits about you, all of you," Freyne said. "I can scout out when needed and protect us from any mancer attacks, but it's physically draining. Let's put a few more miles between us and that hermit before we find a place to stop for lunch."

"What's wrong with Nika?" Lana asked.

"I think he has a little aftersickness from the encounter in the mountains, so I gave him something to prevent it. He'll be fine once he sleeps it off."

"Aren't you worried he'll fall off?" She frowned.

"Like I said, he'll be fine. If he moves, I'll catch him."

"Enough talking. Let's take advantage of this rain while we can," Chardi said, wincing as he shifted his weight.

"He's right." Ur'Shad nodded. "Let's keep moving. We'll rest up when we get to a nice warm inn in Rarn."

Freyne spent the next few hours monitoring the realm and ensuring they weren't being followed. He didn't care to admit that the mancer's attack was powerful and hurt, and that he too was feeling a little nauseous from it. To his relief, though, they weren't followed. *I'm too old for this,* he thought ruefully.

It was some time after noon when Ur'Shad led the party into a small grove of trees that offered considerable shelter from the rain. Freyne shook Nika's knee, but he didn't stir.

"I need help to get him down," he called to Ur'Shad.

Ur'Shad nodded and helped lift him down. He rested Nika against a tree, then hurried back to help Chardi dismount. Freyne stretched his aching back and legs, then sat down beside Nika and yawned. Nika stirred briefly, murmuring in his sleep, then settled and fell silent again. Freyne buried his face in his hands and massaged his temples. He, too, felt exhausted, and longed to lie down and sleep.

A gentle hand patted him on his shoulder. He looked up to see Lana peering at him, looking concerned.

"Are you okay?" she asked, handing him his lunch.

"I'm fine. Just tired," Freyne said. "Mancery is very draining. What about you, though. How are you holding up?"

Lana sat down next to him and cast a look over her shoulder at the princess.

"Can I ask you something personal?"

"Of course." Freyne nodded.

"Chardi is my best friend. Yes we share a bed, but our relationship is strictly non-physical. Nika told me that I should tell him that I have feelings for him, but I don't know. He once told me that he wants to get married and to start a family. I absolutely do not want children and it's not something I'm willing to compromise on. I don't know what to do."

"Are you sure—"

"Of course I'm sure!" she exploded. "No one will ever make me change my mind!"

"That's not what I was going to ask." Freyne held up his hand to silence her, surprised by her outburst. "Don't just assume that because I'm partnered with a man, I haven't faced this problem myself. I was married once, a long time ago, and I was the one who didn't want children in that relationship."

"I'm so sorry." Lana sucked in a deep breath and her cheeks turned red. "I—"

"Having children is a decision that only you can make. It's your body and your life. If Chardi is absolutely certain that he does want children, then you aren't a compatible pairing. It's not fair to try and change each other's mind about this, nor is it fair on any children should you cave and be miserable while raising them. They deserve to be loved and cared for."

"You're the only person who has ever understood me," Lana said softly. "Thank you."

"I'm curious. What's your reason for not wanting children?"

"If you haven't noticed, I'm actually enjoying this adventure and would like to go on more in the future. I can't do that with a child hanging off me."

"There's more to it, isn't there?" Freyne prompted.

"Pregnancy." Lana sighed and looked at her lap. "It absolutely terrifies me. It's the thought of having something growing inside me, plus the fact that people die while giving birth. So many say it's beautiful but I think it's gross. Not only that, but If I hear one more person tell me that things are different when it's your own, I think I'll scream."

"So that's why your relationship is non-physical."

"Well, yes. I can't risk getting pregnant."

Lana blushed and looked away. Freyne took a bite of his lunch and chewed slowly, waiting for her to speak, but she remained silent.

"You do know there's several different herbs and remedies that stop that from happening, don't you?" he said gently once he'd swallowed.

"I've heard of it. I mean, Iryna has something she drinks every night before she sleeps. I don't know where to get it or make it or even how to take it, and I don't feel comfortable asking her. She just thinks I'm not interested in men or *that*."

"Why don't you ask Priye? She may be abrupt, but she's a great healer and I know that deep down she has a caring heart. There's no shame in having intimate relationships with people that aren't for the sole purpose of procreation. You deserve to experience that without any guilt or shame."

"Alright. I'll ask her later."

"Have you spoken to Chardi yet and explained how you feel about all of this?"

"Not yet." Lana sighed again. "I guess I'm just sick of people dismissing how I feel. I don't think I could handle hearing those words from him, too."

"The only advice I can give you is to talk to him. Tell him how you feel, your fears, what you want and don't want in life, everything. No relationship will ever survive without communication and respect from both sides. If he can't respect your feelings, then it's not meant to be."

"I suppose you're right," she said.

"Wait for a quiet moment when it's just the two of you and have an honest conversation with him. If you don't speak up now, one day someone might just come along and win his heart."

"You're so right," Lana said, a look of determination crossing her face. "I'll talk to Priye about options first, and then I'll sit down and talk with him. Thank you so, so much."

It wasn't until early evening that Nika started to come out of his deep sleep. He felt the horse come to a stop and he could hear voices talking quietly to one another. Someone shook his shoulder and a groan escaped his lips.

"He's coming to," a man said.

Someone lifted him from the horse and carried him a short distance, then lowered him to the ground and leaned him against a tree. Nika's mind was still groggy and his head felt heavy. He focused on the familiar voices and sounds around him as his friends set up camp for the night. Something soft climbed onto his lap, and even with his mind clouded in fog he knew it was Arnie-Kyn. He reached down and stroked Arnie's fur, drawing comfort from the cat. Arnie began to purr and knead his leg with his paws.

Nika sensed Freyne approaching and felt his face twitch into a smile. Freyne sat down beside him and gently drew Nika's head onto his shoulder. He felt Freyne brush a strand of hair from his face, followed by gentle kisses on his forehead.

"Hello, old man," he rasped.

"Hello, young whelp. How are you feeling?"

"So sleepy," Nika said.

"Me too. Lana is cooking dinner. As soon as we've eaten we can go to bed and have a decent sleep."

The fog slowly lifted from Nika's mind and he was finally able to force his eyes open. It was dark already, the only light coming from a tiny fire. As his eyes adjusted, the images of the dying militia flooded into his memory. He started shaking as he relived the horror he'd witnessed in the mountains.

"What's wrong?" Freyne asked with concern in his voice.

"As much as they're horrible and corrupt, those people didn't deserve to die like that," Nika said quietly. "How can anyone do that? Just watch them rip their own faces off?"

"I wish I could answer that, but I can't," he said softly. "Sadly, there are people in this world who commits the most atrocious crimes and murders. I can't even comprehend what goes through their minds. I guess that's what sets us apart from evil in the first place. We feel empathy and compassion, love. They feel nothing and have zero regard for others."

"There are twisted people in my world, too." Nika sighed. "I guess I'm just not used to seeing such things with my own eyes."

"No one is ever prepared for such a thing," Freyne said.

Dinner was a simple ham soup with the last of the bread from Grima. Nika ate slowly and quietly, hardly tasting his food. He was exhausted and his mood was low, still disgusted by what he'd seen. His stomach was churning and painful, but he managed to eat all of his dinner and keep it down.

"Come on boo, let's go to bed," Freyne said once they'd finished eating. "I think we're going to need all of our strength over the next few days."

18

The journey through the lower foothills took much longer than Nika anticipated. Every few days they were forced to hide from the increasing numbers of militia who were scouring the hills, looking for them. It took two long weeks to reach the edge of the plains which stretched all the way from the mountains to River Fraal.

Nika followed Freyne and Gaitan up a low hill on his hands and knees, then flopped onto his stomach, peering at Rarn in the distance. From their vantage point, he could see an army of militia gathering and setting up camp on the plains below. The single bridge leading to the city was heavily guarded by soldiers from the King's Army, the sun glinting off their polished steel armour.

"There's no way we can slip through without being seen," Gaitan whispered. "The militia will have scouts posted all around with far-sights. If they haven't seen us already, the moment we're spotted they'll be all over us."

"I agree." Freyne glanced around, then pointed towards the mountains. "We don't have a choice. We're going to have to head back up there and see if we can find a safe place to cross—"

A scream behind them made Nika's blood run cold. Gaitan gasped and his face turned white. At the base of the hill, more of the militia had surrounded them and were holding a knife to Iryna's throat. Nika tried to enter the realm, but his efforts were somehow blocked.

"It's Captain Brigal," Gaitan whimpered.

"Drop your weapons and join us or the princess dies,"

Captain Brigal shouted. "Don't try anything funny. We have mancers and you're outnumbered!"

Nika sucked in a deep breath, memories of their time in Fraal flooding back to him. He followed Freyne and Gaitan's lead and raised his hands above his head. A group of militia swarmed up the hill and tied his hands tight behind his back. Nika's heart was pounding and he felt like he wanted to throw up. The guards dragged them down the hill to the captain, who's face turned from menacing to triumphant.

"Well, well. Look who it is. Gaitan, the pathetic coward. Did you really think you could get away with deserting?"

"Drop dead," Gaitan spat.

The captain punched him in the mouth and laughed as Gaitan sank to his knees, blood dripping from his lip.

"I hereby find you guilty of desertion, murder, disobeying orders, and for travelling with known fugitives. In the name of Governor Drim, I sentence you to immediate death."

"No!" Lana yelled.

The militia laughed and held her firm despite her struggling. Nika watched helplessly, unable to move or help, as the captain drew his sword. The soldier holding Gaitan pulled his head back, exposing his neck even as the captain readied to swing.

Somewhere behind them, a single brassy note of a horn blared, stopping the captain mid-swing. The gathered militia all turned as one and drew their swords as dozens of mounted soldiers wearing polished armour galloped towards them, cutting down the militia in their path. The block on the realm lifted, allowing Nika to untie his bonds and break free. He rushed forward and punched the soldier holding Gaitan in the face, knocking him onto his back.

"Get up," he hissed, pulling his friend to his feet.

Ur'Shad pushed himself backwards and landed on his captor. He squirmed for a moment, then leapt up, his hands free. Nika, Gaitan and Ur'Shad freed the others and they retreated away from the skirmish, no longer the attention of the dwindling militia.

"Shouldn't we make a run for it?" Nika asked.

"If we run, we'll just be captured again," Gaitan said shakily. "Maybe the King's Army can help us, though I doubt it."

"Wait!" Iryna looked at Chardi with a frown. "Did you bring my father's stupid crest with you?"

"Of course I did. You know that high-ranking officers must have one at all times. Why do you ask, princess?"

"Because it's not so stupid now. Where is it?"

Chardi rummaged around in one of his packs for a moment and extracted a neatly folded square of fabric. He wordlessly unfolded it, revealing To'Rel's crest embroidered in gold thread, looking confused.

"Oh." His eyes widened. "Oh! Why didn't I think of this?"

He snatched a tent pole and tied the flag to it, then winced as he raised it in the air. Nika looked back towards the battle that was already over; the ground was littered with bodies of the militia, the King's Army swarming around the hills looking for deserters. A group of ten soldiers broke away from the main force and rode towards them.

"Halt! Who dares to fly the crest of King To'Rel of Al'Obrel?" one of them demanded.

Iryna tossed her hair and drew herself up straight.

"Her Royal Highness, Princess Iryna, daughter of King To'Rel," Ur'Shad declared formally. "Identify yourself!"

"Captain Nurmal of King's Army, loyal only to His Majesty, King Kaiton!" The captain eyed them suspiciously for a moment, then bowed deeply in his saddle. "Your Highness! What brings you to these dangerous lands?"

"I am on official business on behalf of my father and seek urgent audience with King Kaiton," she said. "Would you and your men kindly escort us to Rarn? I will see to it that you are duly compensated."

"Most certainly, Your Highness."

He bowed again then motioned to his men, who quickly moved into formation around them. Nika scrambled into the saddle behind Freyne, and once they'd all mounted, the captain waved to move out. As they rode, Nika looked closer at the soldiers; they wore full polished steel armour with royal blue cloaks fastened around their necks, and rode with an air of pride that indicated they would willingly die for their king. He frowned, unable to comprehend how anyone would give their lives so willingly for others.

"These militia have been harassing us ever since we reached Rybor," Iryna was saying to the captain. "I don't wish to sound conceited, but I fear all of this bloodshed is somehow because of us. What's your take on it, Captain?"

"The militia have never behaved like this in all my years of being King's Army. It's quite concerning. They're in direct violation of the Independent Treaty. Your father and my king are firm allies. We will guard you with our lives."

"Thank you."

They left the cover of the foothills and galloped across the open plains. Nika fidgeted nervously, all too aware of the growing numbers of militia nearby. He was certain they were vastly outnumbered, yet the militia did not attack. They rode for several hours until they crossed the stone bridge which spanned the River Rarn and stopped outside the city gates.

"Captain Nurmal! I have an urgent message for you, sir."

One of the guards hurried forward and saluted sharply, then handed the captain a folded sheet of parchment. Nurmal read the letter and furrowed his brow.

"Light the beacon and inform the garrison. I want this entire stretch of river guarded so thickly that those militia scum can't cross. Send some reinforcements down to the southern listening post just in case they try and come through the mountains. I'll be in the war room shortly."

"Yes, sir."

Nika's stomach twisted uneasily as they followed Nurmal into the city. *Why would the militia want to start a war to capture us?* he wondered. *Something isn't right here. I doubt any of this has anything to do with that lord and his goat.*

The streets of Rarn were wide and clean, devoid of the narrowly-packed terraces that Nika had grown used to. The buildings were mostly built from stone, but small flowering pots placed by the doors and on the upper balconies gave the homes a sense of tranquillity. Each door was painted a different colour, brightening up the cobbled roads with a splash of rainbow. People stood aside politely to allow the party to pass, and the captain waved his thanks.

Nurmal called to halt outside an inn with a nice flowering garden, then dismounted with two of his men and hurried inside. The captain soon returned and bowed deeply to Iryna.

"The innkeeper has offered his entire inn to your disposal for the evening. You and your people have full use of any rooms you desire, and I will post my guards for your protection," he said. "I'm going to debrief with the general and I'll organise an escort to Riz'Hra for you. If there is anything else you require, please let us know."

Once they'd bathed and settled into their room, Nika and Freyne ate their dinner together by the fire, then sprawled out comfortably on the couch, basking in their afterglow. It felt strange to be indoors, warm and protected from the icy mountain wind, and even stranger to finally have some privacy. Freyne opened his journal to read over his work on the prophecy while Nika snuggled into his chest. He'd managed to separate most of the passages and place them in the correct order, but the remaining sections were still incomprehensible.

The sea will flood, the colour of blood.
Many will drown from the grip of the glove.

He's not on our side and cannot be trusted,
Don't lose sight of that murderous bastard.

"How long have we been travelling?" Nika asked.

Freyne flicked through his journal and checked his calendar. "A little over two months. Why do you ask?"

"I was just figuring out when my birthday is." Nika started counting on his fingers. "My birthday would have been 126 days from the date that I came here."

Freyne counted the days on his calendar and worked it out.

"This won't be accurate since there's 365 days in your year and 420 in ours, so your birthday is roughly the 33rd of Neron. I have no idea what day mine is. I'm too old to even worry about another year."

"Do people celebrate their birthday here?" Nika asked.

"We never acknowledged them in the monastery, but that doesn't mean others don't."

"In my world, we usually eat cake, give gifts, and then get

drunk," Nika said. "What else do people celebrate here? Like special days or religious days?"

Freyne shifted slightly so he could run his fingers through Nika's hair and thought back to his time in the monastery.

"Kharung is the major event of the year. It's celebrated on the night of the 42nd of Messai, and usually involves lots of food and drinking. People decorate their homes and towns with bright colours and buy gifts for one another. There's also a celebration to welcome in the new year."

He closed his journal and trailed his fingers down Nika's back.

"There are some other minor celebrations, but because of my upbringing, I only celebrated religious occasions. There's an entire schedule of events that are celebrated each year. At the monastery, we priests held sermons, prayer, and vigils for special days such as The Coming, The Pleading, and Acceptance. These days refer to when Am first came to this world…" Freyne trailed off as Nika's eyes drooped. He smiled and continued to run his fingers through his hair. "Marriage is a big deal here. I lost count of how many ceremonies I officiated over the years. Couples would come from all over Ayrillis just to be married in the most beautiful of Am's places of worship. Many people believe that getting married in our monastery would give them extra blessings from Am, but that was never true.

"I remember looking into the couples' eyes and seeing their love for each other. They were always so happy and excited to be starting their life together. And yet, when I stood there with Alira, I felt nothing but dread. No love or happiness, just miserable at the thought of being trapped. How I envied all those other couples and wished I had that too."

Freyne paused when he noticed that Nika had fallen asleep.

"I never knew love before I met you," he whispered. "I would marry you in a heartbeat."

Nika felt tired and drained the next morning despite having a good sleep. He stomped grumpily down the stairs behind Freyne, looking forward to his breakfast. The wait staff had already filled the table with platters of food, a combination of eggs cooked in different ways, fried ham, hot buttery toast, and porridge. Gaitan, Priye, Ur'Shad and Iryna had already started eating, though he noticed the porridge remained untouched.

He sat next to Gaitan and loaded his plate with everything except the runny oats. When he looked up he saw Lana and Chardi walking towards the table, their hands clasped tightly together. Freyne put his hand on Nika's knee under the table as one of the waiters poured their tea.

"Morning," Lana said with a smile.

"Morning," Nika and Freyne answered at the same time.

Lana laughed, her cheeks a little flushed. Nika could sense exactly what both she and Chardi were feeling and his heart swelled for them.

Iryna ignored Lana's greeting and instead was eyeing Nika with a cheeky expression on her face.

"Did you get hungry last night?" she asked Freyne.

"I'm not sure I follow," Freyne replied quizzically.

She pointed at Nika's neck and Ur'Shad burst out laughing.

Nika was confused for a moment, and then it dawned on him. He felt his face burn. Gaitan and Chardi soon joined in the laughter. Freyne inspected his handiwork and his mouth curled into a grin.

"Come to think of it, I may have had a little snack."

Nika pulled up his shirt to cover the mark, then shoved Freyne playfully to try and hide his embarrassment.

"What are we doing today?" Gaitan asked.

"We're going to the market," Iryna said, indicating Lana, Chardi and Ur'Shad.

"Not you," Priye said firmly to Chardi. "You're staying here and resting. I need to clean your wound."

Chardi looked crestfallen.

"How much longer does this need to go on for?" he grumbled.

"Another week or two of twice daily dressing changes, but even once it's healed, it could take months for you to be back to normal," she said. "I want to inspect the wound closer while we've stopped and make sure everything is healing properly."

"What about you?" Gaitan asked Freyne.

"I have some reading to catch up on," Freyne said. "I think I'll just stay here and have a break from riding."

Gaitan turned lastly to Nika.

"And you?" he asked.

"I have no plans," Nika replied. "Why?"

"I'm going to go down to the wharf to check out those river ferry boats. Want to come?"

"Sure, why not." Nika nodded.

Once they finished eating, Nika kissed Freyne goodbye and left the inn with Gaitan. A cold breeze blew down from the mountains and Nika could feel a cold mist of rain on his face. He pulled up his hood and tightened his cloak around him.

"So, where are you from, anyway?" Gaitan asked.

"A long way from here. You wouldn't know it."

"The mainland, huh?"

"I lived on a platform in the middle of the sea. It was self-contained and there were over two hundred of us living and working there. I maintained and fixed the machinery."

"Wow," Gaitan said. "So why are you here with these people?"

Nika shrugged. Gaitan and Priye hadn't been told about their quest, and Nika didn't want to give anything away.

"I needed a change of pace," he fibbed. "I first met Freyne at the University near Al'Obrel where I got into a bit of trouble. Then we got caught up in the princess' business and we've been travelling with her ever since."

"I see." Gaitan nodded. "They seem like good people."

"They are." Nika nodded. "I wouldn't have made it very far had I not met Freyne when I did."

Gaitan looked thoughtful for a moment.

"What's it like being with a man?" he asked.

"It's just like being with a woman. Two people who care for each other. The only difference is how things work in the bedroom, but when you think about it, they're both good."

"You've been with women too?"

"I've been with lots of women," Nika admitted. "Freyne's the only man I've been with."

"Which is better? I mean…you know."

"Look at it this way. I will never sleep with women again," Nika said. "Maybe you should try it and see what it's like for yourself. You might enjoy it more, too."

"Sorry for all the questions. I've never spoken to someone… like you before," Gaitan said.

"I'm just a normal everyday guy," Nika said. "My choice of partner doesn't change that."

"Back in H'Rak, we are raised to believe that people like you and Freyne are disgusting. A part of me wants to go back there and show everyone how wrong they are."

"You know what?" Nika asked.

"What?"

"I'm glad I didn't kill you."

Nika laughed and slapped Gaitan on his back, who also joined in the laughter. He couldn't help but like the young man and was truly grateful that his life was spared. *I hope he isn't the blood descendant. He's too nice to have to die for the prophecy.*

They soon reached a long wharf that stretched along the bank of the river. There were several steam-powered boats bobbing gently in the water, and Nika could see one paddling up the river towards them.

"Are you two looking for a ferry?" a voice called.

Nika turned and spotted a man peering down at them from one of the boats.

"We're just admiring them," Nika said. "We're not from here."

"Where are you from?" he asked.

"Al'Obrel," Nika replied.

"You're a long way from home, friend. Have you ever been on a paddle steamer before?"

"No."

"Why don't you jump up on board and I'll show you around." The man grinned and beckoned.

Nika hurried aboard, keen to see how the boats worked.

"I'm Navis, the captain of this craft. My engineer is up in the workshop repairing one of the parts that broke, so I'm grounded for the next few days and I'm already bored."

"Did you say they're powered by steam?" Nika asked.

"Yes. These boats are fitted with large steam turbines which turn those paddle wheels. That way we can sail upstream without oars." Navis pointed to the large wheels on the side of the boat. "Come and I'll show you the boiler room."

Navis led them below deck to the stuffy room that contained the engine. Nika gazed in awe at the ingenious engineering. Although the boiler was cold and unlit, he could visualise how everything worked clearly as though he were looking at a schematic.

"This is brilliant," he breathed.

"Is this like the machines you work on?" Gaitan asked.

Nika shook his head.

"The ones I worked on were very different to this."

"Oh, you're an engineer?" Navis asked, his eyes lighting up.

"No. I'm a diesel mechanic by trade. My focus is internal combustion engines and maintenance, not steam," he replied.

"I've never heard of internal combustion. What is it?"

"Um. It's hard to explain," Nika said, wanting to change the subject. "What's that noise?"

In the distance he could hear a soft chugging sound.

"Oh, that's just another steamer coming up the river," Navis replied. "Come and I'll show you upstairs."

He led them from the boiler room and up to the wheelhouse where they could see the approaching vessel in the distance. It was much larger than the one they were on and was flying a royal blue flag with an unfamiliar crest.

"Ah, it's one of the King's Army's vessels," Navis said. "They patrol the river and transport troops up and downstream when needed. Those ferries are much more stable than these smaller boats, faster, and more powerful."

They watched as the steamboat manoeuvred skilfully into its berth and came to a stop. A ramp was lowered over the side and wave after wave of armoured soldiers marched onto the wharf where they formed into ranks and stood at attention. Someone shouted an order and they turned as one, the sound of eighty synchronised stomps echoing around the wharf. Another order was shouted and the soldiers marched away in step.

The army vessel pulled up the ramp and reversed away from the wharf. As it turned to head back down the river, another boat flying the same flag came into view.

"This is most unusual," Navis said, scratching his chin. "I've never seen so many soldiers here before. I wonder if this has anything to do with the fighting over the bridge."

"We heard that the militia are after a group of travellers," Gaitan said, still watching the army vessel approaching. "I wonder if this has anything to do with them?"

"Who knows? So long as it doesn't kill business."

"We'd better get going," Nika said, a bad feeling gnawing at his insides. "Thanks for the tour."

Once they returned to the wharf, Nika dragged Gaitan back along the road as the second boat began to unload even more of the soldiers.

"Do you think the others will mind if I keep riding with you?" Gaitan asked as they walked. "I don't want to admit it to Ur'Shad and Chardi because they scare me, but the thought of being captured by the militia again is terrifying. I don't want to die like that. Or at all, for the matter."

Nika's stomach lurched and his heart broke for his friend.

"It's no problem at all," he said. "We're happy for you to come."

"Really?"

"Yeah."

"Thanks. So where are we going?"

"Riz'Hra," Nika replied. "Let's see if we can find Ur'Shad and the girls. I don't think we're far from the market."

They walked along a busy road lined with armourers, tanners and other trades, and sure enough found themselves at a sprawling market. Merchants in brightly coloured clothing called to them as they walked past, but Nika ignored them, scanning the crowd for his friends. The misty rain didn't hamper the merchants or shoppers' moods as people haggled animatedly around them.

"Nika!"

Nika stopped and spun around; Lana was waving from the next row of stalls. He waved back with a grin and hurried to join her and the others. Ur'Shad looked bored, his arms laden with Iryna's purchases.

"I should have gone with you two," he grumbled. "Were the ferry boats at least interesting?"

"We'll tell you about it later," Nika said quietly. "Here. Let us help with those."

Ur'Shad looked relieved as Nika and Gaitan took their share of things to carry.

"Nika! Come here a moment," Iryna called out.

Nika looked sideways at Ur'Shad then hurried over to the ladies. Before he could object, Iryna tugged back his hood and wrapped a light grey scarf around his neck while giggling.

"There you go. Just in case Freyne gets hungry again." The princess laughed so hard she snorted and Lana giggled.

Nika's face burned hotter than the sun and he stalked back to Ur'Shad and Gaitan.

"Remind me to never go shopping with her again."

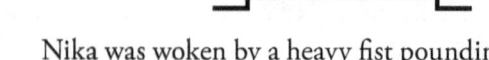

It was lunch time by the time they made it back to the inn. Nika trudged upstairs to deposit the newly purchased supplies in Iryna's room then hurried downstairs to meet the others. His arms were sore from carrying so much for so long. As he approached the table, Freyne eyed Nika's scarf with a raised eyebrow.

"Don't ask," Nika mumbled, sitting next to him.

Freyne chuckled. Nika waited for the wait staff to disappear, then lowered his voice.

"While Gaitan and I were down at the wharf, we saw two boatloads of soldiers come ashore," he said. "Do you really think the militia will try and break through them to get to us?"

"Nurmal already ordered the beacons to be lit and the reinforcement of the lines here. Kaiton is probably preparing for the possibility of invasion." Chardi frowned. "He has always taken border protection seriously and has one of the most powerful armies in the world. I wouldn't put it past him to send his troops over to wipe out the militia for good and regain control of the Independent District."

"Maybe I should stay here, just in case war does break out and they need my help," Priye said thoughtfully.

"Let's not jump to any conclusions yet," Ur'Shad said. "I think we should just here at the inn for the rest of the day and relax so we can leave in a hurry if necessary."

"Agreed." Freyne nodded. "I don't think we'll get to rest much between here and Riz'Hra."

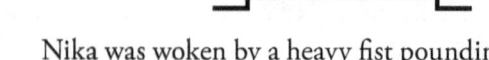

Nika was woken by a heavy fist pounding on the door. He stumbled off the couch and opened the door a crack, still fuzzy from sleep. One of Nurmal's guards had his helm tucked under his arm, a look of concern on his face. He bowed deeply and

Nika opened the door wider, sensing his urgency.

"Sorry to disturb you, sir. I have a message from the captain. We've been ordered to evacuate the princess and will be leaving shortly. Please gather your belongings as quickly as possible and rendezvous at the front of the inn."

Nika yawned and nodded. The guard saluted sharply and moved on to Gaitan's door.

"What's going on?" Freyne asked sleepily from the couch.

"We have to go. Now."

Nika pulled on his trousers and dressed quickly. He gathered his things together while Freyne scurried to get ready. As he reached out to open the door, Freyne caught his arm.

"One more thing," he said quietly. He pulled Nika into a quick hug and planted a lingering kiss on his lips. "You and I will need to be careful over the next few days. Bar'Am used to be unsafe for couples like us and I have no idea if it's still that way. These soldiers are not necessarily our friends and wouldn't hesitate to arrest us if they felt we broke any of their laws."

Nika nodded, his stomach twisting uncomfortably. He kissed Freyne on the cheek one last time, then hid Arnie under his cloak and hurried downstairs. Around thirty mounted soldiers were waiting in formation seemingly unfazed by the rain pelting down on them. Chardi and Lana were the last to reach the front of the inn. Three of the soldiers dismounted and strode towards them.

"Your highness." Captain Nurmal bowed deeply. "I sincerely apologise for disturbing you so late. We must leave at once. Your horses have been prepared for you."

The other two soldiers helped to carry the packs back to the horses for loading.

"What's going on, Captain?" Iryna asked.

"Our spies have indicated that the militia are planning a full-scale attack just before dawn. Even now, they are massing their forces on the other side of the river and are preparing to fight their way across. There's almost a thousand of them now."

"But surely we'll be safe here behind the lines?" she asked.

"We can't afford to take such risk. We must leave now before the battle starts. This isn't some petty grab for land or resources. They're still out to get you and your staff, Your Highness. We'll talk about it more when we reach the first checkpoint. Now, let's move it out. We have a long way to go."

Captain Nurmal bowed again, then motioned for them to hurry. Gaitan mounted the packhorse and offered his hand to help Priye up. She scowled at him and pointed to the front of the saddle. With a sigh, Gaitan slid forward. Priye hitched up her dress and mounted easily behind him.

Once they were all ready, the captain waved for them to move out. The soldiers split into two and formed a protective force around Nika and his friends. He urged his horse into a walk and followed Ur'Shad and Iryna through the streets of the city. They rode in silence, the heavy rain muffling the echoes of the horses' hooves.

The northern gates had already been opened. The guards stood back and saluted sharply as they rode through. Once they were outside, the soldiers formed a protective ring around the companions and kicked their horses into a swift gallop.

They rode steadily, slowing only to rest the horses in short regular intervals and never stopping. Nika couldn't help but feel miserable. He was cold, wet, and tired, and longed to be back at the inn snuggled up with Freyne. A part of him was tired of travelling, and for a moment he missed his old life of routine and discipline on the rig. Freyne shifted slightly in the saddle so their legs touched and gently squeezed Nika's waist.

"I'm here," he said softly.

The rain still fell heavily as the sun began to rise, and as the sky grew brighter, Nika could make out the miserable black clouds rolling overhead. The plains between Rarn and Riz'Hra were dotted with rolling hills and shallow valleys. Trees, shrubs and rocks dotted the landscape. In the distance a bright light shone from the top of a hill. As they rode closer, Nika could just make out a stone building with a flame flickering on its roof.

"Halt! Rank and password?" a voice challenged.

Nurmal held up his hand and ordered the party to halt.

"Captain Nurmal. Lorelei," he shouted back.

"Come on through, captain. Welcome to the checkpoint."

Nurmal waved his hand and they resumed their trek up the hillside. Perched at the top was a stone fort with a large beacon on top. An intricate network of trenches surrounded the fort, and soldiers could be seen moving about inside, patrolling their section and keeping watch.

Captain Nurmal held up his hand again, then stopped and dismounted. He turned and beckoned to Iryna.

"Your horses will be safe here. Please, follow me."

Nurmal led them inside to a small dining hall and removed his helm. He gestured to the rows of tables and bench seats.

"Please make yourselves comfortable. Latrines are down the hall. I'll go and inform the kitchen that you've arrived. We'll have a quick breakfast and then continue." Nurmal bowed and backed out of the room.

As soon as the door closed, Iryna and Ur'Shad fell into each other's arms. Nika looked longingly at Freyne, hating that he couldn't risk being affectionate. Shortly after, Nurmal returned with two of the cooks carrying a large tray each. Breakfast was over-sweetened porridge with honey and sugar and a mug of the strongest sweetened tea Nika had ever tasted.

"I apologise for the crude meal," Nurmal said, sitting with them at the table. "Being soldiers, we need frequent high energy meals so we can perform optimally. You will find that the tea will keep you awake for the next few hours."

"We are most grateful for your help," Iryna said politely. "Would you mind telling us what's going on back in Rarn?"

"King Kaiton has spies deep within the militia. One of them managed to get through to us last night and warn us about the attack." Nurmal stifled a yawn. "We knew they were planning something, especially once they learnt that you're heading towards Rarn. It was just a matter of time before they would launch their full-scale attack."

"I don't suppose you know why they are so desperate to capture us?" Ur'Shad asked.

"The spy report was limited. All we know is that the militia have been ordered to capture the cretins – that's you – no matter what. No one knows who is driving them to attack or why. In all my years in His Majesty's service I've never seen them like this. They know they're not to patrol beyond the boundaries of the Independent District, so like I said the other day, they are in direct violation of the treaty. Therefore, King Kaiton has every right to push them back into the fetid swamp where they belong."

"How long will it take us to get to Riz'Hra?" Freyne asked.

"Usually around two weeks, but if we stick to the schedule, we'll be there in nine days," Nurmal replied.

"So, why are *you* escorting us to Riz'Hra?" Chardi asked, narrowing his eyes. "You're a captain. Your place is back there with your men, especially on the eve of battle."

"I've been ordered back to Riz'Hra immediately to meet with my king," Nurmal replied, standing up. "My place is wherever he orders me to be. Now if you'll excuse me, I need to go and organise my men. We leave in fifteen minutes."

19

Travelling with the King's Army was brutal. Fourteen hours of riding each day was not only physically draining, but mentally exhausting too. When they reached the checkpoint late on the second day, Captain Nurmal informed them that the militia had commenced their attack that very morning. The mood was sombre as Nurmal sat reading out the casualty report, many of the deaths from his own company.

Nika's dreams were plagued with ghosts and undead. The thought of all those deaths just because of some lord wanting revenge on King To'Rel made him sick to his stomach. As he tossed and turned, his dream shifted to the mad hermit and the senseless slaughter of the militia. He watched as the terrifying memory played out before him, only this time the hermit reanimated the corpses and turned them into an undead army.

Something soft and warm climbed onto his chest and the nightmares vanished. He sighed, forgetting the horrors of his dream, and settled into a deep sleep. It wasn't until he was shaken awake that he realised Arnie was laying on his chest, purring softly. Nika reached out and scratched behind his ears.

"It's time to get up, everyone," Nurmal called. "Please dress, relieve yourselves, then eat your breakfast. We leave in under the hour."

Despite the icy wind, the sky was blue with very few clouds to be seen. No one spoke as they rode across the plains towards the next checkpoint. It wasn't until late afternoon that Nika felt a strange pull on the realm. He looked up and saw the sky filling with dark unnatural clouds, and something felt wrong.

"Captain!" Freyne yelled. "Stop!"

Nurmal held up his hand and shouted to halt.

"What is it?" he demanded.

Freyne turned in the direction of Rarn and pointed. The sky was growing darker than night, the only light an occasional flash of lightning. The soldiers looked uneasy. Nika checked that his shield was still strong, then entered the lowest realm. The usual purple tint looked skewed, like the energy was being drawn towards Rarn by some ungodly force.

Without warning, the strange pulling snapped and an almighty shockwave rang out through the realm. He could hear screaming, hundreds if not thousands of lives being extinguished all at once. Nika reefed his mind back just in time for the horse to rear up on her hind legs in fright. Both Nika and Freyne were thrown from her back and landed roughly on the ground. Arnie-Kyn hissed and shot from Nika's cloak.

"What in the gods just happened?" Nurmal shouted.

The soldiers were fanning out, their swords drawn, looking around wildly for an enemy. Nika groaned and sat up, rubbing his throbbing head.

"Are you alright?" he asked, helping Freyne to sit up.

"I – all those screams," he whispered, looking at Nika in horror. "Someone just murdered a vast number of people. I've never seen anything like this before."

"Fall in, men!" Nurmal ordered.

The captain dismounted and helped Nika and Freyne to their feet. He looked uneasy and his hands were trembling. Nika brushed himself off and wiped the blood off a small cut.

"Something major just happened back at Rarn," Freyne said shakily. "I don't know what exactly, but there were many deaths. May Am be with us all."

"How do you know this?" the captain asked uneasily.

"Mancery. We both felt it." Freyne indicated himself and Nika. "We really need to know what happened at Rarn. How long will it take for a messenger pigeon to reach the checkpoint?"

"If it's something major like you think, the update will go directly to King Kaiton himself and bypass the checkpoints. We won't know what's going on for a few days until he issues a statement or new orders."

"We need to get moving, then," Chardi interrupted. "If your emergency protocols are anything like Al'Obrel's, Kaiton will already be summoning his war cabinet."

"Let's just hope there's someone still alive in Rarn to send him a report," Nurmal said. "Move it out!"

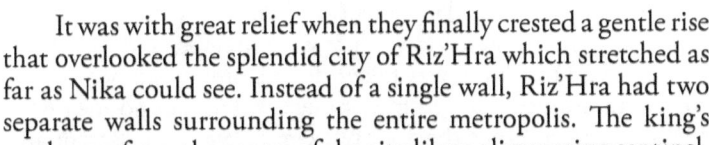

It was with great relief when they finally crested a gentle rise that overlooked the splendid city of Riz'Hra which stretched as far as Nika could see. Instead of a single wall, Riz'Hra had two separate walls surrounding the entire metropolis. The king's castle rose from the centre of the city like a glimmering sentinel.

Nurmal led them to the south entrance where the guards immediately opened the gates to let them through. People milled about in the streets, going about their business with an air of importance. Nika noticed that they dressed more fashionably compared to the other cities he'd visited, though he couldn't tell if their finery was a status symbol or if the people just had a greater appreciation of luxury clothing.

"It's human foolishness," Arnie-Kyn said when Nika asked him about it. *"One does not understand your need to cover up in the first place. Unlike other species, humans have devolved and become reliant on their clothing and tools. One does wonder how you became the dominant race."*

"Sorry I asked," Nika grumbled.

They turned into a wide cobblestone boulevard which was lined with tall metal poles flying the king's crest. On either side of the boulevard was a lush green park with beautiful oaks and plum trees. Despite the winter chill, many people were sitting in the shade of the trees, reading or in small chatty groups. Nika pulled his cloak tighter around him to ward off the chill and shook his head.

"Captain Nurmal, sir! We've been expecting you. You are to meet in the war room at sunrise for an emergency briefing. We're just waiting on some of the generals to arrive. Please take our guests to the south wing and dismiss your men. The attendants are waiting for Her Highness and her staff."

"Thank you, lieutenant."

Nurmal bowed his head and continued through the gates.

He led them past the grand entrance and around to the southern side where a row of servants stood waiting.

"The attendants will take care of you from here," Nurmal said. "Leave your horses and belongings."

"Thank you for everything, Captain," Iryna said.

"It was my pleasure, Your Highness." Nurmal bowed in his saddle, then wheeled his horse and led his men away.

A maid curtsied deeply to Iryna and swept her and Lana into the castle. One by one they were greeted and led inside by an attendant. Nika was taken downstairs into a hot steamy room, his stomach twisting with nerves. He had no idea what to do or expect. Once the door was closed, two more attendants materialised out of the steam and started pulling at Nika's cloak. He swatted their hands away and took a step back.

"Hey! What are you doing?" he demanded.

"We are preparing you for your visit with His Majesty, King Kaiton. Chop chop, we have lots to do," a flippant man said in a business-like tone. "I'm Tanuj, senior groomer."

"It's ok. I can bathe myself," Nika said.

"No, no, absolutely not! You're an honoured guest so you must look and smell the part. I will not have you embarrass me in front of my king. Now, what's your name?"

Nika introduced himself, then extracted Arnie from his cloak and sat him on the floor.

"What in the gods? You can't have a cat in here!"

"If anyone so much as touches a whisker on him, there will be hell to pay." Nika glared at him.

"Er. I'm not sure His Majesty would appreciate a cat in his presence. Last time an animal got loose in court, it caused bedlam and now they're banned."

"Fine. I'll put him outside as soon as we're done. Do you want me to bathe or not?"

"Very well. Please undress, sir."

Nika did as he was told and quickly stripped off. He covered himself with his hands, uncomfortable being nude in front of so many attendants. Tanuj pointed at the bath and Nika climbed into the water. The attendants began lathering lotions and ointments into his skin while Tanuj focused on cutting and styling his hair.

"You humans really are the strangest of creatures," Arnie said.

"Are all those extra people because you smell so bad, or because you can't clean yourself properly?"

"You don't exactly smell like roses, either. You smell worse than that rotting rabbit we passed yesterday. Are you planning to come with us to see the king?"

"One goes where you go," Arnie said, flicking his tail.

"You're going to need a bath, then. Come here." Nika tapped the edge of the tub, earning a glare from the cat. *"Or, you can go and wait in the stables with the horses. Your choice."*

Arnie-Kyn stalked across the room and leapt up on the edge of the bath, eyeing the water with his hackles raised.

"I will hold you so you don't fall in. I promise I won't drop you. But no claws on my bare skin or else!" Nika warned.

He reached out and carefully lifted the cat into his arms. The attendants paused and watched with surprised looks on their faces. Nika held Arnie to his chest and gently trickled some warm water through his fur.

"I have never seen a cat willingly bathe before," Tanuj said.

"He's not a typical cat," Nika replied. "Just don't splash him. I wouldn't want to bleed in front of your king."

"This is most humiliating," Arnie said.

"If I have to suffer through this, so do you."

Nika took a bar of soap and lathered Arnie's fur, then rinsed him off carefully. He could sense the cat's anger.

"There. Was that so bad?"

Arnie said nothing. Nika sat him back on the edge of the tub and the cat retreated into the far corner or the room.

"May I trim your goatee, sir?" Tanuj asked.

"Whatever."

Once he was clean, Nika was ushered into another room where he was fitted for fancy clothes and new shoes. The black woven trousers were soft against his skin, much nicer than the ones he'd accumulated during his time in Ayrillis. As Tanuj was about to hand him a pale green tunic, the door opened and a red-faced servant bustled into the room carrying a bundle of clothes.

"What is it?" Tanuj demanded.

The servant whispered something to him and handed him the bundle. Tanuj's eyes widened and he nodded his head.

"I see. Go and prepare the private antechamber."

The servant bowed and hurried from the room. Tanuj returned the green tunic to the hanging rack and carefully unfolded the garment that the servant gave him. Muttering to himself, he helped Nika into a long-sleeved white shirt followed by an extravagant black and grey waistcoat of the finest quality. Symbols that were similar to Freyne's writing were embroidered onto the collar in fine gold thread.

"I think you're done, sir. You look dashing." Tanuj winked. "I suppose your cat can come too since you've proven it can behave. Now come and I'll take you to the waiting room."

Nika looked around for Arnie and spotted him sitting on a dressing table, his tail swishing angrily. Someone had tied a dark grey and silver ribbon around his neck and brushed the prickles from his fur. Nika grinned and scratched him gently behind his ears.

"Come on," he said. *"Let's get this over and done with."*

Nika was led through the castle to a small antechamber not far from the throne room. He sat on a divan, worried that he'd mess up his finery and nervous for what was to come. After what felt like an eternity, there was a gentle knock at the door and Freyne was ushered into the room. The servant bowed and left them alone. Nika stood up and fell into Freyne's arms.

"I missed you," Freyne said quietly. "You smell so good."

He let go and straightened Nika's collar. Freyne's outfit was similar to Nika's, only instead of grey, Freyne's was a deep burgundy. Nika took a step back and looked him up and down.

"You look great," he breathed.

"So do you. I like what you've done to your hair."

"Thanks. What happens next? I have no idea what I'm supposed to do when we go see the king. Do we just waltz into the court like we did in Al'Obrel, or is it somehow different this time? I don't want to embarrass anyone, especially Iryna, by saying or doing the wrong thing."

Freyne's smile faded and he motioned to Nika to sit.

"I may have backed myself into an uncomfortable situation earlier," Freyne said. "I'm so sorry, boo."

"What do you mean?" Nika swallowed.

Freyne reached into his pocket and withdrew an amulet on a fine silver chain, then wordlessly clipped it around Nika's neck. The disc was cold on Nika's skin.

"The attendants were bad-mouthing Am and the entire religion. I'm sorry, but I couldn't just sit there and say nothing. I outed my position at the monastery and reprimanded them, so now I have no choice but to play the part. This means I'm going to be announced as a high priest in front of everyone, and you will be announced as my neophyte."

"What the fuck is a neophyte?"

"Someone who is new to the monastery, just beginning their training. Just stay with me and I'll guide you along where necessary. Apparently Kaiton is very formal and loves theatrics in his court, but he will probably still question who I am."

"Can't I just go and wait with the horses or something?"

"I really need you here with me." Freyne reached out and took Nika's hands. He was shaking. "I can't do this alone. Please?"

"Ok. But you know I have absolutely no idea what to do or say." Nika's stomach churned, making him feel nauseous.

"I've already taken care of that. You're under a vow of silence and are not permitted to speak out loud, not even to me. Watch closely and I'll show you what to do."

Freyne proceeded to show Nika how to walk, hold his hands, bow, and behave in the king's presence. Nika couldn't help but feel stupid.

"Is that it?" he asked when Freyne finally sat down.

"One more thing. I have something for you." He took Nika's hand and wrapped an intricately woven leather band around his wrist. "I was saving this for your birthday, but I thought it would be nice to wear it somewhere formal. I started making it for you while we were at sea but had trouble with the lock. It was a good thing Gaitan came along when he did. He fixed the lock for me."

Freyne turned Nika's wrist so he could see the clasp. It was shaped like a tiny padlock.

"This is an ancient courtship tradition I read about that I'm not even sure exists anymore. The band is a symbol of my feelings for you. Once it's been locked, the only way to remove it is to cut it off." He removed the band and gently pressed it into Nika's hand. "According to the tradition, if you choose to wear it, it means that you reciprocate those feelings or something like that."

"That's so tacky and cute at the same time." Nika laughed, but deep down he was touched. "Thank you. Help me do it up."

Freyne fastened the band around Nika's wrist then kissed him deeply. Nika grew hot under his collar and for a moment he forgot where they were. A knock on the door made them both jump and scramble to their feet.

"We're ready to announce you, your eminence. This way, please." The servant bowed deeply then beckoned.

Nika looked at Freyne, his cheeks burning from the close call. *"Your eminence?"*

"I've had worse. Come on, boo. Remember, no talking out loud."

Gaitan, Priye, Ur'Shad and Chardi were standing outside the antechamber. Another door opened and Iryna emerged with Lana. She was wearing a stunning lilac gown with gold embroidery shimmering in the light. Her hair cascaded down her back, and she wore a pretty gold tiara to keep it in place. She looked in every essence a royal princess.

Ur'Shad and Chardi's chainmail had been polished and they wore cloaks in the colours of King To'Rel. Chardi's bushy hair and beard had been trimmed and groomed, and Ur'Shad had shaved his head and face, making the big man even more menacing. Lana, Priye, and Gaitan wore plain black formal attire reserved only for the highest ranking servants. The servant fussed about, lining them up in order and ensuring everything was perfect. He paired Ur'Shad and Chardi directly behind the princess, followed by Freyne and Nika. Lana, Priye, and Gaitan stood at the back.

"Are you ready?" Freyne asked.

"Too bad if I'm not," Nika replied, feeling nervous.

A loud fanfare sounded from inside the court and the heavy doors swung open. Iryna took a few steps inside and paused, allowing the lords and ladies of the court to gaze upon her. The room fell silent.

"Her Royal Highness, Princess Iryna, daughter of King To'Rel of the House of Obrel!" a loud voice boomed.

Iryna walked gracefully down the royal blue carpet towards

the throne. The servant motioned to Ur'Shad and Chardi to stand inside the doors and wait their turn.

"Chardi, chief of King To'Rel's elite guard, and Ur'Shad, protector and chaperone of Princess Iryna."

Ur'Shad and Chardi walked in step with Iryna and followed her down the carpet. Freyne nudged Nika and together they stepped through the doorway, pausing as the others had done.

"His eminence, Worshipful Master Christophe Saul Du Freyne, high priest of the Great Monastery of Am, and his neophyte, Nikolai Mikhailov."

Nika walked stiff-legged beside Freyne down the blue carpet, feeling everyone's eyes on him. The court was much larger than King To'Rel's, and much more opulent. The blue carpet lined a raised walkway which ran along the back wall and led to the foot of the throne. Plush pouffes in that same royal blue lined the edges of the court, matching the crests hung around the walls.

The walkway ended at the base of a dais where the king and queen sat on their thrones. Nika stopped behind Chardi and Ur'Shad, noting that Gaitan, Priye and Lana were behind him with no announcement. King Kaiton held up his hand; Ur'Shad and Chardi fell to their knees. Freyne nudged Nika and they followed suit. Iryna curtsied elegantly.

King Kaiton stood and opened his arms wide.

"My friends!" he said loudly, his voice echoing through the silent court. "The House of Mherr welcomes the House of Obrel. What brings you to my lands?"

"It is an honour to stand here before you, Your Majesty," Iryna said, throwing her voice so every noble could hear. "I am here on urgent business on behalf of my father and have important matters to discuss with you."

"Let us retire to my office while the banquet is being prepared. I'm sure there is much to discuss." He turned to face the court. "My friends! You are all invited to dine with us and our honoured guests this evening. Court is now over. You're dismissed."

King Kaiton offered his hand to his queen and together they walked down the steps of the dais. Iryna offered him her hand and he kissed it formally, then led them through a door behind the throne.

The room was small and cosy, furnished with lush armchairs arranged in a semi-circle, all facing an ornate divan. King Kaiton beckoned to a servant who quickly snapped to attention.

"Take Her Royal Highness' wait staff to the servant's quarters and make them feel welcome."

"Yes, Your Majesty." The servant bowed deeply, then turned to Lana, Gaitan and Priye. "This way, please."

Once they were gone, Kaiton lounged on his divan and gestured for everyone to sit. The queen sat in a separate armchair beside him, her back straight and her hands folded in her lap. Kaiton took off his heavy crown and sat it on the divan next to him.

"This is my wife, Queen Astara," he said, smiling at her.

"Hello, everyone." The queen returned his smile.

"Princess Iryna. Last time I saw you, you were just a child playing on your father's lap while we discussed matters of state. And now look at you, a young woman handling your father's business. Tell me, are you betrothed yet?"

"My father is in the process of considering a worthy husband," Iryna replied.

"Wonderful. I shall write to him and offer my middle son Raylon for consideration. Such a marriage would forever cement our alliance," the king said. "I shall introduce you to him later."

Iryna inclined her head. Nika had never seen her act so formal in the time they'd been travelling together and found the shift in her attitude interesting. Seated behind her, Ur'Shad shifted uncomfortably, a scowl on his face.

"Worshipful Master." The king turned to Freyne and eyed him up and down, his expression changing to one of distrust. "Tell me. Who are you really?"

Freyne stiffened and Nika could feel his sudden fear.

"I am who I say I am, Your Majesty."

"Is that so? I received a communique from the monastery just two days ago and there was no mention of you. If you were indeed a high priest, I would know."

"One swears this oath as a sign of my absolute devotion to my God who is Am and only Am. Never will I falsely claim a position that has not been bestowed upon me by my God, lest I be banished from Ayrillis and denied entry to the afterlife," Freyne quoted.

"Law three thousand and thirty-two, tome sixty-four, page four hundred and eighty-one. My personal record is located in the monastery's archives under IT.2999.HPA-du Freyne"

Kaiton's eyes narrowed and Nika could see that he still did not believe a word Freyne said. The silence was palpable and Nika realised he was holding his breath.

"Very well. If you are indeed who you say you are, you will have no problem with saying a prayer before the banquet tonight and invoking Am's blessing, since we all know that only a *real* high priest has the power to do that. And should you fail, I will have you arrested and hanged for lying. Understood?"

"Y-yes, Your Majesty," Freyne croaked.

The king turned back to Iryna, smiling once again. The princess suddenly didn't look so confident.

"Let's put aside the fact that you may be associating with a criminal posing as a priest for a moment and get on with business. What matters did you wish to discuss with me?"

"The militia from the Independent District, for a start," she replied, seeming to regain her composure. "They've been harassing us ever since we reached the port and have bestowed physical harm on myself and my party. What's going on with them, and what happened at Rarn?"

"I've had mixed reports from intelligence, so I'll know more when I sit with my war cabinet in the morning."

"I will sit in too if that's alright with you," she said.

"A war room is hardly the place for a *princess*," Kaiton said, waving his hand dismissively.

"My father would not have sent me here if he didn't deem me worthy of such things," she countered, tossing her hair with defiance. "Under the terms of the alliance with Al'Obrel, we have every right to have a representative sit in and participate in that meeting."

"On that note, why *are* you here? To'Rel's only daughter with minimal staff and no royal escort. Did he even send you here or are you running away from your responsibilities at home?"

"My father wrote to you recently regarding the prophecy. Did you receive his letter?" Iryna asked.

"Around two months ago, yes." Kaiton nodded. "What has this got to do with anything? Let's not get sidetracked here."

"We've been sent to fulfil that prophecy."

"To'Rel doesn't get to decide when or who fulfills anything." Kaiton snorted. "Even I know that only the gods have the power to control these things."

"The time *is* now, Your Majesty," Freyne said quietly.

"And what would you know?" he snapped.

"Freyne knows more about the prophecy than anyone and has been working on translating it since we left Dol'Am!" Iryna exploded, shooting to her feet. "I'm done talking about this for today. We will resume this conversation tomorrow after Freyne has had the opportunity to defend himself."

Kaiton's face reflected his anger, but to Nika's surprise he nodded and stood.

"Very well." He pulled on a cord and a servant hurried into the room. "Take *his eminence* and his neophyte here to my private chapel and extend every courtesy to them as they prepare for this evening. And double the guard at the chapel so they are not disturbed by anyone."

"Yes, My King." The servant bowed. "This way please, your eminence."

Freyne's stomach was twisting from nerves as he followed the servant through a maze of drab service corridors. His chest felt tight and he took several gulping breaths to try and calm himself. *I'm so stupid! I should have just shut up and not said anything,* he berated himself. *If Kaiton doesn't believe me, this whole mission could fail and it will all be my fault. What the fuck was I thinking?*

Nika's hand slipped into his, startling him.

"It's going to be alright," Nika said, squeezing his hand.

"Is it?"

"Well. You are or were a high priest, so why won't it be alright? I know you can do this."

Freyne turned to look at him, then sighed.

"I'm scared, boo. It's been seven hundred years since I've performed a public blessing. It's not as simple as standing up and delivering a speech. Proper prayer and blessings are a special type of magic of their own. If I can't pull this off, we're going to have to

fight our way out of here, and then we're going to have the entirety of the King's Army on our back for the rest of this journey. Five fighters against an entire army of elite solders? I don't like our odds."

"I'm pretty sure both you and Orison told me to trust in Am and they will guide us. Maybe this will be a good thing."

"You're right." Freyne sighed again. *"I keep kicking myself for opening my mouth in the first place, but one of the many oaths I have taken was that I will not stay silent if I hear people being disrespectful to Am. I guess I'll just have to do my best."*

The servant stopped abruptly and pushed open a heavy wooden door. Freyne almost collided with him.

"Here it is, your eminence."

"Thank you. Please wait outside."

Freyne stepped into the chapel and was awed by its beauty. Four bench seats faced a stained-glass mural depicting Am with their wings spread, floating above the ground and grasping a large sword in their clasped hands. A torch or lantern shone from behind the likeness, bathing the chapel in dazzling rainbow lights. Behind him, he heard Nika catch his breath. Freyne made sure the door was closed then pulled him into his arms. Nika held him tight and rubbed his back, comforting him.

"I'll admit I feel a little embarrassed at the thought of showing my religious side to you and the others. None of you have seen that side of me," Freyne whispered.

"I'm bound to see it some time, so it may as well be now," Nika whispered back. "Is there anything I can do to help?"

"Yes." Freyne released him and stood back. "You will need to stand to my right, one step behind me, at all times. During the prayer, hold your hands like I showed you – yes, like that – and don't move from that position until you hear the affirmation from the guests."

"Ok." Nika nodded.

"I really need to concentrate now and get into the right headspace," he said, kissing his Nika gently. "Have a seat. We'll talk about it afterwards."

He knelt on a cushion towards the front of the chapel and faced Am's likeness. The thin layer of dust showed that the king rarely visited to pay his respects. Freyne made himself comfortable, then closed his eyes and focused on his breathing until he was able to relax his mind. It had been so long since his last prayer, and yet everything came flooding back as though he'd done so that very morning. He sifted through his arsenal of sermons, invocations, and blessings, building his prayer in his mind as easily as if he were writing it on paper.

Once he was satisfied with his choices, Freyne reached inward to his heart where he could feel Am's presence swirling deep inside him. He began to draw the energy from his surroundings into his body and directed it to join with Am's presence. The stained-glass mural glowed and flickered and he could feel the warmth of the energy flowing through him. With each breath, each beat of his heart, Am's presence infused into his very being.

Freyne was so deep in his trance that he hardly registered the servant nor the guards escorting them to the banquet hall. He could feel Am's energy flowing and whirling through his body, his skin prickling as he concentrated to keep it contained within him. The door opened and the king called for silence.

He stepped onto the podium with Nika and gazed down at his audience. The guests stood by their chairs waiting to hear the prayer, some of them in anticipation and some were sniggering. King Kaiton was watching on from the head of the table, a smug look on his face, while Iryna, Chardi, and Ur'Shad looked terrified.

Freyne held up his hand; the torches flickered and flared, and although they continued to burn, the light in the great hall dimmed. A faint murmur rippled through the crowd.

"There was a time when our world had no god. We were alone, vulnerable, an under-developed race of savages. We fought amongst ourselves, driven by greed, vengeance, and power. We saw others as beneath us and believed that our own lives mattered more than anyone else's. We were on the path to destroy our very race, our culture, our histories.

"Our world had no one to guide us, love us, and protect us. Our forefathers beseeched the skies, sending their prayers beyond our world, in the hopes to find a god of our own. Only one god heard those prayers, though, and came unto our world to behold our sorry race."

Freyne swept the guests' faces, making eye contact and

throwing his voice as he spoke. His audience were no longer sniggering but watching him in awe, mesmerised.

"Our forefathers begged and implored Am to stay and rule over them, to help shape the world into a better place. But Am refused; to rule over another is to dictate how one should live their life. Am went away.

"Once more, the desperate pleas of our forefathers called them back. 'God, will you stay and rule *with* us, instead of *for* us?' they pleaded. Still, Am refused; a race should be able to rule themselves. Again, Am went away.

"Our forefathers sat down together and for the first time, instead of fighting and arguing, they talked amongst each other and discussed ways to better themselves and their people. They realised that their problems could not be fixed by a god, and instead they must work together to change themselves and the world for the better. For they were all people with beating hearts, neither better nor worse than the ones they deemed below them.

"Am sat watching and could see that our forefathers finally understood the errors of their ways. They learnt friendship, teamwork, and the meaning of empathy, but most importantly they learnt respect towards others."

Freyne gazed around his audience; they were watching him with their mouths open, hanging on his every word. He released some of Am's energy from his body which shimmered around him like speckles of gold.

"On the tenth day, Am returned and agreed to be our god. They taught our forefathers the meaning of life and love. And even now, Am spreads their love to us all equally, regardless of our status. Am does not discriminate on skills, looks, or wealth. Am cares only that you are kind to one another and treat others with respect and dignity. Together, let us pray."

Freyne dimmed the lights even more so he could only just make out the faces of his audience, then began his prayer.

"Beloved Am, hear our prayers. We ask for your guidance, that you may show us how to grow as both individuals and as a race. For without growth, we are stagnant.

"We ask that you teach us how to love and treat others with kindness, just as you taught our forefathers. And we ask that you teach us respect for the people and land around us.

"Teach us to hold our hand, lest we beat our servants. Teach us not to hate that which we do not understand or agree with. And teach us not to hold ourselves over those less fortunate."

Freyne raised his arms over his head and looked up at the roof; the energy was making him glow, lighting up the dim hall. He released some of the energy and directed it towards the ceiling. There was a gasp as the energy swirled and shimmered, allowing everyone to see the night sky above, the stars blinking down at them.

"Beloved Am, I beseech you to bless these people before us, with the kindness and understanding that you have bestowed upon me and my loved ones.

"Beloved Am, I ask that you bless this fair king, as he fights against the evil that is plotting against the tasks you have given us. Please guide him in his quest for peace and fairness within his kingdom.

"Beloved Am, may we forever hold you in our hearts!"

"May we forever hold you in our hearts," the crowd murmured together as one.

Freyne released the last of the energy he was holding and the tiny specks of light swirled around the nobles and the king. A wave of Am's presence spread through the room like a powerful wave and the crowd gasped. As the sparkles began to fade, the lights slowly returned to their former brightness. The guests stood there in silence as Freyne dropped his arms to his sides.

"B-be seated," King Kaiton stammered. "Y-you may commence the banquet."

Freyne half-turned and noticed that more than a dozen guards were right behind them. A wave of dizziness washed over him and he would have fallen had Nika not caught him.

"You're dismissed, gentlemen."

The guards saluted as one, then turned and filed out of the hall. Freyne looked up to see Kaiton strolling towards him, his expression unreadable.

"There is no doubt that you are who you say you are, your eminence," he said, extending his hand. "I apologise sincerely for my rudeness and mistrust, and hope that you can find it in your heart to forgive me."

Freyne accepted his outstretched hand and shook it firmly.

"Thank you, Your Majesty," he said. "Would it be possible for us to be excused from the banquet? To bestow such a blessing is physically and mentally exhausting. I need to rest."

"Of course, my friend. I'll have someone take you to your rooms immediately."

20

"This has gone on for long enough. They have violated the treaty for the last time! I say we wipe their miserable army and take their cities for the crown!"

"They no longer have an army. You heard what happened. They were wiped out by that freak storm!"

"There is no way a storm can do that. I say it was a mancer."

"There's no such thing as a mancer that powerful!"

"Either way, we cannot take southern Bar'Am without the support of the other kings!"

"Of course we can! We have the largest and strongest army in the East. The militia, or what's left of it, is vastly inferior."

Nika sat at the back of the war room, listening to Kaiton's generals and officials bickering back and forth. He stifled a yawn and tried to pay attention.

"Do not underestimate the enemy," Captain Nurmal said firmly. "They almost broke through our lines at Rarn. Their forces are much stronger than we anticipated."

"What do you suggest, captain?" the king asked him.

"I suggest we spread out and fan the plains to assess if there are any more militia waiting in reserve, and re-secure Grima. That way we can reinforce the line and patrol the border to prevent any more forces from trying to break through." Nurmal stood and pointed at the large model of the isle in the middle of the room. "We can easily reinforce the positions by shipping men down the river. The mountains are snowed under which is protecting us on our southern flank, and the swamp will protect us from the north."

"That will spread our line too thin," one of the generals barked. "It leaves us wide open for invasion from the east."

"Gentlemen," the king interjected.

"That's what the warships are for. To patrol and guard our coastal borders," someone else said loudly.

"GENTLEMEN!" Kaiton yelled.

The room fell silent. Nika fidgeted uncomfortably.

"Now is hardly the time to mount a full-scale war, especially without the support of To'Rel and Lok's armies. We'll send out patrols as far as Grima and assess the situation first, while I quietly liaise with the other kings," Kaiton said firmly. "One of my spies said just this morning that he thinks the militia are receiving reinforcements from somewhere, possibly the mainland."

"Reinforcements? We need to act now, then!"

"Until this is confirmed or disproved, we will hold our positions," Kaiton ordered.

Iryna stood and walked over to the model.

"If the militia are receiving reinforcements, you're going to need my father and Lok's armies for additional support. We will need to hit Rybor and take out the militia there first so we can send our forces by sea. We don't have as many warships as you do, so we would need to commandeer some merchant vessels to get the troops across. This could work in our favour."

"You're right, Your Highness. If our allies can take control of Rybor and the port, they can stop the other ships from sailing and the port authority won't be able to get a message across to Fraal," one of the generals said thoughtfully. "To'Rel and Lok can land troops all along the west coast and sweep inland, and no one would realise until it's too late."

"Providing that To'Rel and Lok agree, what then?" Kaiton asked. "We still don't know how many militia are left after the incident at Rarn."

"I say we disband the Independent District and reclaim the area as crown land," another man said. "That cesspool has been allowed to fester for far too long. We absorb their army into ours and the problem is solved."

"I'll write to the kings immediately and send my fastest enchanted birds. I also have some new intelligence reports that

I need to read through this morning. We shall meet again on the morrow. Dismissed, gentlemen."

The generals and advisors filed out of the room, leaving Nika and his friends alone with the king. Kaiton sighed and sank wearily onto his divan and motioned for them to move closer.

"Something just doesn't feel right," he blurted out. "I seem to be missing a part of the story. Can one of you fill me in on your journey so far?"

"If I may, Your Majesty." Chardi cleared his throat and recounted their journey from Al'Obrel to Riz'Hra. "Freyne; didn't you say there was a mancer in the mountains?"

"Yes." Freyne nodded. "Both Nika and I witnessed him wipe out an entire patrol of twenty militia. I can't help but wonder if it's the same one who attacked the army."

"Interesting. He's obviously on our side, then." Kaiton shrugged. "I have spies deep within the ranks of militia. There's been no reports of reinforcements, mancers, or any unusual activity. Lately, though, their reports have been contradictory. Nothing is consistent. I suspect that some of my spies, if not all of them, have been compromised. It just doesn't make sense."

"I still fail to see why they would wage war for Iryna." Ur'Shad frowned. "It doesn't make any sense."

"This prophecy you're chasing," Kaiton said slowly. "Could there possibly be anyone who might be aware of it and not want you to fulfil it?"

Iryna covered her mouth, looking horrified at the thought. Freyne jolted in his seat and his hand shot out and grasped Nika's. Their minds joined at once and Nika's consciousness slipped away.

They sat in a small sitting room on a couch by a fireplace. Bookcases lined the walls, but there were no windows. Nika was sitting on a couch, looking through Freyne's eyes. He was facing a topless young man covered in cuts and bruises; between them was a table with a bag of parchment and scrolls resting on top.

"Thank you for taking me in," the young man said, drying his sandy hair with a towel.

"It's the least we could do. Your people have suffered enough." Freyne's voice came from his mouth. "So tell me, what happened?"

"The rumour is true. The Black Ibis cult prevails. It was they who attacked our village," the man replied. "When I had the vision and saw that they were coming, I told the shaman and we tried to burn as much as we could. She then gave me these and a box and ordered me to run to you. So, I ran."

Freyne's eyes swept to the table then back to the man.

"A box?"

"I buried it in the swamp for safe keeping. This is all I have left." The man looked despairingly at the bag, then at his feet. Nika could sense his anguish.

"There's something else, isn't there?" Freyne asked.

"They – they managed to take one of the prophecies," the man replied, burying his face in his hands. "There were several different versions, all penned by different seers, intended for specific people. One of them was recovered before the flames took hold and survived. You had better pray that the Black Ibis don't decipher the language, because if they do, all hope is lost."

The view swirled and shifted, and Nika was no longer confined within Freyne's body. They were floating, looking down on a burning village. Men dressed in black robes and wearing pointed ibis masks were ransacking the buildings and killing the innocent people below.

A spectral figure appeared between Nika and Freyne, and with a wave of both sadness and anger, raised their hand. Nika felt a surge of power and the robed cultists paused. A second later, they started screaming, then bolted towards the south-west.

Nika was pulled along with Freyne and the figure, following the fleeing cultists through the forest. They burst from the trees and into a grassy field, running in sheer terror. Up ahead, Nika spotted a familiar altar. Instead of stopping at the edge of the cliff, the robed people kept running and plunged to their deaths far below.

"Nika? Freyne? Hello?" someone was calling to them.

"Why in the devil is he holding his hand?" Kaiton asked.

Nika blinked his eyes and slowly slipped back into his own body. For a moment he was confused, then realised he was still sitting in the war room. He looked at Freyne; Freyne was looking at him with a tormented expression on his face.

302

"What's going on?" Kaiton demanded.

Freyne slowly let go of Nika's hand.

"The Black Ibis cult," he whispered.

"The what?"

"The Black Ibis cult. No, it can't be." He stood up and started pacing. "The Brotherhood of the Black Ibis was a cult who were against the coming of Am, and the later coming of Gri'Ran. They believed that the world was just fine being godless. During the holy wars of 1817, the Black Ibis rose up and forged a false alliance with Gri'Ran's forces and attacked the followers of Am. Once that battle was over, they turned on Gri'Ran's army and inflicted great damage before being wiped out. Or so we thought."

Freyne stopped pacing and glanced around the room.

"In the year 3091, the village of the seers and swamp people north of Al'Obrel was destroyed. It wasn't marauders like it says in the history books, it was the Black Ibis cult." He levelled his gaze at Kaiton. "They managed to steal one of the versions of the prophecy."

"That was almost nine hundred years ago. Surely that shouldn't matter to us now?" the king asked.

"Later, in 3287, they destroyed the village south of the monastery." Freyne paused his pacing and looked at Nika. "But why would they attack a village with so little wealth?"

"The Black Ibis were looking for something," Nika said out loud, no longer caring about his fake vow. He crossed the floor and stood facing Freyne. "Am was protecting something. They wouldn't have intervened were it not important."

"What, though? The journal was always with me until I dumped it in my house."

Nika frowned and thought back to the vision they shared in the swamp on Kia-Mor.

"The dagger?" he asked.

Kaiton and the others were watching Nika and Freyne's exchange with confusion etched on their faces.

"A dagger of little or no significance? I don't think so. I used it as a letter opener."

"But what if...what if their copy told them something about that dagger that ours doesn't? What if...what if the blood descendant has to use it?" Nika's jaw dropped.

"Could it really be, though?" Freyne asked, scratching his cheek. "Nothing about a weapon of choice was ever mentioned in my copy of the prophecy, nor the other version I've been working on. Surely if it were that important there'd be some mention of it somewhere?"

"Why else would I have picked it up with the journal? Am must have intended them to be left there for me to find." Nika frowned. "This explains all of those people in the black robes that we saw travelling with the militia!"

"This is a big problem. It was written that the cult would be destroyed, not thrive," Arnie-Kyn said from his seat on the couch.

Nika and Freyne turned and stood facing the cat.

"How can we be sure that it is them?" Nika asked.

"Am wouldn't have shown us the vision if it weren't," Freyne replied. *"This raises another question, though. Why was that memory hidden from me? And what other memories have been taken or are being withheld?"*

"Am would have their reasons," Arnie replied.

"Would someone mind filling me in? I have no idea what you're talking about," Kaiton grumbled.

"I'm sorry, Your Majesty." Freyne took a deep breath. "We now believe that the Black Ibis cult are the ones reinforcing the militia. They've managed to decipher their copy of the prophecy and are trying to stop us from fulfilling it!"

"But why did they attack Rarn and not try to cut us off on the way to Riz'Hra?" Chardi asked.

"They don't know where we're going," Nika said slowly, looking back at Freyne. "We have that nautical chart from the swamp, but they still have no idea where to go next."

"It's possible." Freyne nodded.

"This still doesn't explain their obsession with capturing Iryna," Ur'Shad pointed out.

"Wait. Let me check something." Freyne pulled his journal from his pocket and flicked through the pages, frowning. "No. I don't believe it."

"What?" Kaiton asked.

"I've been stuck on this passage for weeks and it only just clicked into place. Listen to this:

A ruse, a lie, politically founded.
Send off your daughter, the lies compounded.

Into the saddle, together they mounted.
Goodbye, be well, the army surrounded.

Imprison, refuse, her space is crowded.
Tell her no, you won't be countered.

Send her to witness the godly end,
Along with he with no ties to this land.

A protector, a warrior, that's all she needs,
Along with the stranger, and the one who reads."

"Are you telling me I've been a part of this prophecy the entire time?" Iryna asked incredulously.

"A key part." Freyne nodded. "So that's why the cult has been trying to capture you."

Nika's stomach gave a lurch as the words of the prophecy sank in. The truth was painful.

"To'Rel and those monks had no intention to help me get home, did they?" he asked.

"I don't think so. I'm so sorry, boo."

"I'll organise an armed detachment to go with you. I can't risk anything happening to To'Rel's only daughter."

"Armed soldiers travelling away from the battle will draw unnecessary attention to us," Freyne said. "Even the prophecy said that we are enough."

"How about a decoy?" Ur'Shad asked. "Send some of your soldiers down to Mar'Am with some people who look like us. Announce it to court and send them off this afternoon. That way, if there are spies in the city, they should follow the decoy and leave us alone."

"Brilliant." Kaiton grinned. "I'll organise this shortly. Is there anything else you need from me?"

"I need you to write to To'Rel and Lok and warn them about the Black Ibis. Update them on everything that we've spoken about and what's going on with the militia. We'll spend today replenishing our supplies and will leave before sunrise."

"I can do that. Where *are* you going next?"

"According to the nautical chart, we set sail from Barthra."

"But what about this blood descendant? Have you found him yet? And do you have everything you need?"

"We have." Freyne nodded.

"Very well. I'll instruct my servants to have your horses ready and arrange for an escort to the north gates," he said. "What do I do about this Black Ibis cult, though?"

"I would be posting guards at every temple and place of worship within your kingdom and have your forces on high alert. Please send a detachment down to Karatha and protect their temple, too. These cultists will stop at nothing to destroy every last trace of the gods from the world."

Nika was glad to be back in his comfortable travelling clothes. He pulled his thick cloak tighter around him and Arnie to ward off the icy chill and stepped closer to Freyne, waiting for the rest of their friends to assemble in the courtyard. Lana, Gaitan, and Priye emerged from the castle and quietly joined them as the king approached. Kaiton shook hands with Chardi and Ur'Shad, then informally hugged Iryna.

"Take care, my dear. Keep in touch," he said.

"I will. Thank you for your hospitality." She smiled warmly.

Kaiton turned to Nika and shook his hand.

"I'm sure you will make a fine priest someday. Your master truly is the best of the best. Take care, lad."

"Thank you, Your Majesty," Nika replied solemnly.

The king fixed his attention on Freyne and pulled a folded piece of parchment from his pocket.

"As for you, my friend. I've only just received a copy of your file that I requested from the monastery. According to this, Christophe Saul du Freyne was born on the 26th of Oelen, 2985. He was accepted in the 2999 intake and attained the highest rank possible before he disappeared without a trace seven hundred years ago." The king raised his eyebrow.

"What can I say, Your Majesty?" Freyne said quietly. "The years of study and worship required to reach such a level take more than one lifetime. Am knew that and blessed me and the other high priests with a long life."

"But where did you go for all those years?"

"With all due respect, Your Majesty, that information is strictly between Am and I. I hope you understand."

"Very well. It has been a great honour to meet you."

"The honour is mine, Your Majesty." Freyne firmly shook Kaiton's hand. "Thank you for all your help."

"Best of luck on your journey, all of you. I don't think you need me to tell you that the fate of the world is in your hands. May you forever hold Am in your hearts."

The streets were dark and eerie, lit only by an occasional oil lamp. It took almost an hour to reach the northern gates of the city, by which time the sun still had not risen. The guards on duty saluted and waved them through, and the escort turned back towards the castle. Freyne kicked his horse into a canter and led them away from the city.

Nika rode at the back on a spare horse, tired and hungry but in good spirits. He was pleased to be on the road again where he could be himself around his friends. He'd missed Lana, Priye, and Gaitan during their stay at the castle and looked forward to catching up with them again.

Slowly the sun rose into the sky, and after another hour of swift riding, Freyne led them from the road and into a cluster of trees by a stream. Nika slid off his horse and immediately helped himself to Freyne's arms.

"I thought you were leaving us?" Iryna said to Priye.

"I was going to," Priye admitted. "I visited the hospital yesterday and handed over my colleague's belongings. They wanted to send me back to Rarn to help in the war."

"What made you change your mind?" Nika asked.

"Something tells me that you'll need a healer in your travels." She shrugged and rolled her eyes. "Ok, I may have taken a liking to you all. Just maybe, though."

Nika grinned and looked at Gaitan.

"What did you get up to?" he asked.

"I got to meet the king's artisan and learn a few new tricks."

"It's pretty sad if you think seducing a woman is a new trick," Priye said slyly.

"That's not what I meant!" Gaitan said defensively.

"I missed you guys." Nika laughed.

"As for you, Christophe something something Freyne. Are you really a thousand years old? You don't look a day over forty," Chardi said.

"A thousand and four," Nika corrected him.

Freyne sighed.

"You were bound to find out eventually," he said, shaking his head. He reached out and messed up Nika's hair. "I liked it better when you were under the vow of silence."

Nika stifled a laugh and Freyne turned back to Chardi.

"Yes. I really was a high priest and esteemed scholar at the Great Monastery. I'd somewhat retired until someone here came and interrupted my life."

Nika shoved Freyne playfully and they both laughed.

"So what's really going on here?" Priye asked, narrowing her eyes. "I think it's only fair that you fill Gaitan and I in on the whole story."

"I agree," Iryna said.

Freyne nodded, then told Priye and Gaitan about their quest to fulfil the prophecy, omitting the part about the blood descendant. Gaitan's eyes widened.

"I never heard a thing about the militia making an alliance or receiving reinforcements from the mainland. But the night before your capture, a group of people in black cloaks arrived at the garrison and met with Captain Brigal. It was odd because only militia are permitted entry, and these people weren't in uniform. That's when I was sent to Grima with that patrol."

"So this entire war happened because no one could catch you?" Priye asked incredulously.

"I guess so," Freyne replied. "These fanatics will stop at nothing to destroy all that is Am."

"Oh my god. Ner'Am!" Nika gasped as a sudden realisation dawned on him.

"What about Ner'Am?" Ur'Shad frowned.

"Orison said that the temple was destroyed, 'attacked out of hatred and nothing more'," Nika said. "I'll bet you anything that it was the cultists looking for that statue. They wanted to find it before us, but Orison protected it."

"It all makes sense now," Freyne said, pacing by the fire. "They've been looking for the objects of the prophecy, hoping to steal them so we can't succeed. But they failed to find them–"

"– And since they couldn't find those objects, they've been trying to capture us instead," Nika finished. "If they *do* find us, they can still prevent us from fulfilling the prophecy."

"I'm starting to get a bad feeling about this," Ur'Shad said.

"Me too. Let's eat up and get going." Chardi nodded. "Let's hope any remaining militia and that that crazy mancer fall for the decoy and leave us alone."

They rode hard for the next few days, emulating the King's Army method of travelling. As they rode further away from Riz'Hra, the gently rolling hills flattened into a never-ending grassy plain. The cold winter wind lashed at them relentlessly and Nika was starting to think he'd never be warm again.

It took them nine days to reach the seaside city of Barthra. Chardi led them through the quiet streets as it grew steadily darker. Eventually they found an inn overlooking the waterfront and dismounted. Nika could see that the docks weren't as busy as Rybor or the Port of Fraal, and there weren't nearly as many ships. The ones that were there were mostly fishing vessels. The innkeeper came bustling outside with a big smile on his face.

"Welcome, welcome!" He beamed. "I'm your host, Lyal. Do you require lodgings for the night?"

"Yes, please." Chardi nodded.

"Wonderful! Business has been slow lately. We'll take care of your horses. Come inside out of the cold before you get sick."

Lyal led them inside and Chardi paid for their rooms.

"Go right on upstairs. The first rooms on the right are yours. The bathhouse is out the back, and I'll have your dinner sent up shortly since the dining room is closed this evening. If you need anything else, come and find me." Lyal bowed.

Nika followed Freyne up a narrow staircase and into the first available room. He sank down onto the bed and gazed at Freyne, who looked tired and preoccupied.

"Are you alright?" Nika asked him.

"I think so." He paused, then sighed. "No, not really."

Freyne sat on the bed and stared at his feet. Nika could sense his frustration and stress about something and pulled him into a tight hug.

"What's troubling you?" he asked.

"I feel like I've either missed something important or I've messed up the translation of a key passage somewhere," Freyne said quietly. "I can't put my finger on it. It's like it's right on the edge of my mind, but every time I'm about to figure it out, it disappears again."

"I'm sure you'll figure it out," Nika said, trying to sound positive. "You've been spot-on with everything else so far."

"That's the thing, though. If I don't figure this out, I could be sending us to our deaths and ruin everything. What if I lead us to the wrong place? There is so much at stake if I mess this up." Freyne drew a shuddering breath and pulled free of Nika's hold. "I never told you this. While we were in the mountains, Am came to me in a dream. We watched as a world tore itself apart to the point of destruction. It was horrible. I'm afraid that if I mess this up, our own world could also be annihilated. Why else would Am show me that if it there isn't a genuine risk of that happening here?"

"That's a lot of responsibility for one person to carry."

"It is, and I'm really feeling it right now." Freyne sighed again. "I also found out that when my village was destroyed, Am wiped my memory to protect me. Every now and then I find myself remembering snippets of other things, but just as quickly as I recall them, they're gone. I can't help feeling like I'm being manipulated."

"Am would have their reasons, though," Nika said. "Maybe it's their way of guiding us along the right path."

"But don't you think our own thoughts and memories are private and should be off limits? How much more do we have to give of ourselves?"

Freyne was too preoccupied with the prophecy and his stress to even taste his meal. The words and verses were going round and round inside his head, drowning out everything else around him. He stared at his bowl of runny soup, seeing nothing but lines of text scrolling before his eyes.

"Are you coming to have a bath?" Nika asked.

"What?" Freyne looked up and realised that Nika had already finished eating. "Oh. Maybe later. Sorry, boo."

"Don't be sorry, old man. I'm a grown boy; I can take a bath by myself." Nika leant down and kissed him on the forehead. "You know where I am if you change your mind."

Freyne watched Nika slip from the room and became angry with himself. Am had given him one task, to unravel the prophecy and ensure that all of the steps were done properly along the way. The survival of the Black Ibis cult should never have happened, and he could only blame himself. He was a failure.

He pulled his journal from his pocket and flicked through the pages in disbelief. None of it made sense anymore; all of the carefully translated passages were a scrambled mess of random letters. All of his hard work was gone.

"Oh, for fuck's sake!" he screamed, dipping into Nika's more colourful vocabulary.

He hurled his journal at the wall with all of his strength, snatched his towel, and stormed out of the room, slamming the door as hard as he could behind him.

Nika eased himself into the hot steaming tub and stretched out. He tried to relax, but he was worried about Freyne and disappointed that he was to bathe alone. With a sigh, he sank down lower so that his lips were level with the water, and lay there blowing bubbles.

"Sir, you can't go in there! That room is in use," the bath attendant's voice rang out.

"Olis fadus!"

Nika startled and strained his ears to listen to the commotion outside. Freyne's voice sounded angry. The faintest whisper came from the realm, followed by a soft *click*. Freyne barged into Nika's room and locked the door behind him, then started to undress.

"Mind if I join you?" he asked stiffly.

"I thought you'd never come," Nika replied.

311

Freyne climbed into the tub and sat with his arms crossed, scowling at the wall. Nika could feel the raw anger wafting from him, something he'd never sensed from Freyne before. He took a washcloth and hesitantly started to wash Freyne's back.

"Want to talk about it?" he asked.

"Nope. I'm done for today. If the world wants to end tonight, then let it!"

"Okay," Nika said. "What does *olis fadus* mean?"

"In your language, it would be equivalent to saying fuck off." Freyne grunted.

Nika slid to the opposite end of the tub and repositioned his legs, then tugged gently on Freyne's arm.

"Come here and don't argue," he ordered.

Freyne obediently moved so that he was sitting between Nika's legs. He was shaking such was his anger. Nika started massaging his neck and shoulders, carefully working on the tight knots to loosen the tension. After a while Freyne started to relax and his anger gradually subsided.

"I'm so sorry, boo." He slumped forward and buried his face in his hands. "I feel so lost right now."

Nika leaned forward and hugged him from behind.

"It's going to be ok, babe." Nika reassured him. "We have the nautical map, we have the blood descendant, we have the other things we need, and we have each other. All we need to do is find a ship and sail to Gri'Ran's Rest. We're almost there."

"I just want all of this to be over," Freyne said quietly. "I long to be free, to finally live my life as I wish and not under someone else's control. Is that too much to ask?"

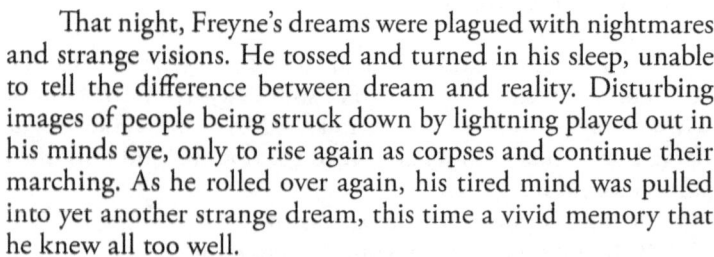

That night, Freyne's dreams were plagued with nightmares and strange visions. He tossed and turned in his sleep, unable to tell the difference between dream and reality. Disturbing images of people being struck down by lightning played out in his minds eye, only to rise again as corpses and continue their marching. As he rolled over again, his tired mind was pulled into yet another strange dream, this time a vivid memory that he knew all too well.

He was standing by the alter in the Inner Sanctum with the other high priests, the Book of Oaths open in front of him.

"Do you, Christophe Saul du Freyne, accept this task bestowed upon you by Am, our god?"

"I accept this responsibility and herby swear an oath in front of our god that I will do all that I can to see this prophecy succeed. Should I become compromised in any way, I promise I will remove myself so I do not sabotage the outcome."

"As Am is our witness, we accept your oath. Please sign here."

The dream shifted…

He stood before a dark tower, gazing at its tip high up in the sky. It wasn't his body, but it felt oddly familiar. Lightning cracked overhead, and in the darkness, a winged beast fluttered through the air. An annoying ticking sound echoed in the back of his mind. Turning his attention back to the door, he reached into his pocket and withdrew the golden gryphon statue. With his hands shaking, he placed it in a notch in the door.

Click.

He pushed open the door, and the view swirled and changed yet again. He was looking down at a small dagger in his hands. The purple gemstones flickered in the light. He held the dagger in both hands and raised it, the tip aimed at his heart…

Everything went black and a deep voice began to speak.

"The time will be signalled by the coming of a stranger,
The world at the time will be in great danger.

"A land from afar, he'll make things right.
Descended from evil, he's one of the light."

"Bring him to me at the place I once dwelled,
And give us his life so balance is upheld."

Freyne wrenched his mind back and bolted upright, sweating and shaking uncontrollably. He looked down at Nika who grunted and rolled over, snoring. His heart was racing as the terrible truth became clear to him, a truth too horrible to comprehend. Freyne stumbled out of bed and rummaged around for a sheet of parchment and his pencil, then scribbled a quick note and placed it on the table while biting back his tears. He quickly dressed and snatched his pack, then tiptoed from the room without looking back.

The wind blowing from the sea was frigid as Freyne led his horse from the stable. He mounted and dared to look up at their room one last time, where his Nika lay sleeping; with a cry of despair, he kicked the horse into a gallop and disappeared into the darkness.

Bar'Am

Part Three

Gri'Ran's Rest

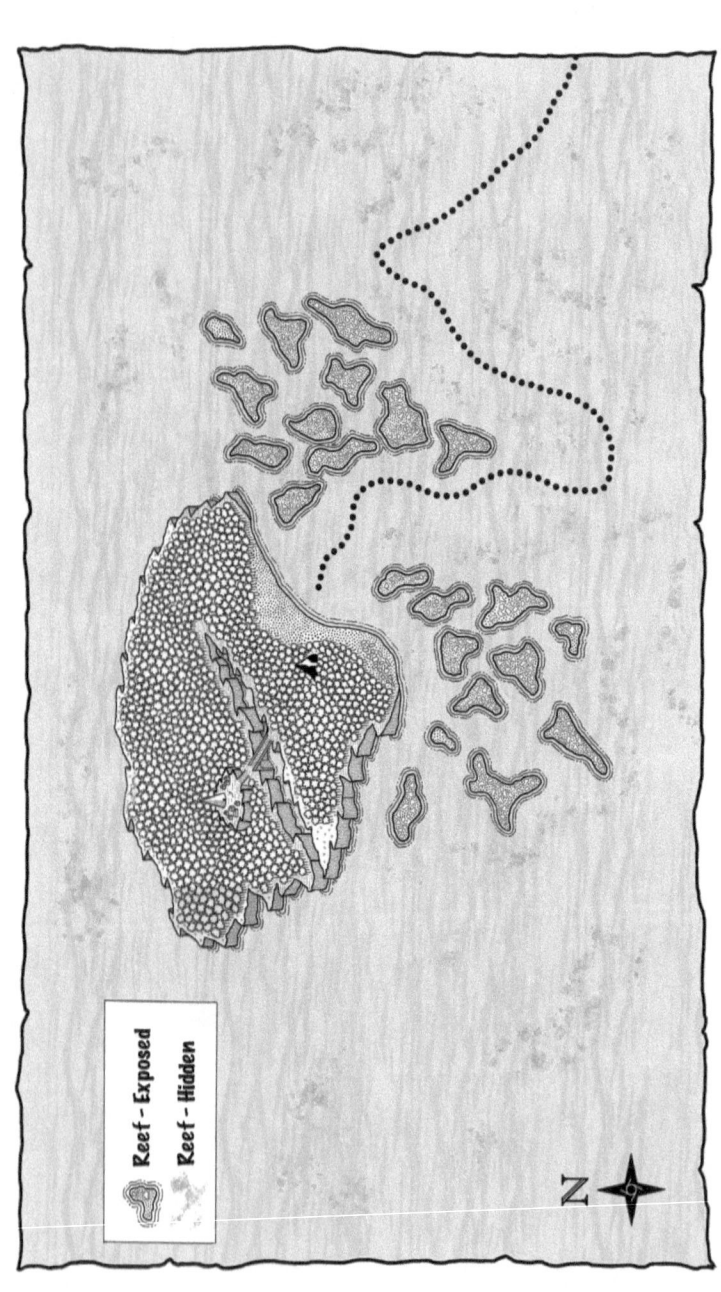

Reef - Exposed

Reef - Hidden

N

21

Nika woke feeling tired and even more drained than the day before. He knew he'd dreamt of the door again, only this time he'd been clutching Freyne's dagger and was pretty sure he was about to plunge it into his own heart. *Why am I seeing this shit? Maybe I'm watching from Gaitan's perspective, but that doesn't make any sense at all.* Unsettled, he rolled over to see if Freyne was awake.

The bed was empty and cold.

He sat up and scanned the room, expecting to see Freyne sitting by the fire, but he was nowhere to be seen. The fire had gone out and the room was icy cold. Something didn't feel right. Confused, he slid out of bed and his eyes fell on the spot where Freyne's pack had been sitting the night before.

It was gone.

Nika's heart started beating a little faster and he looked slowly around the room, taking in every tiny detail. Freyne's clothes, shoes, and cloak were all gone. A single sheet of parchment was on the table and he picked it up with a sinking feeling in his stomach.

My dearest Nikolai,

There are not enough words to tell you how sorry I am.
I cannot go any further with you lest I break my oath to the gods.
You need to know that I love you with all that I am.
Do not come looking for me.

Freyne.

Nika read the words again and felt his entire world start crashing down around him. He took a few steps backwards and thudded into the corner as the room started to spin before his eyes. It felt as though the walls were closing in on him. He slid slowly down the wall to the floor, gasping for breath and shaking uncontrollably. His eyes darted around the room as the harsh reality sunk in.

Freyne was gone.

Arnie-Kyn emerged from the corner of his vision and sat by his side. He placed his little paw on Nika's leg and meowed softly. Nika pulled him into his arms and buried his face in the cat's fur as the tears began to flow. He'd never felt so much pain and didn't know how to deal with it. A part of him wanted to be angry that Freyne could just get up and leave him.

Once he was able to get his sobs under control, he wiped his eyes and looked down at Arnie. The cat rubbed his face on Nika's goatee, purring.

"Why?" he found himself asking. *"Why?"*

"He finally figured it out," Arnie replied. *"The final piece of the puzzle. And he knew that if he stayed with us, he would interfere in the outcome and forever doom the world. It had to be."*

"But why couldn't I go with him?" Nika asked.

"You are needed to perform a task at our destination," Arnie said. *"Perhaps the most important task of us all."*

"What do you mean?"

"Take his journal and see for yourself."

Nika looked across at Freyne's journal where it still sat on the floor after his fit of rage the night before. He held out his hand and used the realm to call it to him. It flew through the air and landed in his hand, open at the page where it had fallen. He felt a sharp pang in his chest as he remembered the day they purchased it; he'd watched Freyne writing in it for hours on end and knew how important it was to him. Nika's eyes brimmed with more tears and he turned back to the open page.

"You know I can't read this," he said, looking at Freyne's beautiful writing.

"Relax your mind and let me in. One will help you," Arnie said.

Nika didn't have the energy to argue. He took a deep breath and felt Arnie's mind join with his. His presence was overwhelmingly strong. Nika looked back at the page and the symbols began to swirl and lift off the page before his eyes.

"…Through a rift in time and space, he of the bloodline will return to us and be met by his guardian. The keeper of knowledge shall join with them, and together they will travel to Gri'Ran's Rest where the deed must take place. He shall bear the lost dagger and Gri'Ran's Gift, and will offer his soul to the gods to fix that which was destroyed…

…He will be joined by a royal witness, her protectors, and an artisan, who shall each have their own tasks to fulfil. These trusted friends shall help him to fulfil his destiny…

…The keeper of knowledge will suffer a time of great conflict. He will be forced to make a choice – either relinquish his friendships or forever to doom our beloved world…"

Nika re-read the words and the image of the door flooded into his mind. With a sick feeling in the pit of his stomach, he recalled his violent dream the night before. There was no way he could deny it; he'd been ready to drive that blade into his own heart, even longed for it, and those feelings were his and his alone. Everything suddenly made sense.

"The blood descendant. It was me all along."

Arnie was silent and gazed deep into Nika's eyes, unblinking.

"So, I'm expected to just waltz into some tower and kill myself for a world I don't even know or understand? Give my life for people who don't give two shits about me?"

"It is your destiny," Arnie replied. *"The death of Ami'Khel tore time and space asunder for a split second for he had no son. However, his lover was pregnant with his child at the time and disappeared without a trace. It is believed that the tear in the world's fabric sucked her into your world, and that's where your bloodline has been ever since."*

"I still don't understand how I got here."

"Am needed you. One is not entirely sure how they did it, but it was Am and the god from your world who got you here. Do you know why Freyne's people built their altar in that place?"

"No?"

"That's where the forefathers met and begged Am to come and be their god. It was the place where Am finally accepted us as their people. That place is sacred and powerful."

"What happens afterwards?" Nika asked. *"Once I'm dead and buried, I mean. Does everyone just go home and pretend nothing ever happened? What about Fr..."* he broke off, unable to finish his sentence.

"One does not know," Arnie said. *"I'm sorry, Nika. I really am."*

Nika felt Arnie's mind slip away and an overwhelming wave of grief washed over him. Arnie leapt from his arms as Nika drew his knees to his chest and rocked backwards and forwards. His heart was breaking and his pain rolled from his eyes, down his cheeks and into his lap.

Time stood still as he broke down and wept. His entire life was built on nothing but false hope. Once again he'd dared to dream, only to have it shattered into a million pieces. And the one person who supposedly cared for him had fled, abandoned him, forcing him to face the truth alone.

His sadness turned to bitterness and he glared down at the leather band on his wrist. *Feelings my arse. Nothing but fucking lies.* He tugged roughly at the band, but the leather would not break. His anger rising, he tugged and pulled harder and harder until the friction broke his skin. The sight of his own blood fuelled his anger into rage and he lashed out, punching the wall, leaving a trail of blood on the mortar until he broke down into a sobbing mess.

He didn't hear the pounding on the door or even Lyal forcing it open. It wasn't until Lana gasped and placed her hand on his shoulder that he realised he wasn't alone. She and Iryna knelt before him and said something he couldn't comprehend. Lana wrapped her arms around him and pulled his head against her chest, cradling him until his tears finally stopped.

Nika stared into space without seeing, vaguely registering what was going on. Priye dabbed something on the cuts that stung but he didn't flinch. He welcomed the pain; pain was the only thing left to feel. She wrapped Nika's hand and wrist in a bandage, then held a small vial to his lips and expertly got the liquid into his mouth.

"Is Ur'Shad and Chardi back yet?" she asked quietly.

"No, but Gaitan's floating around somewhere. I'll go and find him," Iryna said.

They helped him off the floor and guided him onto the bed. A sense of calm washed over him, his mind finally silent, and he fell into a dreamless sleep.

"What in the gods happened here?" Ur'Shad asked when he returned from the docks.

"Freyne took off. He left Nika a note," Iryna said.

"Really? Wow. I assume Nika's not taking it well at all?"

"Of course he isn't. The poor man's heart is broken," Iryna snapped. "He was in a terrible state when we found him."

"He looks calm enough," Chardi said. He turned to Priye. "What did you do to him?"

"I gave him a little something to calm him down before he gave himself a heart attack," Priye said. "He should wake up soon, and I imagine he will be hungry."

"How long has he been sleeping?" Ur'Shad asked.

"Around an hour. It was only a very small dose," she replied. "He's not to be left alone for the next few days. Understood?"

Everyone nodded in agreeance.

"Did you find a ship?" Iryna asked.

"Yes. We leave tomorrow when the tide changes," Ur'Shad replied. "The captain refuses to load the horses, though. We're going to have to sell them."

"Do we even know where we're going?"

"Somewhere north, I think," Chardi replied. "Freyne did mention having a nautical chart. Let's pray that he didn't take it with him."

The rest of the day and night passed before Nika's eyes like a blur. It felt like he was lying in the bottom of a deep dark well, only he couldn't see a light in the distance. He was vaguely aware of his friends always being around, occasionally making him eat or drink something, but all he wanted to do was sleep and shut out the world around him.

Morning came all too soon. Nika slowly collected the few things that Freyne had left behind and put them in his pack. He took one last look around the room and noticed that one of Freyne's pencils had rolled under the bed. Biting back more tears, he picked it up and shoved it in his pocket, then followed Gaitan from the room. They found Ur'Shad and Iryna downstairs, talking to Lyal.

"Are you ready?" Ur'Shad asked as they approached.

Nika brushed past him and stalked towards the waiting ship. He could see Chardi and Priye on the dock with the captain, overseeing their belongings being loaded.

"Head on through the hold and follow the signs to the berths," the captain said, pointing inside. "We leave in half an hour."

After dumping his pack and Arnie in his room, Nika made his way to the stern and watched as the land slipped away behind them. He'd never felt so alone in all his life. A part of him hoped that Freyne would appear at the last moment and rejoin them, but there was no sign of him. Nika brushed his tears away and pulled Freyne's journal from his pocket.

As he flicked through the pages, he realised there was more than just snippets of prophecy. He'd written notes and drawn diagrams, trying to piece things together in a timeline. Every now and then, he came across a page covered in doodles. On one such page there was even a sketch of Nika's tattoo.

After a few more pages of prophecy he found another doodle page, and once again his eyes filled with tears. On the right was a detailed drawing of the pattern Freyne had woven into the leather band, with *Nikolai* etched in the middle. The left page had a rough drawing of the two of them standing in front of a house or cottage with wild flowers growing up the side. Sitting between them was Arnie-Kyn.

Nika wiped his eyes and he continued to flick through the pages one by one until he came across a calendar which was similar to the one on the back of the map. Freyne had traced their journey back to Nika's arrival and filled in parts of their journey along the way. As his eyes swept the timeline, he saw that his birthday had been added and was only ten days away. He sighed miserably and closed the journal, clutching it tightly to his chest as the first drops of rain started to fall.

"There you are. I've been looking for you," Priye said, joining him on the stern. "How are you feeling?"

He closed his eyes and shook his head, still not ready to talk about it. Priye rubbed his back and he opened his eyes.

"I get it." She unstoppered a small flask and offered it to him. "Take a swig of this. It helps."

Nika accepted it and took a gulp of fiery liquid. He coughed and spluttered as it burnt all the way down to his stomach.

"What *is* that?" he asked, eyeing the flask suspiciously.

"Medicinal alcohol, better known as fire water." She laughed and took a deep swig. "It helps take the edge off of life, if you get my drift."

She offered the flask again and he helped himself to a much deeper drink. The burn dulled the pain just a little.

"Now, let me check your dressing."

Nika held out his hand and Priye slowly unwrapped the bandage. The skin was missing from his knuckles and his hand was dark purple and swollen. She gently tested each of his fingers, and as she moved his pinkie, a sharp pain shot up his hand. Nika flinched and sucked in a deep breath.

"You did a nice job of it. That wall really had it coming." Priye smirked. "Your finger is broken."

He watched in silence as she strapped his broken finger to his ring finger, then dabbed some ointment on his cuts and the graze around his wrist.

"Did he give you this?" she asked, pointing at the leather band.

"Yeah. He made it for me."

"He's very skilled," she said, nudging him gently. "He could teach Gaitan a thing or two."

Nika felt a small grin form on his face.

"That's the way." She shot him a warm smile. "Losing the love of your life is never easy. You'll soon learn to approach it with cynicism and sarcasm."

"You lost someone too?" Nika asked.

"My first husband died of sickness years ago. We were young and in love, so it cut me deeply. A few years later, I met another man and we married. Things were great until I found him in bed with a woman half my age."

"What did you do?"

"I snatched his hunting knife and chased them out of my house, and told him that if I ever see either of them again, they'll get cut. People don't like it when their peen is being threatened with a knife."

"Ugh. I was chased by a lady's husband one time," Nika said, feeling his cheeks flush. "She never told me she was married. He had something a bit more deadly than a knife, too. It wasn't my proudest moment."

Priye laughed and gulped down more of her fire water.

"How did you deal with it, though?" Nika asked. "You know. The hurt, betrayal."

"I dedicated my time to helping others," she said. "If you have a creative outlet, bury yourself in it. Focus on what you enjoy doing, and heal from within."

"Ok." Nika nodded.

Priye stood and looked expectantly at him.

"Well, come on. Lunch will be ready soon. Let's get you inside and out of the rain."

Nika spent his days at sea mostly by himself, sitting on the stern and watching the dark swells trailing in the water. He'd taken Priye's advice and busied himself in his music. He started writing a song and poured his emotions into the music. At first his hand was too sore to play the cittern, but as he healed, he was able to pluck away at the strings a little more each day until he perfected his song.

He quickly learnt to put on his happy face around his friends, but deep down he was struggling. Everything reminded him of Freyne, and at times he resented having given his heart so easily. Late at night when he knew his friends were asleep, he'd let his emotions run free and quietly sob himself to sleep. The dream about the door became more frequent, and each time it grew more and more violent. He no longer felt afraid and instead welcomed his fate. Soon, he would be free of the pain that bound him to Ayrillis.

After almost five weeks at sea, the appearance of sharp jagged reefs and rocks announced that they were close to Gri'Ran's Rest. Nika could sense a powerful presence growing stronger by the day and knew without a doubt that it belonged to Gri'Ran. Unlike the warm and loving presence he'd felt from Am, Gri'Ran's was commanding and not to be trifled with.

On the eve of reaching the island, a wild storm rolled in and raged above them. Nika swung in his hammock as the ship rolled in the swells, quietly humming his song to calm his nerves. He'd hardly slept that night; he knew from the nautical chart in Freyne's journal that they were in a narrow channel surrounded by reefs and ridges, and one wrong move could spell disaster.

As though to confirm his fears, the ship suddenly jolted and flung Nika from his hammock. He landed painfully as a loud grinding sound reached his ears. The ship shuddered and tilted to one side, then grew eerily still. Nika stumbled to his feet and snatched his pack.

"Arnie!" he yelled, searching frantically for the cat.

Arnie-Kyn bolted from his hiding place and Nika grabbed him. The ship shuddered as a wave crashed over her deck and water splashed down the stairs and into the cabins.

"Everybody out!" he yelled, thumping on the cabin doors. "Hurry! We're sinking!"

Nika's companions scrambled into the hallway, groggy from sleep, and gasped as they stepped in the freezing water.

"What's going on?" Chardi grumbled, wiping the sleep from his eyes. "Gri'Ran's claws!"

"Just grab what you can and come with me. We have to get off this ship, now!" Nika yelled.

He turned and led the way upstairs as another wave crashed into the ship, spilling more icy water on them. As soon as he reached the deck, he could see that the ship had grounded on a rocky outcrop and was in danger of breaking apart. A bright flash of lightning forked across the sky, followed by a deafening crack of thunder.

"Hold on!" he called as another wave broke over the deck, spraying them all with salty water.

Nika led his friends up the sloping deck and clung onto the rail with his spare hand. The captain and his sailors were all gone. He looked down and eyed the rocks below.

"We're going to have to jump," Ur'Shad yelled. "Nika and Gaitan, you two go first!"

Nika leapt over the side and landed roughly. He released Arnie and threw his pack up higher to safety as Gaitan landed beside him. Ur'Shad and Chardi lowered Iryna and Priye over the side and Nika and Gaitan caught them. Chardi reached out his hand to Lana, but before he could grip her hand, another wave smashed into the ship. Lana screamed as Chardi and Ur'Shad were knocked over the rail and tumbled onto the rocks below. A loud cracking sound reverberated around the reef as the ship broke apart and splintered in the waves.

"Lana?" Iryna screamed. "Where's Lana?"

Nika slipped into the realm and searched frantically for her aura, but she was gone.

"I-I can't see her!" he stammered. "She was only just there!"

A large section of the ship broke free and the angry sea rammed it against the rocks, showering them with splinters and debris.

"We need to move higher," Gaitan called urgently.

Chardi sat up, holding his head in his hands. Ur'Shad was lying unmoving nearby on the ground. Priye knelt down beside him and checked him over.

"He's unconscious, but he should be ok. Can any of you help carry him?" she called.

Chardi stood, holding his hand to his side, and limped towards Ur'Shad as another wave sprayed them with icy water. Gaitan and Nika took a leg each as Chardi staggered backwards, half dragging the big man up the rocky outcrop. Iryna stood rooted to the spot, still staring at the wreck. Priye took her arm and pulled her away up the rocks.

They found a flat rock and laid Ur'Shad on it gently. Chardi clutched at his side and sat next to Ur'Shad, then glanced around.

"Where's Lana?" he asked, a hint of panic in his voice.

"Chardi…" Iryna wavered.

She broke down sobbing and hugged the big man.

"No." Chardi shook his head in disbelief. "It can't be. She was right there with us."

Nika felt a deep pang in his heart as the reality of everything set in. In the space of a few seconds, he'd lost another friend. He slid back down the reef to collect his pack and scanned the realm again, but still he could not locate her.

She was gone.

The darkness surrounded him, and once again he felt himself slipping into the well of despair. He staggered away and found a secluded place to sit, then rummaged through his pack to ensure everything was still inside. Freyne's journal and the firestone were wrapped neatly in one of his shirts, but the makeshift pouch that held the golden gryphon was nowhere to be seen. Nika frantically pulled everything out and checked again, but the little statue was gone.

"Fuck!"

He spent the rest of the night and early morning biting his nails and fretting. Without the statue, there was no way he could open the door and fulfil the prophecy. The storm eventually blew itself away and the wild waves calmed themselves as the sun rose slowly to the middle of the sky. In the distance, he could see the cove where they needed to go. They were so close, yet so far.

A flicker of movement caught his attention and he turned to see a small boat rowing towards the wreck. Nika stood and made his way back to the others as quickly as he could.

"Where have you been?" Ur'Shad asked.

He was sitting up, his head wrapped in a bandage, and his eyes were puffy and rimmed with red. Chardi was nowhere to be seen.

"There's a boat coming," Nika said, dodging the question. "Let's go before we're stuck here."

They gathered the few packs they'd managed to save and hurried down to the water's edge. Gaitan waved until he caught the sailors' attention. Out of the corner of his eye, Nika spotted Chardi staring forlornly out to sea. His heart broke and he quickly averted his gaze.

"Hey! You folks need help?"

"I'm not planning on swimming across," Gaitan mumbled.

Nika recognised the two sailors as Bren and Rhill from the fated ship. As their boat drifted towards the rock, he reached out and grasped the side to help steady them.

"Are there any other survivors?" he asked.

"None that we know of," Bren said. "Now tha' the storm is broken we're gonna keep looking, though."

"Hop in and we'll row you across to that island." Rhill pointed at Gri'Ran's Rest is the distance. "We can take three of you across at a time."

Ur'Shad, Iryna and Priye crossed first, allowing Nika time to search the wreckage for Gri'Ran's Gift. Splintered wood and debris floated on the current, a further reminder of the tragedy that took place only hours before. The statue was nowhere to be seen. He'd failed.

He was quiet as the sailors rowed him across to the cove. The deep sadness wafting from Chardi added to Nika's own pain. He cradled Arnie-Kyn in his arms and cuddled into him, desperate to feel comforted.

The only safe place to go ashore was a small sandy beach. Sharp rocks and reefs made up the rest of the coastline that Nika could see. Beyond the beach was a dark forest. Priye emerged from the trees and waved, then headed towards them.

"Head on over there." Bren pointed to the tree line behind her. "Just a few paces into the trees is a cave."

"Have you been here before?" Gaitan asked.

"Well, sort of." Rhill shifted and shot a look at Bren. "We, er, had a disagreement with the captain last night. He treated us like dirt and we'd had enough. When we warned him about the storm and suggested we drop anchor before we entered the reefs, he laughed at us and called us idiots. Said that we're fired the moment we get back to Barthra. So, we stole this boat and abandoned ship. The wreck was entirely his fault."

Nika's sadness turned to anger, but he kept his mouth shut and leapt over the side of the boat.

"Are you coming?" he asked.

"Not yet. We'll go and see if there are any more survivors."

"I'll go with you," Chardi said quietly.

"No you won't," Priye said firmly. "I still need to check you over. Don't think I didn't notice that cut on your arm."

Chardi held up his left arm; an angry cut ran from his elbow to his wrist, caked in dried blood. He sighed nodded, then wordlessly followed her. Priye beckoned and led them back to a rocky cave. Iryna and Ur'Shad were seated by the mouth, wrapped in each other's arms. Nika could tell they'd both been crying. Biting back more tears of his own, he stumbled away and busied himself with gathering wood for a fire. It didn't take him long to have a decent pile stacked inside the cave and he soon had a warm fire going.

"What are we going to do?" Iryna asked. "We've got nothing. No food. No clothes. No weapons."

"We'll be okay," Nika said, patting her on the shoulder. "Check the packs to see what equipment we do have. I'll go and see what I can do about some food."

He made his way back to the beach and walked slowly through the sand towards the rocky area. Despite his words of reassurance to Iryna, deep down he had no idea what to do for food. He stopped and gazed out at the now calm waters, feeling utterly lost, when he heard a gentle *meow* behind him. Turning, he saw that Arnie had followed him.

"Are you okay?" Nika asked.

"One is fine," Arnie replied. *"I wanted to thank you for saving my life. One is grateful."*

"I've already lost enough of those I care for."

"What's wrong, human?" Arnie sat and gazed into his eyes. *"One can sense that something else is troubling you."*

"I've lost Gri'Ran's Gift."

"Oh dear." Arnie's tail flicked.

"What am I going to do?"

"Let's focus on the problem at hand first. What do you plan to hunt? It's easier to think with a full stomach."

"You know I'm no hunter," Nika said. *"I did go fishing a lot with my foster family, though. We used to catch crabs and fish in the rock pools at low tide. It's worth a try."*

"Very well."

Together, Nika and Arnie walked slowly over the exposed reefs, looking for something edible. He watched as the cat stopped and crouched over a pool with his paw at the ready, his tail weaving slowly from side to side. Arnie swiped at the water and caught himself a small fish.

"Your turn," he said.

Nika could feel his face transform into a slight grin. He continued to walk carefully amongst the rocks until he saw something move. A giant crab backed itself up against the wall of a pool, its claws raised threateningly. Using a rock, Nika stunned and killed it. He held it up for Arnie to see.

"See? I'm not completely useless."

"One shall reserve judgement for the time being," Arnie said.

"Behave, or I'll use you for bait."

He took off his over-shirt and tied the sleeves together, filling it with his catch. He soon had enough crab for everyone, plus a few fish caught by Arnie-Kyn. They turned to head back to camp and spotted the sailors rowing back towards the cove. Nika hurried to meet them.

"How'd you go?" he asked.

"No more survivors," Rhill said bleakly. "Only bodies. And…"

"And?" Nika asked.

"We found your friend. I'm so sorry."

Nika closed his eyes for a moment, fighting back more tears.

"We did manage to salvage a few useful things, too," Rhill added. "A section of the hold was still intact, though it was flooded. Can you give us a hand?"

Nika helped Bren and Rhill to unload the bodies and laid them in a neat row along the beach. Once they were done, he gazed sadly at Lana's lifeless body. Her face was pale beneath her midnight black hair.

"I'll go and let the others know that you found her," he said. "I'll be back soon."

Nika, Gaitan, Priye, and the sailors sat together at the edge of the forest, keeping a respectful distance from Chardi, Iryna, and Ur'Shad while they mourned their lost friend.

"You know, no matter how many people I've seen die, it's never easy losing a friend," Priye said sadly. "She was such a lovely lass."

"She was the kindest person I've ever met." Gaitan nodded. "Why did she always carry that knife with her though?"

"It was for self-defence."

"I'm sure it was just for show."

"I can assure you, it wasn't." Nika sighed and looked at his feet. "Lana would have done anything to help her friends. She has helped me so much and she never even realised it. I just wish I had the opportunity to thank her for everything."

Ur'Shad broke away from the others and made his way back to where Nika sat.

"Chardi and Iryna have agreed on burial," he said quietly. "The tradition in Al'Obrel is to hold vigil for a day, then lay them to rest at sunrise the next morning. She deserves nothing less."

"Is there anything we can help with?" Nika asked.

"We'll need to dig the hole for her grave and make some sort of marker," Ur'Shad replied. "We also need to take care of the rest of the bodies."

"They won't need any special treatment," Rhill said. "We can bury them all together in one big hole. Anything is better than being lost at sea."

"Gaitan and I will help you and Bren with the sailors," Nika offered, standing up. "I don't suppose you were able to recover a pick or spade?"

"Actually, I did," Rhill said.

"Good. You can start digging. Go find a spot over there." Nika pointed at the tree line further up the beach. "Bren, you go and see if anything has washed up from the wreck that we can use for a marker. Gaitan and I will start moving the bodies before the tide comes in."

The afternoon felt surreal for Nika. Iryna brushed and braided Lana's hair and prepared her for burial. Chardi found a nice spot overlooking the beach and dug a small grave. He lined the bottom with fern fronds, then sat by Lana's side while Iryna fussed over her body. Everyone pitched in to help in some way or another, and by late afternoon, everything was sorted. Nika cooked the crabs and fish on the open fire and they ate in silence, exhausted. He leant back against the wall of the cave while he picked at his food, his thoughts turning to his own impending death. He didn't want his friends to be sad and mourn for him, too; they had already mourned enough.

Something within the highest realm seemed to stir, but Nika had no idea what it meant. As beautiful as that realm was, he couldn't understand it like Freyne did. Feeling restless, he stood up and slipped away from the others, and headed back down to the beach. He found a secluded place in between some rocks and nestled himself down, watching the sun dip below the horizon. The sky rippled with different hues of red, orange, yellow, and the faintest hint of purple. A renewed sense of sadness washed over him, and he allowed his tears to run down his cheeks and into the sand.

Looking back towards the shipwreck, he replayed the

dramatic events in his mind, visualising everything that had happened. He watched as the ship slowly crept towards the dangerous outcrop, then held his breath as he waited for the waves to slam it onto the rocks.

The ship didn't crash.

Nika blinked and sat up. He wasn't imagining the ship being wrecked; he was looking at another ship creeping towards the cove. It drifted slowly past the wreck, then dropped anchor. Nika watched in disbelief as a single rowboat was lowered into the water. The sole occupant slowly rowed ashore. Nika frowned as the person leapt from the boat and pulled it onto the beach, then stopped and looked around. His heart leapt into his throat as the tall figure started walking towards him.

He knew who it was before his feet had even touched the sand. In a sudden burst of anger, Nika summoned a wall of energy between them and watched as Freyne collided with it and fell backwards. With a sob, Nika turned and fled into the darkness.

22

He ran through the forest, branches and shrubs whipping at his face and arms in his haste to get away. His eyes stung and his chest was tight. *The audacity! How dare he abandon me then waltz back as though nothing happened?*

"Nika! Come back, please," Freyne called.

The sound of snapping twigs and crunching leaves grew louder behind him. Nika's anger intensified and he pushed himself to keep going. He clutched at a stitch in his side and broke free from the trees.

"Watch ou–"

Nika's stomach lurched as his foot landed on nothing but air. Before he could stop his momentum, he stumbled and fell. His anger turned to panic as he plunged down a steep cliff, his arms and legs flailing.

"Freyne!"

Something soft like a net caught him and broke his fall. He squirmed frantically until he realised he was suspended in the air, an invisible force keeping him from smashing into the jagged rocks below. That same force began to draw him back towards the top of the cliff, inch by terrifying inch. Nika sucked in several rasping breaths to try and calm his panic. He was too scared to move in case whatever was lifting him were to lose its grip.

As he reached the top, he spotted Freyne at the edge of the cliff, his hand extended and a look of absolute concentration on his face. He was sweating and shaking from the effort of saving Nika's life. Freyne guided him towards safety and released him.

Nika stumbled and almost fell backwards, but Freyne caught his hand and pulled him roughly away from danger. His grip was so tight that Nika winced at the pressure on his little finger. He wrenched his hand free and collapsed on the ground, shaking and gasping for breath. Panting, Freyne sank to the ground next to him and reached out to take Nika's hand. Nika wriggled out of reach and crossed his arms defiantly.

"Are we going to talk about this?" Freyne asked.

"What's there to talk about? *You* abandoned *me*, remember? You left me to face this stupid prophecy all by myself when I needed you more than ever."

"I panicked, ok?" Freyne snapped and sat upright. "You pulled me in to your dream and I saw it all. How would you feel if you had to witness your loved one be taken from you and be powerless to stop it?"

Nika stood and brushed himself off angrily.

"It fucking sucks, but it happens!" he shouted. "Just like I had to watch as Lana was swept away and killed. But hey, at least *you* didn't have to witness that! I didn't get to say goodbye and thank her for her friendship, or even get to comfort her before her death. At least you and I would have had each other and we would have been able to say a proper goodbye!"

He spun abruptly on his heel and stormed back towards the trees, his blood boiling.

"Nika, wait!" Freyne dashed after him and landed his hand on Nika's shoulder. "What happened to Lana?"

"Didn't you see the wreck? It's a miracle the rest of us even made it out alive. But you would have known that if you were here."

Nika could just make out the look of chagrin on his face. Freyne let his hand drop and stood gaping at Nika, his mouth opening and closing but nothing came out. Tears sprang to his eyes and rolled down his cheeks.

"I needed you," Nika continued hotly. "Every single night since you left, I had to try and come to terms with the fact that I eventually have to face that door by myself. Run that dagger into my own heart and die alone. No goodbye. No comfort. How would *you* feel if you knew you had to sacrifice your life to gods or people you don't even know? This isn't even my world and I have no fucking say in the matter!"

"Y-you don't understand. I-I had to leave," Freyne choked. "If I didn't, I would have tried to save you, and that would have been disastrous—"

"Then why come back at all?"

"Because I think you'll need this."

Freyne reached into his pocket and balanced something golden in the palm of his hand. Nika's stomach twisted painfully; there was the missing statue of Gri'Ran that he thought was lost at the bottom of the sea.

"Where did you get that?" he demanded, snatching it out of Freyne's hand.

"It was in my pack. I have no idea how it got there, but the fact that I had it meant that I had no choice but to find you and give it back. So now you have it."

Nika stared at the statue in his hand, feeling the familiar warmth radiate from his palm up his arm and to the rest of his body. His anger was rapidly draining while being replaced by a deep sadness. Freyne wordlessly sidestepped him and disappeared into the jungle, leaving him alone on the clifftop. A surge of guilt rose in his chest.

"Wait!" he called.

The crunching of leaves was growing fainter and Freyne didn't stop. Nika shoved the statue into his pocket and ran after him, pushing his way back through the thick foliage. He could no longer hear Freyne's footsteps up ahead and felt the panic rising once more. With tears streaming down his cheeks, he didn't notice the dark outline in front of him until it was too late. Nika collided with him and they both fell roughly onto their backsides.

"Oof!" Freyne gasped.

Nika scrambled to his feet, dazed. In the darkness he could see Freyne sitting up, rubbing his head. Nika reached down and helped him up.

"I'm so sorry," he blubbered, trying to control his emotions. "Please, don't go. I don't want you to leave."

"I'm the one who should be sorry, boo," Freyne said, sliding his hands into his pockets and looking at his feet. "I never wanted to leave you, and I will regret it until the day I die. I'll never forgive myself for hurting you and abandoning you in your time of need."

"I still don't understand *why* you left." Nika sniffed.

"Because I'm a coward." Freyne took a step back. "It seems like whenever something bad happens, I run away with my tail between my legs. Last time, I hid in a forest for seven hundred years. How long would it have been this time? A thousand?"

"You're not a coward."

"I am. It's true."

Nika lowered his eyes to the ground and shook his head. He was exhausted, grieving, hungry, and terrified about his upcoming appointment with death. The last thing he needed was for his heart to be broken all over again.

"I'm going to be dead soon. If you need to leave, I'll understand. But at least have the decency to let me say goodbye first. So until you make up your mind, I'm going back to camp."

He brushed past Freyne and pushed his way through the trees towards where he thought the cave was. After several paces, he heard Freyne crashing through the branches behind him.

"Nika!"

Nika stopped and turned around just in time to be swept into Freyne's arms. His shoulders were heaving in time with his sobs. Raw pain and regret radiated from him. Nika hugged him back and buried his face in Freyne's neck, and for the first time since Barthra, allowed himself to mourn for his own impending death.

"I'm so scared," Nika wept.

"Me too. I've never known happiness until I met you. After all I've done for Am, the one and only person I've ever truly loved is fated to be taken from me. How is this fair?"

Nika shook his head, unable to answer. They held each other tight until Nika finally got his tears under control.

"Can you stay with me tonight? I don't think I can handle being alone right now."

"You won't be alone again, I promise. I'll stay by your side until the very end. You deserve nothing less."

Freyne ran his fingers along Nika's cheek and gently lifted his chin. He lent forward and pressed his lips to Nika's almost hesitantly. Nika's belly filled with butterflies and he accepted Freyne's kiss with every fibre of his body. He pulled back only to stifle a yawn.

"I'm so tired," he said, feeling a wave of fatigue come over him. "Let's go and get some sleep. We need to be up at sunrise to say goodbye to Lana."

"Everything I do, I do for a reason. Only I can see the bigger picture. Trust me, my son. All will be clear soon..."

Freyne felt his shoulder being shaken and his dream vanished. He opened his eyes to see Ur'Shad and Iryna peering down at him. Nika twisted out of his arms and sat up, yawning.

"What are you doing here?" Iryna demanded angrily.

Freyne tried to hide his unease by sitting up, but her gaze bore into him. He'd expected his friends to be mad, not hostile.

"I know you're angry with me and you have every right to be," he said. "I'm so sorry."

"Sorry isn't going to bring Lana back! Sorry isn't going to get us off this stinking island! You should have—"

"Er. Princess?" Ur'Shad interrupted.

"What?!"

"He came here on a ship. We're no longer trapped here."

"Oh. Well. Still, you shouldn't have run off like that!"

"I know, and it's something I will regret for the rest of my life," Freyne said. "You have every right to be angry with me."

"Can we discuss this later?" Ur'Shad asked. "The sun will begin to rise soon. We need to prepare to lay Lana to rest."

"Alright." Iryna nodded.

Nika stood and pulled Freyne to his feet. They dusted the sand from each other's backs then followed Iryna and Ur'Shad to a small cave. Chardi was sitting on a ledge of rock next to Priye, looking as though he hadn't slept a wink.

"You're back," he grunted.

"I am. How are you holding up?"

Freyne sat next to him and hesitated before placing his hand on Chardi's shoulder.

"N-not very well. I can't help but blame myself. I should have been protecting her, but instead I failed her."

"There was nothing you could have done to save her," Freyne said softly. "When it's time, it's time."

"You're a man of faith. What happens to her now?"

"If she was an active follower, Am would have already taken her soul to the afterlife where she'll rest eternally. Since she wasn't, she'll remain where her body is laid to rest."

"So her soul will just linger here forever?" Chardi choked.

"Usually, yes."

"Usually?"

"I was a high priest, remember? As her lover, you get to decide if you'd like me to say a prayer of deliverance and have her soul taken to the afterlife. This is an important decision, though, because you need to respect her thoughts and beliefs. No one should be bound into the afterlife if they do not subscribe to the gods."

"Lana would always join in the prayers at court and held absolute respect for Am. I think she would approve of this."

"Understand that while her body will remain here, it will decay and become of the earth in which she was buried. The only tie she will have to this life is our memory of her. She will live on through us honouring her."

"Are you saying I can't come back here to visit her grave?"

"You can, but she won't be here. If you want to feel close to her, I suggest you pray. Visit the Sanctuary at the monastery or any place of Am and you will be even closer to her."

"All right. Do it." Chardi nodded. "I feel a bit better knowing that she will be resting peacefully with Am."

"So do I."

"Thank you. I'm glad you came back."

A faint hint of orange touched the horizon. Ur'Shad stood and looked meaningfully at Chardi.

"Come on, brother. It's time," he said.

Chardi nodded and stood. Priye patted him on the back, her usual sarcasm replaced with compassion for once.

"It's going to be alright," she said soothingly. "Let's go."

Freyne accepted Nika's proffered hand and followed Ur'Shad through the trees until they reached Lana's resting place. They made a circle around her lifeless body and stood in silence. Freyne knelt down and took her hand, a knot forming in his throat. His heart broke for her; she didn't deserve to die so young. He said his silent goodbye and brushed away his tears, then stood and rejoined Nika.

One by one they knelt down and said their own goodbyes.

Chardi was last and carefully pulled her into one final embrace. He buried his face in her hair and wept quietly. After some time had passed, Freyne patted his shoulder and the big man nodded.

"I love you so much," he whispered.

Chardi laid her back down and took his place in the circle.

"Let us bow our heads in prayer," Freyne said quietly. "Dearest Lana was the kindest of souls. She joined us on this journey to help in any way she could, and that she did in so many ways. She was our light on the darkest of days. We stand together in this circle to show the never-ending cycle of life and death, and that life continues even after we take our final breath.

"Beloved Am. We implore you, please deliver our Lana into your eternal care. May you watch over her soul as she is freed from the bonds that hold her to this physical life. May we forever hold you in our hearts."

"May we forever hold you in our hearts."

Freyne felt Am's presence pulsating inside him, growing and spreading throughout his body. He opened his eyes in time to see a faint swirl of light flow from him to Lana's body and form a glowing figure that hovered just above her chest. Chardi gasped and the figure turned to face him. It stretched out its hand, and as Chardi reached over to touch it, it shattered into thousands of tiny light particles and shot up towards the sky. The entire clearing twinkled for a moment, then settled back into darkness.

Once the lights were gone, Lana lay lifeless, even more pale than before, her body nothing but an empty vessel. Ur'Shad and Chardi gently lifted her into the grave, then stood back as Iryna laid her father's crest on her chest. Ur'Shad took the spade and wiped a tear from his eye.

"I'll finish off here," he said quietly.

Chardi pulled him into a big bear hug, then disappeared into the forest, leaving Iryna and Ur'Shad alone with their grief. Freyne took Nika's hand and led him from the clearing, desperate to find somewhere private so that he too could grieve. His prayer, uttered for so many during his time as a high priest, reminded him that very soon he would be grieving for Nika as well. His hope for a happy and peaceful life once the prophecy was fulfilled was now just a realm of darkness. *There is nothing left for me in this life,* he thought miserably. *I'm so done with this.*

The day passed like a blur for Nika. Freyne left his side only to hunt, after which they rejoined the others to cook lunch. Nika sat in the mouth of the cave, chewing slowly but hardly tasting his food. Gri'Ran's presence was surrounding him and growing stronger with each passing minute. The ticking sound was back, only it was much slower than usual. He dropped the leaf that was his makeshift plate and stared into space. His mind felt detached from his body and full of fog.

"Are you okay, boo?" Freyne asked.

"Gri'Ran's coming," Nika whispered. "I can feel them getting closer and closer. It's almost time."

"I'm here for you." Freyne whispered back.

"But what if you try to save me?" Nika argued. "I don't want all of this to be for nothing."

"I've found peace within myself. We'll be together in the afterlife so I'll just have to wait."

Nika glanced at the others sitting around the fire sharing their memories of Lana. Chardi had since returned, though he still looked miserable.

"The others don't know yet, do they?" Nika asked.

Freyne shook his head.

"Do you want them to know? So you can say goodbye?"

"At first, I thought that would just make it harder. But then I realised that they deserve some closure, too. Maybe it will lessen the blow so to speak."

Nika shook his head to try and clear some of the fog. He still felt detached, as though his body no longer belonged to him. It was as if he were a puppet being controlled by his master. When he looked up, he spotted Arnie-Kyn emerging from the forest. The cat stalked towards him and helped himself to Nika's lap.

"*Where have you been, flea bag?*" he asked.

"*Hunting. Being a cat. It is almost time. Are you ready?*"

"*I don't think anyone is ever ready for death,*" Nika said. "*But if that's what's needed to fix this world, then who am I to refuse? One life for the benefit of humanity is a small sacrifice.*"

"*Such wise words for a whelp,*" Arnie said. "*One will be there with you. Don't be afraid.*"

"What will you do afterwards?" Nika asked.

"Whatever Am bids me to do," Arnie replied. *"Perhaps I will return to Al'Obrel with the other humans and return to the monastery. One misses the warmth and comfort of the library."*

Nika rested his head on Freyne's shoulder and scratched behind Arnie's ears. Time seemed to be dragging by slowly.

"I hate sitting around and waiting. Can't we just go and get it over and done with?"

"Just be patient," Freyne said. *"Do you have all the things you need? The dagger and statue?"*

"Yeah." Nika nodded. *"What about you? What will you do once I'm...once it's done?"*

"I'll make sure your body is taken care of and you're at rest. Then, I'll make sure the others get back on the ship and sail to Al'Obrel. Once they're gone I'll meet you in the afterlife."

Nika shot him a look, but Freyne shook his head and held up his hand for quiet.

"My mind is made up. Don't try and talk me out of it."

"I don't have the energy to even try. I think I'll go and tell the others now. The time is close."

Freyne kissed Nika's hair then helped him to his feet. Nika picked up Arnie-Kyn and walked slowly towards the fire. Iryna looked up as he approached and her face grew concerned.

"Are you ok?" she asked.

"No. I have something important to tell you all." Nika swallowed and tried to clear the fog in his head. "You'll recall that we were sent to find the blood descendant in order to fulfil this prophecy. Well, it happens tonight."

Iryna, Ur'Shad and Chardi exchanged long worried glances with one another.

"Who's the descendant?" Chardi asked.

"At first we thought it was Gaitan," Nika said, eyeing his friend across the fire. "That night in Barthra, though, we learned the truth. It was me all along."

"No!" Iryna shot to her feet. "It can't be true."

"Oh, it's true," Freyne said.

"Are you sure? I mean, how would you know?" she asked.

"I've been dreaming about it," Nika said. "Ever since I got sick that time when we were heading towards Rybor. At first they were few and far between, but ever since Barthra, I've been having the same dream every fucking night. I know in gory detail exactly what I have to do. So, I'm here to say goodbye to you all. You're the only friends I've ever really had and I'm so glad I got to meet and travel with you all."

"Oh, Nika."

To his surprise, Iryna pulled him into a hug and squeezed him for a moment before letting go. One by one his friends took their turn to hug him and say their goodbyes. While the fog dulled his emotions, he still felt a deep sadness. Just as he shook Bren and Rhill's hands, an overpowering surge of Gri'Ran's presence flooded into him. Nika froze.

"Come, Nickolai!" Gri'Ran commanded. *"It is time."*

The walk through the forest took several hours and the sky was rapidly losing daylight. Giant ferns and shrubs blanketed the floor of the forest, and thick vines snaked down from the trees, making the trek difficult. Overhead, giant bats chattered from their perches within the canopy. Nika walked quietly with Freyne's arm wrapped protectively around him. His mind was so foggy he couldn't think or feel. Iryna, Ur'Shad and Chardi walked behind them in silence.

After a while the trees thinned and they came to the edge of a deep chasm. Below, a river raged and the only way to cross was a crumbling stone bridge. Two stone gryphon statues stood either side of the bridge, weathered over countless years, only one of the heads was broken and covered in moss on the ground.

"Do you think it's safe?" Chardi asked.

Nika nodded and continued across the bridge. His feet moved on their own and he was no longer in control of his body. The far side of the chasm was shrouded in fog, but as he drew closer he could make out a steep flight of stairs leading up the side of a rocky hill. Step by step he climbed until he reached the top. He stepped onto an ancient overgrown plaza.

"What is this place?" Ur'Shad asked.

"It's the only surviving temple of Gri'Ran," Freyne said in a hushed tone. "I think this is where they once dwelled in physical form."

A gust of wind blew from the west and stirred the fog around them. Around the edges of the plaza were ruined buildings taken back by nature, and in the centre, a small pond in the shape of a hook. Freyne gasped.

"Are you okay?" Iryna demanded.

"By the gods! That symbol. It's Gri'Ran's mark. Why didn't I realise this before?"

"What do you mean?" she asked.

"Nika's scar. Look at it."

Nika felt his expression form into a frown as they ogled his face. Freyne was right; the pond was shaped exactly like his scar. The wind blew again and the fog eddied and swirled, and it was Nika's turn to gasp. At the opposite end of the plaza was the tower from his dreams, exactly as he remembered it. He drifted towards it, drawn by Gri'Ran's power and ignoring the shouts behind him.

"Halt!"

Someone grabbed his arm and spun him roughly around, tearing him back to the present. They were surrounded by around twenty people wearing black cloaks and hideous ibis masks. A chill travelled down his spine when he saw that his friends were all being held captive.

"Damir! We got them!" one of the cultists called.

Another group of cloaked figures emerged from one of the ruined buildings and hurried towards them, each of them wielding sword or daggers.

"Well done, Garlyn my love. See, I told you that this would work. Our Lord has never lead us astray. Perhaps he'll hold us in higher regard for this and maybe even reward us."

"Should we kill them first, or summon Our Lord first?"

"Kill them now and be done with it. The prophecy can't be fulfilled if they're all dead."

Gri'Ran's presence stirred within Nika's body, making him tingle all over. The cultists manoeuvred him and his friends into a line and shoved them to their knees. Nika could see Ur'Shad and Chardi struggling to break free, but without their swords they had no chance to defend themselves.

"Ith vu wader in laven, toso rifkin he roneth," Nika warned.

The voice that parted his lips was not his own, nor was the

language he spoke. He watched without emotion as the cultists positioned themselves to carry out the execution, ignoring him. One of the cultists barked an order and they raised their swords ready to strike. Iryna squirmed and tried to break free.

A surge of Gri'Ran's power exploded from Nika's body and struck the cultists. They screamed and fell writhing to the ground. Chardi and Ur'Shad scrambled to their feet and snatched a sword each.

"Neen ma cide tri mahsan Gri'Ran!" the voice roared from Nika's mouth and echoed around the ruins.

Dark clouds filled the sky and the ground shook. Raw power sizzled in the air as lightning cracked overhead. The cultists screamed and tried to crawl away, but something invisible pinned them down. Out of nowhere, glowing spikes of energy shot up from the ground and impaled them, killing them all instantly.

"Nika!" Freyne scrambled to his feet and hugged him fiercely. "Are you ok?"

Nika shook his head and tried to clear his mind, but the hold of Gri'Ran was too powerful.

"Come now, Nickolai."

"F-fine," he managed. "We have to go. Gri'Ran is calling me."

He walked slowly towards the doors, his body moving on its own accord. Freyne squeezed his hand and didn't let go. Nika stopped in front of the doors and turned to look at Freyne. He could hear his heart beating and the constant ticking sound which was slowing down with every *tick*. Freyne pulled him into his arms for one final embrace.

"I love you," Nika whispered in his ear.

"I love you too. I'll see you on the other side."

Nika pulled back and saw a single tear in the corner of Freyne's eye. He reached up and wiped it away, then kissed him one final time before glancing up at the sky. A giant bat swooped effortlessly around the tower before disappearing towards the forest. Nika looked back at the door and reached into his pocket for the key. The warmth of the statue greeted him and he knew exactly what to do with it.

Click.

He was shaking as he reached out and pushed open the doors. They swung open and the tower lit up before him with bright swirls of light. Atop a raised dais was an enormous stone gryphon, lying with its head buried under its wing. The gryphon began to glow brighter and brighter until it morphed into the living embodiment of Gri'Ran in their physical form. The mighty god blinked their piercing yellow eyes and flapped their wings, ruffling their feathers.

Two beams of light shot down from above and in a flash, Am and another god stood at the base of the dais. Am was no longer in spectral form, but instead wore a majestic cream robe. A dark void was where their face would be, hidden beneath their hood. Am's beautiful wings unfolded behind them, glowing like crystals. The other god was dressed similarly to Am, only their wings were much smaller. Nika felt a sense of familiarity to the third god, but his mind was too foggy to recognise them.

Nika glanced back at his friends. They were sitting together on a stone bench, a look of awe on their faces. Freyne squeezed his hand and Nika turned back in time to see Arnie-Kyn sit directly in front of him.

"Is this the true blood descendant from the lost line of Za'Haal?" Gri'Ran asked formally.

"Undeniably," Am replied. "He bears your mark."

"I do not sense his allegiance," Gri'Ran said.

"Nor do I," the third god added.

"His allegiance unsurprisingly lies with me," Am mused.

"Very well. So long as he proves loyal to one of us, we can proceed." Gri'Ran looked down at Arnie. "Arnie-Kyn. Come up here, my faithful friend."

Arnie stood and trotted up the dais. Gri'Ran lowered their head and allowed Arnie to rub against them in a show of mutual affection.

"You have served us well, my friend. I thank you."

Arnie sat at Gri'Ran's side and gazed down at Nika and Freyne, his tail weaving slowly from side to side.

"My son," Am said, speaking directly to Freyne. "Come and kneel before me."

Freyne seemed to hesitate, then let go of Nika's hand and knelt before Am. Nika could see that he was trembling.

347

"You, too, have served us well. You've proven your loyalty many, many times. It saddens me that you have experienced far more pain than one should in their lifetime, and have given up all that is precious and loved to you in order to serve me. Don't think that I do not appreciate your sacrifice. I hereby bestow unto you the title of disciple." Am raised their hand, and for a moment Freyne's body glowed. "Go back to your Nika, my son. We will talk after."

The gods all turned back to Nika.

"Nikolai, true descendant of noble Za'Haal. Are you aware of the pact which binds your bloodline?" Gri'Ran asked.

Nika nodded his head, unsure of what to say.

"And do you willingly offer us your life in return for restoring balance to your people?"

Nika nodded again.

"Very well. Kneel before us," Gri'Ran commanded.

Nika fell to his knees, vaguely aware that everyone was staring at him, and gazed up at the mighty god.

"For many years, we have seen corruption, greed, and hatred run strife in our cities. We've felt pure evil walking our lands and disrupting nature's course. Our people have prayed to us, begging for balance to be restored.

"It is, however, forbidden for the gods to directly intervene in the affairs of their people. And so we joined hands with the elder gods and answered our people's prayers indirectly. You, Nikolai, are the answer to their prayers. It is time. Proceed, and restore balance and hope to this pained world."

Nika pulled the dagger from his belt and looked back at Gri'Ran. The ticking sound in his mind had slowed right down, almost to a stop. There was one final *tick*, and he drove the dagger into his chest.

There was no pain. A bright beam of light shot from the wound and Nika felt warmth envelop him. He floated off the ground and hovered as more blinding rays of light shot from his body. Am's comforting presence joined with his, and for a moment he felt connected with Freyne and Arnie for one final time as his life drained from his body. As he fell to the floor, he caught one final glimpse of his beloved Freyne, then drifted towards the afterlife.

23

reyne fell to the ground and pulled Nika's body into his
arms, weeping uncontrollably. His face was cold and pale,
devoid of any life. Freyne pulled the dagger from his chest
and tossed it aside, unable to look at it. His entire world lay in
his arms, dead.

"It is done," Gri'Ran declared.

"No. Something's not right," Am said.

"I feel deception, betrayal," the third god added.

"But how?" Gri'Ran asked. "How does a mere human
deceive not one, but many gods?"

"We must summon the elders and seek council," Am said.

"Very well," both Gri'Ran and the third god said together.

Freyne felt a powerful surge and shielded his eyes as more
beams of light flooded into the room, encircling him and Nika.
Once the light subsided, eleven gods stood in the tower, each
with their own overpowering presence.

"Gri'Ran! Why have you summoned us?" one of the gods
demanded. "You know our combined presence is too powerful
for this world to handle."

"We have been deceived, Bałal. The bloodline still lives."

"Still lives? Is that not the end of it laying right there?"

"The Miscreant, Ami'Khel, still lives and taints the soils of
this world," Am said. "Somehow, he has deceived all of us and
violated our pact and laws."

"This is an outrage!" another god roared. "These vessels
have given up everything to fulfil this prophecy, and still things
are not right. Does this mean their sacrifices were all in vain?"

"Yes. Unless..." The third god broke off. "Let us join minds and find the source of this treachery."

The gods took a step closer together, tightening the ring around Freyne and his Nika. They bowed their heads and a low hum reverberated throughout the temple. Freyne was too numb from grief to fully comprehend what was going on. He held Nika tightly, his tears still streaming down his cheeks. The humming faded to a mere whisper and echoed around the walls until fading to silence. The gods raised their heads, and going around the circle one by one, they spoke.

"Can it really be?"

"It is truth. He is alive."

"How did he hide from us?"

"That rift we felt when we believed he died."

"Khel created the rift deliberately."

"The Black Ibis cult prevails."

"The rift leads to Jehovah's world."

"There is more than one."

"We must close them immediately."

"No. We cannot directly interfere."

"Then to whom shall we delegate this task?"

"Mancery cannot be undone."

"Except by the person who willed it, or a blood relative."

"His only blood relative lies dead at our feet."

"To reverse death is to go against nature."

"To leave the rifts open is also to go against nature."

"They have more than proven themselves."

"Khel is powerful. He has stolen access to the darkest realm."

"Then they must obtain this knowledge too."

"Do we restore that forbidden knowledge to the Keeper?"

"Yes. Restore all that we have hidden from him."

"Agreed. We must vanquish the Miscreant."

"Are they strong enough for this task?"

"No. We must enhance their powers."

"Enhance the young one's time also."

"Am. Their allegiance lies with you. Therefore, you will watch over them and ensure they succeed. Are we agreed?"

"We are," the gods said together.

"Very well."

The gods bowed their heads again and dazzling sprites of light encircled Freyne and Nika's body. At first the sprites drifted lazily through the air, but once the gods joined their minds, the lights began to spin. Faster and faster they whirled until memories and images flashed before Freyne's eyes. He became disoriented and bile rose in his chest. There was a bright flash of light, and the feeling of a thousand white-hot nails stabbed at his mind. Freyne screamed and clutched his head as the memories shifted to dark images of forbidden mancery and things he didn't even remember learning. Knowledge and powers that were taken from him were returned with such force that he thought his brain was about to explode.

"Argh!"

Freyne swayed on his knees, disoriented and in agony. The swirling lights began to slow and drift towards the ceiling. Somewhere beneath them, a deep gong pierced the silence and shook the floor of the temple.

"It is done," Gri'Ran declared. "Arnie-Kyn. Go and continue to watch over them. We will talk with you soon."

The gods shimmered, then one by one they turned into bright beams of light and disappeared in a flash. Gri'Ran sat upright and flapped their wings, then turned into solid stone. The entire temple began to shake and chunks of mortar crumbled from the walls and ceiling.

Someone shook Freyne's shoulder and he slowly opened his eyes. He was dazed and confused and his head hurt. His eyes landed on Nika's lifeless body and he became overwhelmed with another wave of grief.

"This entire place is going to collapse. Let's go!" Chardi yelled, pulling Freyne to his feet. "Can you walk?"

"I-I think so."

"Here. I'll carry Nika," Ur'Shad offered.

"No. I-I'll carry him," Freyne stammered.

He bent down unsteadily and hoisted Nika over his shoulder. His body was much lighter than Freyne remembered, almost weightless. He held Nika tightly and staggered from the tower.

"Wait!" Iryna called.

She dashed back to the tower and retrieved Gri'Ran's Gift from the door, then hurried to catch up. In her other hand was the bloodied dagger. Freyne tore his eyes away from it and followed Chardi back towards the stairs. He almost tripped as one of the ruined buildings collapsed and caused the ground to shake even more violently. They ran past the bodies of the cultists which still lay where they fell, staining the plaza with their pools of blood, and picked their way down the stairs.

"Go go go!" Chardi urged.

Freyne adjusted his grip on Nika's body and followed the others across the bridge, panting for air. With a deafening roar, the last of Gri'Ran's temples collapsed. The bridge shuddered and a section behind them tumbled into the chasm. He made it across just as a giant cloud of dust spewed from the ruins behind them.

"Get down!" Ur'Shad bellowed.

Freyne lowered Nika to the ground and protected his body with his own. Splinters and debris rained down, covering him in thick choking dust. Chardi's strong grip pulled him out of the rubble and helped to brush him off. Freyne coughed and gasped for breath. The ruins of Gri'Ran's temple were gone, obliterated.

"Is everyone ok?" he spluttered.

"We're fine," Ur'Shad said. "Come on. Let's get back to camp."

The trek back to camp was long and exhausting. Freyne followed Ur'Shad's makeshift torch through the trees, stumbling under Nika's weight. He was no longer weightless and Freyne was certain he was growing heavier with each step. It was around midnight when he spotted the glow of the campfire through the trees. Gaitan, Priye, Bren and Rhill were all seated around the fire, waiting for them.

"It's about time you came back. We were getting worried and were going to come and look for you," Gaitan said.

Freyne wordlessly laid Nika on the ground away from the fire and sat by his side, holding his hand and tracing the pattern of the leather band on his wrist. His body was sore and he craved sleep, but the thought of leaving Nika was more than he could bare.

"He gave his life for us. For everyone in this world," Iryna said quietly. "I've never known anyone so selfless. He deserves a hero's burial."

"No. He doesn't want any fuss," Freyne objected. "He wants a simple burial and for you all to get back to Al'Obrel safely."

"Well, too bad. He's our friend," Chardi said. "We need to honour him. Are we done with this prophecy business?"

"I'm not sure," Iryna replied. "I think something is wrong. Could you understand what the gods were saying?"

"No."

Freyne was only half listening. His head ached, he felt sick, and he desperately wanted to grieve alone. He sat holding Nika's hand to his lips, weeping silently and staring into his handsome face. Nika's hand felt warm in his, and in his grief, he thought he could feel a weak pulse. Arnie climbed onto Nika's chest and crouched into a ball, gazing into Freyne's eyes. Freyne reached out and scratched behind the cat's ears.

"Are you okay?" he asked.

"One is fine," Arnie replied.

"Don't you feel any emotion at all?"

"Only when necessary. One is a cat, after all."

Freyne laid Nika's hand down gently and wiped his eyes.

"I don't suppose you're going to let me go and bury him?"

"Of course not. And don't think for a moment that you're taking yourself to the afterlife. You have more important things to do here. Your quest is far from over."

"I've given Am over a thousand years of my life. I'm done."

"It'll be awful lonely for you there."

"What's that supposed to mean?"

Arnie shifted slightly and lay watching Nika's face, his tail twitching. Freyne followed his gaze; in the dim light of the fire, Nika didn't look so pale. Freyne reached out and brushed his hair from his face, then placed the back of his hand on his cheek.

"He's warm. He shouldn't feel warm," Freyne said. In his grief, his voice sounded hysterical. "What's going on?"

Priye bent down and held her fingers to his neck for a moment, then frowned and checked his wrist. Her eyes widened.

"He shouldn't have a pulse, either," she said.

"I can't deal with this," Freyne said. "Is this some sick joke?"

"No. Check for yourself," she said.

Freyne pressed his fingers to Nika's wrist and felt a weak pulse. He was so overwhelmed, so overloaded with grief and confusion that nothing made sense. He glanced around the circle of his friends; everything spun and became a blur. Before he could steady himself, Freyne fainted.

⌐

He was floating around in the darkness, no body, no pain, just a mere untethered consciousness. At first he felt at peace, content, but something disturbed him and his mind had awoken. He tried to close it off, but he couldn't. He felt a presence join with him, only instead of feeling it inside his mind, the presence was detached and separate. He vaguely recognised the presence from when he was alive.

"Nikolai, my son," Am's voice said. "I'm so proud of you."

"Why?" Nika asked. "I didn't do anything special."

"Oh, but you did. You gave up your life for a world you barely knew. Instead of trying to dodge your fate, you accepted it willingly and did what was required of you."

"I didn't really have a choice," Nika pointed out. "Even if I wanted to run, I'm sure you or Gri'Ran would have found me and marched me all the way to that tower."

"But you didn't. You accepted your fate and did so unselfishly," Am said. "Some of your predecessors were much less giving."

"You mean Ami'Khel, don't you?"

"I do."

Am fell silent.

"There's a problem, isn't there?" Nika asked. "I saw something strange as I died."

"Yes, there's a big problem. That's why I am talking to you here now, *before* I deliver you to the afterlife."

"Where's here?" Nika asked.

"You could call this limbo, the space between death and the afterlife," Am explained. "Your soul is still trapped within your body. That's where the godless people's souls remain, unless someone prays for them."

"Like Lana?" Nika asked.

"Oh, yes. I was more than happy to deliver her beautiful soul," Am said. "She sends her love, by the way. She too is proud of you."

"What's in the afterlife?" Nika asked.

"That is something you will only know if you are delivered there. And this brings me to the point of this visit."

"Oh?" Nika asked.

"As I said before, we have a big problem. As you rightly deduced at Riz'Hra, the Brotherhood of the Black Ibis has been operating right under our noses for all these years. I discovered this when his village was destroyed. What we didn't know is that the Miscreant, Ami'Khel, is still alive and has been hiding from us for all this time."

"But how?" Nika asked. "I'm sorry. I don't know much about gods and powers."

"That's okay, my son. I do understand," Am replied. "The original history states that when Ami'Khel was killed, a temporary rift was opened that wreaked havoc on the world. It threw nature out of balance. We have since learned that he used a darker forbidden form of mancery to create the rift himself and hide from us. We believe that rift opened to your world."

"Was it the cult who sent the militia after us?" Nika asked.

"Indeed it was. But more importantly, the rifts remain open and if they're not closed soon, they'll grow unstable and collapse. It will tear this world apart and your sacrifice would have been for nothing."

"Can't you close them?" Nika asked.

"No. Mancery cannot be undone by another mancer. Only someone from the same bloodline can."

"But I was the last of his bloodline. I guess that means the rifts will stay open."

"It means you need to make a choice. You can choose to pass over into the afterlife and rest in peace. Or, I can restore your life, on the condition that you find and close the rifts."

"What about Khel? He'll probably try to fight us."

"You will need to find and destroy him. While he lives, this world will forever be in peril."

"Is Freyne still alive?" Nika asked.

"Of course he is. Arnie-Kyn won't let him do anything stupid. He's protecting your body now."

"Arnie's not a normal cat, is he?"

"I think he would be most offended by that question." Am sounded amused. "Felines were gifted to us by the elder god Bałal. They are an intelligent creature and the ancient people of your world were wise to worship them.

"Back to our problem, though. We need to hurry. If you choose to go after the Miscreant, you will need to undergo intense training in the darkest realm. This is death mancery, all that is forbidden, and you will need to learn it to defeat Khel."

"Who will teach me?" Nika asked.

"My disciple, of course. He has learnt all there is to know about almost every aspect of mancery. It was his chosen field of study at the monastery."

"Why didn't he say so? He always seemed so unsure of himself and acted like he didn't know much about it."

"After the Black Ibis destroyed his village, I had to block a lot of his knowledge and memories to protect him. We have since restored this knowledge to him."

"So, I get to choose between death, or have a third attempt at life," Nika mused.

"Well, if you want to put it that way, yes." He could hear the amusement in Am's tone. "Which will you choose?"

"Death seems so peaceful and I feel it calling to me. And yet, I cannot sit by and allow an entire world to suffer. I have to go back and do what I can to help."

"Very well. As a final consequence of your decision, your life will become a lot more complicated than before. Have Freyne teach you how to pray so that you can commune with me."

"Alright," Nika said. "Wait. I mean, yes, My God."

"You're already learning. Return now to life, my son, and sail henceforth to Al'Obrel. Hold me in your heart, always, and you will never be alone."

Nika's consciousness swirled and rejoined with his body. At once he felt a stabbing pain in his chest and his head began to ache. Something warm was sitting on him, pressing down on the wound and causing it to throb. His hearing returned but his body was still frozen.

"Freyne? Oh dear, Freyne's fainted."

"Lay him out so he doesn't choke on his tongue," a stern voice instructed. "He'll come to soon enough."

"That poor man."

"What did Priye say before?" a man asked.

"She said that Nika has a pulse," a woman replied.

Nika felt the back of someone's hand on his face, then

someone poked around his neck for a moment.

"No way. He *does* have a pulse. Nika's alive!" she exclaimed.

Everyone gasped, then babbled excitedly.

"Someone try and wake Freyne," a young man said.

"Let him sleep, Gaitan," Iryna said.

"He should be awake for this," Gaitan argued.

"Gaitan's right for once. Bren, fetch me that bucket of water. Quickly," Priye ordered.

Nika heard a splash followed by splutters and coughing. A few drops landed on his face and he felt himself twitch.

"What the fuck?" someone said angrily.

Nika's heart soared at the sound of Freyne's voice.

"We thought you might want to be awake before Nika comes to," Gaitan said.

"Is this some sort of a sick joke?" Freyne snapped.

"No. See for yourself."

Nika managed to wriggle his fingers. He focused on trying to move his hand and could feel the stiffness slowly easing. Freyne took his hand and Nika felt his face crease into a smile.

"You're alive," Freyne wept.

Someone lifted Arnie off his chest. The pain was sharp and Nika sucked in a deep breath.

"Can't I die in peace?" he croaked.

"No." Freyne sniffed.

"I'm not very good at it. That's two failed attempts so far."

"Oh, boo."

Nika opened his eyes and gazed up at Freyne. His tears had already dried and he wore a warm smile instead. Am's warning flooded back to him and his heart started racing as he remembered the urgency of his new assignment.

"We need to go."

He tried to push himself up but a sharp pain in his chest made him gasp and collapse. He felt around his wound and was surprised to find fresh blood on his hands.

"You need to stay there until you're in a fit state to move," Freyne scolded him. "You're not out of harm's way yet."

"But–"

"No buts." Priye appeared above him and fixed him with a stern look. "You're bleeding again. Has anyone got a knife?"

Freyne drew one of his daggers from his boot and handed it to her. She cut Nika's shirt open and frowned.

"How could such a small blade cut such a big hole?" she mumbled. "What a mess. I don't have enough supplies to fix this."

"Maple should have plenty on board," Freyne said.

"Maple's here?" Nika demanded. "Why didn't you tell me?"

"We kind of had more pressing issues," Freyne said.

"How did you find her?"

"She found me, actually. I was searching for a captain who was willing to help me find you. She was offloading some supplies from Fiz'Am in her new ship, The Scruffy Mongrel II."

"What was wrong with the other ship?"

"The maintenance would have been too costly to repair, so she sold it and purchased the new one. It's much bigger and faster than the old ship."

"No wonder I didn't recognise it." Nika frowned. "We have to go. Every minute is a minute wasted. You can fix me up on board."

Nika held out his hand, determined to get moving. Freyne sighed and helped him into sitting position. Nika grimaced at the pain but didn't complain. A fresh trail of blood dripped down his torso. Priye tore off a larger section of his shirt and pressed it to the wound.

"Hold this and press firmly or you'll bleed out," she said. "Do you have the strength to walk?"

"I don't know."

Freyne helped Nika to his feet, then caught him as his legs almost gave way.

"I've got you." Freyne grunted and slipped his arm around Nika's waist. "Why do you have to be so stubborn?"

"The fate of the world is now in our hands," Nika said. "We have lots to do."

Nika stood at the stern with Freyne by his side, watching Gri'Ran's Rest slip away in the distance. The sun was rising, filling the sky with brilliant pink and orange hues. His wound had been treated and bandaged, and Nika wore a clean shirt under his cloak. He still felt weak and clung to the rail for support.

"Why did you come back?" Freyne asked quietly once the island had disappeared from view.

"Am gave me a choice," Nika replied. "Death, with an eternity in the afterlife, or come back and save the world. Of course I had to come back."

"You died for this world, and now you live for this world. Do you really care for it that much?"

"In my—no—in the *other* world, there is a saying, 'home is where the heart is.' My home is here with you, even if we are doomed to roam the world chasing evil until the end of days." Nika pulled Freyne's arm around his shoulder and cuddled into him. "Am was never going to let you stay and end your own life. Had I not returned to life, you would have been forced to roam this world, alone."

Freyne sighed and squeezed Nika gently.

"After all those years I spent studying the prophecy, I never thought I'd live to see it fulfilled. Yet here we are. It feels so surreal."

"This is the calm before the storm," Nika said grimly. "We will soon be heading into darkness. The journey up until this point has been a walk in the park, carefully scripted by the gods. We are on our own now and we have to make our own path."

"You're starting to sound very prophetic," Freyne said with a raised eyebrow. "I like it. Careful or I'll be forced to come out of retirement and make you my neophyte for real."

"What, and live to be a thousand and four like you?" Nika laughed, then winced from the pain. "Come on, oh great disciple. Let's go and have some breakfast. Death makes you hungry, you know."

The story continues in book 2, The Darkest Realm.

About The Author

Amy-Alex Campbell is a queer Aussie author living in Western Sydney, Australia. In addition to writing, they love to draw fantasy maps for both commissions and fun. When they're not writing, Amex enjoys gaming, reading, and taking care of their two axolotls, Chernobyl & Pripyat.

Books By This Author

The Miscreant
The Lowest Realm
The Darkest Realm
The Final Realm (forthcoming)
Tysion's Story (forthcoming)

The Marsden Park Series
Beneath the Grandstand

Acknowledgements

I would like to sincerely thank my friends and family for all their support in getting this second edition up of the ground. It wouldn't have been possible without you.

Visit
amyalexcampbell.com
for lore, artwork, maps, pronunciation, and more!

The Darkest Realm

The Miscreant - Book Two

Amy-Alex Campbell

General Ashavan crept through the darkened city streets, being careful to remain unseen. He was a large, hulking man, able to whittle bodies into latticework with a single stroke of his sword. To risk being caught roaming the streets after curfew by the city guards would cost him precious time, time he could not afford. He knew that should he slip up in the slightest way, Lord Du'Rakis would show him no mercy, just as he showed none to the soldiers of the Brotherhood. Men and women who he'd spent years of his life training. The thought of their smoking bodies littering the battlefield and the stench of the burning flesh made him want to throw up.

The patter of the heavy rain hitting the weathered bluestone street muffled his footsteps as he hurried down a dark alleyway. Rounding a corner, a lone mutt started barking from the shadows.

"Halt! Who's prowlin' around out there?" someone shouted.

Ashavan snatched a key from his pocket and jiggled it in a lock as the sound of running feet grew louder. He slipped inside and pressed his ear to the door.

"It's just a mongrel dog," a gruff voice said. "Ter hell with it. Let's git outta this rain."

Ashavan let out a deep breath as the guards moved away.

"Who's there?" a voice called behind him.

"It's me," Ashavan said quickly.

A beam of light pierced the darkness as Tysion unshuttered his lantern and placed it on a table. The small room had hardly changed since Ashavan was there last; a cot against the back wall, a wardrobe, a small table with two chairs, and a bench to prepare meals. The air was cold and frigid; the usually welcoming fire was unlit.

"What are you doing here?" Tysion demanded.

Ashavan eyed him in the dim light; his body looked strong and healthy as always. His brown wavy hair matched the soft curls on his chest which disappeared into a trail leading below his under garments. Tysion's green eyes twinkled in the light of the lantern, betraying his confusion.

"I had to see you," Ashavan blurted out. "You are no longer safe here. The Brotherhood of the Black Ibis is being expunged by our Lord. He's coming to destroy what's left. You need to get out tonight."

"Our Lord? He's yours, not mine. I left that ridiculous cult years ago," Tysion snapped.

"I came here to warn you, not to argue. If I get caught, I'm a dead man. You and I both know that." Ashavan's stomach twisted and turned unpleasantly. "Please. Just pack your things and hurry. We don't have much time."

"And where will I go?" Tysion countered. "You know this place and my workshop is all I have left. You come barging in here and try to uproot my life as though I can just go and start over like nothing ever happened—"

"If you don't leave tonight, you'll die!" Ashavan shouted, his frustration getting the better of him. "He is on a rampage, and this entire city is at risk. I may have made some poor choices in my life, but I swore when I did to always protect you no matter what. Now please start packing. You can hate me while you get ready."

Tysion glared at him for a moment, then huffed and pulled on his tunic and hose.

"Where will I go?" he repeated.

"Head east, as far as you can. Avoid the cities. Hide by day and travel by night."

A wave of sadness washed over him as Tysion turned and stuffed a few tools of his craft into another pack.

"I never meant to get in this deep," Ashavan said softly. "I thought I was doing the right thing. That I was helping to make the world a better place. I never thought it could go this far and that I was the one doing wrong. Once again I've failed you."

"You need to get out now," Tysion said, his tone changing. He paused and looked Ashavan in the eyes. "Only now are you waking up to the level of brainwashing that goes on in that place. Any cult that defies the gods is going to have evil intent. If only you'd woken up when I did."

"I can't leave, and you know that." Ashavan groaned. "Unless he is killed, I am bound to him until the very end. I'm so sorry. I never wanted this to happen."

"Sorry isn't going to change anything." Tysion pulled on his heavy cloak and boots, then stood and slid his sword into the scabbard on his belt. "Let's go."

The rain was still bucketing down outside, making it hard to see in the shadows. Ashavan was grateful they at least had some cover to help keep them hidden from the patrols. After a few close calls and almost being discovered by guards, they made it safely to the entrance of the sewers.

"Down there is the only way out," Ashavan whispered.

Tysion nodded and scurried down the ladder. Ashavan followed, pausing only to pull the heavy cover back over the entrance. The smell of human waste greeted his nose, almost choking him. He heard a splash below followed by gagging.

"Disgusting." Tysion retched.

"It's better than being killed," Ashavan said grimly. "Pass me the lantern. We should be safe here."

Tysion unshuttered the lantern and handed it over. Ashavan flinched from the bright light after being in the darkness for so long. He held it up so they could see and sheathed his sword.

"This way. Be careful, it's slippery."

The sewers were ancient and robustly built from large blocks of basalt stone. The walls and ledges were covered in green moss and grime, and as they carefully picked their way through the gloom, rats fled in every direction. The sound of rushing water was almost deafening; the level in the channel had risen considerably since Ashavan passed through earlier.

A gloomy stairway materialised from the darkness. Ashavan led Tysion up the slippery steps then paused once more to shutter the lantern. He handed it back to Tysion, then cracked open the door and stepped into a stone hut.

"Who's there? Show yourself!" someone yelled. "Hey!"

Ashavan cursed and drew his sword in time to parry a blow from a polearm, throwing his attacker off-guard. Ashavan swung his blade with ease and buried it into the man's abdomen, just below his breastplate. A look of disbelief crossed the man's face, and with a gurgle, he fell to his knees and slumped to the ground.

Without a word, Ashavan wiped the blood from his blade, then dragged the dead guard into the sewers. He listened to the thumps of the body as it tumbled down the stairs, then closed the door and turned to Tysion.

"Are you ok?" he asked.

"I'm standing next to someone who kills without conscience. I'm not even sure how to answer that."

"It was us or him," Ashavan said firmly. "He swung at me first. Come on. I have a horse waiting for you."

They walked in silence until they reached the edge of a large forest. Ashavan led them deeper into the brush to where he'd tethered two horses. Wordlessly, he took Tysion's packs and buckled them to the saddle.

"Take this horse and get as far away from here as you can. There's food and coin in one of the packs. Now, remember what I said. Hide by day, ride by night." Ashavan looked at Tysion for a moment, then lowered his eyes to his feet. "If things had been different...if I left when you did, do you think we'd still be together?"

"You mean if you had've listened to me when I warned you that the Brotherhood was brainwashing you? Or left when your lord tried to kill me? Your heart is ensnared by that cult, and unless you can break away from it, your heart will never be your own." Tysion stepped forward and planted a soft yet firm kiss on Ashavan's lips. "If that day ever arrives, come and find me."

Before Ashavan could say anything else, Tysion leapt into the saddle and sped off into the night.